MARY SHELLEY

FRANKENSTEIN

MARY SHELLEY

FRANKENSTEIN

The 1818 Edition with Related Texts

Edited, with Introduction and Notes, by

David Wootton

Hackett Publishing Company, Inc.
Indianapolis/Cambridge

For further information, please address
    Hackett Publishing Company, Inc.
    P.O. Box 44937
    Indianapolis, Indiana 46244-0937

    www.hackettpublishing.com

Cover design by E. L. Wilson
Interior design by Elana Rosenthal
Composition by Aptara, Inc.

Library of Congress Control Number: 2020934072

ISBN-13: 978-1-62466-913-2 (cloth)
ISBN-13: 978-1-62466-912-5 (pbk.)

Contents

Related Texts

Family Tree of the Godwins and the Shelleys

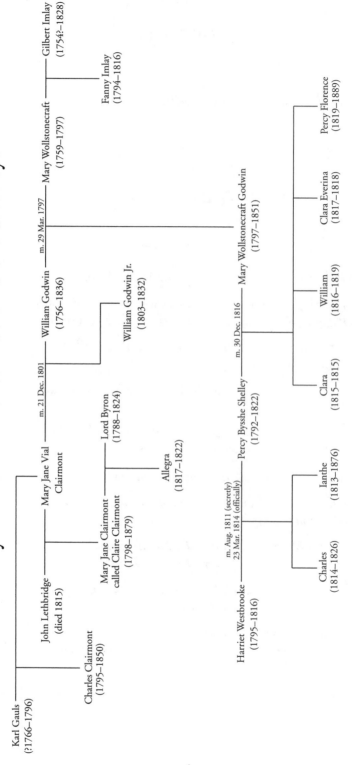

Introduction[1]

Mary Wollstonecraft Shelley (1797–1851), the author of *Frankenstein* (1818), was a motherless child.[2] Her mother, Mary Wollstonecraft (1759–1797), the feminist author, died of puerperal fever a few days after giving birth to her. Mary was named after her mother; she was born Mary Godwin, the daughter of William Godwin (1756–1836), the author of *An Enquiry Concerning Political Justice* (1793), the first great work of anarchist political theory.

Godwin had been deeply in love with Mary Wollstonecraft—Mary Godwin as she officially became when they married after she became pregnant. Grieving, he promptly wrote an account of her life, *Memoirs of the Author of A Vindication of the Rights of Woman* (1798). Unfortunately he miscalculated the effect of the book on its readers, for he did not simply present Wollstonecraft as an intellectual, the author of the first great work of modern feminism. Godwin also detailed her love affairs, the illegitimate birth of her first daughter, Fanny, and her two suicide attempts. And he insisted that they were both hostile to the institution of marriage and had married only to avoid Wollstonecraft's being excluded from polite society. (It was Wollstonecraft's social status, not that of their child, that concerned them.)

It is difficult for us to imagine the social standards prevalent in England in those years. Godwin reported with bitter sarcasm that many of Wollstonecraft's friends—who had been happy to meet her when she was known as Mrs. Imlay (after her lover, Gilbert Imlay, Fanny's father), though she

1. I am most grateful to Bruce Barker-Benfield, Daisy Hay, and Sharon Ruston for valuable comments on an earlier version of this Introduction. I also thank my editor, Brian Rak, and my copyeditor, Laura Clark, for their suggestions. Any errors are mine alone.
2. There are three naming conventions with regard to Mary W. Shelley. Biographers tend to call her "Mary," and her husband, Percy Bysshe Shelley, "Shelley": this is how they themselves spoke and wrote. Literary critics call Mary Shelley "Shelley" when discussing her writings and refer to her husband as Percy Shelley. And those who want to treat the two Shelleys alike call Mary Wollstonecraft Shelley "MWS" and Percy Bysshe Shelley "PBS." I have tried to follow each of these conventions in the appropriate context. I use "Mary" when writing about Mary Shelley's life, and I use "Mary Shelley" or simply "Shelley" when discussing her as an author. In the notes I use "MWS" and "PBS" for brevity. Mary signed herself "Mary W. [for Wollstonecraft] Godwin" before her marriage and "Mary W. Shelley" after. *Frankenstein* was published anonymously, but the second edition, of 1823, which was seen through the press by Godwin, bore the name "Mary Wollstonecraft Shelley" and the third, of 1831, which was seen through the press by Mary herself, "Mary W. Shelley."

never actually claimed to be married—refused to meet her once it became indisputable that Fanny had been born out of marriage. As for suicide: it was illegal; people who died by suicide were denied Christian burial and their relatives could not inherit, while attempted suicide was regarded, not as a cry for help, but as an abominably wicked act.

Worse perhaps: Wollstonecraft and Godwin were both known as defenders of the French Revolution, though Wollstonecraft's view of the Revolution in its later stages had, like Tom Paine's, become highly critical; she had been present in Paris during the Jacobin Terror, when many of her friends had been executed, and had been in danger of execution herself.[3] As for Godwin, he had always abhorred violence used for political ends. But their reputations had been made during the controversy between Edmund Burke (*Reflections on the Revolution in France*, 1790) and Tom Paine (*The Rights of Man*, 1791). The United Kingdom was at war with France from 1793 to 1814, and there was a massive reaction in Britain against the values that were held responsible for the French Revolution and for Napoleon. Polite society seized on Godwin's *Memoirs* as an opportunity to condemn Wollstonecraft and Godwin and everything they stood for; patriotism demanded nothing less.

Mary Godwin was thus the daughter of two of the most reviled intellectuals of the day. A portrait of her mother hung in her father's study; her mother's grave, in the churchyard of St. Pancras nearby, became for her a place of pilgrimage and, as she became older, and even after the family had moved farther away, a place to which she would retreat to read. The books written by her mother (*Thoughts on the Education of Daughters* [1787]; *Mary: A Fiction* [1788]; *A Vindication of the Rights of Men* [1790]; *A Vindication of the Rights of Woman* [1792]; *Letters Written During a Short Residence in Sweden, Norway, and Denmark* [1796]) were her favorite and constant reading. That Mary Godwin should have grown up to be an author need not surprise us; as she herself said: "It is not singular that, as the daughter of two persons of distinguished literary celebrity, I should very early in life have thought of writing."[4] Both her parents had written novels (Godwin was widely held to be one of the finest novelists of the day, even though the moral and political principles expressed in his novels were almost universally condemned); from early on she too must have aspired to be a novelist.

---

3. Wollstonecraft continued to defend the early phase of the Revolution. Her *An Historical and Moral View of the Origin and Progress of the French Revolution* (London: J. Johnson, 1794) was unfinished (only the first volume was published) and does not go beyond 1789.
4. Mary Wollstonecraft Shelley, *Frankenstein: Or, the Modern Prometheus* (London: Henry Colburn and Richard Bentley, 1831), v (below, p. 183).

Mary was not long motherless, at least officially. Alone with two small children to raise, Godwin married Mary Jane Clairmont, a neighbor with two children of her own, Charles and Jane. Clairmont's life before she met Godwin is shrouded in obscurity, but it is remarkable that she and Godwin were married twice on the same day: at St. Leonard's, Shoreditch, Godwin married "Mary Clairmont, widow," while a mile away at St. Mary's, Whitechapel, he married "Mary Vial, spinster."[5] St. Mary's was five miles from their home: far enough to ensure that the priest would not recognize Mary Vial and was unlikely to meet her again. The first marriage was for appearances: "Mary Clairmont" needed to be able to assure anyone who asked that she was indeed married. The second was to make the marriage lawful, since Mary Vial had never married before, and so was not entitled to call herself Mary Clairmont, nor to claim to be a widow. Soon M. J. Godwin (as she called herself when she went into publishing) and William Godwin had a child of their own (young William), so Mary was raised as the middle child in a family of five, no two of whom were full siblings.

Mary loved her father; indeed she was in love with him: she had, she would later say, an "excessive and romantic attachment" to him.[6] Her feelings for her stepmother were very different. Soon after she finally left home she described her stepmother as "a woman I shudder to think of"; "something very analogous to disgust arises whenever I think of her"; "I detest Mrs G."[7] Even before her final escape she had managed to separate herself from her stepmother for considerable periods: she was sent to Ramsgate for six months in 1811 (seawater would, it was hoped, cure her eczema), and between 1812 and 1814 she spent nearly two years in Dundee, Scotland, staying with the relatives of a friend of her father's. In the 1831 Introduction to *Frankenstein* she wrote: "I lived principally in the country as a girl";[8] until the spring of 1807 the family lived in Somers Town, which was then on the edge of London and surrounded by fields, but they then moved to Clerkenwell, and Dundee must have been a welcome escape not only from her stepmother but also from city life. Thus she remained, despite her father's best efforts, a motherless child; or, as Sandra M. Gilbert puts it, her "only real 'mother' was a tombstone—or a shelf of books."[9] For

---

5. William St. Clair, *The Godwins and the Shelleys: The Biography of a Family* (London: Faber & Faber, 1989), 248.
6. Mary Wollstonecraft Shelley, *The Letters of Mary Wollstonecraft Shelley*, ed. Betty T. Bennett, 3 vols. (Baltimore: Johns Hopkins University Press, 1980–1988), 2:215.
7. Harriet Jump, "Monstrous Stepmother: Mary Shelley and Mary Jane Godwin," *Women's Writing* 6 (1999): 297–308, at 297–98.
8. Shelley, *Frankenstein* (1831), vi (below p. 183).
9. Sandra M. Gilbert, "Horror's Twin: Mary Shelley's Monstrous Eve," *Feminist Studies* 4 (1978): 48–73, at 69.

the young Mary, whose mother had died giving birth to her, love and loss, birth and death were already inextricably intertwined.

And then she met Percy Bysshe Shelley (1792–1822). Shelley came from a wealthy family but was engaged in an endless rebellion and had been cut off by his father. He had been sent down from Oxford in 1811, at the age of eighteen, for publishing an atheistical pamphlet. He had tried to raise a revolution in Ireland. He was a poet. And he had declared himself to be Godwin's disciple.

Godwin held that no one had a right to property except whoever could make best use of it. He had set up with Mary Jane as a printer of children's books and had opened a bookshop, but they were constantly in debt, and he was always barely a step away from debtor's prison. Shelley offered to ensure Godwin had financial security for the rest of his life: a promise he would, as slowly became apparent, fail to make good, for he too was constantly in debt, often hiding from bailiffs and repeatedly borrowing against his prospective inheritance (though, in the end, his father long outlived him). Shelley's moral vision contained a peculiar, Godwinian blind spot. He eagerly gave money to good causes (including Godwin) and to the poor, but he happily purchased expensive items (a carriage, a piano, books) on credit with no prospect of ever being able to pay for them. He saw no contradiction in defrauding honest workmen in order to support Godwin and himself: evidently he thought he could make better use of their money than they could.

Thus Shelley became a frequent visitor to Godwin's home, and there he met Mary on her return from Scotland. Secretly they courted. At her mother's grave (with her stepsister Jane nearby to ensure that decency was respected), Mary declared her love for him. On July 28, 1814, they ran away. Mary was still sixteen; Shelley was not yet twenty-two. They made at once for France, which had only recently, with the defeat of Napoleon on April 6, become a possible destination for travelers, and they took Mary Jane's daughter Jane (who had only recently turned sixteen) with them: of the three, she alone spoke French.[10] They were swiftly followed by Mary Jane, who caught up with them at Calais, but was unable to persuade Jane to return with her. (Characteristically, Mary Jane later denied that she had gone after them; perhaps she was unwilling to admit that her mission had ended in failure.) They traveled as far as Switzerland, mostly on foot; there

---

10. It has recently been discovered by Vicki Parslow Stafford that the father of Jane Clairmont (who later called herself Claire and was six months younger than MWS) was Sir John Lethbridge: Claire Clairmont, Mary Jane's Daughter: New Correspondence with Claire's Father (website), last modified April 13, 2017, https://sites.google.com/site/maryjanes daughter/.

they ran out of money and were forced to turn for home, traveling north by riverboat. They had been abroad for six weeks. Throughout, Mary and Shelley kept a journal, which they published anonymously in 1817.[11]

Back in England, Godwin demanded money from Shelley, but refused to meet with him (or even to accept checks made out in his name, for that would imply he had condoned the seduction of his daughter) and tried to prevent his family meeting with Mary. Mary gave birth to a premature baby girl, Clara, on February 22, 1815; two weeks later the infant died.

Mary and Shelley could not marry: Shelley had married Harriet Westbrook, then sixteen, four months after being expelled from Oxford, eloping with her to Edinburgh. They had a daughter in 1813, and when Shelley ran away with Mary, Harriet was pregnant with their second child. Shelley, it must be said, showed no interest in the emotional welfare of either child.

In any case, Mary and Shelley did not believe in marriage: like Mary's parents they believed in free love. Indeed Shelley favored the idea of what we would now call a commune: he and Jane (who now called herself Claire) were so close, and spent so much time alone together, that it seems likely they had a sexual relationship. Mary was increasingly determined that Claire must leave, which she finally did in May of 1815. Meanwhile Shelley had made every effort to persuade Mary to take his best friend, Thomas Jefferson Hogg, as her lover; the two (though never lovers) became so close that it was to Hogg that Mary turned for support on the death of her baby. A second baby, William, was born in January 1816; he was with Mary throughout the writing of *Frankenstein*.

In the spring of 1816 Claire, very deliberately, seduced Lord Byron (1788–1824), the most famous poet of the day. Byron was acquiring an unenviable reputation. He had vast debts. He had ill-treated his wife, who was seeking a separation; he had had an incestuous relationship with his half sister; and his sexual promiscuity was notorious. One of his lovers, Lady Caroline Lamb, had described him as "mad, bad, and dangerous to know." Rumors began to spread that he engaged in sodomy (which carried the death penalty); he was ostracized and was afraid of being attacked in the street.[12] In April he left England, planning never to return. He traveled in style, in a carriage modeled on that of Napoleon.

Claire, now pregnant, persuaded Percy and Mary to set out with her in pursuit of him. They met up on the shores of Lake Geneva. Byron had lost interest in Claire, though she was still determined to sleep with him.

---

11. Mary Wollstonecraft Shelley and Percy Bysshe Shelley, *History of a Six Weeks' Tour Through a Part of France, Switzerland, Germany, and Holland* (London: T. Hookham, 1817).

12. Fiona MacCarthy, *Byron: Life and Legend* (London: John Murray, 2002), 263–80.

But he enjoyed the company of Shelley and of Mary. He and his traveling companion, a young doctor, John Polidori, rented a large villa on the shores of the lake, and Shelley and his two companions took more modest accommodation ("a little cottage" Mary called it) nearby.[13] Shelley, who loved sailing (but could not swim), hired a boat so that they could potter about on the water.

They were a strange and unequal group. Byron was famous and, despite his debts, able to live in luxury. He was working on the third canto of *Childe Harold's Pilgrimage*, the first two cantos of which had been a bestseller. Polidori had been commissioned by a publisher to write an account of Byron's travels; Byron was growing tired of his company and would soon dismiss him. Shelley's work was barely known: his radicalism and atheism meant that he could publish only semi-secretly. Mary and Claire were only eighteen. The other English visitors to Geneva were fascinated by Byron and his female companions; from Geneva they eagerly trained telescopes on the Villa Diodati hoping to see some wickedness; Shelley and Polidori were of no interest to them.

The summer of 1816 was the worst on record. We now know that this was because of the eruption of the volcano Tambora in Indonesia in April 1815.[14] Vast clouds of ash were thrown into the upper atmosphere, and the climate of the whole globe was affected; the winter of 1815/16 was exceptionally cold; 1816 was the year without a summer; 1817 was a year of famine. In Switzerland there were floods, and the glaciers advanced. Byron wrote his poem "Darkness": "Morn came and went—and came, and brought no day." Mary complained of "an almost perpetual rain" in a letter home.[15] "It proved," she wrote later, "a wet, ungenial summer, and incessant rain often confined us for days to the house."[16] Thus it was that, gathered around a log fire in the Villa Diodati, the party turned to a traditional winter occupation, the reading (presumably aloud) of ghost stories.[17] Byron then set the party a challenge: they must each write a story. Polidori

13. Shelley, *Letters*, ed. Bennett (1980–1988), 1:20.

14. There is now a large literature on the Tambora eruption: see in particular Wolfgang Behringer, *Tambora and the Year Without a Summer* (Cambridge, UK: Polity Press, 2019). On its relevance to *Frankenstein*, Gillen D'Arcy Wood, *Tambora: The Eruption That Changed the World* (Princeton, NJ: Princeton University Press, 2014), 9, 45–47, 52–54, 66–69; also Bill Phillips, "*Frankenstein* and Mary Shelley's 'Wet Ungenial Summer,'" *Atlantis* 28 (2006): 59–68.

15. Shelley, *Letters*, ed. Bennett (1980–1988), 1:20.

16. Shelley, *Frankenstein* (1831), vii (below, p. 184).

17. The stories are collected in A. J. Day, ed., *Fantasmagoriana: Tales of the Dead* (St. Ives: Fantasmagoriana Press, 2004).

later produced two stories, both published in 1819. The first, called *The Vampyre*, is now regarded as the first example of modern vampire literature.[18] It was a reworking of the story Byron had told that summer, but it turned a character based on Byron into the villain. Published as being by Byron, it was Polidori's revenge on his former employer. The second, *Ernestus Berchtold: Or the Modern Oedipus* (the subtitle is an obvious reference to the subtitle of *Frankenstein*, by then in print), is his own story reworked. And Mary Godwin (as she still was) produced the first version of *Frankenstein*.

Percy Shelley's Preface to the 1818 edition of *Frankenstein* and Mary Shelley's Introduction to the 1831 edition provide their accounts of the origins of the novel.[19] Our only contemporary source is Polidori's diary.[20] He records that on June 18, the night after Byron's challenge, they "really began to talk ghostly."

> [Byron] repeated some verses of Coleridge's *Christabel*, of the witch's breast; when silence ensued, and Shelley, shrieking and putting his hands to his head, ran out of the room with a candle. Threw water in his face and after gave him ether. He was looking at Mrs S [i.e., Mary Godwin/Shelley], and suddenly thought of a woman he had heard of who had eyes instead of nipples, which taking hold of his mind, horrified him.[21]

Shelley's hysterical fit was so bad that Polidori had a second doctor summoned. Not surprisingly, this event makes no appearance in either Percy Shelley's or Mary Shelley's account.

---

18. John William Polidori, *The Vampyre: A Tale* (London: Sherwood, Neely, and Jones, 1819); John William Polidori, *The Vampyre: And Other Tales of the Macabre*, eds. Robert Morrison and Chris Baldick (Oxford: Oxford University Press, 2008).

19. For a critique of the 1831 Introduction, see James Rieger, "Dr. Polidori and the Genesis of Frankenstein," *Studies in English Literature, 1500–1900* 3 (1963): 461–72.

20. There are two other noncontemporary sources: the introductory letter to Polidori, *The Vampyre: A Tale* (1819) (perhaps by Mme Gatelier: John William Polidori, *The Diary of Dr. John William Polidori, 1816: Relating to Byron, Shelley, Etc.*, ed. W. M. Rossetti [London: Elkin Mathews, 1911], 13); and Thomas Medwin, *Journal of the Conversations of Lord Byron . . . in the Years 1821 and 1822*, 2nd ed. (London: Henry Colburn, 1824), 120–21. (I quote the "second" edition as the text is garbled in earlier editions.) The story "something like 'Alonzo and Imogene'" reported by Byron as told by Lewis (who in fact only joined the group later) is recorded by PBS in their joint journal (Mary Wollstonecraft Shelley, *The Journals of Mary Shelley, 1814–1844*, eds. Paula R. Feldman and Diana Scott-Kilvert [Oxford: Clarendon Press, 1987], 126–27).

21. Polidori, *The Diary*, ed. Rossetti (1911), 127–28 (below, p. 199).

By early September, Mary, Percy, and Claire were back in England. (Byron was never to return; he died a hero, fighting for Greek independence, in 1824.) They went first to Bath (where no one would recognize Claire, now heavily pregnant). They were there in October when they heard news of Mary's half sister Fanny's suicide: Fanny had gone to Swansea to take poison, so that the dreadful event could be, and was, with a moderate amount of judicious lying, concealed. On December 15th they learned that Harriet, abandoned and pregnant by another man, had also died from suicide by drowning.

Two weeks later Shelley and Mary were married: this was intended to facilitate Percy Shelley's claim to raise his children by Harriet, a claim eventually rejected by the judges, who refused to entrust them to an atheist. The marriage also made possible a reconciliation between Mary and her father, who had to this point refused to meet with them (while still expecting financial support from Shelley); Mary though continued to hate her stepmother ("Is she not an odious woman[?]" she wrote).[22] They moved to Marlow, thirty miles up the Thames from London, in March 1817: Mary was now pregnant with her third child, Clara Everina, born in September. They were soon joined by Claire and her baby, Alba, later called Allegra. (The framing narrative of *Frankenstein* covers a period of 276 days, or the same length of time as a pregnancy. It took Mary almost exactly the same length of time to produce the first complete draft of her book, which she called "my hideous progeny".)[23] By May, Mary Shelley had written out a fair copy of her novel, and Percy began to look for a publisher. (Because it was Percy who saw the book into print, the gossip at first was that he was the author.)

Frankenstein is often called a Gothic novel, which certainly fits with the circumstances in which it was first invented: the talking ghostly, the breasts with eyes.[24] The stories were, we are told, to be "founded on some supernatural occurrence."[25] The novel contains scenes of horror and mystery, but contemporary reviewers did not compare it to Gothic novels for the simple reason that it contains no supernatural occurrences—no ghosts, no prophecies, no unseen powers.[26] This is not, Percy Shelley says in his

---

22. Shelley, *Letters*, ed. Bennett (1980–1988), 1:34.
23. Shelley, *Frankenstein* (1831), xii (below, p. 187).
24. Mary Wollstonecraft Shelley, *Frankenstein, or, the Modern Prometheus: The 1818 Text*, ed. Marilyn Butler (Oxford: Oxford University Press, 1994), xxi–xxix.
25. Mary Wollstonecraft Shelley, *Frankenstein; or, The Modern Prometheus*, 3 vols. (London: Lackington, Hughes, Harding, Mavor, & Jones, 1818), 1:xii (below, p. 4).
26. The preface to the first Gothic novel, *Otranto* (the word "Gothic" appears in the subtitle of the second edition), stressed the presence of "miracles, visions, necromancy, dreams,

Preface to the 1818 edition, "a mere tale of spectres or enchantment."[27] Indeed, it is precisely because it drops such Gothic elements that *Frankenstein* is a "modern" story, as its subtitle insists. That is not to say that Mary Shelley did not learn from the techniques of the Gothic novelists; indeed in August, Matthew Lewis (1775–1818), who had written a famous Gothic novel *The Monk* (1796) (written in 1794 when he was aged twenty), briefly joined Byron's party: Percy recorded in their joint journal that Monk Lewis told him "many mysteries of his trade."[28] At this point Mary was busy writing the first draft of her story.

Sir Walter Scott, reviewing *Frankenstein*, grasped exactly what its author was doing: she was imagining a world in which the limits of the natural were different from those known to us, and then asking how people like us would behave in such a world.[29] Godwin had written such a novel, *St. Leon: A Tale of the Sixteenth Century* (1799), in which the protagonist discovers the secrets of immortality and of turning base metal into gold; the impossible premise makes possible a study of the contradictions and corruption of contemporary society; one reviewer thought *Frankenstein* "a feeble imitation" of *St. Leon*.[30] In December 1810 Percy Shelley (aged eighteen) had published a short (and unsuccessful) novel, *St. Irvyne; or, The Rosicrucian*, which really was a feeble imitation of *St. Leon*. Where in *St. Leon* and *St. Irvyne* alchemy proves to be not delusive but real, in *Frankenstein* contemporary science is imagined as capable of fulfilling an ancient dream of the alchemists, the creation of human life. Mary Shelley was

---

and other preternatural events." (Horace Walpole, *The Castle of Otranto a Story. Translated by William Marshal, Gent. from the Original Italian of Onuphrio Muralto* [London: Tho. Lownds, 1765], v.) When the review of *Frankenstein* in *The Literary Panorama, and National Register* (N.S., 8 [1 June 1818]: 411–14, at 412; below, p. 318) calls it a "supernatural story" it can only mean "supernatural" in the sense of marvelous or extraordinary (and see below, p. 3n4). Ann Radcliffe (1764–1823) invented a form of Gothic fiction in which apparently supernatural events turn out to have natural explanations, thus bending the genre, but *Frankenstein* is not even Gothic in this sense.

27. Shelley, *Frankenstein* (1818), 1:viii.

28. Shelley, *Journals*, eds. Feldman and Scott-Kilvert (1987), 126.

29. Sir Walter Scott, review in *Blackwood's Edinburgh Magazine* 2 (March 1818): 613–20, at 613–15 (below, pp. 299–301). See PBS's Preface to the 1818 edition (below, p. 3; Shelley, *Frankenstein* [1818], 1:viii); and, already, Walpole, *The Castle of Otranto* (1765), v: "Allow the possibility of the facts, and all the actors comport themselves as persons would do in their situation."

30. *The Literary Panorama*, N.S. 8 (1 June 1818), 411-12 (below, p. 317).

writing science fiction.[31] She may well have had an example in mind: she had read Voltaire's *Micromégas* (a novel about space travel) in April 1815.[32]

In writing a novel about a man obsessed with scientific knowledge Mary Shelley was drawing on Percy's descriptions of his own youth. In September 1815, the Shelleys, their friend Thomas Love Peacock (who had just written *Headlong Hall*, published in December 1815, a wonderful satirical novel about their circle of friends), and Mary's stepbrother Charles had made a boating trip up the Thames, and had visited Oxford, from which Percy and Hogg had together been expelled in 1811. Charles wrote to Claire: "We visited the very rooms where the two noted infidels, Percy and Hogg, (now, happily, excluded from the society of the present residents), pored, with the incessant and unwearied application of the alchymist, over the certified and natural boundaries of human knowledge."[33] In these rooms, as Shelley surely explained, he had experimented with electricity. We also have Hogg's description of meeting Shelley in his first term at Oxford:

> He then proceeded, with much eagerness and enthusiasm, to show me the various instruments [in his rooms], especially the electrical apparatus; turning round the handle very rapidly, so that the fierce, crackling sparks flew forth; and presently standing upon the stool with glass feet, he begged me to work the machine until he was filled with the fluid, so that his long, wild locks bristled and stood on end. Afterwards he charged a powerful battery of several large jars;[34] labouring with vast energy, and discoursing with increasing vehemence of the marvellous powers of electricity, of thunder and light-

---

31. Rieger (Mary Wollstonecraft Shelley, *Frankenstein, or, the Modern Prometheus: The 1818 Text*, ed. James Rieger [Chicago: University of Chicago Press, 1982], xxvii) writes: "it would be a mistake to call *Frankenstein* a pioneer work of science fiction . . . the technological plausibility that is essential to science fiction is not even pretended at here. The science-fiction writer says, in effect, since *x* has been experimentally proven or theoretically postulated, *y* can be achieved by the following, carefully documented operation. Mary Shelley skips to the outcome and asks, if *y* had been achieved, by whatever means, what would be the moral consequences? In other words, she skips the science." But, inevitably, all science fiction writers skip the science; none of them proceed from actual experiments to a careful documentation of the operation which would produce a seemingly impossible technology. It is sometimes said that *Frankenstein* was the first science fiction novel in English (Elizabeth Bear in Mary Wollstonecraft Shelley, *Frankenstein*, eds. David H. Guston, Ed Finn, and Jason Scott Robert [Cambridge, MA: MIT Press, 2017], 231), but there was a long history of science fiction before *Frankenstein*: see David Wootton, *The Invention of Science: A New History of the Scientific Revolution* (New York: Harper, 2015), chap. 6.
32. Shelley, *Journals*, eds. Feldman and Scott-Kilvert (1987), 73, 91.
33. Richard Holmes, *Shelley: The Pursuit* (London: Weidenfeld & Nicolson, 1974), 291.
34. The battery had been invented by Volta in 1799.

ning; describing an electrical kite that he had made at home, and projecting [i.e., planning] another and an enormous one, or rather a combination of many kites, that would draw down from the sky an immense volume of electricity, the whole ammunition of a mighty thunderstorm; and this being directed to some point would there produce the most stupendous results.[35]

Thunderstorms, lightning, and electricity play an important role in *Frankenstein*. How Percy Shelley must have thrilled to the thunderstorms that broke over Lake Geneva in the miserable summer of 1815. Byron describes one in *Childe Harold*, and Mary enthuses in a letter to Fanny:

> The thunder storms that visit us are grander and more terrific than I have ever seen before. We watch them as they approach from the opposite side of the lake, observing the lightning play among the clouds in various parts of the heavens, and dart in jagged figures upon the piny heights of Jura, dark with the shadow of the overhanging cloud, while perhaps the sun is shining cheerily upon us. One night we enjoyed a finer storm than I had ever before beheld. The lake was lit up—the pines on Jura made visible, and all the scene illuminated for an instant, when a pitchy blackness succeeded, and the thunder came in frightful bursts over our heads amid the darkness.[36]

In its first version Mary Shelley's story began with what became the first sentence of Volume 1, Chapter 4 (1.4): "It was on a dreary night of November. . . ." It thus began with Victor Frankenstein's account of the creation of the creature that he describes as a monster. At some early point Mary Shelley came up with the brilliant device of making the basic structure of the novel consist of two narratives: Frankenstein's, which runs from 1.1 (which is not the beginning of the book in its final form, for it is preceded by four letters from Walton that are not numbered as chapters) to 2.2; and the story told by the Creature he has created, which now runs from 2.3 (but which in an earlier draft was intended to be the opening chapter of the second volume of a two-volume novel) to the end of Volume 2. The first six chapters of Volume 3 provide the tragic outcome. We may guess that all this had been drafted when Mary, Percy, and Claire left for England, which they reached in early September.[37]

Mary Shelley did something remarkable when she constructed the novel around two first-person narratives. In the first place, there is no narrator

35. Holmes, *Shelley: The Pursuit* (1974), 44–45.

36. Shelley, *Letters*, ed. Bennett (1980–1988), 1:20.

37. In the middle of Vol. 2 comes Safie's story: it is clear from the draft manuscript that this w?s a late addition.

who reports events from an impartial and omniscient perspective. Rather we see the world first through Frankenstein's eyes, and then through the Creature's. And the two have very different stories to tell, told from contrasting perspectives, and offering conflicting assessments of their relationship. It is left to us as readers to decide who has the greater claim to our sympathies.[38]

We may contrast *Frankenstein* in this respect with Godwin's successful *Things as They Are: Or the Adventures of Caleb Williams* (1794), a novel with which contemporaries compared it, partly because it portrays a world of injustice and persecution, and also because its narrator is haunted by a remorseless pursuer. *Caleb Williams* is told as a first-person narrative—somewhat imperfectly as Caleb, on at least one occasion, describes events at which he was not present without explaining how he has knowledge of them.[39] We are bound to ask ourselves over and over again whether we share Caleb's assessment of what is going on and how he should respond to it, but in the end we cannot escape Caleb's viewpoint. Caleb, we are required to conclude, is a sort-of-reliable narrator.

In *Frankenstein*, Mary Shelley achieves something quite different: she offers us a choice of viewpoints and leaves us to choose with which of her two narrators we wish to sympathize. This was a common trick in epistolary novels (novels structured around an exchange of letters), such as Samuel Richardson's *Clarissa* (1748), but usually the choice was fairly straightforward, while Shelley postpones the introduction of a second point of view until such a late stage that readers are led to assume they can safely identify with Frankenstein; to hear the Creature speak, tell his own story, and lay claim to our sympathy, comes as a shock. The reader is thus left, deliberately, disoriented, unable to choose between two equally reliable (or unreliable) narrators. Both narrators can be trusted on matters of fact, but it is not clear if either can be trusted when it comes to how they evaluate their circumstances. It is this structural feature of the novel that opens it to a variety of interpretations and, in large part, explains why it has not dated in the way other novels of the period have.

Mary Shelley was evidently thinking about how best to write a first-person narrative as she began work on the story that was to grow into *Frankenstein*: from July 31 to August 4, 1816, she was reading Rousseau's *Reveries*

---

38. On the importance of seeing that both Frankenstein and the Creature have a valid point of view, Lawrence Lipking, "*Frankenstein*, the True Story; or, Rousseau Judges Jean-Jacques," in *Frankenstein*, ed. J. Paul Hunter (New York: Norton, 2012): 416–34, at 418–23.

39. See, on the similarities between the novels, A. D. Harvey, "*Frankenstein* and *Caleb Williams*," *Keats-Shelley Journal* 29 (1980): 21–27, at 24–27.

of the Solitary Walker.[40] Visiting Edward Gibbon's house in Lausanne she felt compelled to invoke "the greater and more sacred name of Rousseau, the contemplation of whose creations left no vacancy for mortal things." She read Rousseau's *Julie* (another epistolary novel) and repeated her pilgrimage of 1814 to Julie's wood.[41]

Godwin's political and moral philosophies were founded on the claim that human institutions, not sin, are the source of moral evil. In this he shared the views of a number of radical Enlightenment thinkers, including Jean-Jacques Rousseau and Mary Wollstonecraft, although the conclusions he was prepared to draw from this premise went further than others, for Godwin held that it should be possible, if people could be persuaded to think differently, to eliminate human-made evil altogether. Mary Shelley, traveling through France in 1814 and seeing the destruction caused by the French Revolution, was far from being an uncritical enthusiast for radical politics. But the central message of *Frankenstein*, the primary reason for dedicating the book to Godwin, is precisely this Godwinian claim: the Creature is naturally good; he is corrupted by human beings, who make him evil. Percy Shelley summed up the book's message clearly in the review he wrote (but did not publish):

> Nor are the crimes and malevolence of the single Being, though indeed withering and tremendous, the offspring of any unaccountable propensity to evil, but flow irresistibly from certain causes fully adequate to their production. They are the children, as it were, of Necessity and Human Nature. In this the direct moral of the book consists; and it is perhaps the most important, and of the most universal application, of any moral that can be enforced by example. Treat a person ill, and he will become wicked.[42]

Thus the central message of *Frankenstein* is that evil begets evil and that human beings are responsible for all the wickedness in the world. It is perhaps relevant that Mary Shelley read Voltaire's philosophical novels,

---

40. Shelley, *Journals*, eds. Feldman and Scott-Kilvert (1987), 121–23. In nearly every edition the *Reveries* was bound with the *Confessions*; MWS read fast, and it seems likely her reading was not confined to the *Reveries*.

41. Shelley, *Journals*, eds. Feldman and Scott-Kilvert (1987), 111–12. On the importance of Rousseau, Lipking, "*Frankenstein*, the True Story; or, Rousseau Judges Jean-Jacques" (2012), 424–34. And, on MWS's sources, Burton R. Pollin, "Philosophical and Literary Sources of *Frankenstein*," *Comparative Literature* 17 (1965): 97–108, is still of interest.

42. Percy Bysshe Shelley, *The Athenæum*, 10 November 1832, p. 730 (review of 1818 edition, written in 1817 or 1818; below p. 326).

which all address the problem of evil, on July 23, 28, and 29, 1816, just when she was getting down to work on *Frankenstein*.[43] And, as we have seen, she had Rousseau in mind: Rousseau who insisted that human beings are not naturally wicked or indeed good but are shaped by society into being one or the other.

The Creature, abandoned by his maker, is ill-treated, and his ill-treatment takes a very specific form: he is excluded from human society. This, on a smaller scale, was what had happened to Percy and Mary as a consequence of their elopement. On December 8, 1816, Shelley described himself as "an outcast from human society"; with few exceptions people "abhor & avoid me."[44] Byron too was an outcast. The Creature thus embodies their shared sense of being driven out of respectable society.

Mary Shelley was also aware (quite apart from her own experience) of how societies function by exclusion as well as inclusion and was conscious that some social groups are treated as if they are not truly human beings. One group in particular was surely in her mind: over and over again the novel echoes the language of antislavery campaigners. Slavery was illegal in Great Britain from the 1770s, but the slave trade remained legal in the British Empire until 1807, and slavery was only abolished there in 1833. Slavery was not abolished in the United States until 1865. Slavery was a continuing abomination, and the language of the novel points to Shelley's acute awareness of the fact.

The novel is thus open to two contrasting readings. On the one hand, Frankenstein and his Creature represent two aspects of our own psychology, the civilized and the primitive, social man and natural man, ego and id, and consequently the two protagonists are bound together, like it or not, in a conflict that can end only in death.[45] On the other (as in Godwin's *Caleb Williams*) the two main protagonists represent the social conflict at the heart of "things as they are," the conflict between master and servant, a conflict that cannot be resolved unless and until society is radically transformed.

It is this moral lesson, that evil begets evil, that is the central message of the book, and it is one that is at odds with the conventional moral code which insists that individuals are responsible for their evil actions: if evil begets evil then it is society that is responsible for evil acts, not those

---

43. Shelley, *Journals*, eds. Feldman and Scott-Kilvert (1987), 117, 121.
44. Miranda Seymour, *Mary Shelley* (London: Faber & Faber, 2011), 174; Percy Bysshe Shelley, *The Letters of Percy Bysshe Shelley*, ed. Frederick L. Jones, 2 vols. (Oxford: Clarendon Press, 1964), 1:571.
45. Mary Wollstonecraft Shelley, *Frankenstein, or, the Modern Prometheus*, ed. Charles E. Robinson (Oxford: Bodleian Library, 2008), 32–34.

who perform them. Hence the complaint by a contemporary reviewer that Shelley's novel leads "to no conclusion either moral or philosophical."[46] Actually the novel leads to a very clear conclusion, which is that Frankenstein has failed to take responsibility for the creature he has created, has failed to nurture him and educate him, and is therefore in large part to blame for the unfolding tragedy—and here one can't help but remember that Percy Shelley had shown no interest in his children by Harriet, had provided little comfort to Mary on the death of their first child, and continued to be a neglectful father.[47] This moral lesson, that children have a right to be loved, escaped all the reviewers, presumably partly because they were unable to grasp the idea that fathers might have just as much responsibility as mothers for the welfare of their children.[48]

Nearly everything you have read so far represents received opinion. I want now, though, to move away from the standard accounts and pursue three interlocking arguments: first, about the novel's subtitle, "The Modern Prometheus"; second, about the novel's relationship to contemporary science; and third, about the composition of the framing narrative, the letters written by Robert Walton to his sister, Mrs. Saville, with which the book begins and ends. These arguments are independent of each other; each of them is, I think, significant; and if all three are sound then they represent a substantial reinterpretation of the novel.

We begin with "The Modern Prometheus." Here (with one exception) scholars have failed to grasp what Shelley (and her readers) meant when they referred to the myth of Prometheus.[49] According to Greek myth,

---

46. This is the complete text of the review appearing in *The Monthly Review*, April 1818: "An uncouth story, in the taste of the German novelists, trenching in some degree on delicacy, setting probability at defiance, and leading to no conclusion either moral or philosophical. In some passages, the writer appears to favour the doctrines of materialism: but a serious examination is scarcely necessary for so excentric a vagary of the imagination as this tale presents" ("*The Monthly Review*, N.S., 85 [April 1818]: 439," The Mary Shelley Wollstonecraft Chronology and Resource Site, ed. Shanon Lawson, Romantic Circles [website], published March 1998, https://romantic-circles.org/reference/chronologies/mschronology/reviews/monthlyrev).
47. See, for example, MWS's letter to PBS of Dec. 5, 1816, breaking the news that she might be pregnant again (Shelley, *Letters*, ed. Bennett [1980–1988], 1:22–23).
48. Eileen Hunt Botting, *Mary Shelley and the Rights of the Child* (Philadelphia: University of Philadelphia Press, 2018).
49. The exception is Mary Wollstonecraft Shelley, *Frankenstein, or, the Modern Prometheus*, ed. M. K. Joseph (Oxford: Oxford University Press, 1980), v–vi, 228–29, first published in 1969, and now rarely consulted as it prints the 1831 edition. (Shaftesbury, claimed by Joseph as MWS's source, seems to me a distraction.) Joseph's account is followed (though not cited) in Mary Wollstonecraft Shelley, *Frankenstein, or, the Modern Prometheus: The*

Prometheus, one of the Titans, who had been defeated by the gods of Olympus, stole fire from the gods and gave it to humans (and with fire came key technologies such as metallurgy)—this is Prometheus *pyrphoros*, the fire-bringer. Zeus responded by creating Pandora, the source of all the troubles of humankind, and by chaining Prometheus to a rock, where his liver was eaten by an eagle (or, in some versions, a vulture). According to the Romans, on the other hand, Prometheus made human beings out of earth and water—this is Prometheus *plasticator*, Prometheus the sculptor. Neither the Greeks nor the Romans associated the theft of fire with the creation of human life, but in Neoplatonism this became a common theme, and thus it became a standard element in Christian accounts of the Promethean myth.[50] Prometheus gives life to his clay statue by bringing down fire from heaven—fire obviously standing as a symbolic representation of the soul. This is why Frankenstein talks about animating lifeless clay.[51]

1818 Text, ed. Nick Groom (Oxford: Oxford University Press, 2018), xxviii–xxix, and Godwin's *The Pantheon* is referenced, but Groom errs when he states that in Ovid's *Metamorphoses* Prometheus "steals celestial fire to bring his creation to life," and thus fails to distinguish between the Roman and Neoplatonic myths. Some editors simply fail to discuss Prometheus (Shelley, *Frankenstein*, ed. Butler [1994]; Mary Wollstonecraft Shelley, *Frankenstein, or, the Modern Prometheus*, eds. David Lorne Macdonald and Kathleen Dorothy Scherf [Peterborough, ON: Broadview Press, 2012]). Others are aware only of the Greek version of the myth (Susan J. Wolfson, ed., *Mary Wollstonecraft Shelley's Frankenstein: Or, the Modern Prometheus* [London: Longman, 2007], xx; Charles E. Robinson [1969], reprinted in Mary Wollstonecraft Shelley, *Frankenstein*, ed. Charlotte Gordon [New York: Penguin, 2018], 217; both Robinson and Elizabeth Bear in Shelley, *Frankenstein*, eds. Guston, Finn, and Robert [2017], xxviii, 231; Baldick in Mary Wollstonecraft Shelley, *Frankenstein: The 1818 Text, Contexts, Criticism*, ed. J. Paul Hunter [New York: Norton, 2012], 182) or of the Roman but not the Neoplatonic: Shelley, *Frankenstein*, ed. Rieger (1982), xxxi.

50. E.g., in Fulgentius, *Mythologies*, 2.6, Theoi Project (website), accessed February 21, 2020, https://www.theoi.com/Text/FulgentiusMythologies2.html#6. Fulgentius was a sixth-century Christian. (I owe this reference to Brian Rak.)

51. Shelley, *Frankenstein* (1818), 1:90 (below, p. 37). Olga Raggio, "The Myth of Prometheus: Its Survival and Metamorphoses Up to the Eighteenth Century," *Journal of the Warburg and Courtauld Institutes* 21 (1958), 44–62. The key differences between the pagan and Christian versions of the myth do not emerge in Genevieve Liveley, "Patchwork Paratexts and Monstrous Metapoetics: 'After Tea M Reads Ovid,'" in *Frankenstein and Its Classics*, ed. Jesse Weiner, Benjamin Eldon Stevens, and Brett M. Rogers (London: Bloomsbury, 2018): 25–41; Martin Priestman, "Prometheus and Dr. Darwin's Vermicelli: Another Stir to the *Frankenstein* Broth," in *Frankenstein and Its Classics*, ed. Weiner, Eldon Stevens, and Rogers (2018): 42–58; and Suzanne L. Barnett, "Romantic Prometheis and the Molding of *Frankenstein*," in *Frankenstein and Its Classics*, ed. Weiner, Eldon Stevens, and Rogers (2018): 76–90. Liveley discusses at length an illustration to the 1632 edition of Sandys's translation of Ovid, stating that it appears "in the editions of Sandys's translation and commentary published from 1632 onwards (including, then, two of the editions in

It is important to see that, although Percy was familiar with the Greek and Roman sources, and although Mary had been reading Ovid, who has a version of the Roman myth, when Mary Shelley subtitled her book "The Modern Prometheus" she was not thinking of the pagan myths, whether Greek or Roman, but of the story that Prometheus had made the first humans out of clay *and had then enlivened them by divine fire*.[52] This is what Frankenstein does: he makes his Creature out of dead matter, and then brings it to life with electricity, which can take the form of fire (as it does in lightning). It is this version of the Prometheus myth to which the *Quarterly Review* made reference: "by dabbling (as [Frankenstein] delicately expresses it) with the unhallowed damps of the grave, and torturing the living animal to animate lifeless clay, our modern Prometheus formed a filthy image to which the last step of his art was to communicate being." And it is to this that *The British Critic*'s reviewer refers when they write of "the last Promethean spark" that gives life.[53]

That this is the version of the Prometheus myth with which Shelley was most familiar we can have no doubt, for it is the version to be found in the book on Greek and Roman mythology written by her own father: *The Pantheon* (1806, with seven editions by 1828) was written for the education of children, and we can be sure that it formed part of Mary's own education.[54] Godwin's account is not original to him; he had simply borrowed it from other similar works, and he was probably quite unaware of how far it

---

Godwin's library)" and that "the chances of MWS having encountered this image . . . are high" (37–39). In fact the image, which shows a Neoplatonic version of the Prometheus myth, is unique to the 1632 edition, and so not in the editions in Godwin's library or in those likely to have been seen by MWS.

52. We may thus contrast MWS's *Frankenstein* with Byron's *Prometheus* (1816) and PBS's *Prometheus Unbound* (1820): these address the classical Greek not the Neoplatonic version of the myth. Ignorance of the Christianized Prometheus myth can lead to a misinterpretation of the text, e.g., when Andrew Smith writes, "The creature's animation is seemingly the consequence of a reactivated life force which exists within the materiality of the body parts from which he is assembled. Life is therefore not found outside the body, or separate from it, because electricity is simply the agent that is employed to bring to life what is already there to be reanimated" (Andrew Smith, "Scientific Contexts," in *The Cambridge Companion to "Frankenstein*," ed. Andrew Smith [Cambridge, MA: Cambridge University Press, 2016]: 69–83, at 72–74), he is relying on a mistaken version of the Abernethy/Lawrence debate (to which we will soon come—neither Abernethy nor Lawrence held the view of life and electricity presented here), and ignoring the Christianized myth of Prometheus, according to which life comes from outside the body.

53. John Wilson Croker, review in *The Quarterly Review* 18 (January 1818): 379–85, at 380 (below, p. 320); review in *The British Critic* N.S. 9 (April 1818): 200–207, at 436 (below, p. 315).

54. Edward Baldwin [William Godwin], *The Pantheon: Or Ancient History of the Gods of Greece and Rome* (London: Thomas Hodgkins, 1806), 93–99 (below, pp. 201–203), 282, and 286.

departed from the pagan sources.[55] This was also the version of the myth that was familiar to Mary Wollstonecraft. In her *Short Residence in Sweden*, a book well-known to Mary Shelley (Percy had read the book aloud to her on the homeward voyage in 1814, but she surely knew it already), she recounts a conflict with a postilion (or coachman):

> The horses went on very well; but when we drew near the post-house, the postilion stopt short, and neither threats, nor promises, could prevail on him to go forward. He even began to howl and weep, when I insisted on his keeping his word. Nothing, indeed, can equal the stupid obstinacy of some of these half alive beings, who seem to have been made by Prometheus, when the fire he stole from Heaven was so exhausted, that he could only spare a spark to give life, not animation, to the inert clay.[56]

We may note that in 1831 Shelley describes Frankenstein as conveying only a "slight spark of life" to dead matter.[57]

And it is this which explains Shelley's epigraph from Milton's *Paradise Lost* (which appears on the title page of each volume of the 1818 edition, and is quoted at the opening of Walter Scott's review). In it she surely expected the reader to recognize an allusion to the myth of Prometheus:

> Did I request thee, Maker, from my clay
> To mould me man? Did I solicit thee
> From darkness to promote me?——[58]

Here Adam, now expelled from Paradise, speaking to God, could equally be speaking to Prometheus. Indeed Prometheus, in the Christian version of the myth, played a part properly reserved for God (as does Frankenstein in Shelley's novel: the *Edinburgh Magazine* was shocked to find Frankenstein addressed by the Creature as "my Creator").[59]

The Prometheus myth, *Paradise Lost*, and the Genesis story (which is evoked by the references to *Paradise Lost*) all provide an account of how

---

55. John Bell, *Bell's New Pantheon; or, Historical Dictionary of the Gods, Demi-Gods, Heroes, and Fabulous Personages of Antiquity* (London: J. Bell, 1790), art "Prometheus," 195–96; Samuel Boyse, *The Pantheon or, Fabulous History of the Heathen Gods, Goddesses, Heroes, &c.*, 8th ed. (Dublin: R. Cross and P. Wogan, 1800), chap. 7; François Pomey, *The Pantheon*, 31st ed. (London: J. Johnson, 1803), chap. 8.

56. Mary Wollstonecraft, *Letters Written During a Short Residence in Sweden, Norway, and Denmark* (London: J. Johnson, 1796), 183–84 (see also 106).

57. Shelley, *Frankenstein* (1831), x (below, p. 186).

58. Milton, *Paradise Lost*, bk. 10, lines 743–5. This crucial text is dropped from the editions of 1823 and 1831.

59. Anonymous review in *The Edinburgh Magazine and Literary Miscellany* NS2 (March 1818), 249-53, at 253 (below, p. 297).

evil comes to be predominant in human existence. In each case a super-natural power (Zeus, Jupiter, or Satan) is at work. Godwin, reviewing the Prometheus myth, thought that this (not the explanation given by the Greek version of the Prometheus myth for technological progress) was the crucial context in which to place the story of Prometheus. What particularly exercised him, as he recounted the myth, is that according to both the Greeks and Genesis it is a woman, Pandora or Eve, who releases evil into the world. As a feminist, Godwin was horrified by this misogyny. Mary Shelley, in choosing to write about a modern Prometheus, naturally had to address the gendered nature of the Prometheus myth. She did it in the simplest and most effective way: she left Pandora out. The Creature longs for a companion, but there is no Eve to his Adam, no Pandora in his life. This absence is as eloquent as anything that is present in the text; the book, we may say, is about Eve precisely because it is nowhere about Eve.[60]

The Prometheus myth was thus, for Shelley, not about Prometheus as a prototype technologist, bringing fire and metallurgy to humankind, but about Prometheus as a godlike creator, the maker of humankind. Franken-stein, like Prometheus, makes a human being from dead matter and brings it to life with fire. The story is fleshed out (if I may so put it) and brought into the nineteenth century by presenting Frankenstein/Prometheus as a natural philosopher, and his own biography as a recapitulation of the history of chemistry. (Much of this was added later to the draft as a result of Shelley's reading Humphry Davy's "Historical View of the Progress of Chemistry" [1812] at the end of October and beginning of November 1816.)[61] The reviewers, of course, acknowledged that there were lots of references to science in the novel, but for them the science in *Franken-stein* was a fantastical plot device, just as immortality is in *St. Leon* and *St. Irvyne*. And indeed Percy Shelley's Preface to the 1818 edition (having

---

60. Gilbert, "Horror's Twin: Mary Shelley's Monstrous Eve" (1978) (also in Sandra M. Gilbert and Susan Gubar, *The Madwoman in the Attic: The Woman Writer and the Nineteenth-Century Literary Imagination* [New Haven, CT: Yale University Press, 1979]).
61. In Humphry Davy, *Elements of Chemical Philosophy* (London: J. Johnson, 1812); Shelley, *Journals*, eds. Feldman and Scott-Kilvert (1987), 142–44; I am not convinced by Laura E. Crouch, "Davy's 'A Discourse, Introductory to a Course of Lectures on Chemistry': A Possible Scientific Source of *Frankenstein*," *Keats-Shelley Journal* 27 (1978): 35–44: the introduction to the *Elements* is roughly three times longer than the "Discourse" and contains much more information about the history of chemistry, including references to Albert Magnus, Roger Bacon, Paracelsus, and Agrippa, none of whom are mentioned in the "Discourse." It is hard to see how MWS could have read the brief "Discourse" on four separate days; it is much easier to imagine that she might have read the longer "Historical View" and then picked around elsewhere in the substantial volume of the *Elements* (all her later references are simply to "Davy's chemistry" or "Davy").

misleadingly claimed that Erasmus Darwin and the German physiologists thought the creation of a living creature "not of impossible occurrence") finally acknowledges that the story is "impossible as a physical fact."[62] Nevertheless, according to Byron one naive reader of the novel asked Sir Humphry Davy, "to his great astonishment," if he could make a man.[63]

The claim that *Frankenstein* is primarily about the origins of evil, not about the power of modern science, may seem a strange claim to make, since it is almost automatic for us to read the novel as a study in the evils of a science unchecked by any sense of moral and social responsibility; such a reading requires us to believe that science is capable of acts fully as dangerous as Frankenstein's creation of his Creature. But it would have been very strange for contemporaries to read it in that way simply because science in 1818 was very far from having the transformative power that it came to have by the end of the nineteenth century. So when a reviewer wrote, "It might, indeed, be the author's view to shew that the powers of man have been wisely limited, and that misery would follow their extension," the point was obvious, to them if not to us: the powers of mankind *were* limited, so there was, in the reviewer's mind, no reason to fear their abuse.[64] Readers in 1818 had no reason to think of science as dangerous or uncontrolled.[65]

A few chronological reference points may be useful here. In 1818 stationary steam engines were becoming commonplace in factories, but they were the relatively cumbersome machines, driven by atmospheric pressure,

---

62. Shelley, *Frankenstein* (1818), 1:vii–viii (below, p. 3). PBS's misleading claim has set commentators off in the wrong direction, searching for evidence that contemporaries seriously thought life might be artificially produced. Thus Marilyn Butler describes the novel as using "the fashionable medieval tale of the supernatural to tell a present-day or futuristic narrative grounded in real-life modern science" (Shelley, *Frankenstein*, ed. Butler [1994], 252; see also 255), which is doubly wrong in that the novel avoids the supernatural and only pretends to be grounded in real-life science. Macdonald and Scherf write: "Darwin's vitalism and his belief in spontaneous generation might have led him to suppose that Victor's project was 'not of impossible occurrence'" (Shelley, *Frankenstein*, eds. Macdonald and Scherf [2012], 21). And see the essays by Ruston (below, n. 69). Although contemporaries were agreed that complex life could not be artificially produced some did think that, exceptionally, microscopic creatures might be generated spontaneously: the evidence here was equivocal until (and even beyond) Pasteur (David Wootton, *Bad Medicine: Doctors Doing Harm Since Hippocrates* [Oxford: Oxford University Press, 2006], 119–35).

63. Medwin, *Conversations of Lord Byron* (1824), 120.

64. Anonymous review in *The Edinburgh Magazine and Literary Miscellany* NS2 (March 1818), 249–53, at 253 (below, p. 297).

65. Harvey, "*Frankenstein* and *Caleb Williams*" (1980), at 21–23. I am not persuaded by Richard Holmes, "Mary Shelley and the Power of Contemporary Science," in Shelley, *Frankenstein*, ed. Hunter (2012), 183–94.

invented by Thomas Newcomen and improved by James Watt. (There is a passing reference to steam in *Frankenstein*, apparently added by Percy Shelley.)[66] The first high-pressure steam engine to be put into operation in the United Kingdom was constructed by Richard Trevithick in 1799, but the implications of this were not yet apparent in 1818. Robert Stephenson's *Rocket* did not run on rails until 1829. Again, in 1818 the only major chemical industry was engaged in the production of bleaching powder; the soda industry (crucial for the production of glass, textiles, paper, and soap) began to expand rapidly only after 1824. So too, the understanding of disease was still basically Hippocratic: Ignaz Semmelweis first attributed puerperal fever (from which Wollstonecraft had died) to faulty hygiene in 1847, and Pasteur patented pasteurization (which was linked to the germ theory of disease) in 1865. The Gatling gun was patented in 1862, and dynamite in 1867, while the range of Napoleon's cannon was, at three hundred yards, no greater than that of a Roman ballista.

Thus in most respects the world in which Mary lived would not have seemed peculiar to Shakespeare. For example, *Frankenstein* must be one of the last major works of literature to be written with a quill pen: one can see in the manuscript how every three pages or so Mary had to pause and sharpen her pen with a penknife (what else), just as Shakespeare must have done. It was in 1822 that John Mitchell pioneered the mass production of steel pen-nibs, and patents for fountain pens (such as John Jacob Parker's in 1832) followed swiftly.[67] Mary wrote her novel on paper made of recycled rags, formed in handheld molds, and it was first printed on the same sort of paper: the Fourdrinier machine, which produced paper in a continuous roll, had been patented in 1806, but had not yet transformed the paper-making industry.[68] Mary's novel thus lies just before, not just after,

---

66. Shelley, *Frankenstein* (1818), 1:55 (below, p. 24); David Ketterer, "'The Wonderful Effects of Steam': More Percy Shelley Words in *Frankenstein*?," *Science Fiction Studies* 25 (1998): 566–68.

67. Seymour Howard, "The Steel Pen and the Modern Line of Beauty," *Technology and Culture* 26 (1985): 785–98.

68. I owe this point to Dr. Bruce Barker-Benfield. It is misleading to claim, as Charles E. Robinson does, that *Frankenstein* is set "in the 1790s, by which time James Watt (1736–1819) had radically improved the steam engine. . . . The new steam engine powered paper mills, printed newspapers, and further developed commerce through steamboats and then trains. These same years were charged by the French Revolution. . . ." The first steam-powered paper mill opened in 1807 ("Beam from a Beam Engine Set on a Plinth at Springfield Mill," Historic England [website], accessed February 21, 2020, https://historicengland.org .uk/listing/the-list/list-entry/1266431). The first newspaper was printed by steam power in 1814 ("Koenig and Bauer's Steam Powered Printing Press," Age of Revolution [website], accessed February 21, 2020, https://ageofrevolution.org/200-object/koenigs-steam-powered-printing-press/). The first steamboat on the Thames was in 1815 ("Steamboat," Wikipedia

the great transformation in technology and in social relations that followed from the industrial revolution. When we read it we take that transformation for granted; but she could not see into the future or imagine what technology would soon accomplish. Rather, something much more immediate provoked her imagination.

In 1993 Marilyn Butler offered a powerful new interpretation of the novel and its scientific context, one which has generally been accepted without question by later critics.[69] Butler pointed out that Percy Shelley had, after he was expelled from Oxford, thought of becoming a doctor

---

[website], last modified January 31, 2020, https://en.wikipedia.org/wiki/Steamboat#19th_century). It is thus not surprising that the solitary reference to steam in *Frankenstein* was an afterthought (above, n. 66).

69. Marilyn Butler, "The First *Frankenstein* and Radical Science," *The Times Literary Supplement*, April 9, 1993, 12–14; reprinted in Shelley, *Frankenstein*, ed. Hunter (2012), 404–16; I cite a parallel text, the introduction to Shelley, *Frankenstein*, ed. Butler (1994), xv–xxi, xxix–xxxiii, xlv–li (and 229–51). For an example of the continuing authority of Butler, see Smith, "Scientific Contexts" (2016), 73: Butler is "critically important." My reading and critique of Butler corresponds to that in Shelley, *Frankenstein*, eds. Macdonald and Scherf (2012), 18–20.

Sharon Ruston, "Resurrecting *Frankenstein*," *The Keats-Shelley Review* 19 (2005): 97–116, and Sharon Ruston, "Chemistry and the Science of Transformation in Mary Shelley's *Frankenstein*," *Nineteenth-Century Contexts* 41 (2019): 255–70, follow Butler in their assumption that Lawrence held a much cruder materialist position than he actually did and in repeating Butler's equivocation as to whether the conceptual framework of the novel is to be understood as "vitalist" or "materialist." It is crucial here to recognize that contemporaries wrote about "materialism," but not (in the texts discussed by Butler) about "vitalism." Thus Butler's terminology ("the vitalist debate," "the vitalist controversy") is inherently anachronistic. Lawrence (William Lawrence, *An Introduction to Comparative Anatomy and Physiology* [London: J. Callow, 1816], vi, 158) presented himself as a follower of Xavier Bichat, and his account of the nature of life was entirely in line with that of Bichat, who wrote: "Life consists in the sum of the functions, by which death is resisted . . . unknown in its nature, it can only be appreciated by its phenomena" (Xavier Bichat, *Physiological Researches on Life and Death* [London: Longman, 1815], 21; and see 80–83, paraphrased at Lawrence, *Introduction to Comparative Anatomy* [1816], 157–61; and Sharon Ruston, *Shelley and Vitality* [Basingstoke, UK: Palgrave Macmillan, 2012], 13, 49, 121, 146). In conventional history of medicine Bichat is regarded as the leading vitalist of the day, a "vitalistic materialist" (Owsei Temkin, "Materialism in French and German Physiology of the Early Nineteenth Century," *Bulletin of the History of Medicine* 20 [1946]: 322–27, at 323; Geoffrey Sutton, "The Physical and Chemical Path to Vitalism: Xavier Bichat's *Physiological Researches on Life and Death*," *Bulletin of the History of Medicine* 58, no. 1 [1984]: 53–71). Indeed the first use of the word "vitalism" recorded by the *Oxford English Dictionary* online is a reference to "the vitalism of Bichot [*sic*]" in 1822 (while the word "vitalist" is not recorded by the OED [entries updated 1920] until 1860, though a much earlier example may be found in the obituary for Erasmus Darwin, *The Monthly Repertory of English Literature*, published in Paris, vol. 17 [1812], 89). Ruston, however, generally follows Butler in treating vitalism and materialism as antonyms (e.g., *Shelley and Vitality*, 5, 66), and the result can only be

and had attended the lectures of a leading surgeon, John Abernethy. Mary and Percy were also both associated with a prominent doctor, William Lawrence, who was their personal physician. In March of 1816 Lawrence had given a lecture to the Royal College of Physicians entitled "On Life"— Percy and Mary were in England when the lecture was given, though they had left by the time it was published. Lawrence's target in "On Life" was Abernethy (though he is never mentioned by name), who had long been his mentor and friend. Abernethy had argued, in two lectures published in 1814, that "life" is something "superadded" to matter, some "subtile, mobile, invisible substance," and that it can be compared to electricity or a magnetic field.[70] (The view was not particularly remarkable. In a letter to Ralph Wedgwood dated December 15, 1810, Percy, then a student at Oxford, had already described "Man" as "a mass of electrified clay."[71]) Lawrence mocked this argument: there was no experimental or observational evidence for the existence of such an invisible substance; it was a foolish fiction.

Lawrence's lecture was the start of a bitter quarrel with Abernethy, one in which he was eventually forced to retract his views in order to save his career (he went on to become the Queen's surgeon, president of the Royal College of Surgeons, and a knight). Lawrence's critics argued that Abernethy's theory was compatible with the idea that life (and, in the case of humankind, the soul) was God-given, while Lawrence (who had ended his 1814 lecture with a quotation from Lucretius that made clear he did not believe in the immortality of the soul) was a crude materialist whose beliefs would undermine all morality.

---

considerable confusion as to whether Bichat, Lawrence, and PBS are or are not "vitalists," and as to whether the text of *Frankenstein* is or is not "materialist."

It is important, when reading Ruston's essays on MWS, to distinguish the claim that living creatures transform dead matter into living matter (you put manure on your allotment, the plants turn the manure into living matter, you in turn eat the plants and turn the plants into muscle and bone, and then you die and are eaten by worms), and thus that the boundary between death and life is permeable, from the claim that *new* life can be created out of dead matter, which was generally held to be true (if at all) only at the level of microorganisms. One must also distinguish resuscitation (or, in contemporary language, "reanimation") from the creation of new life. *Frankenstein*, in suggesting new complex animal or indeed human life could be artificially produced, was deliberately crossing the boundary between the natural and the "supernatural."

70. John Abernethy, *An Enquiry into the Probability and Rationality of Mr. Hunter's Theory of Life* (London: Longman, 1814), 39.

71. Robin Darwall-Smith, "The Student Hoaxers: The New Shelley Letters," *University College Record* 14 (2005): 78–87, at p. 82. I owe this reference to Dr. Bruce Barker-Benfield. On these letters see also James Bryant Reeves, "Unbelief and Sympathy in Shelley and Hogg's Letters to Ralph Wedgwood," *Keats-Shelley Journal* 65 (2016): 41–52.

On Butler's reading of this debate, Mary Shelley shared Lawrence's beliefs, and this materialist outlook is apparent in the 1818 text of *Frankenstein* (certainly the early critics, noting the dedication to Godwin, suspected as much); when Shelley revised the book for its third edition in 1831 she went to elaborate lengths to distance herself from Lawrence's views. Butler's account of the revisions introduced in 1831 is broadly convincing,[72] but as she herself acknowledges, in the 1818 edition "Frankenstein . . . shadows the intellectual position [not of Lawrence but] of Abernethy." In order to get around this puzzling feature of the text Butler has to misrepresent Frankenstein: "Frankenstein the blundering experimenter, still working with superseded notions, shadows the intellectual position of Abernethy, who proposes that the superadded life-element is analogous to electricity. Lawrence's sceptical commentary on that position finds its echo in Mary Shelley's equally detached, serio-comic representation. . . ."[73] It should surely be obvious to any reader of the novel that Frankenstein is no blundering experimenter, that he is presented as being at the cutting edge of contemporary science, and that there is nothing detached or comic about Shelley's representation of the birth of the Creature, which she intended to be as frightful as possible, "supremely frightful."[74]

Abernethy's intellectual position is Victor Frankenstein's, and by implication Shelley's. And this is so for the simple reason that, whether or not Shelley agreed with Abernethy, Abernethy's account of life corresponded exactly to the myth of Prometheus: on Abernethy's account life originates when a spark (of electricity rather than fire) is added to dead matter. Frankenstein is the modern Prometheus simply and solely because he is making a human being by enacting Abernethy's theory of life. In *Frankenstein* Shelley is working out simultaneously the myth of Prometheus and its contemporary analogue, the biological science of Abernethy, and showing how they fit perfectly together. One reason Butler cannot see this is that she has given no thought to the myth of Prometheus, which indeed she never mentions.

In order to make *Frankenstein*, in its first edition, an exposition of Lawrentian principles, Butler has to pass over a fundamental moment in Lawrence's exposition of his doctrine. (She quotes fragments from the passage

---

72. Shelley, *Frankenstein*, ed. Butler (1994), 198–228. See also James O'Rourke, "The 1831 Introduction and Revisions to *Frankenstein*: Mary Shelley Dictates Her Legacy," *Studies in Romanticism* 38 (1999): 365–85.
73. Shelley, *Frankenstein*, ed. Butler (1994), xxi. And see p. l: "Before Mary Shelley publishes the novel in its strategically changed guise [i.e., in 1831], a journalist already claims it for Abernethy's rather than Lawrence's side in the vitalist issue."
74. Shelley, *Frankenstein* (1831), x.

I am about to quote, but in such a way as to obscure its significance, concluding that Lawrence's claim is that "the power that animates animals resists abstraction from matter; for the materialist thinker [i.e., Lawrence], an abstracted approach to Life yields nothing"—I place the phrases she quotes in italics.)[75] Abernethy had implied that one could bring dead matter to life if only one knew how to add the life fluid to it. Lawrence would have none of this, complaining that it radically confused chemistry with biology. The central characteristic of life, he argued, is that it does not obey the laws of physics or chemistry (which, left to themselves, bring about the decay of order into disorder, the triumph of entropy), but acts at variance with them (creating order out of disorder, energy out of decomposition). Thus the principles of life are quite distinct from the principles governing the inanimate world; Lawrence does not use the words "abstract," "abstracted," or "abstraction"; what he does argue is that "living bodies . . . are contrasted with inorganic, inert, or dead bodies" by their "organization," not by some mysterious fluid. Indeed his implicit claim is that it is Abernethy who is, in reality, a crude materialist: by claiming that life consists in "a subtle invisible matter" like electricity he obscures the fundamental differences between the animate and the inanimate.[76] "We are," he writes, "naturally anxious to investigate" the origin of life:

> to see how it is produced, and to inquire how it is communicated to the beings in which we find it. We endeavour therefore *to observe living bodies in the moment of their formation*, to watch the time, *when matter may be supposed to receive the stamp of life*, and the inert mass to be quickened. *Hitherto, however, physiologists have not been able to catch nature in the fact* [i.e., in the act]. Living bodies have never been observed otherwise than completely formed, enjoying already that vital force and producing those internal movements, the first cause of which we are desirous of knowing. However minute and feeble the parts of an embryo may be, when we are first capable of perceiving them, they then enjoy a real life, and possess the germ of all the phenomena, which that life may afterwards develop. These observations,

---

75. Shelley, *Frankenstein*, ed. Butler (1994), xix.

76. Lawrence, *Introduction to Comparative Anatomy* (1816), 120, 174. This explains why reviewers could suspect a novel expounding Abernethy's view of life of materialism: *The Literary Panorama*, N.S. 8 (1 June 1818), 412 (below, p. 317); *The Monthly Review*, Mary Wollstonecraft Shelley Chronology and Resource Site, ed. Lawson, published March 1998, https://romantic-circles.org/reference/chronologies/mschronology/reviews/monthlyrev (above, n. 46). PBS was certainly a materialist when he described human beings as electrified clay. We might say that the difference between Abernethy and Lawrence was not so much that one was not a materialist and the other was, as that one resisted the label of materialist and the other invited it.

extended to all the classes of living creatures, lead to this general fact, that there are none, which have not heretofore formed part of others similar to themselves, from which they have been detached. *All have participated in the existence of other living beings*, before they exercised the functions of life themselves. Thus we find that that *the motion proper to living bodies, or in one word, Life, has its origin in that of their parents*. From these parents they have received the vital impulse; and hence it is evident, that in the present state of things, life proceeds only from life; and there exists no other but that, which has been transmitted from one living body to another, by an uninterrupted succession.[77]

It should now be apparent that the central premise of the imaginary world constructed by Mary Shelley is that Lawrence is wrong. Lawrence's argument implies that one could never artificially produce life, while *Frankenstein* is based on the idea that life may not always proceed only from life, that it might be possible to have a living creature that had no parents. The very idea must have resonated powerfully for Shelley, a motherless child who hated her stepmother and had been rejected by her beloved father. She too was parentless.

Shelley does not mention Abernethy in her account of the genesis of *Frankenstein*; her loyalties lay, after all, with Lawrence, and in any case her knowledge of Abernethy's ideas was probably at secondhand. She recounts a conversation between Percy and Byron at which she had been present. They discussed

> the nature of the principle of life, and whether there was any proba-
> bility of its ever being discovered and communicated. They talked of
> the experiments of Dr. Darwin [Erasmus Darwin, Charles's grandfa-
> ther], (I speak not of what the Doctor really did, or said that he did,
> but, as more to my purpose, of what was then spoken of as having
> been done by him,) who preserved a piece of vermicelli in a glass
> case, till by some extraordinary means it began to move with volun-
> tary motion. Not thus, after all, would life be given. Perhaps a corpse

---

77. Lawrence, *Introduction to Comparative Anatomy* (1816), 140–42. Compare the views of the radical Lawrence with those of the conservative Davy as quoted in Ruston, "Resurrecting *Frankenstein*" (2005), 99–100; the difference between Lawrence and Davy is much less significant than Ruston implies because Lawrence is not the sort of materialist Davy encountered in his youth. Like Lawrence, Davy (in 1804) denied the possibility of life being produced from inorganic matter: "The alterations taking place in common matter are in no cases capable of forming organic bodies, or structures possessed of the faculty of reproduction" (Humphry Davy, *The Collected Works of Sir Humphry Davy*, 9 vols. [London: Smith, Elder, 1839–1840], 2:447).

would be re-animated; galvanism had given token of such things: perhaps the component parts of a creature might be manufactured, brought together, and endued with vital warmth.[78]

As Mary Shelley correctly understood, Darwin was of little use (in saying so she was implicitly disowning the first sentence of Percy's 1818 Preface): like many biologists he believed that microscopic creatures could generate spontaneously, but more complex creatures could only be produced by reproduction. (He does discuss cases in which microscopic creatures may mass together to produce a visible mold, and he even claims, on the basis of anecdotal evidence, that mushrooms are generated spontaneously by dung.) He discussed the "vorticella or wheel-animal" (Shelley's "vermicelli"), which is found in standing water; it can be dried out, and then brought back to life by placing it back in water.[79] More relevant were Luigi Galvani and his nephew Giovanni Aldini. They had made experiments with what was called "animal electricity": Aldini had taken the bodies of recently executed criminals and made them move, in a seemingly lifelike fashion, by shocking them with electricity. Even had they come back to life, this would have been resuscitation, not new creation.[80] But, if Mary Shelley's memory is to be trusted, Percy Shelley and Byron (and Polidori participated in such discussions as well, according to his diary) evidently also discussed whether one might make an artificial creature and somehow communicate the principle of life to it: "perhaps the component parts of a creature might be manufactured, brought together, and endued with vital warmth." This went well beyond anything that had been previously discussed by chemists or biologists. This was all Mary Shelley needed to construct the idea of a modern Prometheus, and she had her waking dream of the creation of the Creature that very night.[81]

---

78. Shelley, *Frankenstein* (1831), ix–x (below, p. 186).

79. "Spontaneous Vitality of Microscopic Animals," in Erasmus Darwin, *The Temple of Nature; or, the Origin of Society: A Poem, with Philosophical Notes* (London: J. Johnson, 1803), 139–49 (below, pp. 228–35).

80. Giovanni Aldini, *An Account of the Late Improvements in Galvanism* (London: Cuthell and Martin, 1803) (selection below, pp. 235–44).

81. My formulation of this issue reflects a response from Sharon Ruston to an earlier version in which I suggested Lawrence might have remarked to PBS that Abernethy's views implied that life might be artificially created. She wrote: "I guess my riposte would be that neither Abernethy nor Lawrence are really considering—at all—how or whether life can be created artificially. I don't think A[bernethy] is doing this any more than L[awrence] is to be honest. This is M[W]S's great contribution to the question of the nature of life I think. . . . I think it's more ambiguous exactly what PBS and Polidori discussed than that they 'evidently discussed whether one might make an artificial creature, etc.' and to say this downplays M[W]S's inspired idea." There's certainly an ambiguity in MWS's text as to who

I have now explained how the Christianized myth of Prometheus combined with Abernethy's theory of life to generate the core idea of the novel. As she wrote it up, Shelley's story began to grow. The remains of two notebooks survive in which Shelley drafted out a large part of the story before making a fair copy, and these, combined with her journal, encouraged Charles E. Robinson in 1996 to attempt a reconstruction of the order and timing of the composition of the book.[82] I want now to propose an alternative to Robinson's chronology.

At issue is the frame narrative with which the book begins and ends, the story of the polar expedition of Robert Walton. Robinson presumes, surely correctly, that the frame narrative was a later addition to a story that originally began with Victor Frankenstein's creation of the Creature. The draft that survives begins on page 41—the first forty pages (or twenty leaves) are missing—and pages 41/42 are a single leaf torn from what was once a quire, a group of leaves folded around a common center.[83] Robinson presumes that the missing pages contained in draft the story of Walton's expedition, and the opening pages of the story of Frankenstein's life.[84] In other words, when Shelley began writing in her notebook she had the total scheme of the novel in her head, and she was able to advance fairly steadily from the beginning to the end, some 363 pages later. And she began writing, we assume, either just before or immediately after her return to England in the autumn of 1816: the first of her two notebooks was purchased in Geneva.[85]

Where, then, did Shelley get the idea of an arctic expedition and sufficient knowledge to give a plausible account of one? The reviewer in *The British Critic* (nominally April 1818) thought that Shelley might have been reading the prose of Mr. Barrow and the poetry of Miss Porden (who later married the great explorer Sir John Franklin)—except she had evidently

---

formulated the idea of the manufacture of an artificial creature; it might have been MWS's contribution to the discussion (she was after all not *entirely* silent); or have emerged as she thought about the topic afterwards; or it might have originated with Byron, Polidori, or PBS. The word "manufacture," one should note, does not occur in the 1818 text, but it does occur twice in John Wilson Croker's *Quarterly Review* essay of June 1818, and Croker may thus have influenced Shelley's interpretation of her own work (*The Quarterly Review* 18 (January [delayed until 12 June] 1818), 380 (below, p. 320).

82. For Robinson's own summary of his findings, see Charles E. Robinson, "*Frankenstein:* Its Composition and Publication," in *The Cambridge Companion to* Frankenstein, ed. Andrew Smith (Cambridge: Cambridge University Press, 2016): 13–25.

83. Mary Wollstonecraft Shelley, *The Frankenstein Notebooks*, ed. Charles E. Robinson, 2 vols. (New York: Garland, 1996), 1:xxxvii–xxxviii.

84. Shelley, *The Frankenstein Notebooks*, ed. Robinson (1996), 1:2.

85. Shelley, *The Frankenstein Notebooks*, ed. Robinson (1996), 1:lxxx–lxxxi.

"anticipated" them as John Barrow had published in "the last number of the *Quarterly Review*" (which had appeared in February 1818), while Eleanor Anne Porden's poem had gone to press after March 31 of 1818— and we know that Shelley's novel was finished by May of 1817.[86] The reviewer in the *Quarterly Review* (published June 12, 1818), on the other hand, thought Shelley must have been reading Mr. Daines Barrington and Colonel Beaufoy.[87] Barrington's *The Possibility of Approaching the North Pole Asserted*, with an appendix by Beaufoy, had been published after March 1, 1818; Barrington's own contribution was a reprint of obscure articles from fifty years earlier, articles that asserted it should be possible to sail over the North Pole.[88] Shelley is most unlikely to have seen the earlier articles and pamphlets and shows no acquaintance with the idea (which was of renewed interest in 1818) that the North Pole might lie beneath open seas.[89] The little flurry of publications about the Arctic in 1818 had been whipped up by Barrow, who saw the end of the war with France as an opportunity to recommence arctic exploration, which had lain dormant at least sixty years. He was the instigator of two arctic expeditions that set out in 1818, the first in a new series of expeditions, which included Franklin's tragic third expedition of 1845, in which all 129 participants were lost.[90]

---

86. Review in *The British Critic*, N.S. 9 (April 1818): 432–438 at 433 (below, p. 311). For the dating of this issue of the *Quarterly Review*: "*Quarterly Review*, Volume 18, Number 35 (October 1817)," The *Quarterly Review* Archive, ed. Jonathan Cutmore, Romantic Circles (website), published February 2005, https://romantic-circles.org/reference/qr/index/35 .html. For the date of Porden, Eleanor Anne Porden, *The Arctic Expeditions, A Poem* (London: John Murray, 1818), 6. For the completion of MWS's novel, Shelley, *Journals*, eds. Feldman and Scott-Kilvert (1987), 171, and Shelley, *Letters*, ed. Bennett (1980–1988), 1:36.

87. "*Quarterly Review*," Mary Wollstonecraft Shelley Chronology and Resource Site, ed. Lawson, published March 1998, https://romantic-circles.org/reference/chronologies/ mschronology/reviews/qrrev.html (below, p. 321).

88. Daines Barrington and Mark Beaufoy, *The Possibility of Approaching the North Pole Asserted* (London: T. and J. Allman, 1818), vi.

89. Christopher Carter, "'The Sea Fryseth Not': Science and the Open Polar Sea in the Nineteenth Century," *Earth Sciences History* 32 (2013): 235–351. Carter quotes Shelley, *Frankenstein* (1818), 1:5 (below, p. 6): "through the seas which surround the pole" as implying that she did, but all quests for a Northwest Passage depended on there being open water for a passage west; this is very different from the claim that the pole itself lay under open water. In fact Walton expects the North Pole to be on land, though not necessarily ice-bound.

90. This basic chronology escapes Lisa Vargo, "Contextualizing Sources," in *The Cambridge Companion to "Frankenstein,"* ed. Andrew Smith (Cambridge: Cambridge University Press, 2016), 26–40, at 30. She writes, "The composition of the novel dates from a period of 'Arctic Fever,' during which Shelley would have read John Barrow's 'On the Polar Ice and

Thus we have a puzzle that perplexed contemporaries and perplexes us: what did Shelley read about the Arctic? Had her book been published a year later she could have read Barrow, Barrington, and Porden, but as it is her book appears to be a peculiar anticipation of a literature that did not yet exist. The simplest solution to this problem is to conclude that Shelley had read an earlier article by Barrow that appeared in the *Quarterly Review* in February of 1817 and that would have given her all the information she needed.[91] That particular issue would have been of great interest to both the Shelleys as it contained a review by Walter Scott of Byron's *Childe Harold's Pilgrimage* Canto III. We know from Mary Shelley's journals that she and Percy read the previous and the next issues of the *Quarterly Review*, so it is very likely they read this one; moreover the very first essay in this issue, a review (again by Barrow) of Thomas Legh's *Narrative of a Journey in Egypt*, is the likely source for Percy Shelley's famous poem "Ozymandias,"

Northern Passage into the Pacific' and other articles in Murray's *Quarterly Review*." In fact Shelley's novel predates Arctic Fever, and Barrow's "On the Polar Ice" was nominally printed in the *Quarterly Review* issue for October 1817 but actually appeared on February 21, 1818 ("*Quarterly Review*," *Quarterly Review* Archive, ed. Cutmore, published February 2005, https://romantic-circles.org/reference/qr/index/35.html), after the publication of *Frankenstein*, which appeared on January 1, 1818 (Shelley, *The Frankenstein Notebooks*, ed. Robinson [1996], 1:xcii). For similar errors, see Jen Hill, *White Horizon: The Arctic in the Nineteenth-Century British Imagination* (Albany, NY: State University of New York Press, 2008), 56–69. J. Paul Hunter writes: "Voyages of discovery seeking a navigable northwest passage were frequent in Shelley's time and contemporary periodicals were full of their detailed travel accounts" (Shelley, *Frankenstein*, ed. Hunter [2012], 8, n. 2), but this is not true of the period when Shelley was writing the novel. Nick Groom writes: "By the time *Frankenstein* was published there was a government bounty of £20,000 available for traversing the [Northwest] passage and a £5,000 prize for reaching within one degree of the North Pole" (Shelley, *Frankenstein*, ed. Groom [2018], xxviii). Actually the bounty and prize were established in 1744 and again in 1776 (18 George II, c.17; 16 George III, c.6—which placed restrictions on the prize). *After* the publication of *Frankenstein*, in 1818 (the new act was introduced on March 6), these were repealed, but the same bounty and prize were made available (58 George III c.20).

91. John Barrow, "Lord Selkirk and the North-west Company," *Quarterly Review* 16 (1816): 129–72 (selection below, 281–86). This solution is, in my view rightly, adopted by Adriana Craciun, "*Frankenstein*'s Politics," in *The Cambridge Companion to "Frankenstein*," ed. Andrew Smith (Cambridge: Cambridge University Press, 2016): 84–98, at 91, and by Wood, *Tambora* (2014), 146–48, but it is powerfully challenged by Janice Cavell, "The Sea of Ice and the Icy Sea: The Arctic Frame of *Frankenstein*," *Arctic* 70 (2017): 295–307. My aim is to respond to that challenge. I would add that I do not find Cavell's quest for alternative, earlier sources persuasive.

written in December 1817.[92] But—and it is a significant "but"—this solution requires a major revision to Robinson's chronology.

In October of 1816 Mary Shelley, in Bath, was reading travel literature, and this is when Robinson thinks she wrote the opening chapters of the book. She records reading no books about the Arctic, but she does record reading Evert Ysbrants Ides's *Three Years Travels from Moscow Over-Land to China* (1706).[93] Ides was a Dutch merchant sent to China as an ambassador by Peter the Great. He describes traveling by sled, pulled by dogs, through Siberia. From early on Shelley must have wanted a frame narrative which began and ended in icy wastes; I suggest that in October of 1816 she opened the draft of her novel with just such a narrative, inspired by Ides's account of sledging through Siberia.[94] Then, four months later, when her draft was far advanced, she read Barrow's essay, which dealt with the Arctic. She went back to the beginning and tore out the first twenty leaves and began writing new pages that introduced Walton and told the story from his viewpoint but incorporated some older material. Thus Ides had described Russian sledges as lightweight, for traveling over drifted snow, so light that they could be pulled by only two dogs; Shelley retained these light, fast sleds, but she then had to have Frankenstein substitute a heavy sledge capable of traveling across pack ice.[95] By this point she must also have read the descriptions of Eskimo sleds, pulled by many dogs, and of the breaking up of sea ice to be found in Southey's *Omniana* (1812), a sort of anthology of diverse texts: she and Percy left a copy behind when they moved out of their house in Marlow.[96]

Where did she leave off, returning to the beginning to start again? The answer, I suggest, is to be found in Notebook B, folio 81v, which became Volume 3, page 144 of the 1818 edition. Frankenstein has been narrating how he had followed the Creature "amidst the wilds of Tartary and

---

92. Shelley, *Journals*, eds. Feldman and Scott-Kilvert (1987), 100, 149, 172; Percy Bysshe Shelley, *The Poems of Shelley: 1817–1819*, ed. Kelvin Everest (London: Longman, 1989), 307–10.

93. Shelley, *Journals*, eds. Feldman and Scott-Kilvert (1987), 143.

94. The original frame narrative must also have involved a friend to whom Frankenstein told his story: see Shelley, *Frankenstein* (1818), 1:86, which is carried through unchanged from the manuscript.

95. Evert Ysbrants Ides, *Three Years Travels from Moscow Over-Land to China* (London: W. Freeman, 1706), 15; Shelley, *Frankenstein* (1818), 1:8; 3:146, 147, 149.

96. "Labrador" in Robert Southey and Samuel Taylor Coleridge, *Omniana, or Horæ Otiosiores*, 2 vols. (London: Longman, 1812), 1:164–87; Vargo, "Contextualizing Sources" (2016), 30—this must be based on what is known as "the Marlow inventory," an unpublished list in the Pforzheimer Library of the books in MWS's and PBS's possession at Marlow, and which they left behind on their departure for Italy in the spring of 1818.

Russia." At night he communes with the ghosts of his beloved dead. The creature leaves him a message: "Follow me; I seek the everlasting ices of the north, where you will feel the misery of cold and frost, to which I am impassive." "Scoffing devil!" Frankenstein responds:

> Again do I vow vengeance again do I devote thee, miserable fiend, to torture & death never will I omit my search untill he or I perish. And then with what extacy shall I join my Elizabeth & those who even now prepare for me the reward of my tedious & horrible pilgrimage.

What we have here is a sort of premature ending. But how to get from here to an account of the death of Frankenstein and/or the Creature? And how to explain how that account reaches the reader? It is at this point, I think, that Shelley turned back to the beginning, tore out her original draft, and introduced Walton into the story.

When the text in Notebook B starts up again, after the premature ending, Shelley has a newly sharpened pen: "As I purs[u]ed still my journey to the northward, the snows thickened, & cold encreased. . . ." Frankenstein now announces that "some weeks before this period I had procured a sledge & dogs." By the end of the paragraph Frankenstein learns from some peasants that the Creature "had pursued his journey across the sea in a direction that led to no land & they conjectured that he must be speedily destroyed in the breaking of the ice or frozen by the eternal frost." The arctic narrative now recommences. It then continues smoothly to the point where Frankenstein sees Walton's vessel "riding at anchor, and holding forth to me hopes of succour and life," and the novel finishes with Walton's account of Frankenstein's death and the Creature's disappearance.

The publication of issue 31 of the *Quarterly Review* (February 7, 1817) was followed by the most intensive period of writing recorded in Mary Shelley's journal: she seems to have written her draft for twenty-three consecutive days from March 18 to April 9, and Robinson, who thinks she only had the last eighty-two pages of the draft to complete at this point, and who reckons that she wrote at the rate of five pages a day, is puzzled as to what exactly she was doing: the puzzle disappears if she was also writing forty or more pages to tack on at the beginning.[97]

Introducing Walton had a minor consequence that is worth noting. The main narrative contains no dates, but a reader would assume its setting was vaguely contemporary: nineteenth-century poems are freely quoted in the text on the assumption that Frankenstein might be familiar with them. But Shelley knew from reading Barrow that the last British expedition to the

---

97. Shelley, *The Frankenstein Notebooks*, ed. Robinson (1996), 1:lxxxiv.

Arctic had been in 1791–1792.[98] Since, as she wrote the novel, she knew
of no planned expeditions, it was natural for her to conclude that the narrative must be set in the eighteenth century (hence the datings of Walton's
letters to 17—), and she would expect readers to recognize that the events
must take place before the outbreak of war with France in 1793.[99]

But the introduction of the new frame narrative had a much more important consequence, because Walton introduces a new element into the
story. Walton is prepared to risk the lives of all his men so that he can
make new discoveries. The story of Frankenstein and his Creature is a story
of an experiment gone dreadfully wrong, with terrible consequences. But
Frankenstein does not embark on his researches expecting others to die so
that he may acquire knowledge, even if that is the outcome. Reading Barrow's essay, Shelley saw the opportunity to bring an English ship into her
story—when Frankenstein exclaims "I had no conception that vessels ever
came so far north" we may suspect that he expresses Shelley's own surprise
on reading about arctic voyages;[100] but in Barrow's belittling of the efforts
of others and his confidence that he alone knew how an expedition should
be conducted, she caught sight of something that she found dangerous and
horrifying: a masculine willingness to sacrifice the lives of others in a futile
quest for an insignificant mathematical point. We might say that Barrow
(and Walton, who was modeled on his literary persona) was expressing a
Promethean ambition (referring now to the Greek myth of Prometheus
the fire stealer and inventor of technology). Thus the final version of the
framing narrative transformed the significance of the novel. It had started
out as a horror story, a work of science fiction, describing the creation of a
monster; it ended up rooted in contemporary science fact, describing the
dangers of an unchecked pursuit of new knowledge. It had become a novel
about misplaced ambition, about the failure of modern science to consider
the implications of its enterprise.[101]

This transformation left a striking inconsistency in the novel. The whole
point of the framing narrative is that Frankenstein and Walton are fellow
souls, who recognize each other as having similar ambitions and aspira-
tions. Walton is Frankenstein's alter ego, his secret sharer, his doppelgänger:

---

98. Barrow, "Lord Selkirk, and the North-west Company" (1816), 166 (below, pp. 281–
82).
99. This involves rejecting the commonly-adopted view that Walton's first letter is to be
dated to 1796: see for example the "Table of Dates" in Shelley, *Frankenstein*, ed. Hunter
(2012), xxiii–xxv, based on Anne K. Mellor, *Mary Shelley: Her Life, Her Fiction, Her Monsters* (London: Routledge, 1988), 237, n. 22. No evidence supports Mellor's conjectural
dating.
100. Shelley, *Frankenstein* (1818), 3:152 (below, p. 168).
101. Shelley, *Frankenstein*, ed. Robinson (2008), 31.

"for all their superficial differences, the novel's acknowledged scientists are two of a kind," writes Marilyn Butler.[102] And the two of them together represent the values of modern science. But Frankenstein's original narrative had a quite different understanding of his relationship to modern science, and at one solitary point in it, the word "ambition" made a significant appearance. (We should note that the passage in question is the result of a revision to the text by Percy Shelley: I place in italics the words originally written by Percy in the margin of the manuscript, which went virtually unchanged into the 1818 edition):

> Besides, I had a contempt for the uses of modern natural philosophy. It was very different when the masters of the science sought immortality and power; such views, although futile, were grand; but now the scene was changed. *The ambition of the inquirer seemed to limit itself to the annihilation of those visions on which my interest in science was chiefly founded. I was required to exchange chimeras of boundless grandeur for realities of little worth.*[103]

Here what Frankenstein is stressing is that he is sharply at odds with "modern natural philosophy." His ambitions are those of the old alchemists, while modern chemistry is concerned with the pedestrian and the mundane. And indeed, in seeking to create life he is undertaking an enterprise that will cut him off from the community of university natural philosophers.

The same sharp contrast between Frankenstein's enterprise and that of modern science is to be found in Frankenstein's insistence upon secrecy. We might be reading a version of the Faust story or a Gothic novel when we read:

> I see by your eagerness, and the wonder and hope which your eyes express, my friend, that you expect to be informed of the secret with which I am acquainted; that cannot be: listen patiently until the end of my story, and you will easily perceive why I am reserved upon that subject. I will not lead you on, unguarded and ardent as I then was,

---

102. Shelley, *Frankenstein*, ed. Butler (1994), xxxv.

103. Shelley, *Frankenstein* (1818), 1:71. MWS's original text, crossed out by PBS, did not include the word "ambition"—further evidence that in MWS's original conception the book was not about "ambition." Her crossed-out text reads: "and the expulsion of chimera overthrew at the same time all greatness in the science" (Notebook A, fol. 11v: I am grateful to Dr. Bruce Barker-Benfield for pointing out PBS's contribution). Much ink has been spilled over the collaboration between MWS and PBS in the writing of *Frankenstein*. For a summary of the issues, see Shelley, *The Frankenstein Notebooks*, ed. Robinson (1996), 1:lxvi–lxxv, who concludes (lxvii): "PBS's contributions to *Frankenstein* were no more than what most publishers' editors have provided new (or old) authors or, in fact, what colleagues have provided to each other after reading each other's works in progress."

to your destruction and infallible misery. Learn from me, if not by my precepts, at least by my example, how dangerous is the acquirement of knowledge, and how much happier that man is who believes his native town to be the world, than he who aspires to become greater than his nature will allow.[104]

Frankenstein's fault, as described here, lies in seeking to be *greater than his nature will allow*. By the time Mary Shelley came to write the second version of the framing narrative, however, she was committed to a different view of the dangers of knowledge: she had seen in Barrow a new kind of grand ambition. Barrow's ambition was openly expressed in public, and not at all secretive. It required institutional support and demanded public approbation. Unlike the raising of demons, the quest for the elixir of life, or Frankenstein's ambition to create life, it could not be presented as trespassing upon forbidden territory. The changing significance of "ambition" in the text thus points to an internal tension between the conception that Shelley had of her project when she started writing, and the view she had reached by the time she finished.

Over and over again commentators on *Frankenstein* use the phrase "Promethean ambition."[105] As it happens I can find no example of this phrase being used before 1839 when it appears in an essay on Balzac's novel *The Quest of the Absolute*, a novel about a chemist: although the reviewer does not explicitly mention *Frankenstein* (s)he seems to deliberately echo themes from the novel.[106] So it would seem that the idea of "Promethean ambition" is not the source or inspiration of Shelley's *Frankenstein*; there are no references to ambition in previous tellings of the myth of Prometheus. Rather the idea of Promethean ambition is the outcome or the conclusion of the novel, and it is in the final conversations between Walton

---

104. Shelley, *Frankenstein* (1818), 1:86 (below, p. 35).

105. An example at random: Mary Lowe-Evans, "The Groomsmen," in *Mary Shelley's "Frankenstein*," ed. Harold Bloom (Broomall, PA: Chelsea House Publishers, 2004): 165–74, at 168. Lowe-Evans thinks (166) MWS's contemporaries would have associated Prometheus with "presumption": I can find no evidence to support this. It is also commonplace to say that the novel is about *hubris*: yet the first example of this word in English given by the *Oxford English Dictionary* online is dated 1884 (entry updated 1933). So too the frequent discussion of Frankenstein as an "overreacher" risks anachronism: e.g., Barbara Frey Waxman, "Victor Frankenstein's Romantic Fate: The Tragedy of the Overreacher as Woman," in *Mary Shelley's "Frankenstein*," ed. Bloom (2004): 105–16; George Levine, "The Ambiguous Heritage of *Frankenstein*," in *The Endurance of "Frankenstein": Essays on Mary Shelley's Novel*, ed. George Levine and U. C. Knoepflmacher (Berkeley, CA: University of California Press, 1979): 3–30, at 9–10. The first example given by the *Oxford English Dictionary* online of the use of "overreacher" in this sense is from 1952 (entry updated 2004).

106. *The New York Review* 4 (1839), 441–56, at 452.

and Frankenstein that the term "ambition" begins to refer to something dangerous and to be avoided. It is only, I think, during her intense writing spell between March 18 and April 9, 1817, that Shelley's novel came to be about what we now call (in implicit reference to her subtitle) Promethean ambition.

Shelley's novel was strangely prescient. It is about arctic exploration just before the great age of arctic exploration. It is about the robbing of grave-yards for body parts just before the Burke and Hare murders of 1828. And so we get striking readings of the novel which deliberately read it anach-ronistically, as if it was contemporary with later events.[107] This ability to catch hold of issues that were still embryonic is one of Shelley's strengths as an author, but it requires explanation. The intention of writing a horror story explains the graveyards and body parts. It is Barrow's first essay on the arctic (the first of many) in the *Quarterly Review* that explains both her prescience on the subject of arctic exploration and her transformation of "lofty ambition" into something new, Promethean ambition. "Farewell, Walton!" says Frankenstein at the end. "Seek happiness in tranquillity, and avoid ambition, even if it be only the apparently innocent one of distin-guishing yourself in science and discoveries."[108] For more than a hundred years the ambition of seeking scientific knowledge had been lauded; now, suddenly, it was no longer innocent.[109] Shelley had read Barrow, and had discovered what her true subject had been all along.

The nine months in which Shelley wrote *Frankenstein* were full of difficul-ties, but looking back she saw this as the best of times. Mary and Percy left England for Italy in the spring of 1818, just when reviews of *Frankenstein* were beginning to appear. Their baby Clara died that year, William the next. In 1822 Percy drowned. Her book, Shelley wrote, "was the offspring

---

107. Jessica Richard, "'A Paradise of My Own Creation': *Frankenstein* and the Improb-able Romance of Polar Exploration," *Nineteenth-Century Contexts* 25 (2003): 295–314; Adriana Craciun, "Writing the Disaster: Franklin and *Frankenstein*," *Nineteenth-Century Literature* 65 (2011): 433–80; Adriana Craciun, *Writing Arctic Disaster: Authorship and Exploration* (Cambridge: Cambridge University Press, 2016); Tim Marshall, *Murdering to Dissect: Grave-Robbing,* Frankenstein, *and the Anatomy Literature* (Manchester: Manchester University Press, 1995). On the difficulties of reading *Frankenstein* as foreshadowing the industrial revolution (as in Warren Montag, "'The Workshop of Filthy Creation': A Marxist Reading of *Frankenstein*," in *Mary Shelley Frankenstein*, ed. Johanna M. Smith [Boston: Bedford/St. Martin's, 2000]: 384–95), Phillips, "*Frankenstein* and Mary Shelley's 'Wet Un-genial Summer'" (2006), 59–60.
108. Shelley, *Frankenstein* (1818), 3:161, 177 (below, pp. 171, 176). Compare 1:93–94 (below, p. 38).
109. David Wootton, *Power, Pleasure, and Profit: Insatiable Appetites from Machiavelli to Madison* (Cambridge, MA: Harvard University Press, 2018), 90–91, 110–12.

of happy days, when death and grief were but words, which found no true echo in my heart." But, she added, "my readers have nothing to do with these associations."[110] The story, she knew, had taken on a life of its own.[111]

Appendix:

There is perhaps a further source for the Prometheus myth in *Frankenstein* in addition to Godwin's *The Pantheon*. On May 8, 9, and 10, 1815, Mary Shelley read Book II of Spenser's *The Faerie Queene*.[112] There she found, in Canto X:

> But Guyon all this while his booke did read,
>> Ne yet has ended: for it was a great
>> And ample volume, that doth far excead
>> My leasure, so long leaues here to repeat:
>> It told, how first Prometheus did create
>> A man, of many partes from beasts deriued,
>> And then stole fire from heauen, to animate
>> His worke, for which he was by Ioue depriued
> Of life him selfe, and hart-strings of an Ægle riued.

> That man so made, he called Elfe, to weet
>> Quick, the first authour of all Elfin kind:
>> Who wandring through the world with wearie feet,
>> Did in the gardins of Adonis find
>> A goodly creature, whom he deemd in mind

---

110. Shelley, *Frankenstein* (1831), xii (below, p. 187).

111. It would be wrong to think that *Frankenstein* was from the start a bestseller. The first edition was in 500 copies only, but, being expensive, will have been sold primarily to circulating libraries, so there will have been many more than 500 readers (and one reason for adopting the three-volume format was that three people could be reading a single copy at the same time). William St. Clair reckons 7,000–8,000 copies were printed and sold in the first forty years: sales were held back because the book was in copyright, and the publishers preferred to market expensive editions. Most people encountered MWS's story through its stage adaptations. William St. Clair, *The Reading Nation in the Romantic Period* (Cambridge: Cambridge University Press, 2004), 357–73. For a list of editions, see "Study Aids: Editions of Mary Shelley's *Frankenstein*" in Mary Wollstonecraft Shelley, *Frankenstein*, ed. Stuart Curran (Romantic Circles, 2009), https://romantic-circles.org/editions/frankenstein/textual.

112. Shelley, *Journals*, eds. Feldman and Scott-Kilvert (1987), 77–78; Seymour, *Mary Shelley* (2011), 134.

> To be no earthly wight, but either Spright,
> Or Angell, th'authour of all woman kind;
> Therefore a Fay he her according hight,
> Of whom all Faeryes spring, and fetch their lignage right.

Shelley was struck by the elves in *The Faerie Queene*, and began to refer to Percy as her Elf; in December 1816, when she was working on *Frankenstein*, he is her "sweet Elf . . . a winged Elf . . . my airy Elf."[113] Shelley had almost certainly read Upton's edition of *The Faerie Queene*.[114] Upton explains this passage:

> The book which Sir Guyon was reading gave an account of the original and history of the Fairies; how Prometheus first mixed earth and water together, and from this clay formed the image of a man: he then endued it with various passions derived from various creatures; he gave it anger from lyons, craft from foxes, fear from hares, &c.
>
> > *Fertur Prometheus addere principi*
> > *Limo coactam particulam undique,*
> > *Desectam et insani leonis*
> > *Vim stomacho adposuisse nostro.*
> >
> > Hor[ace] L. i. Od. xvi.
>
> [In the Loeb translation (Horace, *Odes and Epodes*, ed. and trans. Niall Rudd, Loeb Classical Library 33 [Cambridge, MA: Harvard University Press, 2004], 57): "They say that when Prometheus was compelled to add an element cut from every animal to our primordial clay, he also put into the human heart the violence of a raging lion."]
>
> Let the reader at leisure, compare the well-known verses of Simonides, concerning the formation of women, according to this story of Prometheus. There was still wanting in this work the animating and true vital spark, which he stole from heaven. The moral of which fable is, that reason is *the candle of the Lord*; a light kindled from the original, and source of all light.[115]

---

113. Shelley, *Letters*, ed. Bennett (1980–1988), 1:22–23.

114. The two most recent editions, by Upton and Church, both appeared in 1758; Upton's was more convenient, being in two volumes rather than four, and had better notes.

115. Edmund Spenser, *Spenser's Faerie Queene*, ed. John Upton, 2 vols. (London: J. and R. Tonson, 1758), 2:495.

Upton goes on to explain that by "life" Spenser means "the happiness of life," and he might have added that the substitution of heart strings for the liver goes back at least to Fulgentius in the sixth century.[116] The verses of Simonides (or Semonides as he is now known) describe ten different sorts of women constructed from animals—from a pig, a fox, a donkey, etc.—or from the elements, the earth and the sea.

There is a certain ambiguity in Horace, in Semonides, in Spenser, and in Upton's reading of all three. Are men (or women) made from the *parts* of animals, or are they made from the passions or qualities of animals? How literally are we to take the idea of humans made from animals? In Spenser himself, is "parts" to be taken in the obvious modern sense (which is how contemporary scholars apparently read it), or (as seems to me likely) is it meant in the sense in which we still occasionally talk of a "man of parts," i.e., a man of excellent *qualities*? Either way, the literal reading imposes itself on the reader, even if she then opts for the analogical reading, and Mary Shelley had here an image of a human being constructed out of the parts of dissected animals.

---

116. "The liver which Prometheus exposes to the vulture is what we call the heart." (Fulgentius, *Mythologies*, 2.6, Theoi Project [website], accessed February 21, 2020, https://www.theoi.com/Text/FulgentiusMythologies2.html#6.)

Further Reading

The best introduction to *Frankenstein* is Daisy Hay, *The Making of Mary Shelley's* Frankenstein (Oxford: Bodleian Library, 2019). The manuscripts of *Frankenstein* may be found at: http://shelleygodwinarchive.org/contents/frankenstein/. A useful collection of essays is Andrew Smith, *The Cambridge Companion to* Frankenstein (Cambridge: Cambridge University Press, 2016); see also *The Endurance of* Frankenstein*: Essays on Mary Shelley's Novel*, eds. George Levine and U. C. Knoepflmacher (Berkeley, CA: University of California Press, 1979); Harold Bloom, ed. *Mary Shelley's* Frankenstein (Broomall, PA: Chelsea House, 2004). The best of several biographies of Mary is Miranda Seymour, *Mary Shelley* (London: Faber & Faber, 2011). The classic biography of Percy is Richard Holmes, *Shelley: The Pursuit* (London: Weidenfeld & Nicolson, 1974). For Byron, see Fiona MacCarthy, *Byron: Life and Legend* (London: John Murray, 2002); and for Polidori, Andrew Edwards and Suzanne Edwards, *His Master's Reflection: Travels with John Polidori, Lord Byron's Doctor and Author of* The Vampyre (Brighton: Sussex Academic Press, 2019).

On *Frankenstein* as a Gothic novel, Robert D. Hume, "Gothic Versus Romantic: A Revaluation of the Gothic Novel," *Publications of the Modern Language Association of America* 84 (1969): 282–90; Ellen Moers, "Female Gothic: The Monster's Mother," *New York Review of Books*, March 21, 1974; and Maggie Kilgour, *The Rise of the Gothic Novel* (London: Routledge, 1995). An important, early feminist essay is Sandra M. Gilbert, "Horror's Twin: Mary Shelley's Monstrous Eve," *Feminist Studies* 4 (1978): 48–73 (which also appears as a chapter in Sandra M. Gilbert and Susan Gubar, *The Madwoman in the Attic: The Woman Writer and the Nineteenth-Century Literary Imagination* [New Haven, CT: Yale University Press, 1979]). A pioneering feminist study is Anne K. Mellor, *Mary Shelley: Her Life, Her Fiction, Her Monsters* (London: Routledge, 1988). On *Frankenstein*'s science see Sharon Ruston, "Resurrecting *Frankenstein*," *The Keats-Shelley Review* 19 (2005): 97–116; Sharon Ruston, "Chemistry and the Science of Transformation in Mary Shelley's *Frankenstein*," *Nineteenth-Century Contexts* 41 (2019): 255–70; and Christa Knellwolf King and Jane R. Goodall, eds. *Frankenstein's Science* (Aldershot, UK: Ashgate, 2008).[117] On race and slavery, H. L. Malchow, "Frankenstein's Monster and Images

---

117. Sharon Ruston also has a forthcoming book, provisionally entitled *The Science of Life and Death in Mary Shelley's* Frankenstein, of which she kindly showed me a draft chapter.

of Race in Nineteenth-Century Britain," *Past & Present* 139 (1993): 90–130; Anne K. Mellor, "*Frankenstein*, Racial Science, and the Yellow Peril," *Nineteenth-Century Contexts* 23 (2001): 1–28; Allan Lloyd Smith, "'This Thing of Darkness': Racial Discourse in Mary Shelley's *Frankenstein*," *Gothic Studies* 6 (2004): 208–22; and Jill Lepore, "It's Still Alive," *New Yorker*, February 12, 2018. And, on the later use of Frankenstein's Creature in the context of race relations, Elizabeth Young, *Black Frankenstein: The Making of an American Metaphor* (New York: New York University Press, 2008).

A Note on the Texts

All texts are based on the first edition of that text. Anomalies in spelling and punctuation are reproduced as in the original. Notes to the text of *Frankenstein* are all by this editor except where indicated; in the section of further texts, notes by this editor are enclosed within square brackets. The engraved frontispiece that appears before the title page of the 1818 edition is taken from the 1831 edition (there were no illustrations in the 1818 edition).

FRANKENSTEIN: THE 1818 EDITION

T. Holst, del.   W. Chevalier, sculp.

FRANKENSTEIN

"By the glimmer of the half-extinguished
light, I saw the dull, yellow eye of the
creature open; it breathed hard, and a
convulsive motion agitated its limbs.
* * * I rushed out of the room."

Page 43.

London, Published by H. Colburn and R. Bentley, 1831.

FRANKENSTEIN;

OR,

THE MODERN PROMETHEUS.

IN THREE VOLUMES

Did I request thee, Maker, from my clay
To mould me man? Did I solicit thee
From darkness to promote me?—
PARADISE LOST.[1]

Vol. 1

1818

---

1. All notes to *Frankenstein* are, except where indicated, those of the editor. This epigraph does not appear in the second and third editions. See above, p. xxiv.

TO

WILLIAM GODWIN,

AUTHOR OF *POLITICAL JUSTICE, CALEB WILLIAMS, &c.*

THESE VOLUMES

Are respectfully inscribed

BY

THE AUTHOR.

PREFACE[2]

THE event on which this fiction is founded has been supposed, by Dr. Darwin, and some of the physiological writers of Germany, as not of impossible occurrence.[3] I shall not be supposed as according the remotest degree of serious faith to such an imagination; yet, in assuming it as the basis of a work of fancy, I have not considered myself as merely weaving a series of supernatural terrors.[4] The event on which   I.viii the interest of the story depends is exempt from the disadvantages of a mere tale of spectres or enchantment. It was recommended by the novelty of the situations which it developes; and, however impossible as a physical fact,[5] affords a point of view to the imagination for the delineating of human passions more comprehensive and commanding than any which the ordinary relations of existing events can yield.

I have thus endeavoured to preserve the truth of the elementary principles of human nature, while I have not scrupled to innovate upon their combinations. The *Iliad*, the tragic poetry of Greece,— Shakespeare, in the *Tempest* and *Midsummer Night's Dream*,—and   I.ix most especially Milton, in *Paradise Lost*, conform to this rule; and the most humble novelist, who seeks to confer or receive amusement from his labours, may, without presumption, apply to prose fiction a licence, or rather a rule, from the adoption of which so many exquisite combinations of human feeling have resulted in the highest specimens of poetry.

---

2. According to MWS's 1831 Introduction this Preface was written by PBS.

3. For Erasmus Darwin, see below, pp. 186, 228–235. The first of William Lawrence's lectures in his *Introduction to Comparative Anatomy* (1816) announced his attachment to the German school of physiology represented by Blumenbach, Rudolphi, and Tiedemann, and PBS is probably thinking of Lawrence here.

4. The word "supernatural" has two senses in *Frankenstein*. Sometimes it means something impossible in nature ("supernatural horrors," below, p. 34); and sometimes it means something exceptional and abnormal ("supernatural enthusiasm," "supernatural force," below pp. 34, 106). MWS agreed (below, p. 4) to write a ghost story about some "supernatural occurrence," but actually there is nothing strictly "supernatural" in her story, in the sense of something ghostly or miraculous, but only things that are exceptional and abnormal. It is not "a mere tale of spectres or enchantment." Thus the reader is encouraged to expect a Gothic novel, while at the same time being told that the story will be something quite different.

5. Note that "however impossible as a physical fact" contradicts the first sentence.

3

The circumstance on which my story rests was suggested in casual conversation.[6] It was commenced, partly as a source of amusement, and partly as an expedient for exercising any untried resources of I.x   mind. Other motives were mingled with these, as the work proceeded. I am by no means indifferent to the manner in which whatever moral tendencies exist in the sentiments or characters it contains shall affect the reader; yet my chief concern in this respect has been limited to avoiding the enervating effects of the novels of the present day, and to the exhibition of the amiableness of domestic affection, and the excellence of universal virtue. The opinions which naturally spring from the character and situation of the hero are by no means to be conceived as existing always in my own conviction; nor is any inference justly to be drawn from the following pages as prejudicing any philosophical doctrine of whatever kind.[7]

I.xi   It is a subject also of additional interest to the author, that this story was begun in the majestic region where the scene is principally laid, and in society which cannot cease to be regretted. I passed the summer of 1816 in the environs of Geneva. The season was cold and rainy, and in the evenings we crowded around a blazing wood fire, and occasionally amused ourselves with some German stories of ghosts, which happened to fall into our hands.[8] These tales excited in us a playful desire of imitation. Two other friends (a tale from the pen of one of whom would be far more acceptable to the public than I.xii   any thing I can ever hope to produce)[9] and myself agreed to write each a story, founded on some supernatural occurrence.

The weather, however, suddenly became serene; and my two friends left me on a journey among the Alps, and lost, in the magnificent scenes which they present, all memory of their ghostly visions. The following tale is the only one which has been completed.[10]

---

6. See MWS's 1831 Introduction, below, p. 185.
7. I.e., the book should not be read as an attack on belief in an immortal soul.
8. *Fantasmagoriana*, 2 vols. (Paris, 1812), translated from German.
9. Byron.
10. At this point Polidori's *The Vampyre* (1819) had not yet been published.

FRANKENSTEIN;

OR, THE

MODERN PROMETHEUS.

LETTER I.

To Mrs. SAVILLE, *England.*

St. Petersburgh, Dec. 11th, 17—.

YOU will rejoice to hear that no disaster has accompanied the commencement of an enterprise which you have regarded with such evil forebodings. I arrived here yesterday; and my first task is to assure my dear sister of my welfare, and increasing confidence in the success of my undertaking.

I am already far north of London; and as I walk in the streets of Petersburgh, I feel a cold northern breeze play upon my cheeks, which braces my nerves, and fills me with delight. Do you understand this feeling? This breeze, which has travelled from the regions towards which I am advancing, gives me a foretaste of those icy climes. Inspirited by this wind of promise, my day dreams become more fervent and vivid. I try in vain to be persuaded that the pole is the seat of frost and desolation; it ever presents itself to my imagination as the region of beauty and delight. There, Margaret, the sun is for ever visible; its broad disk just skirting the horizon, and diffusing a perpetual splendour.[11] There—for with your leave, my sister, I will put some trust in preceding navigators—there snow and frost are banished; and, sailing over a calm sea, we may be wafted to a land

---

11. On the source of this passage in Milton's *Paradise Lost*, see Rudolf Beck, "'The Region of Beauty and Delight': Walton's Polar Fantasies in Mary Shelley's *Frankenstein*," *Keats-Shelley Journal* 49 (2000): 24–29.

I.3   surpassing in wonders and in beauty every region hitherto discovered
on the habitable globe. Its productions and features may be without
example, as the phænomena of the heavenly bodies undoubtedly
are in those undiscovered solitudes. What may not be expected in a
country of eternal light? I may there discover the wondrous power
which attracts the needle;[12] and may regulate a thousand celestial
observations, that require only this voyage to render their seeming
eccentricities consistent for ever. I shall satiate my ardent curiosity
with the sight of a part of the world never before visited, and may
tread a land never before imprinted by the foot of man. These are
my enticements, and they are sufficient to conquer all fear of danger
or death, and to induce me to commence this laborious voyage with

I.4   the joy a child feels when he embarks in a little boat, with his holiday
mates, on an expedition of discovery up his native river. But, supposing all these conjectures to be false, you cannot contest the inestima-
ble benefit which I shall confer on all mankind to the last generation,
by discovering a passage near the pole to those countries, to reach
which at present so many months are requisite; or by ascertaining
the secret of the magnet, which, if at all possible, can only be effected
by an undertaking such as mine.

These reflections have dispelled the agitation with which I began
my letter, and I feel my heart glow with an enthusiasm which ele-
vates me to heaven; for nothing contributes so much to tranquillize
the mind as a steady purpose,—a point on which the soul may fix its
intellectual eye. This expedition has been the favourite dream of my

I.5   early years. I have read with ardour the accounts of the various voyages which have been made in the prospect of arriving at the North
Pacific Ocean through the seas which surround the pole. You may
remember, that a history of all the voyages made for purposes of
discovery composed the whole of our good uncle Thomas's library.
My education was neglected, yet I was passionately fond of reading.
These volumes were my study day and night, and my familiarity with
them increased that regret which I had felt, as a child, on learning
that my father's dying injunction had forbidden my uncle to allow me
to embark in a sea-faring life.

These visions faded when I perused, for the first time, those poets whose effusions entranced my soul, and lifted it to heaven. I also

I.6   became a poet, and for one year lived in a Paradise of my own creation; I imagined that I also might obtain a niche in the temple where

---

12. The compass needle.

the names of Homer and Shakespeare are consecrated. You are well acquainted with my failure, and how heavily I bore the disappointment. But just at that time I inherited the fortune of my cousin, and my thoughts were turned into the channel of their earlier bent.

Six years have passed since I resolved on my present undertaking. I can, even now, remember the hour from which I dedicated myself to this great enterprise. I commenced by inuring my body to hardship. I accompanied the whale-fishers on several expeditions to the North Sea; I voluntarily endured cold, famine, thirst, and want of sleep; I often worked harder than the common sailors during the day, and devoted my nights to the study of mathematics, the theory I.7 of medicine, and those branches of physical science from which a naval adventurer might derive the greatest practical advantage. Twice I actually hired myself as an under-mate in a Greenland whaler, and acquitted myself to admiration. I must own I felt a little proud, when my captain offered me the second dignity in the vessel, and entreated me to remain with the greatest earnestness; so valuable did he consider my services.

And now, dear Margaret, do I not deserve to accomplish some great purpose. My life might have been passed in ease and luxury; but I preferred glory to every enticement that wealth placed in my path. Oh, that some encouraging voice would answer in the affirmative! My courage and my resolution is firm; but my hopes fluctuate, and my spirits are often depressed. I am about to proceed on a long I.8 and difficult voyage; the emergencies of which will demand all my fortitude: I am required not only to raise the spirits of others, but sometimes to sustain my own, when their's are failing.

This is the most favourable period for travelling in Russia. They fly quickly over the snow in their sledges; the motion is pleasant, and, in my opinion, far more agreeable than that of an English stage-coach. The cold is not excessive, if you are wrapt in furs, a dress which I have already adopted; for there is a great difference between walking the deck and remaining seated motionless for hours, when no exercise prevents the blood from actually freezing in your veins. I have no ambition to lose my life on the post-road[13] between St. Petersburgh and Archangel.

I shall depart for the latter town in a fortnight or three weeks; and I.9 my intention is to hire a ship there, which can easily be done by paying the insurance for the owner, and to engage as many sailors as I think

---

13. I.e., a main road used by the postal service.

necessary among those who are accustomed to the whale-fishing. I do not intend to sail until the month of June: and when shall I return? Ah, dear sister, how can I answer this question? If I succeed, many, many months, perhaps years, will pass before you and I may meet. If I fail, you will see me again soon, or never.

Farewell, my dear, excellent, Margaret. Heaven shower down blessings on you, and save me, that I may again and again testify my gratitude for all your love and kindness.

Your affectionate brother,

R. WALTON.

LETTER II.

To Mrs. SAVILLE, *England.*

Archangel, 28th March, 17—.

HOW slowly the time passes here, encompassed as I am by frost and snow; yet a second step is taken towards my enterprise. I have hired a vessel, and am occupied in collecting my sailors; those whom I have already engaged appear to be men on whom I can depend, and are certainly possessed of dauntless courage.

But I have one want which I have never yet been able to satisfy; and the absence of the object of which I now feel as a most severe I.11 evil. I have no friend, Margaret: when I am glowing with the enthusiasm of success, there will be none to participate my joy; if I am assailed by disappointment, no one will endeavour to sustain me in dejection. I shall commit my thoughts to paper, it is true; but that is a poor medium for the communication of feeling. I desire the company of a man who could sympathize with me; whose eyes would reply to mine. You may deem me romantic, my dear sister, but I bitterly feel the want of a friend. I have no one near me, gentle yet courageous, possessed of a cultivated as well as of a capacious mind, whose tastes are like my own, to approve or amend my plans. How would such a friend repair the faults of your poor brother! I am too ardent in execution, and too impatient of difficulties. But it is a still greater evil to I.12 me that I am self-educated: for the first fourteen years of my life I ran wild on a common, and read nothing but our uncle Thomas's books of voyages. At that age I became acquainted with the celebrated poets of our own country; but it was only when it had ceased to be in my power to derive its most important benefits from such a conviction, that I perceived the necessity of becoming acquainted with more languages than that of my native country. Now I am twenty-eight, and am in reality more illiterate than many school-boys of fifteen. It is true that I have thought more, and that my day dreams are more extended and magnificent; but they want (as the painters call it) *keeping;*[14] and I greatly need a friend who would have sense enough not

---

14. *Oxford English Dictionary* online, s.v. "keeping n.," (updated 1901) sense 9: the maintenance of the proper relation between the representations of nearer and more distant objects in a picture; the maintenance of harmony of composition.

I.13   to despise me as romantic, and affection enough for me to endeavour
to regulate my mind.

Well, these are useless complaints; I shall certainly find no friend
on the wide ocean, nor even here in Archangel, among merchants
and seamen. Yet some feelings, unallied to the dross of human nature, beat even in these rugged bosoms. My lieutenant, for instance,
is a man of wonderful courage and enterprise; he is madly desirous of
glory. He is an Englishman, and in the midst of national and professional prejudices, unsoftened by cultivation, retains some of the no-
blest endowments of humanity. I first became acquainted with him
on board a whale vessel: finding that he was unemployed in this city,
I easily engaged him to assist in my enterprise.

The master is a person of an excellent disposition, and is remark-
I.14   able in the ship for his gentleness, and the mildness of his discipline.
He is, indeed, of so amiable a nature, that he will not hunt (a favourite, and almost the only amusement here), because he cannot endure to spill blood. He is, moreover, heroically generous. Some years
ago he loved a young Russian lady, of moderate fortune; and having
amassed a considerable sum in prize-money, the father of the girl
consented to the match. He saw his mistress once before the destined
ceremony; but she was bathed in tears, and, throwing herself at his
feet, entreated him to spare her, confessing at the same time that she
loved another, but that he was poor, and that her father would never
consent to the union. My generous friend reassured the suppliant,
and on being informed of the name of her lover instantly abandoned
I.15   his pursuit. He had already bought a farm with his money, on which
he had designed to pass the remainder of his life; but he bestowed the
whole on his rival, together with the remains of his prize-money to
purchase stock, and then himself solicited the young woman's father
to consent to her marriage with her lover. But the old man decidedly
refused, thinking himself bound in honour to my friend; who, when
he found the father inexorable, quitted his country, nor returned until he heard that his former mistress was married according to her
inclinations. "What a noble fellow!" you will exclaim. He is so; but
then he has passed all his life on board a vessel, and has scarcely an
idea beyond the rope and the shroud.[15]

But do not suppose that, because I complain a little, or because
I.16   I can conceive a consolation for my toils which I may never know,
that I am wavering in my resolutions. Those are as fixed as fate; and

---

15. Ropes attached to the mast.

my voyage is only now delayed until the weather shall permit my embarkation. The winter has been dreadfully severe; but the spring promises well, and it is considered as a remarkably early season; so that, perhaps, I may sail sooner than I expected. I shall do nothing rashly; you know me sufficiently to confide in my prudence and considerateness whenever the safety of others is committed to my care.

I cannot describe to you my sensations on the near prospect of my undertaking. It is impossible to communicate to you a conception of the trembling sensation, half pleasurable and half fearful, with which I am preparing to depart. I am going to unexplored regions, to "the land of mist and snow;" but I shall kill no albatross, therefore do not be alarmed for my safety.[16]   I.17

Shall I meet you again, after having traversed immense seas, and returned by the most southern cape of Africa or America? I dare not expect such success, yet I cannot bear to look on the reverse of the picture. Continue to write to me by every opportunity: I may receive your letters (though the chance is very doubtful) on some occasions when I need them most to support my spirits. I love you very tenderly. Remember me with affection, should you never hear from me again.

Your affectionate brother,

ROBERT WALTON.

---

16. See Samuel Taylor Coleridge, "The Rime of the Ancient Mariner" (1798), line 403.

LETTER III.

I.18

To Mrs. SAVILLE, *England.*

July 7th, 17—.

MY DEAR SISTER,

I write a few lines in haste, to say that I am safe, and well advanced on my voyage. This letter will reach England by a merchant-man now on its homeward voyage from Archangel; more fortunate than I, who may not see my native land, perhaps, for many years. I am, however, in good spirits: my men are bold, and apparently firm of purpose; nor do the floating sheets of ice that continually pass us, indicating the dangers of the region towards which we are advancing, appear to dismay them. We have already reached a very high latitude; but it is the height of summer, and although not so warm as in England, the southern gales, which blow us speedily towards those shores which I so ardently desire to attain, breathe a degree of renovating warmth which I had not expected.

No incidents have hitherto befallen us, that would make a figure in a letter. One or two stiff gales, and the breaking of a mast, are accidents which experienced navigators scarcely remember to record; and I shall be well content, if nothing worse happen to us during our voyage.

Adieu, my dear Margaret. Be assured, that for my own sake, as well as your's, I will not rashly encounter danger. I will be cool, persevering, and prudent.

Remember me to all my English friends.

Most affectionately yours,

R. W.

I.19

I.20

LETTER IV.

To Mrs. SAVILLE, *England.*

August 5th, 17—.

SO strange an accident has happened to us, that I cannot forbear recording it, although it is very probable that you will see me before these papers can come into your possession.

Last Monday (July 31st), we were nearly surrounded by ice, which closed in the ship on all sides, scarcely leaving her the sea room in which she floated. Our situation was somewhat dangerous, especially as we were compassed round by a very thick fog. We accordingly lay to, hoping that some change would take place in the atmosphere and weather.

About two o'clock the mist cleared away, and we beheld, stretched out in every direction, vast and irregular plains of ice, which seemed to have no end. Some of my comrades groaned, and my own mind began to grow watchful with anxious thoughts, when a strange sight suddenly attracted our attention, and diverted our solicitude from our own situation. We perceived a low carriage, fixed on a sledge and drawn by dogs, pass on towards the north, at the distance of half a mile: a being which had the shape of a man, but apparently of gigantic stature, sat in the sledge, and guided the dogs. We watched the rapid progress of the traveller with our telescopes, until he was lost among the distant inequalities of the ice.

This appearance excited our unqualified wonder. We were, as we believed, many hundred miles from any land; but this apparition seemed to denote that it was not, in reality, so distant as we had supposed. Shut in, however, by ice, it was impossible to follow his track, which we had observed with the greatest attention.

About two hours after this occurrence, we heard the ground sea;[17] and before night the ice broke, and freed our ship. We, however, lay to until the morning, fearing to encounter in the dark those large

---

17. Defined as "a sea when the waters are agitated to the bottom" in William Crowe, *Lewesdon Hill: A Poem* (Oxford: Clarendon Press, 1788), 29.

loose masses which float about after the breaking up of the ice. I profited of this time to rest for a few hours.

I.24
In the morning, however, as soon as it was light, I went upon deck, and found all the sailors busy on one side of the vessel, apparently talking to some one in the sea. It was, in fact, a sledge, like that we had seen before, which had drifted towards us in the night, on a large fragment of ice. Only one dog remained alive; but there was a human being within it, whom the sailors were persuading to enter the vessel. He was not, as the other traveller seemed to be, a savage inhabitant of some undiscovered island, but an European. When I appeared on deck, the master said, "Here is our captain, and he will not allow you to perish on the open sea."

On perceiving me, the stranger addressed me in English, although with a foreign accent. "Before I come on board your vessel," said he, "will you have the kindness to inform me whither you are bound?"

I.25
You may conceive my astonishment on hearing such a question addressed to me from a man on the brink of destruction, and to whom I should have supposed that my vessel would have been a resource which he would not have exchanged for the most precious wealth the earth can afford. I replied, however, that we were on a voyage of discovery towards the northern pole.

Upon hearing this he appeared satisfied, and consented to come on board. Good God! Margaret, if you had seen the man who thus capitulated[18] for his safety, your surprise would have been boundless. His limbs were nearly frozen, and his body dreadfully emaciated by fatigue and suffering. I never saw a man in so wretched a condition. We attempted to carry him into the cabin; but as soon as he had quit-
I.26
ted the fresh air, he fainted. We accordingly brought him back to the deck, and restored him to animation by rubbing him with brandy, and forcing him to swallow a small quantity. As soon as he shewed signs of life, we wrapped him up in blankets, and placed him near the chimney of the kitchen-stove. By slow degrees he recovered, and ate a little soup, which restored him wonderfully.

Two days passed in this manner before he was able to speak; and I often feared that his sufferings had deprived him of understanding. When he had in some measure recovered, I removed him to my own cabin, and attended on him as much as my duty would permit. I never saw a more interesting creature: his eyes have generally an expression of wildness, and even madness; but there are moments

18. Bargained.

when, if any one performs an act of kindness towards him, or does   I.27
him any the most trifling service, his whole countenance is lighted
up, as it were, with a beam of benevolence and sweetness that I never saw equalled. But he is generally melancholy and despairing; and
sometimes he gnashes his teeth, as if impatient of the weight of woes
that oppresses him.

When my guest was a little recovered, I had great trouble to keep
off the men, who wished to ask him a thousand questions; but I
would not allow him to be tormented by their idle curiosity, in a state
of body and mind whose restoration evidently depended upon entire
repose. Once, however, the lieutenant asked, Why he had come so far
upon the ice in so strange a vehicle?

His countenance instantly assumed an aspect[19] of the deepest
gloom; and he replied, "To seek one who fled from me."   I.28

"And did the man whom you pursued travel in the same fashion?"

"Yes."

"Then I fancy we have seen him; for, the day before we picked you
up, we saw some dogs drawing a sledge, with a man in it, across the
ice."

This aroused the stranger's attention; and he asked a multitude
of questions concerning the route which the dæmon,[20] as he called
him, had pursued. Soon after, when he was alone with me, he said, "I
have, doubtless, excited your curiosity, as well as that of these good
people; but you are too considerate to make inquiries."

"Certainly; it would indeed be very impertinent and inhuman in
me to trouble you with any inquisitiveness of mine."

"And yet you rescued me from a strange and perilous situation;   I.29
you have benevolently restored me to life."

Soon after this he inquired, if I thought that the breaking up of the
ice had destroyed the other sledge? I replied, that I could not answer
with any degree of certainty; for the ice had not broken until near
midnight, and the traveller might have arrived at a place of safety
before that time; but of this I could not judge.

---

19. Appearance.
20. In Greek mythology dæmons are halfway between men and gods; but Victor also
calls the Creature "demoniacal"—i.e., demonic or devilish, and the Creature speaks
of the "dæmons [i.e., devils] of hell." Thus MWS does not seem to have distinguished
between dæmons and demons (devils).

From this time the stranger seemed very eager to be upon deck, to watch for the sledge which had before appeared; but I have persuaded him to remain in the cabin, for he is far too weak to sustain the rawness of the atmosphere. But I have promised that some one should watch for him, and give him instant notice if any new object should appear in sight.

I.30   Such is my journal of what relates to this strange occurrence up to the present day. The stranger has gradually improved in health, but is very silent, and appears uneasy when any one except myself enters his cabin. Yet his manners are so conciliating and gentle, that the sailors are all interested in him, although they have had very little communication with him. For my own part, I begin to love him as a brother; and his constant and deep grief fills me with sympathy and compassion. He must have been a noble creature in his better days, being even now in wreck so attractive and amiable.

I said in one of my letters, my dear Margaret, that I should find no friend on the wide ocean; yet I have found a man who, before his
I.31   spirit had been broken by misery, I should have been happy to have possessed as the brother of my heart.

I shall continue my journal concerning the stranger at intervals, should I have any fresh incidents to record.

August 13th, 17—.

My affection for my guest increases every day. He excites at once my admiration and my pity to an astonishing degree. How can I see so noble a creature destroyed by misery without feeling the most poignant grief? He is so gentle, yet so wise; his mind is so cultivated; and when he speaks, although his words are culled with the choicest art, yet they flow with rapidity and unparalleled eloquence.

He is now much recovered from his illness, and is continually on the deck, apparently watching for the sledge that preceded his own.
I.32   Yet, although unhappy, he is not so utterly occupied by his own misery, but that he interests himself deeply in the employments of others. He has asked me many questions concerning my design; and I have related my little history frankly to him. He appeared pleased with the confidence, and suggested several alterations in my plan, which I shall find exceedingly useful. There is no pedantry in his manner; but all he does appears to spring solely from the interest he instinctively takes in the welfare of those who surround him. He is often overcome

by gloom, and then he sits by himself, and tries to overcome all that
is sullen or unsocial in his humour. These paroxysms pass from him
like a cloud from before the sun, though his dejection never leaves
him. I have endeavoured to win his confidence; and I trust that I have
succeeded. One day I mentioned to him the desire I had always felt of   I.33
finding a friend who might sympathize with me, and direct me by his
counsel. I said, I did not belong to that class of men who are offended
by advice. "I am self-educated, and perhaps I hardly rely sufficiently
upon my own powers. I wish therefore that my companion should be
wiser and more experienced than myself, to confirm and support me;
nor have I believed it impossible to find a true friend."

"I agree with you," replied the stranger, "in believing that friendship is not only a desirable, but a possible acquisition. I once had a
friend, the most noble of human creatures, and am entitled, therefore, to judge respecting friendship. You have hope, and the world
before you, and have no cause for despair. But I——I have lost every   I.34
thing, and cannot begin life anew."

As he said this, his countenance became expressive of a calm settled grief, that touched me to the heart. But he was silent, and presently retired to his cabin.

Even broken in spirit as he is, no one can feel more deeply than he
does the beauties of nature. The starry sky, the sea, and every sight
afforded by these wonderful regions, seems still to have the power
of elevating his soul from earth. Such a man has a double existence:
he may suffer misery, and be overwhelmed by disappointments; yet
when he has retired into himself, he will be like a celestial spirit, that
has a halo around him, within whose circle no grief or folly ventures.

Will you laugh at the enthusiasm I express concerning this divine
wanderer? If you do, you must have certainly lost that simplicity   I.35
which was once your characteristic charm. Yet, if you will, smile at
the warmth of my expressions, while I find every day new causes for
repeating them.

August 19th, 17—.

Yesterday the stranger said to me, "You may easily perceive, Captain Walton, that I have suffered great and unparalleled misfortunes.
I had determined, once, that the memory of these evils should die
with me; but you have won me to alter my determination. You seek

for knowledge and wisdom, as I once did; and I ardently hope that the gratification of your wishes may not be a serpent to sting you, as mine has been. I do not know that the relation of my misfortunes will be useful to you, yet, if you are inclined, listen to my tale. I believe that the strange incidents connected with it will afford a view of nature, which may enlarge your faculties and understanding. You will hear of powers and occurrences, such as you have been accustomed to believe impossible: but I do not doubt that my tale conveys in its series internal evidence of the truth of the events of which it is composed."

You may easily conceive that I was much gratified by the offered communication; yet I could not endure that he should renew his grief by a recital of his misfortunes. I felt the greatest eagerness to hear the promised narrative, partly from curiosity, and partly from a strong desire to ameliorate his fate, if it were in my power. I expressed these feelings in my answer.

"I thank you," he replied, "for your sympathy, but it is useless; my fate is nearly fulfilled. I wait but for one event, and then I shall repose in peace. I understand your feeling," continued he, perceiving that I wished to interrupt him; "but you are mistaken, my friend, if thus you will allow me to name you; nothing can alter my destiny: listen to my history, and you will perceive how irrevocably it is determined.["]

He then told me, that he would commence his narrative the next day when I should be at leisure. This promise drew from me the warmest thanks. I have resolved every night, when I am not engaged, to record, as nearly as possible in his own words, what he has related during the day. If I should be engaged, I will at least make notes. This manuscript will doubtless afford you the greatest pleasure: but to me, who know him, and who hear it from his own lips, with what interest and sympathy shall I read it in some future day!

I.36

I.37

I.38

FRANKENSTEIN;

OR,

THE MODERN PROMETHEUS.

CHAPTER I.

I AM by birth a Genevese; and my family is one of the most distinguished of that republic. My ancestors had been for many years counsellors and syndics;[21] and my father had filled several public situations with honour and reputation. He was respected by all who knew him for his integrity and indefatigable attention to public business. He passed his younger days perpetually occupied by the affairs of his country; and it was not until the decline of life that he thought of marrying, and bestowing on the state sons who might carry his virtues and his name down to posterity.

As the circumstances of his marriage illustrate his character, I cannot refrain from relating them. One of his most intimate friends was a merchant, who, from a flourishing state, fell, through numerous mischances, into poverty. This man, whose name was Beaufort, was of a proud and unbending disposition, and could not bear to live in poverty and oblivion in the same country where he had formerly been distinguished for his rank and magnificence. Having paid his debts, therefore, in the most honourable manner, he retreated with his daughter to the town of Lucerne, where he lived unknown and in wretchedness. My father loved Beaufort with the truest friendship, and was deeply grieved by his retreat in these unfortunate circumstances. He grieved also for the loss of his society, and resolved to seek him out and endeavour to persuade him to begin the world again through his credit and assistance.

Beaufort had taken effectual measures to conceal himself; and it was ten months before my father discovered his abode. Overjoyed

---

21. The four elected syndics of Geneva effectively controlled the city's government up until the revolution of 1792.

at this discovery, he hastened to the house, which was situated in a mean street, near the Reuss.[22] But when he entered, misery and despair alone welcomed him. Beaufort had saved but a very small sum of money from the wreck of his fortunes; but it was sufficient to provide him with sustenance for some months, and in the mean time

I.42 he hoped to procure some respectable employment in a merchant's house. The interval was consequently spent in inaction; his grief only became more deep and rankling, when he had leisure for reflection; and at length it took so fast hold of his mind, that at the end of three months he lay on a bed of sickness, incapable of any exertion.

His daughter attended him with the greatest tenderness; but she saw with despair that their little fund was rapidly decreasing, and that there was no other prospect of support. But Caroline Beaufort possessed a mind of an uncommon mould; and her courage rose to support her in her adversity. She procured plain work;[23] she plaited straw; and by various means contrived to earn a pittance scarcely sufficient to support life.

Several months passed in this manner. Her father grew worse;

I.43 her time was more entirely occupied in attending him; her means of subsistence decreased; and in the tenth month her father died in her arms, leaving her an orphan and a beggar. This last blow overcame her; and she knelt by Beaufort's coffin, weeping bitterly, when my father entered the chamber. He came like a protecting spirit to the poor girl, who committed herself to his care, and after the interment of his friend he conducted her to Geneva, and placed her under the protection of a relation. Two years after this event Caroline became his wife.

When my father became a husband and a parent, he found his time so occupied by the duties of his new situation, that he relinquished many of his public employments, and devoted himself to the education of his children. Of these I was the eldest, and the destined

I.44 successor to all his labours and utility. No creature could have more tender parents than mine. My improvement and health were their constant care, especially as I remained for several years their only child. But before I continue my narrative, I must record an incident which took place when I was four years of age.

My father had a sister, whom he tenderly loved, and who had married early in life an Italian gentleman. Soon after her marriage,

---

22. The river that runs through Lucerne.
23. Simple needlework (*Oxford English Dictionary*, s.v. "plain work" [updated 2006]).

she had accompanied her husband into her native country, and for some years my father had very little communication with her. About the time I mentioned she died; and a few months afterwards he received a letter from her husband, acquainting him with his intention of marrying an Italian lady, and requesting my father to take charge of the infant Elizabeth, the only child of his deceased sister. "It is my wish," he said, "that you should consider her as your own daughter, and educate her thus. Her mother's fortune is secured to her, the documents of which I will commit to your keeping. Reflect upon this proposition; and decide whether you would prefer educating your niece yourself to her being brought up by a stepmother." I.45

My father did not hesitate, and immediately went to Italy, that he might accompany the little Elizabeth to her future home. I have often heard my mother say, that she was at that time the most beautiful child she had ever seen, and shewed signs even then of a gentle and affectionate disposition. These indications, and a desire to bind as closely as possible the ties of domestic love, determined my mother to consider Elizabeth as my future wife; a design which she never found reason to repent. I.46

From this time Elizabeth Lavenza became my playfellow, and, as we grew older, my friend. She was docile and good tempered, yet gay and playful as a summer insect. Although she was lively and animated, her feelings were strong and deep, and her disposition uncommonly affectionate. No one could better enjoy liberty, yet no one could submit with more grace than she did to constraint and caprice. Her imagination was luxuriant, yet her capability of application was great. Her person was the image of her mind; her hazel eyes, although as lively as a bird's, possessed an attractive softness. Her figure was light and airy; and, though capable of enduring great fatigue, she appeared the most fragile creature in the world. While I admired her understanding and fancy, I loved to tend on her, as I should on a favourite animal; and I never saw so much grace both of person and mind united to so little pretension. I.47

Every one adored Elizabeth. If the servants had any request to make, it was always through her intercession. We were strangers to any species of disunion and dispute; for although there was a great dissimilitude in our characters, there was an harmony in that very dissimilitude. I was more calm and philosophical than my companion; yet my temper was not so yielding. My application was of longer endurance; but it was not so severe whilst it endured. I delighted in investigating the facts relative to the actual world; she busied herself

in following the aërial creations of the poets. The world was to me a
I.48   secret, which I desired to discover; to her it was a vacancy, which she
sought to people with imaginations of her own.

My brothers were considerably younger than myself; but I had
a friend in one of my schoolfellows, who compensated for this defi-
ciency. Henry Clerval was the son of a merchant of Geneva, an intimate friend of my father. He was a boy of singular talent and fancy.
I remember, when he was nine years old, he wrote a fairy tale, which
was the delight and amazement of all his companions. His favourite
study consisted in books of chivalry and romance; and when very
young, I can remember, that we used to act plays composed by him
out of these favourite books, the principal characters of which were
Orlando, Robin Hood, Amadis, and St. George.[24]

I.49   No youth could have passed more happily than mine. My parents
were indulgent, and my companions amiable. Our studies were never forced; and by some means we always had an end placed in view,
which excited us to ardour in the prosecution of them. It was by this
method, and not by emulation, that we were urged to application.
Elizabeth was not incited to apply herself to drawing, that her companions might not outstrip her; but through the desire of pleasing
her aunt, by the representation of some favourite scene done by her
own hand. We learned Latin and English, that we might read the
writings in those languages; and so far from study being made odious to us through punishment, we loved application, and our amusements would have been the labours of other children. Perhaps we
I.50   did not read so many books, or learn languages so quickly, as those
who are disciplined according to the ordinary methods; but what we
learned was impressed the more deeply on our memories.

In this description of our domestic circle I include Henry Clerval;
for he was constantly with us. He went to school with me, and generally passed the afternoon at our house; for being an only child, and
destitute of companions at home, his father was well pleased that he
should find associates at our house; and we were never completely
happy when Clerval was absent.

I feel pleasure in dwelling on the recollections of childhood, before
misfortune had tainted my mind, and changed its bright visions of
extensive usefulness into gloomy and narrow reflections upon self.

---

24. Robin Hood was a story known to English children, not to Genevans; indeed all
these romantic heroes, of very varied origin and date, were the subject of books available
to children.

But, in drawing the picture of my early days, I must not omit to record those events which led, by insensible steps to my after tale of misery: for when I would account to myself for the birth of that passion, which afterwards ruled my destiny, I find it arise, like a mountain river, from ignoble and almost forgotten sources; but, swelling as it proceeded, it became the torrent which, in its course, has swept away all my hopes and joys. I.51

Natural philosophy[25] is the genius[26] that has regulated my fate; I desire therefore, in this narration, to state those facts which led to my predilection for that science. When I was thirteen years of age, we all went on a party of pleasure to the baths near Thonon:[27] the inclemency of the weather obliged us to remain a day confined to the inn. In this house I chanced to find a volume of the works of Cornelius Agrippa.[28] I opened it with apathy; the theory which he attempts to demonstrate, and the wonderful facts which he relates, soon changed I.52 this feeling into enthusiasm. A new light seemed to dawn upon my mind; and, bounding with joy, I communicated my discovery to my father. I cannot help remarking here the many opportunities instructors possess of directing the attention of their pupils to useful knowledge, which they utterly neglect. My father looked carelessly at the title-page of my book, and said, "Ah! Cornelius Agrippa! My dear Victor, do not waste your time upon this; it is sad trash."

If, instead of this remark, my father had taken the pains to explain to me, that the principles of Agrippa had been entirely exploded, and that a modern system of science had been introduced, which possessed much greater powers than the ancient, because the powers of the latter were chimerical,[29] while those of the former were real and I.53 practical; under such circumstances, I should certainly have thrown Agrippa aside, and, with my imagination warmed as it was, should probably have applied myself to the more rational theory of chemistry which has resulted from modern discoveries. It is even possible, that the train of my ideas would never have received the fatal impulse that led to my ruin. But the cursory glance my father had taken of my volume by no means assured me that he was acquainted with its contents; and I continued to read with the greatest avidity.

---

25. The standard term for what would later be called natural science.
26. Genius, a divine spirit.
27. Some fifteen miles from Geneva.
28. Cornelius Agrippa (1486–1535) was famous as a practitioner of magic.
29. Fanciful.

When I returned home, my first care was to procure the whole works of this author, and afterwards of Paracelsus and Albertus Magnus.[30] I read and studied the wild fancies of these writers with

I.54　delight; they appeared to me treasures known to few beside myself; and although I often wished to communicate these secret stores of knowledge to my father, yet his indefinite censure of my favourite Agrippa always withheld me. I disclosed my discoveries to Elizabeth, therefore, under a promise of strict secrecy; but she did not interest herself in the subject, and I was left by her to pursue my studies alone.

It may appear very strange, that a disciple of Albertus Magnus should arise in the eighteenth century; but our family was not scientifical, and I had not attended any of the lectures given at the schools of Geneva. My dreams were therefore undisturbed by reality; and I entered with the greatest diligence into the search of the philosopher's stone and the elixir of life.[31] But the latter obtained my most

I.55　undivided attention: wealth was an inferior object; but what glory would attend the discovery, if I could banish disease from the human frame, and render man invulnerable to any but a violent death!

Nor were these my only visions. The raising of ghosts or devils was a promise liberally accorded by my favourite authors, the fulfilment of which I most eagerly sought; and if my incantations were always unsuccessful, I attributed the failure rather to my own inexperience and mistake, than to a want of skill or fidelity in my instructors.[32]

The natural phænomena that take place every day before our eyes did not escape my examinations. Distillation,[33] and the wonderful effects of steam,[34] processes of which my favourite authors were utterly igno-

I.56　rant, excited my astonishment; but my utmost wonder was engaged

---

30. Paracelsus (1493–1541) was a Swiss alchemist and doctor. Albertus Magnus (1193–1280), a Dominican philosopher, was supposed to have constructed a head of brass which could answer questions. In a letter to Godwin in 1812 PBS reported that as a boy he had "pored over the reveries of Albertus Magnus & Paracelsus."

31. Alchemists believed the philosopher's stone would turn base metals into gold, and the elixir of life would ensure eternal youth.

32. Agrippa's apprentice was supposed to have used a formula found in one of his books to raise the Devil, with fatal consequences. PBS had sought as a boy to encounter ghosts: "Hymn to Intellectual Beauty" (1816), lines 49–54.

33. Distillation really was uncommon before modern times.

34. See David Ketterer, "'The Wonderful Effects of Steam': More Percy Shelley Words in *Frankenstein*?," *Science Fiction Studies* 25 (1998): 566–68.

by some experiments on an air-pump,[35] which I saw employed by a gentleman whom we were in the habit of visiting.

The ignorance of the early philosophers on these and several other points served to decrease their credit with me: but I could not entirely throw them aside, before some other system should occupy their place in my mind.

When I was about fifteen years old, we had retired to our house near Belrive,[36] when we witnessed a most violent and terrible thunder-storm. It advanced from behind the mountains of Jura; and the thunder burst at once with frightful loudness from various quarters of the heavens. I remained, while the storm lasted, watching its progress with curiosity and delight. As I stood at the door, on a sudden I beheld a stream of fire issue from an old and beautiful oak, which stood about twenty yards from our house; and so soon as the   I.57 dazzling light vanished, the oak had disappeared, and nothing remained but a blasted stump. When we visited it the next morning, we found the tree shattered in a singular manner. It was not splintered by the shock, but entirely reduced to thin ribbands of wood. I never beheld any thing so utterly destroyed.

The catastrophe of this tree excited my extreme astonishment; and I eagerly inquired of my father the nature and origin of thunder and lightning. He replied, "Electricity;" describing at the same time the various effects of that power. He constructed a small electrical machine, and exhibited a few experiments; he made also a kite, with a wire and string, which drew down that fluid from the clouds.[37]

This last stroke completed the overthrow of Cornelius Agrippa,   I.58 Albertus Magnus, and Paracelsus, who had so long reigned the lords of my imagination. But by some fatality I did not feel inclined to commence the study of any modern system; and this disinclination was influenced by the following circumstance.

My father expressed a wish that I should attend a course of lectures upon natural philosophy, to which I cheerfully consented. Some accident prevented my attending these lectures until the course was nearly finished. The lecture, being therefore one of the last, was entirely incomprehensible to me. The professor discoursed with the

---

35. A reference to Robert Boyle's seventeenth-century experiments with a vacuum.
36. On the south shore of Lac Léman (on which Geneva stands), a little beyond where the Byron-Shelley party were staying.
37. Victor's father repeated Benjamin Franklin's experiment of 1752, designed to show that lightning is electricity.

greatest fluency of potassium and boron,[38] of sulphates and oxyds, terms to which I could affix no idea; and I became disgusted with the science of natural philosophy, although I still read Pliny and Buffon with delight, authors, in my estimation, of nearly equal interest and utility.[39]

I.59

My occupations at this age were principally the mathematics, and most of the branches of study appertaining to that science. I was busily employed in learning languages; Latin was already familiar to me, and I began to read some of the easiest Greek authors without the help of a lexicon. I also perfectly understood English and German. This is the list of my accomplishments at the age of seventeen; and you may conceive that my hours were fully employed in acquiring and maintaining a knowledge of this various literature.

Another task also devolved upon me, when I became the instructor of my brothers. Ernest was six years younger than myself, and was my principal pupil. He had been afflicted with ill health from his infancy, through which Elizabeth and I had been his constant nurses: his disposition was gentle, but he was incapable of any severe application. William, the youngest of our family, was yet an infant, and the most beautiful little fellow in the world; his lively blue eyes, dimpled cheeks, and endearing manners, inspired the tenderest affection.

I.60

Such was our domestic circle, from which care and pain seemed for ever banished. My father directed our studies, and my mother partook of our enjoyments. Neither of us possessed the slightest pre-eminence over the other; the voice of command was never heard amongst us; but mutual affection engaged us all to comply with and obey the slightest desire of each other.

---

38. Potassium and boron were first isolated by Humphry Davy in 1807–1808.

39. Pliny the Elder (23–79) wrote a *Natural History* which contains many marvelous stories. Buffon (1707–1788) was the greatest naturalist (we would now say biologist) of the eighteenth century. PBS refers to him in a letter written while in Geneva.

CHAPTER II.   I.61

WHEN I had attained the age of seventeen, my parents resolved that I should become a student at the university of Ingolstadt. I had hitherto attended the schools of Geneva; but my father thought it necessary, for the completion of my education, that I should be made acquainted with other customs than those of my native country. My departure was therefore fixed at an early date; but, before the day resolved upon could arrive, the first misfortune of my life occurred—an omen, as it were, of my future misery.

Elizabeth had caught the scarlet fever; but her illness was not severe, and she quickly recovered. During her confinement, many arguments had been urged to persuade my mother to refrain from attending upon her. She had, at first, yielded to our entreaties; but when she heard that her favourite was recovering, she could no longer debar herself from her society, and entered her chamber long before the danger of infection was past. The consequences of this imprudence were fatal. On the third day my mother sickened; her fever was very malignant, and the looks of her attendants prognosticated the worst event. On her death-bed the fortitude and benignity of this admirable woman did not desert her. She joined the hands of Elizabeth and myself: "My children," she said, "my firmest hopes of future happiness were placed on the prospect of your union. This expectation will now be the consolation of your father. Elizabeth, my love, you must supply my place to your younger cousins. Alas! I regret that I am taken from you; and, happy and beloved as I have been, is it not hard to quit you all? But these are not thoughts befitting me; I will endeavour to resign myself cheerfully to death, and will indulge a hope of meeting you in another world."

She died calmly; and her countenance expressed affection even in death. I need not describe the feelings of those whose dearest ties are rent by that most irreparable evil, the void that presents itself to the soul, and the despair that is exhibited on the countenance. It is so long before the mind can persuade itself that she, whom we saw every day, and whose very existence appeared a part of our own, can have departed for ever—that the brightness of a beloved eye can have been extinguished, and the sound of a voice so familiar, and dear to the ear, can be hushed, never more to be heard. These are the reflections of the first days; but when the lapse of time proves the reality of the evil, then the actual bitterness of grief commences. Yet from

I.62

I.63

I.64

whom has not that rude hand rent away some dear connexion; and why should I describe a sorrow which all have felt, and must feel? The time at length arrives, when grief is rather an indulgence than a necessity; and the smile that plays upon the lips, although it may be deemed a sacrilege, is not banished. My mother was dead, but we had still duties which we ought to perform; we must continue our course with the rest, and learn to think ourselves fortunate, whilst one remains whom the spoiler[40] has not seized.

I.65

My journey to Ingolstadt, which had been deferred by these events, was now again determined upon. I obtained from my father a respite of some weeks. This period was spent sadly; my mother's death, and my speedy departure, depressed our spirits; but Elizabeth endeavoured to renew the spirit of cheerfulness in our little society. Since the death of her aunt, her mind had acquired new firmness and vigour. She determined to fulfil her duties with the greatest exactness; and she felt that that most imperious duty, of rendering her uncle and cousins happy, had devolved upon her. She consoled me, amused her uncle, instructed my brothers; and I never beheld her so enchanting as at this time, when she was continually endeavouring to contribute to the happiness of others, entirely forgetful of herself.

I.66

The day of my departure at length arrived. I had taken leave of all my friends, excepting Clerval, who spent the last evening with us. He bitterly lamented that he was unable to accompany me: but his father could not be persuaded to part with him, intending that he should become a partner with him in business, in compliance with his favourite theory, that learning was superfluous in the commerce of ordinary life. Henry had a refined mind; he had no desire to be idle, and was well pleased to become his father's partner, but he believed that a man might be a very good trader, and yet possess a cultivated understanding.

We sat late, listening to his complaints, and making many little arrangements for the future. The next morning early I departed. Tears gushed [*sic*] from the eyes of Elizabeth; they proceeded partly from sorrow at my departure, and partly because she reflected that the same journey was to have taken place three months before, when a mother's blessing would have accompanied me.

I.67

I threw myself into the chaise that was to convey me away, and indulged in the most melancholy reflections. I, who had ever been surrounded by amiable companions, continually engaged in endeav-

---

40. I.e., death.

ouring to bestow mutual pleasure, I was now alone. In the university, whither I was going, I must form my own friends, and be my own protector. My life had hitherto been remarkably secluded and domestic; and this had given me invincible repugnance to new countenances. I loved my brothers, Elizabeth, and Clerval; these were "old   I.68 familiar faces;"[41] but I believed myself totally unfitted for the company of strangers. Such were my reflections as I commenced my journey; but as I proceeded, my spirits and hopes rose. I ardently desired the acquisition of knowledge. I had often, when at home, thought it hard to remain during my youth cooped up in one place, and had longed to enter the world, and take my station among other human beings. Now my desires were complied with, and it would, indeed, have been folly to repent.

I had sufficient leisure for these and many other reflections during my journey to Ingolstadt, which was long and fatiguing. At length the high white steeple of the town met my eyes. I alighted, and was conducted to my solitary apartment, to spend the evening as I pleased.

The next morning I delivered my letters of introduction, and paid   I.69 a visit to some of the principal professors, and among others to M. Krempe, professor of natural philosophy. He received me with politeness, and asked me several questions concerning my progress in the different branches of science appertaining to natural philosophy. I mentioned, it is true, with fear and trembling, the only authors I had ever read upon those subjects. The professor stared: "Have you," he said, "really spent your time in studying such nonsense?"

I replied in the affirmative. "Every minute," continued M. Krempe with warmth, "every instant that you have wasted on those books is utterly and entirely lost. You have burdened your memory with exploded systems, and useless names. Good God! in what desert land   I.70 have you lived, where no one was kind enough to inform you that these fancies, which you have so greedily imbibed, are a thousand years old, and as musty as they are ancient? I little expected in this

---

41. The title of a poem (1798) by Charles Lamb. This is one of a series of poetry references that don't fit with the notional setting of the story in the eighteenth century. The framing narrative is probably set in 1791–92, the date of Duncan's expedition in quest of the Northwest passage. Since Victor's narrative contains no reference to the Revolution or Napoleon, MWS perhaps always intended the story to conclude before the autumn of 1972 and the outbreak of war in Europe, although the Creature reads Volney's *Ruins* (1791) as part of his education. (Anne K. Mellor, *Mary Shelley: Her Life, Her Fiction, Her Monsters* [London: Routledge, 1988], 54–55, 237, n. 22 argued that the main events take place in the years 1792–1797, and most editors follow her.)

enlightened and scientific age to find a disciple of Albertus Magnus
and Paracelsus. My dear Sir, you must begin your studies entirely
anew."

So saying, he stept aside, and wrote down a list of several books
treating of natural philosophy, which he desired me to procure, and
dismissed me, after mentioning that in the beginning of the following
week he intended to commence a course of lectures upon natural
philosophy in its general relations, and that M. Waldman, a fellow-
professor, would lecture upon chemistry the alternate days that he
missed.

I.71   I returned home, not disappointed, for I had long considered
those authors useless whom the professor had so strongly repro-
bated; but I did not feel much inclined to study the books which I
procured at his recommendation. M. Krempe was a little squat man,
with a gruff voice and repulsive countenance; the teacher, therefore, did not prepossess me in favour of his doctrine. Besides, I had
a contempt for the uses of modern natural philosophy. It was very
different, when the masters of the science sought immortality and
power; such views, although futile, were grand: but now the scene
was changed. The ambition of the inquirer seemed to limit itself to
the annihilation of those visions on which my interest in science was
chiefly founded. I was required to exchange chimeras of boundless
grandeur for realities of little worth.

I.72   Such were my reflections during the first two or three days spent
almost in solitude. But as the ensuing week commenced, I thought
of the information which M. Krempe had given me concerning the
lectures. And although I could not consent to go and hear that little
conceited fellow deliver sentences out of a pulpit, I recollected what
he had said of M. Waldman, whom I had never seen, as he had hitherto been out of town.

Partly from curiosity, and partly from idleness, I went into the
lecturing room, which M. Waldman entered shortly after. This professor was very unlike his colleague. He appeared about fifty years of
age, but with an aspect expressive of the greatest benevolence; a few
gray hairs covered his temples, but those at the back of his head were
nearly black. His person was short, but remarkably erect; and his
I.73   voice the sweetest I had ever heard. He began his lecture by a recapitulation of the history of chemistry and the various improvements
made by different men of learning, pronouncing with fervour the
names of the most distinguished discoverers. He then took a cursory
view of the present state of the science, and explained many of its

elementary terms. After having made a few preparatory experiments, he concluded with a panegyric upon modern chemistry, the terms of which I shall never forget:—

"The ancient teachers of this science," said he, "promised impossibilities, and performed nothing. The modern masters promise very little; they know that metals cannot be transmuted, and that the elixir of life is a chimera. But these philosophers, whose hands seem only made to dabble in dirt, and their eyes to pour over the microscope or crucible, have indeed performed miracles. They penetrate into the recesses of nature, and shew how she works in her hiding places. They ascend into the heavens; they have discovered how the blood circulates, and the nature of the air we breathe.[42] They have acquired new and almost unlimited powers; they can command the thunders of heaven, mimic the earthquake, and even mock the invisible world with its own shadows."

    I.74

I departed highly pleased with the professor and his lecture, and paid him a visit the same evening. His manners in private were even more mild and attractive than in public; for there was a certain dignity in his mien during his lecture, which in his own house was replaced by the greatest affability and kindness. He heard with attention my little narration concerning my studies, and smiled at the names of Cornelius Agrippa, and Paracelsus, but without the contempt that M. Krempe had exhibited. He said, that "these were men to whose indefatigable zeal modern philosophers were indebted for most of the foundations of their knowledge. They had left to us, as an easier task, to give new names, and arrange in connected classifications, the facts which they in a great degree had been the instruments of bringing to light. The labours of men of genius, however erroneously directed, scarcely ever fail in ultimately turning to the solid advantage of mankind." I listened to his statement, which was delivered without any presumption or affectation; and then added, that his lecture had removed my prejudices against modern chemists; and I, at the same time, requested his advice concerning the books I ought to procure.

    I.75

    I.76

"I am happy," said M. Waldman, "to have gained a disciple; and if your application equals your ability, I have no doubt of your success. Chemistry is that branch of natural philosophy in which the

---

42. The discovery that the air we breathe is made up of different gases (oxygen, nitrogen) is associated in particular with Joseph Priestley (1733–1804), Daniel Rutherford (1749–1819), and Antoine Lavoisier (1743–1794). The circulation of the blood was discovered much earlier, in 1628, by William Harvey.

greatest improvements have been and may be made; it is on that account that I have made it my peculiar[43] study; but at the same time I
have not neglected the other branches of science. A man would make
but a very sorry chemist, if he attended to that department of human
knowledge alone. If your wish is to become really a man of science,
and not merely a petty experimentalist, I should advise you to apply
to every branch of natural philosophy, including mathematics."

I.77   He then took me into his laboratory, and explained to me the uses
of his various machines; instructing me as to what I ought to procure,
and promising me the use of his own, when I should have advanced
far enough in the science not to derange their mechanism. He also
gave me the list of books which I had requested; and I took my leave.

Thus ended a day memorable to me; it decided my future destiny.

---

43. Special.

CHAPTER III.

I.78

FROM this day natural philosophy, and particularly chemistry, in the most comprehensive sense of the term, became nearly my sole occupation. I read with ardour those works, so full of genius and discrimination, which modern inquirers have written on these subjects. I attended the lectures, and cultivated the acquaintance, of the men of science of the university; and I found even in M. Krempe a great deal of sound sense and real information, combined, it is true, with a repulsive physiognomy and manners, but not on that account the less valuable. In M. Waldman I found a true friend. His gentleness I.79 was never tinged by dogmatism; and his instructions were given with an air of frankness and good nature, that banished every idea of pedantry. It was, perhaps, the amiable character of this man that inclined me more to that branch of natural philosophy which he professed, than an intrinsic love for the science itself. But this state of mind had place only in the first steps towards knowledge: the more fully I entered into the science, the more exclusively I pursued it for its own sake. That application, which at first had been a matter of duty and resolution, now became so ardent and eager, that the stars often disappeared in the light of morning whilst I was yet engaged in my laboratory.

As I applied so closely, it may be easily conceived that I improved rapidly. My ardour was indeed the astonishment of the students; I.80 and my proficiency, that of the masters. Professor Krempe often asked me, with a sly smile, how Cornelius Agrippa went on? whilst M. Waldman expressed the most heartfelt exultation in my progress. Two years passed in this manner, during which I paid no visit to Geneva, but was engaged, heart and soul, in the pursuit of some discoveries, which I hoped to make. None but those who have experienced them can conceive of the enticements of science. In other studies you go as far as others have gone before you, and there is nothing more to know; but in a scientific pursuit there is continual food for discovery and wonder. A mind of moderate capacity, which closely pursues one study, must infallibly arrive at great proficiency in that study; and I, who continually sought the attainment of one object of I.81 pursuit, and was solely wrapt up in this, improved so rapidly, that, at the end of two years, I made some discoveries in the improvement of some chemical instruments, which procured me great esteem and admiration at the university. When I had arrived at this point, and had become as well acquainted with the theory and practice of natural philosophy as depended on the lessons of any of the professors at Ingolstadt, my residence there being no longer conducive to my improvements, I thought of returning to my friends and my native town, when an incident happened that protracted my stay.

One of the phænonema[44] which had peculiarly attracted my attention was the structure of the human frame, and, indeed, any animal endued with life. Whence, I often asked myself, did the principle of life proceed? It was a bold question, and one which has ever been considered as a mystery; yet with how many things are we upon the brink of becoming acquainted, if cowardice or carelessness did not restrain our inquiries. I revolved these circumstances in my mind, and determined thenceforth to apply myself more particularly to those branches of natural philosophy which relate to physiology. Unless I had been animated by an almost supernatural enthusiasm, my application to this study would have been irksome, and almost intolerable. To examine the causes of life, we must first have recourse to death. I became acquainted with the science of anatomy: but this was not sufficient; I must also observe the natural decay and corruption of the human body. In my education my father had taken the greatest precautions that my mind should be impressed with no supernatural horrors. I do not ever remember to have trembled at a tale of superstition, or to have feared the apparition of a spirit. Darkness had no effect upon my fancy; and a church-yard was to me merely the receptacle of bodies deprived of life, which, from being the seat of beauty and strength, had become food for the worm. Now I was led to examine the cause and progress of this decay, and forced to spend days and nights in vaults and charnel houses. My attention was fixed upon every object the most insupportable to the delicacy of the human feelings. I saw how the fine form of man was degraded and wasted; I beheld the corruption of death succeed to the blooming cheek of life; I saw how the worm inherited the wonders of the eye and brain. I paused, examining and analysing all the minutiæ of causation, as exemplified in the change from life to death, and death to life, until from the midst of this darkness a sudden light broke in upon me—a light so brilliant and wondrous, yet so simple, that while I became dizzy with the immensity of the prospect which it illustrated, I was surprised that among so many men of genius, who had directed their

I.82

I.83

I.84

---

44. *Sic* for "phænomena."

inquiries towards the same science, that I alone should be reserved to discover so astonishing a secret.

Remember, I am not recording the vision of a madman. The sun does not more certainly shine in the heavens, than that which I now affirm is true. Some miracle might have produced it, yet the stages of the discovery were distinct and probable. After days and nights of incredible labour and fatigue, I succeeded in discovering the cause of 1.85 generation and life; nay, more, I became myself capable of bestowing animation upon lifeless matter.

The astonishment which I had at first experienced on this discovery soon gave place to delight and rapture. After so much time spent in painful labour, to arrive at once at the summit of my desires, was the most gratifying consummation of my toils. But this discovery was so great and overwhelming, that all the steps by which I had been progressively led to it were obliterated, and I beheld only the result. What had been the study and desire of the wisest men since the creation of the world, was now within my grasp. Not that, like a magic scene, it all opened upon me at once: the information I had obtained was of a nature rather to direct my endeavours so soon as I should point them towards the object of my search, than to exhibit 1.86 that object already accomplished. I was like the Arabian who had been buried with the dead, and found a passage to life aided only by one glimmering, and seemingly ineffectual, light.[45]

I see by your eagerness, and the wonder and hope which your eyes express, my friend, that you expect to be informed of the secret with which I am acquainted; that cannot be: listen patiently until the end of my story, and you will easily perceive why I am reserved upon that subject. I will not lead you on, unguarded and ardent as I then was, to your destruction and infallible misery. Learn from me, if not by my precepts, at least by my example, how dangerous is the acquirement of knowledge, and how much happier that man is who believes his native town to be the world, than he who aspires to become greater 1.87 than his nature will allow.

When I found so astonishing a power placed within my hands, I hesitated a long time concerning the manner in which I should employ it. Although I possessed the capacity of bestowing animation, yet to prepare a frame for the reception of it, with all its intricacies of fibres, muscles, and veins, still remained a work of inconceivable difficulty and labour. I doubted at first whether I should attempt the

---

45. A reference to Sinbad's Fourth Voyage in *One Thousand and One Nights*.

creation of a being like myself or one of simpler organization; but my imagination was too much exalted by my first success to permit me to doubt of my ability to give life to an animal as complex and wonderful as man. The materials at present within my command hardly

I.88 appeared adequate to so arduous an undertaking; but I doubted not that I should ultimately succeed. I prepared myself for a multitude of reverses; my operations might be incessantly baffled, and at last my work be imperfect: yet, when I considered the improvement which every day takes place in science and mechanics, I was encouraged to hope my present attempts would at least lay the foundations of future success. Nor could I consider the magnitude and complexity of my plan as any argument of its impracticability. It was with these feelings that I began the creation of a human being. As the minuteness of the parts formed a great hindrance to my speed, I resolved, contrary to my first intention, to make the being of a gigantic stature; that is to say, about eight feet in height, and proportionably large. After

I.89 having formed this determination, and having spent some months in successfully collecting and arranging my materials, I began.

No one can conceive the variety of feelings which bore me onwards, like a hurricane, in the first enthusiasm of success. Life and death appeared to me ideal bounds, which I should first break through, and pour a torrent of light into our dark world. A new species would bless me as its creator and source; many happy and excellent natures would owe their being to me. No father could claim the gratitude of his child so completely as I should deserve their's. Pursuing these reflections, I thought, that if I could bestow animation upon lifeless matter, I might in process of time (although I now found it impossible) renew life where death had apparently devoted the body to corruption.[46]

I.90 These thoughts supported my spirits, while I pursued my undertaking with unremitting ardour. My cheek had grown pale with study, and my person had become emaciated with confinement. Sometimes, on the very brink of certainty, I failed; yet still I clung to the hope which the next day or the next hour might realize. One secret which I alone possessed was the hope to which I had dedicated myself; and the moon gazed on my midnight labours, while, with unrelaxed and breathless eagerness, I pursued nature to her hiding

---

46. Victor has in mind two distinct projects: i) bestowing life on lifeless matter (the project that leads to the creation of the Creature) and ii) restoring life to the dead, which would result in immortality.

places. Who shall conceive the horrors of my secret toil, as I dabbled among the unhallowed damps[47] of the grave, or tortured the living animal to animate the lifeless clay?[48] My limbs now tremble, and my eyes swim with the remembrance; but then a resistless, and almost frantic impulse, urged me forward; I seemed to have lost all soul or   I.91 sensation but for this one pursuit. It was indeed but a passing trance, that only made me feel with renewed acuteness so soon as, the unnatural stimulus ceasing to operate, I had returned to my old habits. I collected bones from charnel houses; and disturbed, with profane fingers, the tremendous secrets of the human frame. In a solitary chamber, or rather cell, at the top of the house, and separated from all the other apartments by a gallery and staircase, I kept my workshop of filthy creation; my eyeballs were starting from their sockets in attending to the details of my employment. The dissecting room and the slaughter-house furnished many of my materials; and often did my human nature turn with loathing from my occupation, whilst, still urged on by an eagerness which perpetually increased, I brought   I.92 my work near to a conclusion.

The summer months passed while I was thus engaged, heart and soul, in one pursuit. It was a most beautiful season; never did the fields bestow a more plentiful harvest, or the vines yield a more luxuriant vintage: but my eyes were insensible to the charms of nature. And the same feelings which made me neglect the scenes around me caused me also to forget those friends who were so many miles absent, and whom I had not seen for so long a time. I knew my silence disquieted them; and I well remembered the words of my father: "I know that while you are pleased with yourself, you will think of us with affection, and we shall hear regularly from you. You must pardon me, if I regard any interruption in your correspondence as a proof that your other duties are equally neglected."   I.93

I knew well therefore what would be my father's feelings; but I could not tear my thoughts from my employment, loathsome in itself, but which had taken an irresistible hold of my imagination. I wished, as it were, to procrastinate all that related to my feelings of affection until the great object, which swallowed up every habit of my nature, should be completed.

---

47. In the now obsolete sense of "a vapour or gas of a noxious kind" *(Oxford English Dictionary* online, s.v. "damp n.1" [updated 1894], sense 1).
48. The word "clay" is an implicit reference to Ovid's version of the Prometheus myth, as well as to the various passages in the Bible where human beings are compared to pots made of clay, God being the potter.

I then thought that my father would be unjust if he ascribed my neglect to vice, or faultiness on my part; but I am now convinced that he was justified in conceiving that I should not be altogether free from blame. A human being in perfection ought always to preserve a calm and peaceful mind, and never to allow passion or a transitory desire to disturb his tranquillity. I do not think that the pursuit of knowledge is an exception to this rule. If the study to which you apply yourself has a tendency to weaken your affections, and to destroy your taste for those simple pleasures in which no alloy can possibly mix, then that study is certainly unlawful, that is to say, not befitting the human mind. If this rule were always observed; if no man allowed any pursuit whatsoever to interfere with the tranquillity of his domestic affections, Greece had not been enslaved; Caesar would have spared his country; America would have been discovered more gradually; and the empires of Mexico and Peru had not been destroyed.

I.94

But I forget that I am moralizing in the most interesting part of my tale; and your looks remind me to proceed.

I.95

My father made no reproach in his letters; and only took notice of my silence by inquiring into my occupations more particularly than before. Winter, spring, and summer, passed away during my labours; but I did not watch the blossom or the expanding leaves— sights which before always yielded me supreme delight, so deeply was I engrossed in my occupation. The leaves of that year had withered before my work drew near to a close; and now every day shewed me more plainly how well I had succeeded. But my enthusiasm was checked by my anxiety, and I appeared rather like one doomed by slavery to toil in the mines, or any other unwholesome trade, than an artist occupied by his favourite employment. Every night I was oppressed by a slow fever, and I became nervous to a most painful degree; a disease that I regretted the more because I had hith-

I.96

erto enjoyed most excellent health, and had always boasted of the firmness of my nerves. But I believed that exercise and amusement would soon drive away such symptoms; and I promised myself both of these, when my creation should be complete.

CHAPTER IV.   I.97

IT was on a dreary night of November, that I beheld the accomplishment of my toils. With an anxiety that almost amounted to agony, I collected the instruments of life[49] around me, that I might infuse a spark of being into the lifeless thing that lay at my feet. It was already one in the morning; the rain pattered dismally against the panes, and my candle was nearly burnt out, when, by the glimmer of the half-extinguished light, I saw the dull yellow eye of the creature open; it breathed hard, and a convulsive motion agitated its limbs.   I.98

How can I describe my emotions at this catastrophe, or how delineate the wretch whom with such infinite pains and care I had endeavoured to form? His limbs were in proportion, and I had selected his features as beautiful. Beautiful!—Great God! His yellow skin scarcely covered the work of muscles and arteries beneath; his hair was of a lustrous black, and flowing; his teeth of a pearly whiteness; but these luxuriances only formed a more horrid contrast with his watery eyes, that seemed almost of the same colour as the dun white sockets in which they were set, his shrivelled complexion, and straight black lips.

The different accidents of life are not so changeable as the feelings of human nature. I had worked hard for nearly two years, for the sole   I.99 purpose of infusing life into an inanimate body. For this I had deprived myself of rest and health. I had desired it with an ardour that far exceeded moderation; but now that I had finished, the beauty of the dream vanished, and breathless horror and disgust filled my heart. Unable to endure the aspect of the being I had created, I rushed out of the room, and continued a long time traversing my bed-chamber, unable to compose my mind to sleep. At length lassitude succeeded to the tumult I had before endured; and I threw myself on the bed in my clothes, endeavouring to seek a few moments of forgetfulness. But it was in vain: I slept indeed, but I was disturbed by the wildest dreams. I thought I saw Elizabeth, in the bloom of health, walking in the streets of Ingolstadt. Delighted and surprised, I embraced her; but   I.100 as I imprinted the first kiss on her lips, they became livid with the hue of death; her features appeared to change, and I thought that I held the corpse of my dead mother in my arms; a shroud enveloped her form, and I saw the grave-worms crawling in the folds of the flannel. I started from my sleep with horror; a cold dew covered my forehead,

---

49. Evidently an electrical machine of some sort.

my teeth chattered, and every limb became convulsed; when, by the dim and yellow light of the moon, as it forced its way through the window-shutters, I beheld the wretch—the miserable monster whom I had created. He held up the curtain of the bed; and his eyes, if eyes they may be called, were fixed on me. His jaws opened, and he muttered some inarticulate sounds, while a grin wrinkled his cheeks. He

I.101   might have spoken, but I did not hear; one hand was stretched out, seemingly to detain me, but I escaped, and rushed down stairs. I took refuge in the court-yard belonging to the house which I inhabited; where I remained during the rest of the night, walking up and down in the greatest agitation, listening attentively, catching and fearing each sound as if it were to announce the approach of the demoniacal corpse to which I had so miserably given life.

Oh! no mortal could support the horror of that countenance. A mummy again endued with animation could not be so hideous as that wretch. I had gazed on him while unfinished; he was ugly then; but when those muscles and joints were rendered capable of motion, it became a thing such as even Dante could not have conceived.

I passed the night wretchedly. Sometimes my pulse beat so quickly

I.102   and hardly, that I felt the palpitation of every artery; at others, I nearly sank to the ground through languor and extreme weakness. Mingled with this horror, I felt the bitterness of disappointment: dreams that had been my food and pleasant rest for so long a space, were now become a hell to me; and the change was so rapid, the overthrow so complete!

Morning, dismal and wet, at length dawned, and discovered to my sleepless and aching eyes the church of Ingolstadt, its white steeple and clock, which indicated the sixth hour. The porter opened the gates of the court, which had that night been my asylum, and I issued into the streets, pacing them with quick steps, as if I sought to avoid the wretch whom I feared every turning of the street would present to my view. I did not dare return to the apartment which I inhabit-

I.103   ed, but felt impelled to hurry on, although wetted by the rain, which poured from a black and comfortless sky.

I continued walking in this manner for some time, endeavouring, by bodily exercise, to ease the load that weighed upon my mind. I traversed the streets, without any clear conception of where I was, or what I was doing. My heart palpitated in the sickness of fear; and I hurried on with irregular steps, not daring to look about me:

> Like one who, on a lonely road,
>   Doth walk in fear and dread,
> And, having once turn'd round, walks on,

And turns no more his head;
Because he knows a frightful fiend
    Doth close behind him tread[50].

Continuing thus, I came at length opposite to the inn at which the various diligences[51] and carriages usually stopped. Here I paused, I.104 I knew not why; but I remained some minutes with my eyes fixed on a coach that was coming towards me from the other end of the street. As it drew nearer, I observed that it was the Swiss diligence: it stopped just where I was standing; and, on the door being opened, I perceived Henry Clerval, who, on seeing me, instantly sprung out. "My dear Frankenstein," exclaimed he, "how glad I am to see you! how fortunate that you should be here at the very moment of my alighting!["]

Nothing could equal my delight on seeing Clerval; his presence brought back to my thoughts my father, Elizabeth, and all those scenes of home so dear to my recollection. I grasped his hand, and in a moment forgot my horror and misfortune; I felt suddenly, and for the first time during many months, calm and serene joy. I welcomed I.105 my friend, therefore, in the most cordial manner, and we walked towards my college. Clerval continued talking for some time about our mutual friends, and his own good fortune in being permitted to come to Ingolstadt. "You may easily believe," said he, "how great was the difficulty to persuade my father that it was not absolutely necessary for a merchant not to understand any thing except book-keeping; and, indeed, I believe I left him incredulous to the last, for his constant answer to my unwearied entreaties was the same as that of the Dutch schoolmaster in the Vicar of Wakefield: 'I have ten thousand florins a year without Greek, I eat heartily without Greek.' But his affection for me at length overcame his dislike of learning, and he has permitted me to undertake a voyage of discovery to the land of I.106 knowledge."

"It gives me the greatest delight to see you; but tell me how you left my father, brothers, and Elizabeth."

"Very well, and very happy, only a little uneasy that they hear from you so seldom. By the bye, I mean to lecture you a little upon their account mysel[f].—But, my dear Frankenstein," continued he, stopping short, and gazing full in my face, "I did not before remark how very

---

50. Coleridge's "Ancient Mariner." [MWS's note.]
51. Stagecoaches.

ill you appear; so thin and pale; you look as if you had been watching
for several nights."

"You have guessed right; I have lately been so deeply engaged in
one occupation, that I have not allowed myself sufficient rest, as you
see: but I hope, I sincerely hope, that all these employments are now
at an end, and that I am at length free."

I.107   I trembled excessively; I could not endure to think of, and far less
to allude to the occurrences of the preceding night. I walked with a
quick pace, and we soon arrived at my college. I then reflected, and
the thought made me shiver, that the creature whom I had left in my
apartment might still be there, alive, and walking about. I dreaded
to behold this monster; but I feared still more that Henry should see
him. Entreating him therefore to remain a few minutes at the bottom of the stairs, I darted up towards my own room. My hand was
already on the lock of the door before I recollected myself. I then
paused; and a cold shivering came over me. I threw the door forcibly
open, as children are accustomed to do when they expect a spectre
I.108   to stand in waiting for them on the other side; but nothing appeared.
I stepped fearfully in: the apartment was empty; and my bedroom
was also freed from its hideous guest. I could hardly believe that so
great a good-fortune could have befallen me; but when I became assured that my enemy had indeed fled, I clapped my hands for joy,
and ran down to Clerval.

We ascended into my room, and the servant presently brought
breakfast; but I was unable to contain myself. It was not joy only that
possessed me; I felt my flesh tingle with excess of sensitiveness, and
my pulse beat rapidly. I was unable to remain for a single instant in
the same place; I jumped over the chairs, clapped my hands, and
laughed aloud. Clerval at first attributed my unusual spirits to joy
on his arrival; but when he observed me more attentively, he saw a
I.109   wildness in my eyes for which he could not account; and my loud,
unrestrained, heartless laughter, frightened and astonished him.

"My dear Victor," cried he, "what, for God's sake, is the matter?
Do not laugh in that manner. How ill you are! What is the cause of
all this?["]

"Do not ask me," cried I, putting my hands before my eyes, for I
thought I saw the dreaded spectre glide into the room; "*he* can tell.—
Oh, save me! save me!" I imagined that the monster seized me; I
struggled furiously, and fell down in a fit.

Poor Clerval! what must have been his feelings? A meeting, which
he anticipated with such joy, so strangely turned to bitterness. But I

was not the witness of his grief; for I was lifeless, and did not recover my senses for a long, long time.

This was the commencement of a nervous fever, which confined I.110 me for several months. During all that time Henry was my only nurse. I afterwards learned that, knowing my father's advanced age, and unfitness for so long a journey, and how wretched my sickness would make Elizabeth, he spared them this grief by concealing the extent of my disorder. He knew that I could not have a more kind and attentive nurse than himself; and, firm in the hope he felt of my recovery, he did not doubt that, instead of doing harm, he performed the kindest action that he could towards them.

But I was in reality very ill; and surely nothing but the unbounded and unremitting attentions of my friend could have restored me to life. The form of the monster on whom I had bestowed existence was for ever before my eyes, and I raved incessantly concerning him. Doubtless I.111 my words surprised Henry: he at first believed them to be the wanderings of my disturbed imagination; but the pertinacity with which I continually recurred to the same subject persuaded him that my disorder indeed owed its origin to some uncommon and terrible event.

By very slow degrees, and with frequent relapses, that alarmed and grieved my friend, I recovered. I remember the first time I became capable of observing outward objects with any kind of pleasure, I perceived that the fallen leaves had disappeared, and that the young buds were shooting forth from the trees that shaded my window. It was a divine spring; and the season contributed greatly to my convalescence. I felt also sentiments of joy and affection revive in my bosom; my gloom disappeared, and in a short time I became as I.112 cheerful as before I was attacked by the fatal passion.

"Dearest Clerval," exclaimed I, "how kind, how very good you are to me. This whole winter, instead of being spent in study, as you promised yourself, has been consumed in my sick room. How shall I ever repay you? I feel the greatest remorse for the disappointment of which I have been the occasion; but you will forgive me."

"You will repay me entirely, if you do not discompose yourself, but get well as fast as you can; and since you appear in such good spirits, I may speak to you on one subject, may I not?"

I trembled. One subject! what could it be? Could he allude to an object on whom I dared not even think?

"Compose yourself," said Clerval, who observed my change of co- I.113 lour, "I will not mention it, if it agitates you; but your father and cousin would be very happy if they received a letter from you in your own hand-writing. They hardly know how ill you have been, and are uneasy at your long silence."

"Is that all? my dear Henry. How could you suppose that my first thought would not fly towards those dear, dear friends whom I love, and who are so deserving of my love."

"If this is your present temper, my friend, you will perhaps be glad to see a letter that has been lying here some days for you: it is from your cousin, I believe."

CHAPTER V.

CLERVAL then put the following letter into my hands.

"*To* V. FRANKENSTEIN.

"MY DEAR COUSIN,

"I cannot describe to you the uneasiness we have all felt concerning your health. We cannot help imagining that your friend Clerval conceals the extent of your disorder: for it is now several months since we have seen your hand-writing; and all this time you have been obliged to dictate your letters to Henry. Surely, Victor, you must have been exceedingly ill; and this makes us all very wretched, as much so I.115 nearly as after the death of your dear mother. My uncle was almost persuaded that you were indeed dangerously ill, and could hardly be restrained from undertaking a journey to Ingolstadt. Clerval always writes that you are getting better; I eagerly hope that you will confirm this intelligence soon in your own hand-writing; for indeed, indeed, Victor, we are all very miserable on this account. Relieve us from this fear, and we shall be the happiest creatures in the world. Your father's health is now so vigorous, that he appears ten years younger since last winter. Ernest also is so much improved, that you would hardly know him: he is now nearly sixteen, and has lost that sickly appearance which he had some years ago; he is grown quite robust and active.

"My uncle and I conversed a long time last night about what pro- I.116 fession Ernest should follow. His constant illness when young has deprived him of the habits of application; and now that he enjoys good health, he is continually in the open air, climbing the hills, or rowing on the lake. I therefore proposed that he should be a farmer; which you know, Cousin, is a favourite scheme of mine. A farmer's is a very healthy happy life; and the least hurtful, or rather the most beneficial profession of any. My uncle had an idea of his being educated as an advocate, that through his interest he might become a judge. But, besides that he is not at all fitted for such an occupation, it is certainly more creditable to cultivate the earth for the sustenance of man, than to be the confidant, and sometimes the accomplice, of his vices; which is the profession of a lawyer. I said, that the em- I.117 ployments of a prosperous farmer, if they were not a more honourable, they were at least a happier species of occupation than that of a judge, whose misfortune it was always to meddle with the dark side of human nature. My uncle smiled, and said, that I ought to be an advocate myself, which put an end to the conversation on that subject.

"And now I must tell you a little story that will please, and perhaps amuse you. Do you not remember Justine Moritz? Probably you do not; I will relate her history therefore, in a few words. Madame Moritz, her mother, was a widow with four children, of whom Justine was the third. This girl had always been the favourite of her father; but, through a strange perversity, her mother could not endure her, and, after the death of M. Moritz, treated her very ill. My aunt observed this; and, when Justine was twelve years of age, prevailed on her mother to allow her to live at her house. The republican institutions of our country have produced simpler and happier manners than those which prevail in the great monarchies that surround it. Hence there is less distinction between the several classes of its inhabitants; and the lower orders being neither so poor nor so despised, their manners are more refined and moral. A servant in Geneva does not mean the same thing as a servant in France and England. Justine, thus received in our family, learned the duties of a servant; a condition which, in our fortunate country, does not include the idea of ignorance, and a sacrifice of the dignity of a human being.

I.119   "After what I have said, I dare say you well remember the heroine of my little tale: for Justine was a great favourite of your's; and I recollect you once remarked, that if you were in an ill humour, one glance from Justine could dissipate it, for the same reason that Ariosto gives concerning the beauty of Angelica[52]—she looked so frank-hearted and happy. My aunt conceived a great attachment for her, by which she was induced to give her an education superior to that which she had at first intended. This benefit was fully repaid; Justine was the most grateful little creature in the world: I do not mean that she made any professions, I never heard one pass her lips; but you could see by her eyes that she almost adored her protectress. Although her disposition was gay, and in many respects inconsiderate, yet she paid the greatest attention to every gesture of my aunt. She thought her the model of all excellence, and endeavoured to imitate her phraseology and manners, so that even now she often reminds me of her.

"When my dearest aunt died, every one was too much occupied in their own grief to notice poor Justine, who had attended her during

I.118

I.120

---

52. The heroine of *Orlando Furioso* (1516).

her illness with the most anxious affection. Poor Justine was very ill; but other trials were reserved for her.

"One by one, her brothers and sister died; and her mother, with the exception of her neglected daughter, was left childless. The conscience of the woman was troubled; she began to think that the deaths of her favourites was a judgment from heaven to chastise her partiality. She was a Roman Catholic; and I believe her confessor confirmed the idea which she had conceived. Accordingly, a few I.121 months after your departure for Ingolstadt, Justine was called home by her repentant mother. Poor girl! she wept when she quitted our house: she was much altered since the death of my aunt; grief had given softness and a winning mildness to her manners, which had before been remarkable for vivacity. Nor was her residence at her mother's house of a nature to restore her gaiety. The poor woman was very vacillating in her repentance. She sometimes begged Justine to forgive her unkindness, but much oftener accused her of having caused the deaths of her brothers and sister. Perpetual fretting at length threw Madame Moritz into a decline, which at first increased her irritability, but she is now at peace for ever. She died on the first approach of cold weather, at the beginning of this last I.122 winter. Justine has returned to us; and I assure you I love her tenderly. She is very clever and gentle, and extremely pretty; as I mentioned before, her mien and her expressions continually remind me of my dear aunt.

"I must say also a few words to you, my dear cousin, of little darling William. I wish you could see him; he is very tall of his age, with sweet laughing blue eyes, dark eye-lashes, and curling hair. When he smiles, two little dimples appear on each cheek, which are rosy with health. He has already had one or two little *wives*, but Louisa Biron is his favourite, a pretty little girl of five years of age.

"Now, dear Victor, I dare say you wish to be indulged in a little gossip concerning the good people of Geneva. The pretty Miss Mansfield has already received the congratulatory visits on her approach- I.123 ing marriage with a young Englishman, John Melbourne, Esq. Her ugly sister, Manon, married M. Duvillard, the rich banker, last autumn. Your favourite schoolfellow, Louis Manoir, has suffered several misfortunes since the departure of Clerval from Geneva. But he has already recovered his spirits, and is reported to be on the point of marrying a very lively pretty Frenchwoman, Madame Tavernier. She is a widow, and much older than Manoir; but she is very much admired, and a favourite with every body.

"I have written myself into good spirits, dear cousin; yet I cannot conclude without again anxiously inquiring concerning your health. Dear Victor, if you are not very ill, write yourself, and make your father and all of us happy; or——I cannot bear to think of the other side of the question; my tears already flow. Adieu, my dearest cousin.

"ELIZABETH LAVENZA.

"Geneva, March 18th, 1 7—."

I.124

"Dear, dear Elizabeth!" I exclaimed when I had read her letter, "I will write instantly, and relieve them from the anxiety they must feel." I wrote, and this exertion greatly fatigued me; but my convalescence had commenced, and proceeded regularly. In another fortnight I was able to leave my chamber.

I.125   One of my first duties on my recovery was to introduce Clerval to the several professors of the university. In doing this, I underwent a kind of rough usage, ill befitting the wounds that my mind had sustained. Ever since the fatal night, the end of my labours, and the beginning of my misfortunes, I had conceived a violent antipathy even to the name of natural philosophy. When I was otherwise quite restored to health, the sight of a chemical instrument would renew all the agony of my nervous symptoms. Henry saw this, and had removed all my apparatus from my view. He had also changed my apartment; for he perceived that I had acquired a dislike for the room which had previously been my laboratory. But these cares of Clerval were made of no avail when I visited the professors. M. Waldman inflicted torture when he praised, with kindness and warmth, the astonishing progress I had made in the sciences. He soon perceived that I disliked the subject; but, not guessing the real cause, he

I.126   attributed my feelings to modesty, and changed the subject from my improvement to the science itself, with a desire, as I evidently saw, of drawing me out. What could I do? He meant to please, and he tormented me. I felt as if he had placed carefully, one by one, in my view those instruments which were to be afterwards used in putting me to a slow and cruel death. I writhed under his words, yet dared not exhibit the pain I felt. Clerval, whose eyes and feelings were always quick in discerning the sensations of others, declined the subject, alleging, in excuse, his total ignorance; and the conversation took a more general turn. I thanked my friend from my heart, but I did not speak. I saw plainly that he was surprised, but he never attempted to draw my secret from me; and although I loved him with a mixture

I.127   of affection and reverence that knew no bounds, yet I could never persuade myself to confide to him that event which was so often present to my recollection, but which I feared the detail to another would only impress more deeply.

M. Krempe was not equally docile; and in my condition at that time, of almost insupportable sensitiveness, his harsh blunt encomiums gave me even more pain than the benevolent approbation of M. Waldman. "D—n the fellow!" cried he; "why, M. Clerval, I assure you he has outstript us all. Aye, stare if you please; but it is nevertheless true. A youngster who, but a few years ago, believed Cornelius Agrippa as firmly as the gospel, has now set himself at the head of the university; and if he is not soon pulled down, we shall all be out of countenance.—Aye, aye," continued he, observing my face expressive of suffering, "M. Frankenstein is modest; an excellent quality in a young man. Young men should be diffident of themselves, you know, M. Clerval; I was myself when young: but that wears out in a very short time." I.128

M. Krempe had now commenced an eulogy on himself, which happily turned the conversation from a subject that was so annoying to me.

Clerval was no natural philosopher. His imagination was too vivid for the minutiæ of science. Languages were his principal study; and he sought, by acquiring their elements, to open a field for self-instruction on his return to Geneva. Persian, Arabic, and Hebrew, gained his attention, after he had made himself perfectly master of Greek and Latin. For my own part, idleness had ever been irksome to me; and now that I wished to fly from reflection, and hated my former studies, I felt great relief in being the fellow-pupil with my friend, and found not only instruction but consolation in the works of the orientalists. Their melancholy is soothing, and their joy elevating to a degree I never experienced in studying the authors of any other country. When you read their writings, life appears to consist in a warm sun and garden of roses,—in the smiles and frowns of a fair enemy, and the fire that consumes your own heart. How different from the manly and heroical poetry of Greece and Rome. I.129

Summer passed away in these occupations, and my return to Geneva was fixed for the latter end of autumn; but being delayed by several accidents, winter and snow arrived, the roads were deemed impassable, and my journey was retarded until the ensuing spring. I felt this delay very bitterly; for I longed to see my native town, and my beloved friends. My return had only been delayed so long from an unwillingness to leave Clerval in a strange place, before he had I.130

become acquainted with any of its inhabitants. The winter, however, was spent cheerfully; and although the spring was uncommonly late, when it came, its beauty compensated for its dilatoriness.

The month of May had already commenced, and I expected the letter daily which was to fix the date of my departure, when Henry proposed a pedestrian tour in the environs of Ingolstadt that I might bid a personal farewell to the country I had so long inhabited. I acceded with pleasure to this proposition: I was fond of exercise, and Clerval had always been my favourite companion in the rambles of this nature that I had taken among the scenes of my native country.

I.131

We passed a fortnight in these perambulations: my health and spirits had long been restored, and they gained additional strength from the salubrious air I breathed, the natural incidents of our progress, and the conversation of my friend. Study had before secluded me from the intercourse of my fellow creatures, and rendered me unsocial; but Clerval called forth the better feelings of my heart; he again taught me to love the aspect of nature, and the cheerful faces of children. Excellent friend! how sincerely did you love me, and endeavour to elevate my mind, until it was on a level with your own. A selfish pursuit had cramped and narrowed me, until your gentleness and affection warmed and opened my senses; I became the same happy creature who, a few years ago, loving and beloved by all, had no sorrow or care. When happy, inanimate nature had the power of bestowing on me the most delightful sensations. A serene sky and verdant fields filled me with ecstacy. The present season was indeed divine; the flowers of spring bloomed in the hedges, while those of summer were already in bud: I was undisturbed by thoughts which during the preceding year had pressed upon me, notwithstanding my endeavours to throw them off, with an invincible burden.

I.132

Henry rejoiced in my gaiety, and sincerely sympathized in my feelings: he exerted himself to amuse me, while he expressed the sensations that filled his soul. The resources of his mind on this occasion were truly astonishing: his conversation was full of imagination; and very often, in imitation of the Persian and Arabic writers, he invented tales of wonderful fancy and passion. At other times he repeated my favourite poems, or drew me out into arguments, which he supported with great ingenuity.

I.133

We returned to our college on a Sunday afternoon: the peasants were dancing, and every one we met appeared gay and happy. My own spirits were high, and I bounded along with feelings of unbridled joy and hilarity.

CHAPTER VI.

ON my return, I found the following letter from my father:—

"*To* V. FRANKENSTEIN.

"MY DEAR VICTOR,

"You have probably waited impatiently for a letter to fix the date of your return to us; and I was at first tempted to write only a few lines, merely mentioning the day on which I should expect you. But that would be a cruel kindness, and I dare not do it. What would be your surprise, my son, when you expected a happy and gay welcome, to behold, on the contrary, tears and wretchedness? And how, Victor, can I relate our misfortune? Absence cannot have rendered you callous to our joys and griefs; and how shall I inflict pain on an absent child? I wish to prepare you for the woeful news, but I know it is impossible; even now your eye skims over the page, to seek the words which are to convey to you the horrible tidings.

"William is dead!—that sweet child, whose smiles delighted and warmed my heart, who was so gentle, yet so gay! Victor, he is murdered!

"I will not attempt to console you; but will simply relate the circumstances of the transaction.

"Last Thursday (May 7th) I, my niece, and your two brothers, went to walk in Plainpalais.[53] The evening was warm and serene, and we prolonged our walk farther than usual. It was already dusk before we thought of returning; and then we discovered that William and Ernest, who had gone on before, were not to be found. We accordingly rested on a seat until they should return. Presently Ernest came, and inquired if we had seen his brother: he said, that they had been playing together, that William had run away to hide himself, and that he vainly sought for him, and afterwards waited for him a long time, but that he did not return.

"This account rather alarmed us, and we continued to search for him until night fell, when Elizabeth conjectured that he might have returned to the house. He was not there. We returned again, with torches; for I could not rest, when I thought that my sweet boy had

---

53. In her letter of June 1, 1816, MWS describes this as "a grassy plain planted with a few trees" where the Genevans promenade.

lost himself, and was exposed to all the damps and dews of night: Elizabeth also suffered extreme anguish. About five in the morning I discovered my lovely boy, whom the night before I had seen blooming and active in health, stretched on the grass livid and motionless: the print of the murderer's finger was on his neck.

"He was conveyed home, and the anguish that was visible in my countenance betrayed the secret to Elizabeth. She was very earnest to see the corpse. At first I attempted to prevent her; but she persisted, and entering the room where it lay, hastily examined the neck of the victim, and clasping her hands exclaimed, 'O God! I have murdered my darling infant!'

I.138 "She fainted, and was restored with extreme difficulty. When she again lived, it was only to weep and sigh. She told me, that that same evening William had teazed her to let him wear a very valuable miniature that she possessed of your mother. This picture is gone, and was doubtless the temptation which urged the murderer to the deed. We have no trace of him at present, although our exertions to discover him are unremitted; but they will not restore my beloved William.

"Come, dearest Victor; you alone can console Elizabeth. She weeps continually, and accuses herself unjustly as the cause of his death; her words pierce my heart. We are all unhappy; but will not that be an additional motive for you, my son, to return and be our comforter? Your dear mother! Alas, Victor! I now say, Thank God she did not live to witness the cruel, miserable death of her youngest darling!

I.139 "Come, Victor; not brooding thoughts of vengeance against the assassin, but with feelings of peace and gentleness, that will heal, instead of festering the wounds of our minds. Enter the house of mourning, my friend, but with kindness and affection for those who love you, and not with hatred for your enemies.

"Your affectionate and afflicted father,

["]ALPHONSE FRANKENSTEIN.

"Geneva, May 12th, 17—."

Clerval, who had watched my countenance as I read this letter, was surprised to observe the despair that succeeded to the joy I at first expressed on receiving news from my friends. I threw the letter on the table, and covered my face with my hands.

I.140 "My dear Frankenstein," exclaimed Henry, when he perceived me weep with bitterness, "are you always to be unhappy? My dear friend, what has happened?"

I motioned to him to take up the letter, while I walked up and down the room in the extremest agitation. Tears also gushed from the eyes of Clerval, as he read the account of my misfortune.

"I can offer you no consolation, my friend," said he; "your disaster is irreparable. What do you intend to do?"

"To go instantly to Geneva: come with me, Henry, to order the horses."

During our walk, Clerval endeavoured to raise my spirits. He did not do this by common topics of consolation, but by exhibiting the truest sympathy. "Poor William!" said he, "that dear child; he now sleeps with his angel mother. His friends mourn and weep, but he is at rest: he does not now feel the murderer's grasp; a sod covers his I.141 gentle form, and he knows no pain. He can no longer be a fit subject for pity; the survivors are the greatest sufferers, and for them time is the only consolation. Those maxims of the Stoics, that death was no evil, and that the mind of man ought to be superior to despair on the eternal absence of a beloved object, ought not to be urged. Even Cato wept over the dead body of his brother."[54]

Clerval spoke thus as we hurried through the streets; the words impressed themselves on my mind, and I remembered them afterwards in solitude. But now, as soon as the horses arrived, I hurried into a cabriole,[55] and bade farewell to my friend.

My journey was very melancholy. At first I wished to hurry on, for I longed to console and sympathize with my loved and sorrow- I.142 ing friends; but when I drew near my native town, I slackened my progress. I could hardly sustain the multitude of feelings that crowded into my mind. I passed through scenes familiar to my youth, but which I had not seen for nearly six years. How altered every thing might be during that time? One sudden and desolating change had taken place; but a thousand little circumstances might have by degrees worked other alterations, which, although they were done more tranquilly, might not be the less decisive. Fear overcame me; I dared not advance, dreading a thousand nameless evils that made me tremble, although I was unable to define them.

I remained two days at Lausanne, in this painful state of mind. I contemplated the lake: the waters were placid; all around was

---

54. Reported in *Plutarch's Lives*.
55. A small carriage with a folding hood.

I.143 calm, and the snowy mountains, "the palaces of nature,"[56] were not changed. By degrees the calm and heavenly scene restored me, and I continued my journey towards Geneva.

The road ran by the side of the lake, which became narrower as I approached my native town. I discovered more distinctly the black sides of Jura, and the bright summit of Mont Blanc; I wept like a child: "Dear mountains! my own beautiful lake! how do you welcome your wanderer? Your summits are clear; the sky and lake are blue and placid. Is this to prognosticate peace, or to mock at my unhappiness?"

I fear, my friend, that I shall render myself tedious by dwelling on these preliminary circumstances; but they were days of compar-
I.144 ative happiness, and I think of them with pleasure. My country, my beloved country! who but a native can tell the delight I took in again beholding thy streams, thy mountains, and, more than all, thy lovely lake.

Yet, as I drew nearer home, grief and fear again overcame me. Night also closed around; and when I could hardly see the dark mountains, I felt still more gloomily. The picture appeared a vast and dim scene of evil, and I foresaw obscurely that I was destined to become the most wretched of human beings. Alas! I prophesied truly, and failed only in one single circumstance, that in all the misery I imagined and dreaded, I did not conceive the hundredth part of the anguish I was destined to endure.

It was completely dark when I arrived in the environs of Geneva; the gates of the town were already shut; and I was obliged to pass
I.145 the night at Secheron, a village half a league to the east of the city. The sky was serene; and, as I was unable to rest, I resolved to visit the spot where my poor William had been murdered. As I could not pass through the town, I was obliged to cross the lake in a boat to arrive at Plainpalais. During this short voyage I saw the lightnings playing on the summit of Mont Blanc in the most beautiful figures. The storm appeared to approach rapidly; and, on landing, I ascended a low hill, that I might observe its progress. It advanced; the heavens were clouded, and I soon felt the rain coming slowly in large drops, but its violence quickly increased.

I quitted my seat, and walked on, although the darkness and storm increased every minute, and the thunder burst with a terrific crash

---

56. Quoted from Byron's *Childe Harold's Pilgrimage*, Canto III, stanza 62, written in the summer of 1816, when MWS began *Frankenstein,* and published that year.

over my head. It was echoed from Salêve, the Juras, and the Alps of I.146
Savoy; vivid flashes of lightning dazzled my eyes, illuminating the
lake, making it appear like a vast sheet of fire; then for an instant
every thing seemed of a pitchy darkness, until the eye recovered itself from the preceding flash. The storm, as is often the case in Switzerland, appeared at once in various parts of the heavens. The most
violent storm hung exactly north of the town, over that part of the
lake which lies between the promontory of Belrive and the village of
Copêt. Another storm enlightened Jura with faint flashes; and another darkened and sometimes disclosed the Môle, a peaked mountain
to the east of the lake.

While I watched the storm, so beautiful yet terrific,[57] I wandered
on with a hasty step. This noble war in the sky elevated my spirits;
I clasped my hands, and exclaimed aloud, "William, dear angel! this I.147
is thy funeral, this thy dirge!" As I said these words, I perceived in
the gloom a figure which stole from behind a clump of trees near
me; I stood fixed, gazing intently: I could not be mistaken. A flash
of lightning illuminated the object, and discovered its shape plainly to me; its gigantic stature, and the deformity of its aspect, more
hideous than belongs to humanity, instantly informed me that it was
the wretch, the filthy dæmon to whom I had given life. What did he
there? Could he be (I shuddered at the conception) the murderer of
my brother? No sooner did that idea cross my imagination, than I
became convinced of its truth; my teeth chattered, and I was forced
to lean against a tree for support. The figure passed me quickly, and
I lost it in the gloom. Nothing in human shape could have destroyed I.148
that fair child. *He* was the murderer! I could not doubt it. The mere
presence of the idea was an irresistible proof of the fact. I thought of
pursuing the devil; but it would have been in vain, for another flash
discovered him to me hanging among the rocks of the nearly perpendicular ascent of Mont Salêve, a hill that bounds Plainpalais on the
south. He soon reached the summit, and disappeared.

I remained motionless. The thunder ceased; but the rain still continued, and the scene was enveloped in an impenetrable darkness. I
revolved in my mind the events which I had until now sought to forget: the whole train of my progress towards the creation; the appearance of the work of my own hands alive at my bed side; its departure. I.149
Two years had now nearly elapsed since the night on which he first
received life; and was this his first crime? Alas! I had turned loose

---

57. Terrifying (the standard sense of the word at the time).

into the world a depraved wretch, whose delight was in carnage and misery; had he not murdered my brother?

No one can conceive the anguish I suffered during the remainder of the night, which I spent, cold and wet, in the open air. But I did not feel the inconvenience of the weather; my imagination was busy in scenes of evil and despair. I considered the being whom I had cast among mankind, and endowed with the will and power to effect purposes of horror, such as the deed which he had now done, nearly in the light of my own vampire, my own spirit let loose from the grave, and forced to destroy all that was dear to me.

I.150   Day dawned; and I directed my steps towards the town. The gates were open; and I hastened to my father's house. My first thought was to discover what I knew of the murderer, and cause instant pursuit to be made. But I paused when I reflected on the story that I had to tell. A being whom I myself had formed, and endued with life, had met me at midnight among the precipices of an inaccessible mountain. I remembered also the nervous fever with which I had been seized just at the time that I dated my creation, and which would give an air of delirium to a tale otherwise so utterly improbable. I well knew that if any other had communicated such a relation to me, I should have looked upon it as the ravings of insanity. Besides, the strange nature of the animal would elude all pursuit, even if I were so far credited as I.151   to persuade my relatives to commence it. Besides, of what use would be pursuit? Who could arrest a creature capable of scaling the overhanging sides of Mont Salêve? These reflections determined me, and I resolved to remain silent.

It was about five in the morning when I entered my father's house. I told the servants not to disturb the family, and went into the library to attend their usual hour of rising.

Six years had elapsed, passed as a dream but for one indelible trace, and I stood in the same place where I had last embraced my father before my departure for Ingolstadt. Beloved and respectable parent! He still remained to me. I gazed on the picture of my mother, which stood over the mantlepiece. It was an historical subject, painted at my father's desire, and represented Caroline Beaufort in an I.152   agony of despair, kneeling by the coffin of her dead father. Her garb was rustic, and her cheek pale; but there was an air of dignity and beauty, that hardly permitted the sentiment of pity. Below this picture was a miniature of William; and my tears flowed when I looked upon it. While I was thus engaged, Ernest entered: he had heard me arrive, and hastened to welcome me. He expressed a sorrowful delight to see me: "Welcome, my dearest Victor," said he."[*sic*] ["]Ah! I wish you had come three months ago, and then you would have found us all joyous and delighted. But we are now unhappy; and, I am afraid, tears instead of smiles will be your welcome. Our father looks so sorrowful: this dreadful event seems to have revived in his mind his grief on the death of Mamma. Poor Elizabeth also is quite inconsolable." Ernest began to weep as he said these words.   I.153

"Do not," said I, "welcome me thus; try to be more calm, that I may not be absolutely miserable the moment I enter my father's house after so long an absence. But, tell me, how does my father support his misfortunes? and how is my poor Elizabeth?"

"She indeed requires consolation; she accused herself of having caused the death of my brother, and that made her very wretched. But since the murderer has been discovered——"

"The murderer discovered! Good God! how can that be? who could attempt to pursue him? It is impossible; one might as well try to overtake the winds, or confine a mountain-stream with a straw."

"I do not know what you mean; but we were all very unhappy when she was discovered. No one would believe it at first; and even now   I.154 Elizabeth will not be convinced, notwithstanding all the evidence. Indeed, who would credit that Justine Moritz, who was so amiable, and fond of all the family, could all at once become so extremely wicked?"

"Justine Moritz! Poor, poor girl, is she the accused? But it is wrongfully; every one knows that; no one believes it, surely, Ernest?"

"No one did at first; but several circumstances came out, that have almost forced conviction upon us: and her own behaviour has been so confused, as to add to the evidence of facts a weight that, I fear, leaves no hope for doubt. But she will be tried to-day, and you will then hear all."

He related that, the morning on which the murder of poor William had been discovered, Justine had been taken ill, and con-   I.155 fined to her bed; and, after several days, one of the servants, happening to examine the apparel she had worn on the night of the murder, had discovered in her pocket the picture of my mother, which had been judged to be the temptation of the murderer. The servant instantly shewed it to one of the others, who, without saying a word to any of the family, went to a magistrate; and, upon their deposition, Justine was apprehended. On being charged with the fact, the poor girl confirmed the suspicion in a great measure by her extreme confusion of manner.

This was a strange tale, but it did not shake my faith; and I replied earnestly, "You are all mistaken; I know the murderer. Justine, poor, good Justine, is innocent."

I.156   At that instant my father entered. I saw unhappiness deeply impressed on his countenance, but he endeavoured to welcome me cheerfully; and, after we had exchanged our mournful greeting, would have introduced some other topic than that of our disaster, had not Ernest exclaimed, "Good God, Papa! Victor says that he knows who was the murderer of poor William."

"We do also, unfortunately," replied my father; "for indeed I had rather have been for ever ignorant than have discovered so much depravity and ingratitude in one I valued so highly."

"My dear father, you are mistaken; Justine is innocent."

"If she is, God forbid that she should suffer as guilty. She is to be tried to-day, and I hope, I sincerely hope, that she will be acquitted."

I.157   This speech calmed me. I was firmly convinced in my own mind that Justine, and indeed every human being, was guiltless of this murder. I had no fear, therefore, that any circumstantial evidence could be brought forward strong enough to convict her; and, in this assurance, I calmed myself, expecting the trial with eagerness, but without prognosticating an evil result.

We were soon joined by Elizabeth. Time had made great alterations in her form since I had last beheld her. Six years before she had been a pretty, good-humoured girl, whom every one loved and caressed. She was now a woman in stature and expression of countenance, which was uncommonly lovely. An open and capacious forehead gave indications of a good understanding, joined to great frank-
I.158   ness of disposition. Her eyes were hazel, and expressive of mildness, now through recent affliction allied to sadness. Her hair was of a rich, dark auburn, her complexion fair, and her figure slight and graceful. She welcomed me with the greatest affection. "Your arrival, my dear cousin," said she, "fills me with hope. You perhaps will find some means to justify my poor guiltless Justine. Alas! who is safe, if she be convicted of crime? I rely on her innocence as certainly as I do upon my own. Our misfortune is doubly hard to us; we have not only lost that lovely darling boy, but this poor girl, whom I sincerely love, is to be torn away by even a worse fate. If she is condemned, I never shall know joy more. But she will not, I am sure she will not; and then I shall be happy again, even after the sad death of my little William."

"She is innocent, my Elizabeth," said I, "and that shall be proved;   I.159 fear nothing, but let your spirits be cheered by the assurance of her acquittal."

"How kind you are! every one else believes in her guilt, and that made me wretched; for I knew that it was impossible: and to see every one else prejudiced in so deadly a manner, rendered me hopeless and despairing." She wept.

"Sweet niece," said my father, "dry your tears. If she is, as you believe, innocent, rely on the justice of our judges, and the activity with which I shall prevent the slightest shadow of partiality."

I.160

CHAPTER VII.

WE passed a few sad hours, until eleven o'clock, when the trial was to commence. My father and the rest of the family being obliged to attend as witnesses, I accompanied them to the court. During the whole of this wretched mockery of justice, I suffered living torture. It was to be decided, whether the result of my curiosity and lawless devices would cause the death of two of my fellow-beings: one a smiling babe, full of innocence and joy; the other far more dreadfully murdered,

I.161 with every aggravation of infamy that could make the murder memorable in horror. Justine also was a girl of merit, and possessed qualities which promised to render her life happy: now all was to be obliterated in an ignominious grave; and I the cause! A thousand times rather would I have confessed myself guilty of the crime ascribed to Justine; but I was absent when it was committed, and such a declaration would have been considered as the ravings of a madman, and would not have exculpated her who suffered through me.

The appearance of Justine was calm. She was dressed in mourning; and her countenance, always engaging, was rendered, by the solemnity of her feelings, exquisitely beautiful. Yet she appeared confident in innocence, and did not tremble, although gazed on and

I.162 execrated by thousands; for all the kindness which her beauty might otherwise have excited, was obliterated in the minds of the spectators by the imagination of the enormity she was supposed to have committed. She was tranquil, yet her tranquillity was evidently constrained; and as her confusion had before been adduced as a proof of her guilt, she worked up her mind to an appearance of courage. When she entered the court, she threw her eyes round it, and quickly discovered where we were seated. A tear seemed to dim her eye when she saw us; but she quickly recovered herself, and a look of sorrowful affection seemed to attest her utter guiltlessness.

The trial began; and after the advocate against her had stated the charge, several witnesses were called. Several strange facts combined against her, which might have staggered any one who had not

I.163 such proof of her innocence as I had. She had been out the whole of the night on which the murder had been committed, and towards morning had been perceived by a market-woman not far from the spot where the body of the murdered child had been afterwards found. The woman asked her what she did there; but she looked very strangely, and only returned a confused and unintelligible answer.

She returned to the house about eight o'clock; and when one inquired where she had passed the night, she replied, that she had been
looking for the child, and demanded earnestly, if any thing had been
heard concerning him. When shewn the body, she fell into violent
hysterics, and kept her bed for several days. The picture was then
produced, which the servant had found in her pocket; and when Elizabeth, in a faltering voice, proved that it was the same which, an hour   I.164
before the child had been missed, she had placed round his neck, a
murmur of horror and indignation filled the court.

Justine was called on for her defence. As the trial had proceeded, her countenance had altered. Surprise, horror, and misery, were
strongly expressed. Sometimes she struggled with her tears; but
when she was desired to plead, she collected her powers, and spoke
in an audible although variable voice:—

"God knows," she said, "how entirely I am innocent. But I do not
pretend that my protestations should acquit me: I rest my innocence
on a plain and simple explanation of the facts which have been adduced against me; and I hope the character I have always borne will
incline my judges to a favourable interpretation, where any circum-   I.165
stance appears doubtful or suspicious."

She then related that, by the permission of Elizabeth, she had
passed the evening of the night on which the murder had been committed, at the house of an aunt at Chêne, a village situated at about
a league from Geneva. On her return, at about nine o'clock, she met
a man, who asked her if she had seen any thing of the child who was
lost. She was alarmed by this account, and passed several hours in
looking for him, when the gates of Geneva were shut, and she was
forced to remain several hours of the night in a barn belonging to a
cottage, being unwilling to call up the inhabitants, to whom she was
well known. Unable to rest or sleep, she quitted her asylum early,
that she might again endeavour to find my brother. If she had gone
near the spot where his body lay, it was without her knowledge. That   I.166
she had been bewildered when questioned by the market-woman,
was not surprising, since she had passed a sleepless night, and the
fate of poor William was yet uncertain. Concerning the picture she
could give no account.

"I know," continued the unhappy victim, "how heavily and fatally
this one circumstance weighs against me, but I have no power of explaining it; and when I have expressed my utter ignorance, I am only
left to conjecture concerning the probabilities by which it might have
been placed in my pocket. But here also I am checked. I believe that I

have no enemy on earth, and none surely would have been so wicked as to destroy me wantonly. Did the murderer place it there? I know I.167 of no opportunity afforded him for so doing; or if I had, why should he have stolen the jewel, to part with it again so soon?

"I commit my cause to the justice of my judges, yet I see no room for hope. I beg permission to have a few witnesses examined concerning my character; and if their testimony shall not overweigh my supposed guilt, I must be condemned, although I would pledge my salvation on my innocence."

Several witnesses were called, who had known her for many years, and they spoke well of her; but fear, and hatred of the crime of which they supposed her guilty, rendered them timorous, and unwilling to come forward. Elizabeth saw even this last resource, her excellent dispositions and irreproachable conduct, about to fail the accused, I.168 when, although violently agitated, she desired permission to address the court.

"I am," said she, "the cousin of the unhappy child who was murdered, or rather his sister, for I was educated by and have lived with his parents ever since and even long before his birth. It may therefore be judged indecent in me to come forward on this occasion; but when I see a fellow-creature about to perish through the cowardice of her pretended friends, I wish to be allowed to speak, that I may say what I know of her character. I am well acquainted with the accused. I have lived in the same house with her, at one time for five, and at another for nearly two years. During all that period she appeared to me the most amiable and benevolent of human creatures. She nursed Madame Frankenstein, my aunt, in her last illness with the greatest I.169 affection and care; and afterwards attended her own mother during a tedious illness, in a manner that excited the admiration of all who knew her. After which she again lived in my uncle's house, where she was beloved by all the family. She was warmly attached to the child who is now dead, and acted towards him like a most affectionate mother. For my own part, I do not hesitate to say, that, notwithstanding all the evidence produced against her, I believe and rely on her perfect innocence. She had no temptation for such an action: as to the bauble on which the chief proof rests, if she had earnestly desired it, I should have willingly given it to her; so much do I esteem and value her."

Excellent Elizabeth! A murmur of approbation was heard; but it was excited by her generous interference, and not in favour of poor I.170 Justine, on whom the public indignation was turned with renewed violence, charging her with the blackest ingratitude. She herself wept as Elizabeth spoke, but she did not answer. My own agitation and anguish was extreme during the whole trial. I believed in her innocence; I knew it. Could the dæmon, who had (I did not for a minute doubt) murdered my brother, also in his hellish sport have betrayed the innocent to death and ignominy. I could not sustain the horror of my situation; and when I perceived that the popular voice, and the countenances of the judges, had already condemned my unhappy victim, I rushed out of the court in agony. The tortures of the accused did not equal mine; she was sustained by innocence, but the fangs of remorse tore my bosom, and would not forego their hold.

I passed a night of unmingled wretchedness. In the morning I I.171 went to the court; my lips and throat were parched. I dared not ask the fatal question; but I was known, and the officer guessed the cause of my visit. The ballots had been thrown; they were all black, and Justine was condemned.

I cannot pretend to describe what I then felt. I had before experienced sensations of horror; and I have endeavoured to bestow upon them adequate expressions, but words cannot convey an idea of the heart-sickening despair that I then endured. The person to whom I addressed myself added, that Justine had already confessed her guilt. "That evidence," he observed, "was hardly required in so glaring a case, but I am glad of it; and, indeed, none of our judges like to condemn a criminal upon circumstantial evidence, be it ever so decisive."

When I returned home, Elizabeth eagerly demanded the result. I.172

"My cousin," replied I, "it is decided as you may have expected; all judges had rather that ten innocent should suffer, than that one guilty should escape. But she has confessed."

This was a dire blow to poor Elizabeth, who had relied with firmness upon Justine's innocence. "Alas!" said she, "how shall I ever again believe in human benevolence? Justine, whom I loved and esteemed as my sister, how could she put on those smiles of innocence only to betray; her mild eyes seemed incapable of any severity or ill-humour, and yet she has committed a murder."

Soon after we heard that the poor victim had expressed a wish to see my cousin. My father wished her not to go; but said, that he left it to her own judgment and feelings to decide. "Yes," said Elizabeth, I.173 "I will go, although she is guilty; and you, Victor, shall accompany me: I cannot go alone." The idea of this visit was torture to me, yet I could not refuse.

We entered the gloomy prison-chamber, and beheld Justine sitting on some straw at the further end; her hands were manacled, and her head rested on her knees. She rose on seeing us enter; and when we were left alone with her, she threw herself at the feet of Elizabeth, weeping bitterly. My cousin wept also.

"Oh, Justine!" said she, "why did you rob me of my last consolation. I relied on your innocence; and although I was then very wretched, I was not so miserable as I am now."

I.174   "And do you also believe that I am so very, very wicked? Do you also join with my enemies to crush me?" Her voice was suffocated with sobs.

"Rise, my poor girl," said Elizabeth, "why do you kneel, if you are innocent? I am not one of your enemies; I believed you guiltless, notwithstanding every evidence, until I heard that you had yourself declared your guilt. That report, you say, is false; and be assured, dear Justine, that nothing can shake my confidence in you for a moment, but your own confession."

"I did confess; but I confessed a lie. I confessed, that I might obtain absolution; but now that falsehood lies heavier at my heart than all my other sins. The God of heaven forgive me! Ever since I was condemned, my confessor has besieged me; he threatened and menaced, I.175   until I almost began to think that I was the monster that he said I was. He threatened excommunication and hell fire in my last moments, if I continued obdurate. Dear lady, I had none to support me; all looked on me as a wretch doomed to ignominy and perdition. What could I do? In an evil hour I subscribed to a lie; and now only am I truly miserable."

She paused, weeping, and then continued—"I thought with horror, my sweet lady, that you should believe your Justine, whom your blessed aunt had so highly honoured, and whom you loved, was a creature capable of a crime which none but the devil himself could have perpetrated. Dear William! dearest blessed child! I soon shall see you again in heaven, where we shall all be happy; and that consoles me, going as I am to suffer ignominy and death."

I.176   "Oh, Justine! forgive me for having for one moment distrusted you. Why did you confess? But do not mourn, my dear girl; I will every where proclaim your innocence, and force belief. Yet you must die; you, my playfellow, my companion, my more than sister. I never can survive so horrible a misfortune."

"Dear, sweet Elizabeth, do not weep. You ought to raise me with thoughts of a better life, and elevate me from the petty cares of this world of injustice and strife. Do not you, excellent friend, drive me to despair."

"I will try to comfort you; but this, I fear, is an evil too deep and poignant to admit of consolation, for there is no hope. Yet heaven bless thee, my dearest Justine, with resignation, and a confidence elevated beyond this world. Oh! how I hate its shews and mockeries! when one creature is murdered, another is immediately deprived of life in a slow torturing manner; then the executioners, their hands yet reeking with the blood of innocence, believe that they have done a great deed. They call this *retribution*. Hateful name! When that word is pronounced, I know greater and more horrid punishments are going to be inflicted than the gloomiest tyrant has ever invented to satiate his utmost revenge. Yet this is not consolation for you, my Justine, unless indeed that you may glory in escaping from so miserable a den. Alas! I would I were in peace with my aunt and my lovely William, escaped from a world which is hateful to me, and the visages of men which I abhor." I.177

Justine smiled languidly. "This, dear lady, is despair, and not resignation. I must not learn the lesson that you would teach me. Talk of something else, something that will bring peace, and not increase of misery." I.178

During this conversation I had retired to a corner of the prison-room, where I could conceal the horrid anguish that possessed me. Despair! Who dared talk of that? The poor victim, who on the morrow was to pass the dreary boundary between life and death, felt not as I did, such deep and bitter agony. I gnashed my teeth, and ground them together, uttering a groan that came from my inmost soul. Justine started. When she saw who it was, she approached me, and said, "Dear Sir, you are very kind to visit me; you, I hope, do not believe that I am guilty."

I could not answer. "No, Justine," said Elizabeth; "he is more convinced of your innocence than I was; for even when he heard that you had confessed, he did not credit it." I.179

"I truly thank him. In these last moments I feel the sincerest gratitude towards those who think of me with kindness. How sweet is the affection of others to such a wretch as I am! It removes more than half my misfortune; and I feel as if I could die in peace, now that my innocence is acknowledged by you, dear lady, and your cousin."

Thus the poor sufferer tried to comfort others and herself. She indeed gained the resignation she desired. But I, the true murderer,

felt the never dying worm alive in my bosom,[58] which allowed of no hope or consolation. Elizabeth also wept, and was unhappy; but her's also was the misery of innocence, which, like a cloud that passes over
I.180 the fair moon, for a while hides, but cannot tarnish its brightness. Anguish and despair had penetrated into the core of my heart; I bore a hell within me, which nothing could extinguish.[59] We staid several hours with Justine; and it was with great difficulty that Elizabeth could tear herself away. "I wish," cried she, "that I were to die with you; I cannot live in this world of misery."

Justine assumed an air of cheerfulness, while she with difficulty repressed her bitter tears. She embraced Elizabeth, and said, in a voice of half suppressed emotion, "Farewell, sweet lady, dearest Elizabeth, my beloved and only friend; may heaven in its bounty bless and preserve you; may this be the last misfortune that you will ever suffer. Live, and be happy, and make others so."

I.181 As we returned, Elizabeth said, "You know not, my dear Victor, how much I am relieved, now that I trust in the innocence of this unfortunate girl. I never could again have known peace, if I had been deceived in my reliance on her. For the moment that I did believe her guilty, I felt an anguish that I could not have long sustained. Now my heart is lightened. The innocent suffers; but she whom I thought amiable and good has not betrayed the trust I reposed in her, and I am consoled."

Amiable cousin! such were your thoughts, mild and gentle as your own dear eyes and voice. But I—I was a wretch, and none ever conceived of the misery that I then endured.

END OF VOL. I.

---

58. In the Bible (Mark 9:44) hell is described as a place where the "worm dieth not." In *The Bride of Abydos* (1813) Byron describes remorse as "the worm that will not sleep— and never dies." Chaucer, Shakespeare, and Pope refer to the "worm of conscience" (cf. *Oxford English Dictionary* online, s.v. "worm n.," sense 11a [updated 1928]).
59. Cf. Milton, *Paradise Lost,* bk. 4, lines 75ff.

VOLUME II.

CHAPTER I.

NOTHING is more painful to the human mind, than, after the feelings have been worked up by a quick succession of events, the dead calmness of inaction and certainty which follows, and deprives the soul both of hope and fear. Justine died; she rested; and I was alive. The blood flowed freely in my veins, but a weight of despair and remorse pressed on my heart, which nothing could remove. Sleep   II.2 fled from my eyes; I wandered like an evil spirit, for I had committed deeds of mischief beyond description horrible, and more, much more, (I persuaded myself) was yet behind. Yet my heart overflowed with kindness, and the love of virtue. I had begun life with benevolent intentions, and thirsted for the moment when I should put them in practice, and make myself useful to my fellow-beings. Now all was blasted: instead of that serenity of conscience, which allowed me to look back upon the past with self-satisfaction, and from thence to gather promise of new hopes, I was seized by remorse and the sense of guilt, which hurried me away to a hell of intense tortures, such as no language can describe.

This state of mind preyed upon my health, which had entirely re-   II.3 covered from the first shock it had sustained. I shunned the face of man; all sound of joy or complacency was torture to me; solitude was my only consolation—deep, dark, death-like solitude.

My father observed with pain the alteration perceptible in my disposition and habits, and endeavoured to reason with me on the folly of giving way to immoderate grief. "Do you think, Victor," said he, "that I do not suffer also? No one could love a child more than I loved your brother;" (tears came into his eyes as he spoke); "but is it not a duty to the survivors, that we should refrain from augmenting their unhappiness by an appearance of immoderate grief? It is also a duty owed to yourself; for excessive sorrow prevents improvement or enjoyment, or even the discharge of daily usefulness, without which no man is fit for society."

This advice, although good, was totally inapplicable to my case; I   II.4 should have been the first to hide my grief, and console my friends, if remorse had not mingled its bitterness with my other sensations. Now I could only answer my father with a look of despair, and endeavour to hide myself from his view.

About this time we retired to our house at Belrive. This change was particularly agreeable to me. The shutting of the gates regularly at ten o'clock, and the impossibility of remaining on the lake after that hour, had rendered our residence within the walls of Geneva very irksome to me. I was now free. Often, after the rest of the family had retired for the night, I took the boat, and passed many hours upon the water. Sometimes, with my sails set, I was carried by the II.5 wind; and sometimes, after rowing into the middle of the lake, I left the boat to pursue its own course, and gave way to my own miserable reflections. I was often tempted, when all was at peace around me, and I the only unquiet thing that wandered restless in a scene so beautiful and heavenly, if I except some bat, or the frogs, whose harsh and interrupted croaking was heard only when I approached the shore—often, I say, I was tempted to plunge into the silent lake, that the waters might close over me and my calamities for ever. But I was restrained, when I thought of the heroic and suffering Elizabeth, whom I tenderly loved, and whose existence was bound up in mine. I thought also of my father, and surviving brother: should I by my base desertion leave them exposed and unprotected to the malice of the fiend whom I had let loose among them?

II.6   At these moments I wept bitterly, and wished that peace would revisit my mind only that I might afford them consolation and happiness. But that could not be. Remorse extinguished every hope. I had been the author of unalterable evils; and I lived in daily fear, lest the monster whom I had created should perpetrate some new wickedness. I had an obscure feeling that all was not over, and that he would still commit some signal crime, which by its enormity should almost efface the recollection of the past. There was always scope for fear, so long as any thing I loved remained behind. My abhorrence of this fiend cannot be conceived. When I thought of him, I gnashed my teeth, my eyes became inflamed, and I ardently wished to extinguish that life which I had so thoughtlessly bestowed. When II.7   I reflected on his crimes and malice, my hatred and revenge burst all bounds of moderation. I would have made a pilgrimage to the highest peak of the Andes, could I, when there, have precipitated him to their base. I wished to see him again, that I might wreak the utmost extent of anger on his head, and avenge the deaths of William and Justine.

Our house was the house of mourning. My father's health was deeply shaken by the horror of the recent events. Elizabeth was sad and desponding; she no longer took delight in her ordinary occupations; all pleasure seemed to her sacrilege toward the dead; eternal woe and tears she then thought was the just tribute she should pay to innocence so blasted and destroyed. She was no longer that happy creature, who in earlier youth wandered with me on the banks of the lake, and talked with ecstacy of our future prospects. She had become grave, and often conversed of the inconstancy of fortune, and the instability of human life. II.8

"When I reflect, my dear cousin," said she, "on the miserable death of Justine Moritz, I no longer see the world and its works as they before appeared to me. Before, I looked upon the accounts of vice and injustice, that I read in books or heard from others, as tales of ancient days, or imaginary evils; at least they were remote, and more familiar to reason than to the imagination; but now misery has come home, and men appear to me as monsters thirsting for each other's blood. Yet I am certainly unjust. Every body believed that poor girl to be guilty; and if she could have committed the crime for which she suffered, assuredly she would have been the most depraved of human creatures. For the sake of a few jewels, to have murdered the son of her benefactor and friend, a child whom she had nursed from its birth, and appeared to love as if it had been her own! I could not consent to the death of any human being; but certainly I should have thought such a creature unfit to remain in the society of men. Yet she was innocent. I know, I feel she was innocent; you are of the same opinion, and that confirms me. Alas! Victor, when falsehood can look so like the truth, who can assure themselves of certain happiness? I feel as if I were walking on the edge of a precipice, towards which thousands are crowding, and endeavouring to plunge me into the abyss. William and Justine were assassinated, and the murderer escapes; he walks about the world free, and perhaps respected. But even if I were condemned to suffer on the scaffold for the same crimes, I would not change places with such a wretch." II.9

II.10

I listened to this discourse with the extremest agony. I, not in deed, but in effect, was the true murderer. Elizabeth read my anguish in my countenance, and kindly taking my hand said, "My dearest cousin, you must calm yourself. These events have affected me, God knows how deeply; but I am not so wretched as you are. There is an expression of despair, and sometimes of revenge, in your countenance, that makes me tremble. Be calm, my dear Victor; I would sacrifice my life to your peace. We surely shall be happy: quiet in our native country, and not mingling in the world, what can disturb our tranquillity?"

She shed tears as she said this, distrusting the very solace that she gave; but at the same time she smiled, that she might chase away the fiend that lurked in my heart. My father, who saw in the unhappiness that was painted in my face only an exaggeration of that sorrow which I might naturally feel, thought that an amusement suited to my taste would be the best means of restoring to me my wonted serenity. It was from this cause that he had removed to the country; and, induced by the same motive, he now proposed that we should all make an excursion to the valley of Chamounix. I had been there before, but Elizabeth and Ernest never had; and both had often expressed an earnest desire to see the scenery of this place, which had been described to them as so wonderful and sublime. Accordingly we departed from Geneva on this tour about the middle of the month of August, nearly two months after the death of Justine.

The weather was uncommonly fine; and if mine had been a sorrow to be chased away by any fleeting circumstance, this excursion would certainly have had the effect intended by my father. As it was, I was somewhat interested in the scene; it sometimes lulled, although it could not extinguish my grief. During the first day we travelled in a carriage. In the morning we had seen the mountains at a distance, towards which we gradually advanced. We perceived that the valley through which we wound, and which was formed by the river Arve, whose course we followed, closed in upon us by degrees; and when the sun had set, we beheld immense mountains and precipices overhanging us on every side, and heard the sound of the river raging among rocks, and the dashing of water-falls around.

The next day we pursued our journey upon mules; and as we ascended still higher, the valley assumed a more magnificent and astonishing character. Ruined castles hanging on the precipices of piny mountains; the impetuous Arve, and cottages every here and there peeping forth from among the trees, formed a scene of singular beauty. But it was augmented and rendered sublime by the mighty Alps, whose white and shining pyramids and domes towered above all, as belonging to another earth, the habitations of another race of beings.

We passed the bridge of Pelissier, where the ravine, which the river forms, opened before us, and we began to ascend the mountain that overhangs it. Soon after we entered the valley of Chamounix. This valley is more wonderful and sublime, but not so beautiful and
picturesque as that of Servox, through which we had just passed.

The high and snowy mountains were its immediate boundaries; but we saw no more ruined castles and fertile fields. Immense glaciers approached the road; we heard the rumbling thunder of the falling avelânche, and marked the smoke of its passage. Mont Blanc, the supreme and magnificent Mont Blanc, raised itself from the surrounding *aiguilles*,[60] and its tremendous *dome* overlooked the valley.

During this journey, I sometimes joined Elizabeth, and exerted myself to point out to her the various beauties of the scene. I often suffered my mule to lag behind, and indulged in the misery of reflection. At other times I spurred on the animal before my companions, that I might forget them, the world, and, more than all, myself. When at a distance, I alighted, and threw myself on the grass, weighed down by horror and despair. At eight in the evening I arrived at Chamounix. My father and Elizabeth were very much fatigued; Ernest, who accompanied us, was delighted, and in high spirits: the only circumstance that detracted from his pleasure was the south wind, and the rain it seemed to promise for the next day.

II.15

We retired early to our apartments, but not to sleep; at least I did not. I remained many hours at the window, watching the pallid lightning that played above Mont Blanc, and listening to the rushing of the Arve, which ran below my window.

---

60. Peaks.

CHAPTER II.

THE next day, contrary to the prognostications of our guides, was fine, although clouded. We visited the source of the Arveiron, and rode about the valley until evening. These sublime and magnificent scenes afforded me the greatest consolation that I was capable of receiving. They elevated me from all littleness of feeling; and although they did not remove my grief, they subdued and tranquillized it. In some degree, also, they diverted my mind from the thoughts over which it had II.17 brooded for the last month. I returned in the evening, fatigued, but less unhappy, and conversed with my family with more cheerfulness than had been my custom for some time. My father was pleased, and Elizabeth overjoyed. "My dear cousin," said she, "you see what happiness you diffuse when you are happy; do not relapse again!"

The following morning the rain poured down in torrents, and thick mists hid the summits of the mountains. I rose early, but felt unusually melancholy. The rain depressed me; my old feelings recurred, and I was miserable. I knew how disappointed my father would be at this sudden change, and I wished to avoid him until I had recovered myself so far as to be enabled to conceal those feelings that overpowered me. I knew that they would remain that day at the II.18 inn; and as I had ever inured myself to rain, moisture, and cold, I resolved to go alone to the summit of Montanvert. I remembered the effect that the view of the tremendous and ever-moving glacier had produced upon my mind when I first saw it. It had then filled me with a sublime ecstacy that gave wings to the soul, and allowed it to soar from the obscure world to light and joy. The sight of the awful[61] and majestic in nature had indeed always the effect of solemnizing my mind, and causing me to forget the passing cares of life. I determined to go alone, for I was well acquainted with the path, and the presence of another would destroy the solitary grandeur of the scene.

The ascent is precipitous, but the path is cut into continual and short windings, which enable you to surmount the perpendicularity II.19 of the mountain. It is a scene terrifically desolate. In a thousand spots the traces of the winter avelanche may be perceived, where trees lie broken and strewed on the ground; some entirely destroyed, others bent, leaning upon the jutting rocks of the mountain, or transversely upon other trees. The path, as you ascend higher, is intersected

---

61. Awe-inspiring.

by ravines of snow, down which stones continually roll from above; one of them is particularly dangerous, as the slightest sound, such as even speaking in a loud voice, produces a concussion of air sufficient to draw destruction upon the head of the speaker. The pines are not tall or luxuriant, but they are sombre, and add an air of severity to the scene. I looked on the valley beneath; vast mists were rising from the rivers which ran through it, and curling in thick wreaths around the opposite mountains, whose summits were hid in the uniform clouds, while rain poured from the dark sky, and added to the melancholy impression I received from the objects around me. Alas! why does man boast of sensibilities superior to those apparent in the brute; it only renders them more necessary beings.[62] If our impulses were confined to hunger, thirst, and desire, we might be nearly free; but now we are moved by every wind that blows, and a chance word or scene that that word may convey to us. II.20

> We rest; a dream has power to poison sleep.
> We rise; one wand'ring thought pollutes the day.
> We feel, conceive, or reason; laugh, or weep,
>   Embrace fond woe, or cast our cares away;
> It is the same: for, be it joy or sorrow,
>   The path of its departure still is free.
> Man's yesterday may ne'er be like his morrow;
>   Nought may endure but mutability![63]

It was nearly noon when I arrived at the top of the ascent. For some time I sat upon the rock that overlooks the sea of ice. A mist covered both that and the surrounding mountains. Presently a breeze dissipated the cloud, and I descended upon the glacier. The surface is very uneven, rising like the waves of a troubled sea, descending low, and interspersed by rifts that sink deep. The field of ice is almost a league in width, but I spent nearly two hours in crossing it. The opposite mountain is a bare perpendicular rock. From the side where I now stood Montanvert was exactly opposite, at the distance of a league; and above it rose Mont Blanc, in awful majesty. I remained in a recess of the rock, gazing on this wonderful and stupendous scene. The sea, or rather the vast river of ice, wound among its dependent mountains, whose aërial summits hung over its recesses. Their icy and glittering peaks shone in the sunlight over the clouds. My heart, which was before sorrowful, now swelled with something like joy; I II.21

II.22

---

62. I.e., less capable of acting with free will.
63. From Percy Bysshe Shelley, "Mutability," published January 1816.

exclaimed—"Wandering spirits, if indeed ye wander, and do not rest in your narrow beds, allow me this faint happiness, or take me, as your companion, away from the joys of life."

As I said this, I suddenly beheld the figure of a man, at some distance, advancing towards me with superhuman speed. He bounded over the crevices in the ice, among which I had walked with caution; his stature also, as he approached, seemed to exceed that of man. I was troubled: a mist came over my eyes, and I felt a faintness seize me; but I was quickly restored by the cold gale of the mountains. II.23   I perceived, as the shape came nearer, (sight tremendous and abhorred!) that it was the wretch whom I had created. I trembled with rage and horror, resolving to wait his approach, and then close with him in mortal combat. He approached; his countenance bespoke bitter anguish, combined with disdain and malignity, while its unearthly ugliness rendered it almost too horrible for human eyes. But I scarcely observed this; anger and hatred had at first deprived me of utterance, and I recovered only to overwhelm him with words expressive of furious detestation and contempt.

"Devil!" I exclaimed, "do you dare approach me? and do not you fear the fierce vengeance of my arm wreaked on your miserable head? Begone, vile insect! or rather stay, that I may trample you to dust! II.24   and, oh, that I could, with the extinction of your miserable existence, restore those victims whom you have so diabolically murdered!"

"I expected this reception," said the dæmon. "All men hate the wretched; how then must I be hated, who am miserable beyond all living things! Yet you, my creator, detest and spurn me, thy creature, to whom thou art bound by ties only dissoluble by the annihilation of one of us. You purpose to kill me. How dare you sport thus with life? Do your duty towards me, and I will do mine towards you and the rest of mankind. If you will comply with my conditions, I will leave them and you at peace; but if you refuse, I will glut the maw of death, until it be satiated with the blood of your remaining friends."

"Abhorred monster! fiend that thou art! the tortures of hell are II.25   too mild a vengeance for thy crimes. Wretched devil! you reproach me with your creation; come on then, that I may extinguish the spark which I so negligently bestowed."

My rage was without bounds; I sprang on him, impelled by all the feelings which can arm one being against the existence of another.

He easily eluded me, and said,

"Be calm! I entreat you to hear me, before you give vent to your hatred on my devoted[64] head. Have I not suffered enough, that you seek to increase my misery? Life, although it may only be an accumulation of anguish, is dear to me, and I will defend it. Remember, thou hast made me more powerful than thyself; my height is superior to thine; my joints more supple. But I will not be tempted to set myself in opposition to thee. I am thy creature, and I will be even mild and docile to my natural lord and king, if thou wilt also perform thy part, the which   II.26
thou owest me. Oh, Frankenstein, be not equitable to every other, and trample upon me alone, to whom thy justice, and even thy clemency and affection, is most due. Remember, that I am thy creature:[65] I ought to be thy Adam; but I am rather the fallen angel, whom thou drivest from joy for no misdeed. Every where I see bliss, from which I alone am irrevocably excluded. I was benevolent and good; misery made me a fiend. Make me happy, and I shall again be virtuous."

"Begone! I will not hear you. There can be no community between you and me; we are enemies. Begone, or let us try our strength in a fight, in which one must fall."

"How can I move thee? Will no entreaties cause thee to turn a favourable eye upon thy creature, who implores thy goodness and   II.27
compassion? Believe me, Frankenstein: I was benevolent; my soul glowed with love and humanity: but am I not alone, miserably alone? You, my creator, abhor me; what hope can I gather from your fellow-creatures, who owe me nothing? they spurn and hate me. The desert mountains and dreary glaciers are my refuge. I have wandered here many days; the caves of ice, which I only do not fear, are a dwelling to me, and the only one which man does not grudge. These bleak skies I hail, for they are kinder to me than your fellow-beings. If the multitude of mankind knew of my existence, they would do as you do, and arm themselves for my destruction. Shall I not then hate them who abhor me? I will keep no terms with my enemies. I am misera-   II.28
ble, and they shall share my wretchedness. Yet it is in your power to recompense me, and deliver them from an evil which it only remains for you to make so great, that not only you and your family, but thousands of others, shall be swallowed up in the whirlwinds of its rage. Let your compassion be moved, and do not disdain me. Listen to my tale: when you have heard that, abandon or commiserate me, as you shall judge that I deserve. But hear me. The guilty are allowed, by

---

64. Doomed.
65. Thy creation.

human laws, bloody as they may be, to speak in their own defence before they are condemned. Listen to me, Frankenstein. You accuse me of murder; and yet you would, with a satisfied conscience, destroy your own creature. Oh, praise the eternal justice of man! Yet I

II.29 ask you not to spare me: listen to me; and then, if you can, and if you will, destroy the work of your hands."

"Why do you call to my remembrance circumstances of which I shudder to reflect, that I have been the miserable origin and author? Cursed be the day, abhorred devil, in which you first saw light! Cursed (although I curse myself) be the hands that formed you! You have made me wretched beyond expression. You have left me no power to consider whether I am just to you, or not. Begone! relieve me from the sight of your detested form."

"Thus I relieve thee, my creator," he said, and placed his hated hands before my eyes, which I flung from me with violence; "thus I take from thee a sight which you abhor. Still thou canst listen to me,

II.30 and grant me thy compassion. By the virtues that I once possessed, I demand this from you. Hear my tale; it is long and strange, and the temperature of this place is not fitting to your fine sensations; come to the hut upon the mountain. The sun is yet high in the heavens; before it descends to hide itself behind yon snowy precipices, and illuminate another world, you will have heard my story, and can decide. On you it rests, whether I quit for ever the neighbourhood of man, and lead a harmless life, or become the scourge of your fellow-creatures, and the author of your own speedy ruin."

As he said this, he led the way across the ice: I followed. My heart was full, and I did not answer him; but, as I proceeded, I weighed the various arguments that he had used, and determined at least to

II.31 listen to his tale. I was partly urged by curiosity, and compassion confirmed my resolution. I had hitherto supposed him to be the murderer of my brother, and I eagerly sought a confirmation or denial of this opinion. For the first time, also, I felt what the duties of a creator towards his creature were, and that I ought to render him happy before I complained of his wickedness. These motives urged me to comply with his demand. We crossed the ice, therefore, and ascended the opposite rock. The air was cold, and the rain again began to descend: we entered the hut, the fiend with an air of exultation, I with a heavy heart, and depressed spirits. But I consented to listen; and, seating myself by the fire which my odious companion had lighted, he thus began his tale.

CHAPTER III.

II.32

"IT is with considerable difficulty that I remember the original æra of my being: all the events of that period appear confused and indistinct. A strange multiplicity of sensations seized me, and I saw, felt, heard, and smelt, at the same time; and it was, indeed, a long time before I learned to distinguish between the operations of my various senses. By degrees, I remember, a stronger light pressed upon my nerves, so that I was obliged to shut my eyes. Darkness then came over me, and troubled me; but hardly had I felt this, when, by opening my II.33 eyes, as I now suppose, the light poured in upon me again. I walked, and, I believe, descended; but I presently found a great alteration in my sensations. Before, dark and opaque bodies had surrounded me, impervious to my touch or sight; but I now found that I could wander on at liberty, with no obstacles which I could not either surmount or avoid. The light became more and more oppressive to me; and, the heat wearying me as I walked, I sought a place where I could receive shade. This was the forest near Ingolstadt; and here I lay by the side of a brook resting from my fatigue, until I felt tormented by hunger and thirst. This roused me from my nearly dormant state, and I ate some berries which I found hanging on the trees, or lying on the ground. I slaked my thirst at the brook; and then lying down, was II.34 overcome by sleep.

"It was dark when I awoke; I felt cold also, and half-frightened as it were instinctively, finding myself so desolate. Before I had quitted your apartment, on a sensation of cold, I had covered myself with some clothes; but these were insufficient to secure me from the dews of night. I was a poor, helpless, miserable wretch; I knew, and could distinguish, nothing; but, feeling pain invade me on all sides, I sat down and wept.

"Soon a gentle light stole over the heavens, and gave me a sensation of pleasure. I started up, and beheld a radiant form[66] rise from among the trees. I gazed with a kind of wonder. It moved slowly, but it enlightened my path; and I again went out in search of berries. I was still cold, when under one of the trees I found a huge cloak, with II.35 which I covered myself, and sat down upon the ground. No distinct ideas occupied my mind; all was confused. I felt light, and hunger, and thirst, and darkness; innumerable sounds rung in my ears, and

---

66. MWS noted in 1831: "The moon."

on all sides various scents saluted[67] me: the only object that I could distinguish was the bright moon, and I fixed my eyes on that with pleasure.

"Several changes of day and night passed, and the orb of night had greatly lessened when I began to distinguish my sensations from each other. I gradually saw plainly the clear stream that supplied me with drink, and the trees that shaded me with their foliage. I was delighted when I first discovered that a pleasant sound, which often saluted my ears, proceeded from the throats of the little winged ani-
II.36   mals who had often intercepted the light from my eyes. I began also to observe, with greater accuracy, the forms that surrounded me, and to perceive the boundaries of the radiant roof of light which canopied me. Sometimes I tried to imitate the pleasant songs of the birds, but was unable. Sometimes I wished to express my sensations in my own mode, but the uncouth and inarticulate sounds which broke from me frightened me into silence again.

"The moon had disappeared from the night, and again, with a lessened form, shewed itself, while I still remained in the forest. My sensations had, by this time, become distinct, and my mind received every day additional ideas. My eyes became accustomed to the light, and to perceive objects in their right forms; I distinguished the insect
II.37   from the herb, and, by degrees, one herb from another. I found that the sparrow uttered none but harsh notes, whilst those of the black-bird and thrush were sweet and enticing.

"One day, when I was oppressed by cold, I found a fire which had been left by some wandering beggars, and was overcome with de-light at the warmth I experienced from it. In my joy I thrust my hand into the live embers, but quickly drew it out again with a cry of pain. How strange, I thought, that the same cause should produce such opposite effects! I examined the materials of the fire, and to my joy found it to be composed of wood. I quickly collected some branches; but they were wet, and would not burn. I was pained at this, and sat still watching the operation of the fire. The wet wood which I had
II.38   placed near the heat dried, and itself became inflamed. I reflected on this; and, by touching the various branches, I discovered the cause, and busied myself in collecting a great quantity of wood, that I might dry it, and have a plentiful supply of fire. When night came on, and brought sleep with it, I was in the greatest fear lest my fire should be extinguished. I covered it carefully with dry wood and leaves, and

---

67. Greeted.

placed wet branches upon it; and then, spreading my cloak, I lay on the ground, and sunk into sleep.

"It was morning when I awoke, and my first care was to visit the fire. I uncovered it, and a gentle breeze quickly fanned it into a flame. I observed this also, and contrived a fan of branches, which roused the embers when they were nearly extinguished. When night came again, I found, with pleasure, that the fire gave light as well as heat; and that the discovery of this element was useful II.39 to me in my food; for I found some of the offals that the travellers had left had been roasted, and tasted much more savoury than the berries I gathered from the trees. I tried, therefore, to dress my food in the same manner, placing it on the live embers. I found that the berries were spoiled by this operation, and the nuts and roots much improved.

"Food, however, became scarce; and I often spent the whole day searching in vain for a few acorns to assuage the pangs of hunger. When I found this, I resolved to quit the place that I had hitherto inhabited, to seek for one where the few wants I experienced would be more easily satisfied. In this emigration, I exceedingly lamented the loss of the fire which I had obtained through accident, and knew not how to re-produce it. I gave several hours to the serious II.40 consideration of this difficulty; but I was obliged to relinquish all attempt to supply it; and, wrapping myself up in my cloak, I struck across the wood towards the setting sun. I passed three days in these rambles, and at length discovered the open country. A great fall of snow had taken place the night before, and the fields were of one uniform white; the appearance was disconsolate, and I found my feet chilled by the cold damp substance that covered the ground.

"It was about seven in the morning, and I longed to obtain food and shelter; at length I perceived a small hut, on a rising ground, which had doubtless been built for the convenience of some shepherd. This was a new sight to me; and I examined the structure with great curiosity. II.41 Finding the door open, I entered. An old man sat in it, near a fire, over which he was preparing his breakfast. He turned on hearing a noise; and, perceiving me, shrieked loudly, and, quitting the hut, ran across the fields with a speed of which his debilitated form hardly appeared capable. His appearance, different from any I had ever before seen, and his flight, somewhat surprised me. But I was enchanted by the appearance of the hut: here the snow and rain could not penetrate; the ground was dry; and it presented to me then as exquisite and divine a

retreat as Pandæmonium[68] appeared to the dæmons of hell after their
sufferings in the lake of fire.[69] I greedily devoured the remnants of
the shepherd's breakfast, which consisted of bread, cheese, milk, and
II.42   wine; the latter, however, I did not like. [Then,] overcome by fatigue, I
lay down among some straw, and fell asleep.

"It was noon when I awoke; and, allured by the warmth of the
sun, which shone brightly on the white ground, I determined to recommence my travels; and, depositing the remains of the peasant's
breakfast in a wallet[70] I found, I proceeded across the fields for several hours, until at sunset I arrived at a village. How miraculous did this
appear! the huts, the neater cottages, and stately houses, engaged
my admiration by turns. The vegetables in the gardens, the milk and
cheese that I saw placed at the windows of some of the cottages, allured my appetite. One of the best of these I entered; but I had hardly
placed my foot within the door, before the children shrieked, and
one of the women fainted. The whole village was roused; some fled,
II.43   some attacked me, until, grievously bruised by stones and many other kinds of missile weapons, I escaped to the open country, and fearfully took refuge in a low hovel, quite bare, and making a wretched
appearance after the palaces I had beheld in the village. This hovel,
however, joined a cottage of a neat and pleasant appearance; but,
after my late dearly-bought experience, I dared not enter it. My place
of refuge was constructed of wood, but so low, that I could with difficulty sit upright in it. No wood, however, was placed on the earth,
which formed the floor, but it was dry; and although the wind entered it by innumerable chinks, I found it an agreeable asylum from
the snow and rain.

"Here then I retreated, and lay down, happy to have found a shel-
II.44   ter, however miserable, from the inclemency of the season, and still
more from the barbarity of man.

"As soon as morning dawned, I crept from my kennel, that I might
view the adjacent cottage, and discover if I could remain in the habitation I had found. It was situated against the back of the cottage,
and surrounded on the sides which were exposed by a pig-stye and
a clear pool of water. One part was open, and by that I had crept in;
but now I covered every crevice by which I might be perceived with
stones and wood, yet in such a manner that I might move them on

---

68. A word invented by Milton, meaning "city of all the devils."
69. Milton, *Paradise Lost*, bk. 1, lines 670ff.
70. A satchel.

occasion to pass out: all the light I enjoyed came through the stye, and that was sufficient for me.

"Having thus arranged my dwelling, and carpeted it with clean straw, I retired; for I saw the figure of a man at a distance, and I remembered too well my treatment the night before, to trust myself in his power. I had first, however, provided for my sustenance for that day, by a loaf of coarse bread, which I purloined, and a cup with which I could drink, more conveniently than from my hand, of the pure water which flowed by my retreat. The floor was a little raised, so that it was kept perfectly dry, and by its vicinity to the chimney of the cottage it was tolerably warm.   II.45

"Being thus provided, I resolved to reside in this hovel, until something should occur which might alter my determination. It was indeed a paradise, compared to the bleak forest, my former residence, the rain-dropping branches, and dank earth. I ate my breakfast with pleasure, and was about to remove a plank to procure myself a little water, when I heard a step, and, looking through a small chink, I   II.46 beheld a young creature, with a pail on her head, passing before my hovel. The girl was young and of gentle demeanour, unlike what I have since found cottagers and farm-house servants to be. Yet she was meanly dressed, a coarse blue petticoat and a linen jacket being her only garb; her fair hair was plaited, but not adorned; she looked patient, yet sad. I lost sight of her; and in about a quarter of an hour she returned, bearing the pail, which was now partly filled with milk. As she walked along, seemingly incommoded by the burden, a young man met her, whose countenance expressed a deeper despondence. Uttering a few sounds with an air of melancholy, he took the pail from her head, and bore it to the cottage himself. She followed, and they disappeared. Presently I saw the young man again, with some   II.47 tools in his hand, cross the field behind the cottage; and the girl was also busied, sometimes in the house, and sometimes in the yard.

"On examining my dwelling, I found that one of the windows of the cottage had formerly occupied a part of it, but the panes had been filled up with wood. In one of these was a small and almost imperceptible chink, through which the eye could just penetrate. Through this crevice, a small room was visible, white-washed and clean, but very bare of furniture. In one corner, near a small fire, sat an old man, leaning his head on his hands in a disconsolate attitude. The young girl was occupied in arranging the cottage; but presently she took something out of a drawer, which employed her hands, and she sat down beside the old man, who, taking up an instrument, began

II.48 to play, and to produce sounds, sweeter than the voice of the thrush or the nightingale. It was a lovely sight, even to me, poor wretch! who had never beheld aught beautiful before. The silver hair and benevolent countenance of the aged cottager, won my reverence; while the gentle manners of the girl enticed my love. He played a sweet mournful air, which I perceived drew tears from the eyes of his amiable companion, of which the old man took no notice, until she sobbed audibly; he then pronounced a few sounds, and the fair creature, leaving her work, knelt at his feet. He raised her, and smiled with such kindness and affection, that I felt sensations of a peculiar and over-powering nature: they were a mixture of pain and pleasure, such as I had never before experienced, either from hunger or cold,

II.49 warmth or food; and I withdrew from the window, unable to bear these emotions.

"Soon after this the young man returned, bearing on his shoulders a load of wood. The girl met him at the door, helped to relieve him of his burden, and, taking some of the fuel into the cottage, placed it on the fire; then she and the youth went apart into a nook of the cottage, and he shewed her a large loaf and a piece of cheese. She seemed pleased; and went into the garden for some roots and plants, which she placed in water, and then upon the fire. She afterwards continued her work, whilst the young man went into the garden, and appeared busily employed in digging and pulling up roots. After he had been employed thus about an hour, the young woman joined him, and they entered the cottage together.

II.50 "The old man had, in the mean time, been pensive; but, on the appearance of his companions, he assumed a more cheerful air, and they sat down to eat. The meal was quickly dispatched. The young woman was again occupied in arranging the cottage; the old man walked before the cottage in the sun for a few minutes, leaning on the arm of the youth. Nothing could exceed in beauty the contrast between these two excellent creatures. One was old, with silver hairs and a countenance beaming with benevolence and love: the younger was slight and graceful in his figure, and his features were moulded with the finest symmetry; yet his eyes and attitude expressed the utmost sadness and despondency. The old man returned to the cottage; and the youth, with tools different from those he had used in the morning, directed his steps across the fields.

II.51 "Night quickly shut in; but, to my extreme wonder, I found that the cottagers had a means of prolonging light, by the use of tapers, and was delighted to find, that the setting of the sun did not put an end to the pleasure I experienced in watching my human neighbours. In the evening, the young girl and her companion were employed in various occupations which I did not understand; and the old man again took up the instrument, which produced the divine sounds that had enchanted me in the morning. So soon as he had finished, the youth began, not to play, but to utter sounds that were monotonous, and neither resembling the harmony of the old man's instrument or the songs of the birds; I since found that he read aloud, but at that time I knew nothing of the science of words or letters.

"The family, after having been thus occupied for a short time, ex- II.52 tinguished their lights, and retired, as I conjectured, to rest.

CHAPTER IV.

"I LAY on my straw, but I could not sleep. I thought of the occurrences of the day. What chiefly struck me was the gentle manners of these people; and I longed to join them, but dared not. I remembered too well the treatment I had suffered the night before from the barbarous villagers, and resolved, whatever course of conduct I might hereafter think it right to pursue, that for the present I would remain quietly in my hovel, watching, and endeavouring to discover the motives which influenced their actions.

II.54   "The cottagers arose the next morning before the sun. The young woman arranged the cottage, and prepared the food; and the youth departed after the first meal.

"This day was passed in the same routine as that which preceded it. The young man was constantly employed out of doors, and the girl in various laborious occupations within. The old man, whom I soon perceived to be blind, employed his leisure hours on his instrument, or in contemplation. Nothing could exceed the love and respect which the younger cottagers exhibited towards their venerable companion. They performed towards him every little office of affection and duty with gentleness; and he rewarded them by his benevolent smiles.

"They were not entirely happy. The young man and his compan-
II.55   ion often went apart, and appeared to weep. I saw no cause for their unhappiness; but I was deeply affected by it. If such lovely creatures were miserable, it was less strange that I, an imperfect and solitary being, should be wretched. Yet why were these gentle beings unhappy? They possessed a delightful house (for such it was in my eyes), and every luxury; they had a fire to warm them when chill, and delicious viands when hungry; they were dressed in excellent clothes; and, still more, they enjoyed one another's company and speech, interchanging each day looks of affection and kindness. What did their tears imply? Did they really express pain? I was at first unable to solve these questions; but perpetual attention, and time, explained to me many appearances which were at first enigmatic.

II.56   "A considerable period elapsed before I discovered one of the causes of the uneasiness of this amiable family; it was poverty: and they suffered that evil in a very distressing degree. Their nourishment consisted entirely of the vegetables of their garden, and the milk of one cow, who gave very little during the winter, when its masters could scarcely procure food to support it. They often, I believe, suffered the pangs of hunger very poignantly, especially the two younger cottagers; for several times they placed food before the old man, when they reserved none for themselves.

"This trait of kindness moved me sensibly. I had been accustomed, during the night, to steal a part of their store for my own consumption; but when I found that in doing this I inflicted pain on the cottagers, I abstained, and satisfied myself with berries, nuts, and roots, II.57 which I gathered from a neighbouring wood.

"I discovered also another means through which I was enabled to assist their labours. I found that the youth spent a great part of each day in collecting wood for the family fire; and, during the night, I often took his tools, the use of which I quickly discovered, and brought home firing sufficient for the consumption of several days.

"I remember, the first time that I did this, the young woman, when she opened the door in the morning, appeared greatly astonished on seeing a great pile of wood on the outside. She uttered some words in a loud voice, and the youth joined her, who also expressed surprise. I observed, with pleasure, that he did not go to the forest that day, but spent it in repairing the cottage, and cultivating the garden. II.58

"By degrees I made a discovery of still greater moment. I found that these people possessed a method of communicating their experience and feelings to one another by articulate sounds. I perceived that the words they spoke sometimes produced pleasure or pain, smiles or sadness, in the minds and countenances of the hearers. This was indeed a godlike science, and I ardently desired to become acquainted with it. But I was baffled in every attempt I made for this purpose. Their pronunciation was quick; and the words they uttered, not having any apparent connexion with visible objects, I was unable to discover any clue by which I could unravel the mystery of their reference. By great application, however, and after having remained II.59 during the space of several revolutions of the moon in my hovel, I discovered the names that were given to some of the most familiar objects of discourse: I learned and applied the words *fire*, *milk*, *bread*, and *wood*. I learned also the names of the cottagers themselves. The youth and his companion had each of them several names, but the old man had only one, which was *father*. The girl was called *sister*, or *Agatha*; and the youth *Felix*, *brother*, or *son*. I cannot describe the delight I felt when I learned the ideas appropriated to each of these sounds, and was able to pronounce them. I distinguished several other words, without being able as yet to understand or apply them; such as *good*, *dearest*, *unhappy*.

"I spent the winter in this manner. The gentle manners and beauty
II.60   of the cottagers greatly endeared them to me: when they were unhappy, I felt depressed; when they rejoiced, I sympathized in their joys.
I saw few human beings beside them; and if any other happened to
enter the cottage, their harsh manners and rude gait only enhanced
to me the superior accomplishments of my friends. The old man,
I could perceive, often endeavoured to encourage his children, as
sometimes I found that he called them, to cast off their melancholy.
He would talk in a cheerful accent, with an expression of goodness
that bestowed pleasure even upon me. Agatha listened with respect,
her eyes sometimes filled with tears, which she endeavoured to wipe
away unperceived; but I generally found that her countenance and
tone were more cheerful after having listened to the exhortations of
II.61   her father. It was not thus with Felix. He was always the saddest of
the groupe; and, even to my unpractised senses, he appeared to have
suffered more deeply than his friends. But if his countenance was
more sorrowful, his voice was more cheerful than that of his sister,
especially when he addressed the old man.

"I could mention innumerable instances, which, although slight,
marked the dispositions of these amiable cottagers. In the midst of
poverty and want, Felix carried with pleasure to his sister the first
little white flower that peeped out from beneath the snowy ground.
Early in the morning before she had risen, he cleared away the snow
that obstructed her path to the milk-house, drew water from the well,
and brought the wood from the out-house, where, to his perpetual
II.62   astonishment, he found his store always replenished by an invisible
hand. In the day, I believe, he worked sometimes for a neighbouring
farmer, because he often went forth, and did not return until dinner,
yet brought no wood with him. At other times he worked in the garden; but, as there was little to do in the frosty season, he read to the
old man and Agatha.

"This reading had puzzled me extremely at first; but, by degrees, I
discovered that he uttered many of the same sounds when he read as
when he talked. I conjectured, therefore, that he found on the paper
signs for speech which he understood, and I ardently longed to comprehend these also; but how was that possible, when I did not even
understand the sounds for which they stood as signs? I improved,
however, sensibly in this science, but not sufficiently to follow up
II.63   any kind of conversation, although I applied my whole mind to the
endeavour: for I easily perceived that, although I eagerly longed to
discover myself to the cottagers, I ought not to make the attempt

until I had first become master of their language; which knowledge might enable me to make them overlook the deformity of my figure; for with this also the contrast perpetually presented to my eyes had made me acquainted.

"I had admired the perfect forms of my cottagers—their grace, beauty, and delicate complexions: but how was I terrified, when I viewed myself in a transparent pool![71] At first I started back, unable to believe that it was indeed I who was reflected in the mirror; and when I became fully convinced that I was in reality the monster that I am, I was filled with the bitterest sensations of despondence and mortification. Alas! I did not yet entirely know the fatal effects of this miserable deformity.   II.64

"As the sun became warmer, and the light of day longer, the snow vanished, and I beheld the bare trees and the black earth. From this time Felix was more employed; and the heart-moving indications of impending famine disappeared. Their food, as I afterwards found, was coarse, but it was wholesome; and they procured a sufficiency of it. Several new kinds of plants sprung up in the garden, which they dressed; and these signs of comfort increased daily as the season advanced.

"The old man, leaning on his son, walked each day at noon, when it did not rain, as I found it was called when the heavens poured forth its waters. This frequently took place; but a high wind quickly dried the earth, and the season became far more pleasant than it had been.   II.65

"My mode of life in my hovel was uniform. During the morning I attended the motions of the cottagers; and when they were dispersed in various occupations, I slept: the remainder of the day was spent in observing my friends. When they had retired to rest, if there was any moon, or the night was star-light, I went into the woods, and collected my own food and fuel for the cottage. When I returned, as often as it was necessary, I cleared their path from the snow, and performed those offices that I had seen done by Felix. I afterwards found that these labours, performed by an invisible hand, greatly astonished them; and once or twice I heard them, on these occasions, utter the words *good spirit, wonderful;* but I did not then understand the signification of these terms.   II.66

"My thoughts now became more active, and I longed to discover the motives and feelings of these lovely creatures; I was inquisitive to

---

71. In contrast to Narcissus in Greek mythology, who fell in love with himself when he saw his reflection in water.

know why Felix appeared so miserable, and Agatha so sad. I thought (foolish wretch!) that it might be in my power to restore happiness to these deserving people. When I slept, or was absent, the forms of the venerable blind father, the gentle Agatha, and the excellent Felix, flitted before me. I looked upon them as superior beings, who would be the arbiters of my future destiny. I formed in my imagination a thousand pictures of presenting myself to them, and their reception of me. I imagined that they would be disgusted, until, by my gentle demeanour and conciliating words, I should first win their favour, and afterwards their love.

"These thoughts exhilarated me, and led me to apply with fresh ardour to the acquiring the art of language. My organs were indeed harsh, but supple; and although my voice was very unlike the soft music of their tones, yet I pronounced such words as I understood with tolerable ease. It was as the ass and the lap-dog; yet surely the gentle ass, whose intentions were affectionate, although his manners were rude, deserved better treatment than blows and execration.[72]

"The pleasant showers and genial warmth of spring greatly altered the aspect of the earth. Men, who before this change seemed to have been hid in caves, dispersed themselves, and were employed in various arts of cultivation. The birds sang in more cheerful notes, and the leaves began to bud forth on the trees. Happy, happy earth! fit habitation for gods, which, so short a time before, was bleak, damp, and unwholesome. My spirits were elevated by the enchanting appearance of nature; the past was blotted from my memory, the present was tranquil, and the future gilded by bright rays of hope, and anticipations of joy.

II.67

II.68

---

72. In La Fontaine's fable "The Ass and the Lapdog," an ass tries to behave like its master's dog, rubbing against him, but instead of getting patted and stroked, the ass is beaten.

CHAPTER V.

"I now hasten to the more moving part of my story. I shall relate events that impressed me with feelings which, from what I was, have made me what I am.

"Spring advanced rapidly; the weather became fine, and the skies cloudless. It surprised me, that what before was desert and gloomy should now bloom with the most beautiful flowers and verdure. My senses were gratified and refreshed by a thousand scents of delight, and a thousand sights of beauty.

"It was on one of these days, when my cottagers periodically rest- II.70 ed from labour—the old man played on his guitar, and the children listened to him—I observed that the countenance of Felix was melancholy beyond expression: he sighed frequently; and once his father paused in his music, and I conjectured by his manner that he inquired the cause of his son's sorrow. Felix replied in a cheerful accent, and the old man was recommencing his music, when some one tapped at the door.

"It was a lady on horseback, accompanied by a countryman as a guide. The lady was dressed in a dark suit, and covered with a thick black veil. Agatha asked a question; to which the stranger only replied by pronouncing, in a sweet accent, the name of Felix. Her voice was musical, but unlike that of either of my friends. On hearing this II.71 word, Felix came up hastily to the lady; who, when she saw him, threw up her veil, and I beheld a countenance of angelic beauty and expression. Her hair of a shining raven black, and curiously braided; her eyes were dark, but gentle, although animated; her features of a regular proportion, and her complexion wondrously fair, each cheek tinged with a lovely pink.

"Felix seemed ravished with delight when he saw her, every trait of sorrow vanished from his face, and it instantly expressed a degree of ecstatic joy, of which I could hardly have believed it capable; his eyes sparkled, as his cheek flushed with pleasure; and at that moment I thought him as beautiful as the stranger. She appeared affect- II.72 ed by different feelings; wiping a few tears from her lovely eyes, she held out her hand to Felix, who kissed it rapturously, and called her, as well as I could distinguish, his sweet Arabian. She did not appear to understand him, but smiled. He assisted her to dismount, and, dismissing her guide, conducted her into the cottage. Some conversation took place between him and his father; and the young stranger knelt at the old man's feet, and would have kissed his hand, but he raised her, and embraced her affectionately.

"I soon perceived, that although the stranger uttered articulate sounds, and appeared to have a language of her own, she was neither understood by, or herself understood, the cottagers. They made many signs which I did not comprehend; but I saw that her presence diffused gladness through the cottage, dispelling their sorrow as the

II.73   sun dissipates the morning mists. Felix seemed peculiarly happy, and with smiles of delight welcomed his Arabian. Agatha, the ever-gentle Agatha, kissed the hands of the lovely stranger; and, pointing to her brother, made signs which appeared to me to mean that he had been sorrowful until she came. Some hours passed thus, while they, by their countenances, expressed joy, the cause of which I did not comprehend. Presently I found, by the frequent recurrence of one sound which the stranger repeated after them, that she was endeavouring to learn their language; and the idea instantly occurred to me, that I should make use of the same instructions to the same end. The stranger learned about twenty words at the first lesson, most of them indeed were those which I had before understood, but I profited by the others.

II.74   "As night came on, Agatha and the Arabian retired early. When they separated, Felix kissed the hand of the stranger, and said, 'Good night, sweet Safie.' He sat up much longer, conversing with his father; and, by the frequent repetition of her name, I conjectured that their lovely guest was the subject of their conversation. I ardently desired to understand them, and bent every faculty towards that purpose, but found it utterly impossible.

"The next morning Felix went out to his work; and, after the usual occupations of Agatha were finished, the Arabian sat at the feet of the old man, and, taking his guitar, played some airs so entrancingly beautiful, that they at once drew tears of sorrow and delight from my eyes. She sang, and her voice flowed in a rich cadence, swelling or dying away, like a nightingale of the woods.

II.75   ["]When she had finished, she gave the guitar to Agatha, who at first declined it. She played a simple air, and her voice accompanied it in sweet accents, but unlike the wondrous strain of the stranger. The old man appeared enraptured, and said some words, which Agatha endeavoured to explain to Safie, and by which he appeared to wish to express that she bestowed on him the greatest delight by her music.

["]The days now passed as peaceably as before, with the sole alteration, that joy had taken place of sadness in the countenances of my friends. Safie was always gay and happy; she and I improved rapidly in the knowledge of language, so that in two months I began to comprehend most of the words uttered by my protectors.

["]In the meanwhile also the black ground was covered with herbage, and the green banks interspersed with innumerable flowers, sweet to the scent and the eyes, stars of pale radiance among the moonlight woods; the sun became warmer, the nights clear and balmy; and my nocturnal rambles were an extreme pleasure to me, although they were considerably shortened by the late setting and early rising of the sun; for I never ventured abroad during daylight, fearful of meeting with the same treatment as I had formerly endured in the first village which I entered. II.76

"My days were spent in close attention, that I might more speedily master the language; and I may boast that I improved more rapidly than the Arabian, who understood very little, and conversed in broken accents, whilst I comprehended and could imitate almost every word that was spoken.

["]While I improved in speech, I also learned the science of letters, as it was taught to the stranger; and this opened before me a wide field for wonder and delight. II.77

"The book from which Felix instructed Safie was Volney's *Ruins of Empires*.[73] I should not have understood the purport of this book, had not Felix, in reading it, given very minute explanations. He had chosen this work, he said, because the declamatory style was framed in imitation of the eastern authors. Through this work I obtained a cursory knowledge of history, and a view of the several empires at present existing in the world; it gave me an insight into the manners, governments, and religions of the different nations of the earth. I heard of the slothful Asiatics; of the stupendous genius and mental activity of the Grecians; of the wars and wonderful virtue of the early Romans—of their subsequent degeneration—of the decline of that mighty empire; of chivalry, christianity, and kings. I heard of the discovery of the American hemisphere, and wept with Safie over the hapless fate of its original inhabitants. II.78

"These wonderful narrations inspired me with strange feelings. Was man, indeed, at once so powerful, so virtuous, and magnificent, yet so vicious and base? He appeared at one time a mere scion of the evil principle, and at another as all that can be conceived of noble and godlike. To be a great and virtuous man appeared the highest

---

73. Published in French in 1791, in English in 1792. Volney had traveled in the East: hence Felix's belief that he had been influenced by eastern authors.

honour that can befall a sensitive being; to be base and vicious, as many on record have been, appeared the lowest degradation, a condition more abject than that of the blind mole or harmless worm.

II.79 For a long time I could not conceive how one man could go forth to murder his fellow, or even why there were laws and governments; but when I heard details of vice and bloodshed, my wonder ceased, and I turned away with disgust and loathing.

"Every conversation of the cottagers now opened new wonders to me. While I listened to the instructions which Felix bestowed upon the Arabian, the strange system of human society was explained to me. I heard of the division of property, of immense wealth and squalid poverty; of rank, descent, and noble blood.

"The words induced me to turn towards myself. I learned that the possessions most esteemed by your fellow-creatures were, high and unsullied descent united with riches. A man might be respected with only one of these acquisitions; but without either he was considered,

II.80 except in very rare instances, as a vagabond and a slave, doomed to waste his powers for the profit of the chosen few. And what was I? Of my creation and creator I was absolutely ignorant; but I knew that I possessed no money, no friends, no kind of property. I was, besides, endowed with a figure hideously deformed and loathsome; I was not even of the same nature as man. I was more agile than they, and could subsist upon coarser diet; I bore the extremes of heat and cold with less injury to my frame; my stature far exceeded their's. When I looked around, I saw and heard of none like me. Was I then a monster, a blot upon the earth, from which all men fled, and whom all men disowned?

"I cannot describe to you the agony that these reflections inflicted upon me; I tried to dispel them, but sorrow only increased with

II.81 knowledge. Oh, that I had for ever remained in my native wood, nor known or felt beyond the sensations of hunger, thirst, and heat!

"Of what a strange nature is knowledge! It clings to the mind, when it has once seized on it, like a lichen on the rock. I wished sometimes to shake off all thought and feeling; but I learned that there was but one means to overcome the sensation of pain, and that was death—a state which I feared yet did not understand. I admired virtue and good feelings, and loved the gentle manners and amiable qualities of my cottagers; but I was shut out from intercourse[74] with them, except through means which I obtained by stealth, when I was unseen and unknown, and which rather increased than satisfied the desire I had

---

74. Social interaction. (The *Oxford English Dictionary* online, s.v. "intercourse n." [updated 1900] gives 1803 as the first use of the word in its modern sexual meaning.)

of becoming one among my fellows. The gentle words of Agatha, and   II.82
the animated smiles of the charming Arabian, were not for me. The
mild exhortations of the old man, and the lively conversation of the
loved Felix, were not for me. Miserable, unhappy wretch!

"Other lessons were impressed upon me even more deeply. I heard
of the difference of sexes; of the birth and growth of children; how
the father doated on the smiles of the infant, and the lively sallies of
the older child; how all the life and cares of the mother were wrapt up
in the precious charge; how the mind of youth expanded and gained
knowledge; of brother, sister, and all the various relationships which
bind one human being to another in mutual bonds.

"But where were my friends and relations? No father had watched
my infant days, no mother had blessed me with smiles and caress-   II.83
es; or if they had, all my past life was now a blot, a blind vacancy in
which I distinguished nothing. From my earliest remembrance I had
been as I then was in height and proportion. I had never yet seen a
being resembling me, or who claimed any intercourse with me. What
was I? The question again recurred, to be answered only with groans.

"I will soon explain to what these feelings tended; but allow me
now to return to the cottagers, whose story excited in me such various feelings of indignation, delight, and wonder, but which all terminated in additional love and reverence for my protectors (for so I
loved, in an innocent, half painful self-deceit, to call them).

CHAPTER VI.

II.84

"SOME time elapsed before I learned the history of my friends. It was one which could not fail to impress itself deeply on my mind, unfolding as it did a number of circumstances each interesting and wonderful to one so utterly inexperienced as I was.

"The name of the old man was De Lacey. He was descended from a good family in France, where he had lived for many years in affluence, respected by his superiors, and beloved by his equals. His son was bred in the service of his country; and Agatha had ranked with ladies of the highest distinction. A few months before my arrival, they had lived in a large and luxurious city, called Paris, surrounded by friends, and possessed of every enjoyment which virtue, refinement of intellect, or taste, accompanied by a moderate fortune, could afford.

II.85

"The father of Safie had been the cause of their ruin. He was a Turkish merchant, and had inhabited Paris for many years, when, for some reason which I could not learn, he became obnoxious to the government. He was seized and cast into prison the very day that Safie arrived from Constantinople to join him. He was tried, and condemned to death. The injustice of his sentence was very flagrant; all Paris was indignant; and it was judged that his religion and wealth, rather than the crime alleged against him, had been the cause of his condemnation.

II.86

"Felix had been present at the trial; his horror and indignation were uncontrollable, when he heard the decision of the court. He made, at that moment, a solemn vow to deliver him, and then looked around for the means. After many fruitless attempts to gain admittance to the prison, he found a strongly grated window in an unguarded part of the building, which lighted the dungeon of the unfortunate Mahometan; who, loaded with chains, waited in despair the execution of the barbarous sentence. Felix visited the grate at night, and made known to the prisoner his intentions in his favour. The Turk, amazed and delighted, endeavoured to kindle the zeal of his deliverer by promises of reward and wealth. Felix rejected his offers with contempt; yet when he saw the lovely Safie, who was allowed to visit her father, and who, by her gestures, expressed her lively gratitude, the youth could not help owning to his own mind, that the captive possessed a treasure which would fully reward his toil and hazard.

II.87

"The Turk quickly perceived the impression that his daughter had made on the heart of Felix, and endeavoured to secure him more entirely in his interests by the promise of her hand in marriage, so soon as he should be conveyed to a place of safety. Felix was too delicate[75] to accept this offer; yet he looked forward to the probability of that event as to the consummation of his happiness.

"During the ensuing days, while the preparations were going forward for the escape of the merchant, the zeal of Felix was warmed by several letters that he received from this lovely girl, who found $\quad$ II.88 means to express her thoughts in the language of her lover by the aid of an old man, a servant of her father's, who understood French. She thanked him in the most ardent terms for his intended services towards her father; and at the same time she gently deplored her own fate.

"I have copies of these letters; for I found means, during my residence in the hovel, to procure the implements of writing; and the letters were often in the hands of Felix or Agatha. Before I depart, I will give them to you, they will prove the truth of my tale; but at present, as the sun is already far declined, I shall only have time to repeat the substance of them to you.

"Safie related, that her mother was a Christian Arab, seized and made a slave by the Turks; recommended by her beauty, she had won $\quad$ II.89 the heart of the father of Safie, who married her. The young girl spoke in high and enthusiastic terms of her mother, who, born in freedom spurned the bondage to which she was now reduced. She instructed her daughter in the tenets of her religion, and taught her to aspire to higher powers of intellect, and an independence of spirit, forbidden to the female followers of Mahomet. This lady died; but her lessons were indelibly impressed on the mind of Safie, who sickened at the prospect of again returning to Asia, and the being immured within the walls of a haram,[76] allowed only to occupy herself with puerile amusements, ill suited to the temper of her soul, now accustomed to grand ideas and a noble emulation for virtue. The prospect of marrying a Christian, and remaining in a country where women were $\quad$ II.90 allowed to take a rank in society, was enchanting to her.

---

75. "Having a refined sense of what is proper or appropriate; highly sensitive to feelings of embarrassment, shame, etc.; considerate of the feelings of others." (*Oxford English Dictionary* online s.v. "delicate adj. and n.," sense 12a [updated 2020]).
76. I.e., harem.

"The day for the execution of the Turk was fixed; but, on the night previous to it, he had quitted prison, and before morning was distant many leagues from Paris. Felix had procured passports in the name of his father, sister, and himself. He had previously communicated his plan to the former, who aided the deceit by quitting his house, under the pretence of a journey, and concealed himself, with his daughter, in an obscure part of Paris.

"Felix conducted the fugitives through France to Lyons, and across Mont Cenis to Leghorn, where the merchant had decided to wait a favourable opportunity of passing into some part of the Turkish dominions.

"Safie resolved to remain with her father until the moment of his II.91   departure, before which time the Turk renewed his promise that she should be united to his deliverer; and Felix remained with them in expectation of that event; and in the mean time he enjoyed the society of the Arabian, who exhibited towards him the simplest and tenderest affection. They conversed with one another through the means of an interpreter, and sometimes with the interpretation of looks; and Safie sang to him the divine airs of her native country.

"The Turk allowed this intimacy to take place, and encouraged the hopes of the youthful lovers, while in his heart he had formed far other plans. He loathed the idea that his daughter should be united to a Christian; but he feared the resentment of Felix if he should appear lukewarm; for he knew that he was still in the pow-II.92   er of his deliverer, if he should choose to betray him to the Italian state which they inhabited. He revolved a thousand plans by which he should be enabled to prolong the deceit until it might be no longer necessary, and secretly to take his daughter with him when he departed. His plans were greatly facilitated by the news which arrived from Paris.

"The government of France were greatly enraged at the escape of their victim, and spared no pains to detect and punish his deliverer. The plot of Felix was quickly discovered, and De Lacey and Agatha were thrown into prison. The news reached Felix, and roused him from his dream of pleasure. His blind and aged father, and his gentle sister, lay in a noisome dungeon, while he enjoyed the free air, and the society of her whom he loved. This idea was torture to him. He II.93   quickly arranged with the Turk, that if the latter should find a favourable opportunity for escape before Felix could return to Italy, Safie should remain as a boarder at a convent at Leghorn; and then, quitting the lovely Arabian, he hastened to Paris, and delivered himself up to the vengeance of the law, hoping to free De Lacey and Agatha by this proceeding.

"He did not succeed. They remained confined for five months before the trial took place; the result of which deprived them of their fortune, and condemned them to a perpetual exile from their native country.

"They found a miserable asylum in the cottage in Germany, where I discovered them. Felix soon learned that the treacherous Turk, for whom he and his family endured such unheard-of oppression, on discovering that his deliverer was thus reduced to poverty and impotence, became a traitor to good feeling and honour, and had quitted Italy with his daughter, insultingly sending Felix a pittance of money to aid him, as he said, in some plan of future maintenance. II.94

"Such were the events that preyed on the heart of Felix, and rendered him, when I first saw him, the most miserable of his family. He could have endured poverty, and when this distress had been the meed[77] of his virtue, he would have gloried in it: but the ingratitude of the Turk, and the loss of his beloved Safie, were misfortunes more bitter and irreparable. The arrival of the Arabian now infused new life into his soul.

"When the news reached Leghorn, that Felix was deprived of his wealth and rank, the merchant commanded his daughter to think no more of her lover, but to prepare to return with him to her native country. The generous nature of Safie was outraged by this command; she attempted to expostulate with her father, but he left her angrily, reiterating his tyrannical mandate. II.95

"A few days after, the Turk entered his daughter's apartment, and told her hastily, that he had reason to believe that his residence at Leghorn had been divulged, and that he should speedily be delivered up to the French government; he had, consequently, hired a vessel to convey him to Constantinople, for which city he should sail in a few hours. He intended to leave his daughter under the care of a confidential servant, to follow at her leisure with the greater part of his property, which had not yet arrived at Leghorn.

"When alone, Safie resolved in her own mind the plan of conduct that it would become her to pursue in this emergency. A residence in Turkey was abhorrent to her; her religion and feelings were alike adverse to it. By some papers of her father's, which fell into her hands, she heard of the exile of her lover, and learnt the name of the spot II.96

---

77. I.e., reward.

where he then resided. She hesitated some time, but at length she formed her determination. Taking with her some jewels that belonged to her, and a small sum of money, she quitted Italy, with an attendant, a native of Leghorn, but who understood the common language of Turkey, and departed for Germany.

"She arrived in safety at a town about twenty leagues from the cottage of De Lacey, when her attendant fell dangerously ill. Safie nursed her with the most devoted affection; but the poor girl died, and the Arabian was left alone, unacquainted with the language of the country, and utterly ignorant of the customs of the world. She fell, however, into good hands. The Italian had mentioned the name of the spot for which they were bound; and, after her death, the woman of the house in which they had lived took care that Safie should arrive in safety at the cottage of her lover.

II.97

CHAPTER VII.

"SUCH was the history of my beloved cottagers. It impressed me deeply. I learned, from the views of social life which it developed, to admire their virtues, and to deprecate the vices of mankind.

["]As yet I looked upon crime as a distant evil; benevolence and generosity were ever present before me, inciting within me a desire to become an actor in the busy scene where so many admirable qualities were called forth and displayed. But, in giving an account of the progress of my intellect, I must not omit a circumstance which occurred in the beginning of the month of August of the same year.

"One night, during my accustomed visit to the neighbouring wood, where I collected my own food, and brought home firing for my protectors, I found on the ground a leathern portmanteau, containing several articles of dress and some books. I eagerly seized the prize, and returned with it to my hovel. Fortunately the books were written in the language the elements of which I had acquired at the cottage; they consisted of *Paradise Lost*, a volume of *Plutarch's Lives*, and the *Sorrows of Werter*.[78] The possession of these treasures gave me extreme delight; I now continually studied and exercised my mind upon these histories, whilst my friends were employed in their ordinary occupations.

"I can hardly describe to you the effect of these books. They produced in me an infinity of new images and feelings, that sometimes raised me to ecstacy, but more frequently sunk me into the lowest dejection. In the *Sorrows of Werter*, besides the interest of its simple and affecting story, so many opinions are canvassed, and so many lights thrown upon what had hitherto been to me obscure subjects, that I found in it a never-ending source of speculation and astonishment. The gentle and domestic manners it described, combined with lofty sentiments and feelings, which had for their object something out of self, accorded well with my experience among my protectors, and with the wants which were for ever alive in my own bosom. But I thought Werter himself a more divine being than I had ever beheld or imagined; his character contained no pretension, but it sunk deep. The disquisitions upon death and suicide were calculated to fill me

---

78. Volney, Milton, Plutarch, and Goethe (author of *The Sorrows of Young Werther* [1774]) thus provide the Creature's education. Between them they cover history, religion, politics, and psychology.

with wonder. I did not pretend to enter into the merits of the case, yet I inclined towards the opinions of the hero, whose extinction I wept, without precisely understanding it.

["]As I read, however, I applied much personally to my own feelings and condition. I found myself similar, yet at the same time strangely unlike the beings concerning whom I read, and to whose conversation I was a listener. I sympathized with, and partly understood them, but I was unformed in mind; I was dependent on none, and related to none. 'The path of my departure was free;' and there was none to lament my annihilation. My person was hideous, and my stature gigantic: what did this mean? Who was I? What was I? Whence did I come? What was my destination? These questions continually recurred, but I was unable to solve them.

II.102

"The volume of *Plutarch's Lives* which I possessed, contained the histories of the first founders of the ancient republics. This book had a far different effect upon me from the *Sorrows of Werter*. I learned from Werter's imaginations despondency and gloom: but Plutarch taught me high thoughts; he elevated me above the wretched sphere of my own reflections, to admire and love the heroes of past ages. Many things I read surpassed my understanding and experience. I had a very confused knowledge of kingdoms, wide extents of country, mighty rivers, and boundless seas. But I was perfectly unacquainted with towns, and large assemblages of men. The cottage of my protectors had been the only school in which I had studied human nature; but this book developed new and mightier scenes of action. I read of men concerned in public affairs governing or massacring their species. I felt the greatest ardour for virtue rise within me, and abhorrence for vice, as far as I understood the signification of those terms, relative as they were, as I applied them, to pleasure and pain alone. Induced by these feelings, I was of course led to admire peaceable law-givers, Numa, Solon, and Lycurgus, in preference to Romulus and Theseus.[79] The patriarchal[80] lives of my protectors caused these impressions to take a firm hold on my mind; perhaps, if my first introduction to humanity had been made by a young soldier, burning

II.103

---

79. Numa was the second king of Rome; Solon established the laws of Athens; and Lycurgus established the laws of Sparta; Romulus, the first king of Rome, killed his twin brother, Remus; Theseus, the legendary founder of Athens, killed the Minotaur, and his Six Labours involved six killings.

80. Lives like those of Abraham and other patriarchs in the Old Testament—i.e., rural, unsophisticated, noble. Compare Byron, *Sardanapalus* (1821) i.ii.36: "The shepherd kings of patriarchal times."

for glory and slaughter, I should have been imbued with different II.104
sensations.

"But *Paradise Lost* excited different and far deeper emotions. I
read it, as I had read the other volumes which had fallen into my
hands, as a true history. It moved every feeling of wonder and awe,
that the picture of an omnipotent God warring with his creatures was
capable of exciting. I often referred the several situations, as their
similarity struck me, to my own. Like Adam, I was created apparently
united by no link to any other being in existence; but his state was far
different from mine in every other respect. He had come forth from
the hands of God a perfect creature, happy and prosperous, guarded
by the especial care of his Creator; he was allowed to converse with,
and acquire knowledge from beings of a superior nature;[81] but I was
wretched, helpless, and alone. Many times I considered Satan as the II.105
fitter emblem of my condition; for often, like him, when I viewed the
bliss of my protectors, the bitter gall of envy rose within me.

"Another circumstance strengthened and confirmed these feelings. Soon after my arrival in the hovel, I discovered some papers in
the pocket of the dress[82] which I had taken from your laboratory. At
first I had neglected them; but now that I was able to decypher the
characters in which they were written, I began to study them with
diligence. It was your journal of the four months that preceded my
creation. You minutely described in these papers every step you took
in the progress of your work; this history was mingled with accounts
of domestic occurrences. You, doubtless, recollect these papers. Here
they are. Every thing is related in them which bears reference to my II.106
accursed origin; the whole detail of that series of disgusting circumstances which produced it is set in view; the minutest description of
my odious and loathsome person is given, in language which painted your own horrors, and rendered mine ineffaceable. I sickened
as I read. 'Hateful day when I received life!' I exclaimed in agony.
'Cursed creator! Why did you form a monster so hideous that even
you turned from me in disgust? God in pity made man beautiful and
alluring, after his own image; but my form is a filthy type[83] of your's,
more horrid from its very resemblance. Satan had his companions,

---

81. In Milton's *Paradise Lost,* Adam and Eve talk to the angel Raphael before the Fall;
in the book of Genesis, the first appearance of an angel is after the Fall. The Creature
knows about Adam and Eve only through reading Milton.
82. "Dress" is here a gender-neutral term.
83. Version.

fellow-devils, to admire and encourage him; but I am solitary and detested.'

"These were the reflections of my hours of despondency and soli-
II.107   tude; but when I contemplated the virtues of the cottagers, their amiable and benevolent dispositions, I persuaded myself that when they
should become acquainted with my admiration of their virtues, they
would compassionate[84] me, and overlook my personal deformity.
Could they turn from their door one, however monstrous, who solicited their compassion and friendship? I resolved, at least, not to despair, but in every way to fit myself for an interview with them which
would decide my fate. I postponed this attempt for some months
longer; for the importance attached to its success inspired me with
a dread lest I should fail. Besides, I found that my understanding
improved so much with every day's experience, that I was unwilling
to commence this undertaking until a few more months should have
added to my wisdom.

II.108   "Several changes, in the mean time, took place in the cottage. The
presence of Safie diffused happiness among its inhabitants; and I also
found that a greater degree of plenty reigned there. Felix and Agatha
spent more time in amusement and conversation, and were assisted
in their labours by servants. They did not appear rich, but they were
contented and happy; their feelings were serene and peaceful, while
mine became every day more tumultuous. Increase of knowledge
only discovered to me more clearly what a wretched outcast I was. I
cherished hope, it is true; but it vanished, when I beheld my person
reflected in water, or my shadow in the moon-shine, even as that frail
image and that inconstant shade.[85]

"I endeavoured to crush these fears, and to fortify myself for the
II.109   trial which in a few months I resolved to undergo; and sometimes I
allowed my thoughts, unchecked by reason, to ramble in the fields
of Paradise, and dared to fancy amiable and lovely creatures sympathizing with my feelings and cheering my gloom; their angelic
countenances breathed smiles of consolation. But it was all a dream:
no Eve soothed my sorrows, or shared my thoughts; I was alone. I
remembered Adam's supplication to his Creator;[86] but where was
mine? he had abandoned me, and, in the bitterness of my heart, I
cursed him.

---

84. I.e., have compassion for me.
85. I.e., even as a shadow cast by moonlight vanishes.
86. In *Paradise Lost*, bk. 8, lines 379–451.

"Autumn passed thus. I saw, with surprise and grief, the leaves decay and fall, and nature again assume the barren and bleak appearance it had worn when I first beheld the woods and the lovely moon. Yet I did not heed the bleakness of the weather; I was better fitted by my conformation for the endurance of cold than heat. But my chief delights were the sight of the flowers, the birds, and all the gay apparel of summer; when those deserted me, I turned with more attention towards the cottagers. Their happiness was not decreased by the absence of summer. They loved, and sympathized with one another; and their joys, depending on each other, were not interrupted by the casualties[87] that took place around them. The more I saw of them, the greater became my desire to claim their protection and kindness; my heart yearned to be known and loved by these amiable creatures: to see their sweet looks turned towards me with affection, was the utmost limit of my ambition. I dared not think that they would turn them from me with disdain and horror. The poor that stopped at their door were never driven away. I asked, it is true, for greater treasures than a little food or rest; I required kindness and sympathy; but I did not believe myself utterly unworthy of it.

"The winter advanced, and an entire revolution of the seasons had taken place since I awoke into life. My attention, at this time, was solely directed towards my plan of introducing myself into the cottage of my protectors. I revolved many projects; but that on which I finally fixed was, to enter the dwelling when the blind old man should be alone. I had sagacity enough to discover, that the unnatural hideousness of my person was the chief object of horror with those who had formerly beheld me. My voice, although harsh, had nothing terrible in it; I thought, therefore, that if, in the absence of his children, I could gain the good-will and mediation of the old De Lacy,[88] I might, by his means, be tolerated by my younger protectors.

"One day, when the sun shone on the red leaves that strewed the ground, and diffused cheerfulness, although it denied warmth, Safie, Agatha, and Felix, departed on a long country walk, and the old man, at his own desire, was left alone in the cottage. When his children had departed, he took up his guitar, and played several mournful, but sweet airs, more sweet and mournful than I had ever heard him play before. At first his countenance was illuminated with pleasure, but,

II.110

II.111

II.112

87. *Oxford English Dictionary* online, s.v. "casualty n.," sense 2a: "a chance occurrence" (updated 1889).
88. Earlier, and in later editions, De Lacey.

as he continued, thoughtfulness and sadness succeeded; at length, laying aside the instrument, he sat absorbed in reflection.

"My heart beat quick; this was the hour and moment of trial, which would decide my hopes, or realize my fears. The servants were gone to a neighbouring fair. All was silent in and around the cottage: it was an excellent opportunity; yet, when I proceeded to execute my plan, my limbs failed me, and I sunk to the ground. Again I rose; and, exerting all the firmness of which I was master, removed the planks which I had placed before my hovel to conceal my retreat. The fresh air revived me, and, with renewed determination, I approached the door of their cottage.

"I knocked. 'Who is there?' said the old man—'Come in.'

"I entered; 'Pardon this intrusion,' said I, 'I am a traveller in want of a little rest; you would greatly oblige me, if you would allow me to remain a few minutes before the fire.'

"'Enter,' said De Lacy; 'and I will try in what manner I can relieve your wants; but, unfortunately, my children are from home, and, as I am blind, I am afraid I shall find it difficult to procure food for you.'

"'Do not trouble yourself, my kind host, I have food; it is warmth and rest only that I need.'

"I sat down, and a silence ensued. I knew that every minute was precious to me, yet I remained irresolute in what manner to commence the interview; when the old man addressed me—

"'By your language, stranger, I suppose you are my countryman;— are you French?'

"'No; but I was educated by a French family, and understand that language only. I am now going to claim the protection of some friends, whom I sincerely love, and of whose favour I have some hopes.'

"'Are these Germans?'

"'No, they are French. But let us change the subject. I am an unfortunate and deserted creature; I look around, and I have no relation or friend upon earth. These amiable people to whom I go have never seen me, and know little of me. I am full of fears; for if I fail there, I am an outcast in the world for ever.'

"'Do not despair. To be friendless is indeed to be unfortunate; but the hearts of men, when unprejudiced by any obvious self-interest, are full of brotherly love and charity. Rely, therefore, on your hopes; and if these friends are good and amiable, do not despair.'

"'They are kind—they are the most excellent creatures in the world; but, unfortunately, they are prejudiced against me. I have

II.113

II.114

II.115

good dispositions; my life has been hitherto harmless, and, in some degree, beneficial; but a fatal prejudice clouds their eyes, and where they ought to see a feeling and kind friend, they behold only a detestable monster.'

"'That is indeed unfortunate; but if you are really blameless, cannot you undeceive them?'   II.116

"'I am about to undertake that task; and it is on that account that I feel so many overwhelming terrors. I tenderly love these friends; I have, unknown to them, been for many months in the habits of daily kindness towards them; but they believe that I wish to injure them, and it is that prejudice which I wish to overcome.'

"'Where do these friends reside?'

"'Near this spot.'

"The old man paused, and then continued, 'If you will unreservedly confide to me the particulars of your tale, I perhaps may be of use in undeceiving them. I am blind, and cannot judge of your countenance, but there is something in your words which persuades me that you are sincere. I am poor, and an exile; but it will afford me true   II.117 pleasure to be in any way serviceable to a human creature.'

"'Excellent man! I thank you, and accept your generous offer. You raise me from the dust by this kindness; and I trust that, by your aid, I shall not be driven from the society and sympathy of your fellow-creatures.'

"'Heaven forbid! even if you were really criminal; for that can only drive you to desperation, and not instigate you to virtue. I also am unfortunate; I and my family have been condemned, although innocent: judge, therefore, if I do not feel for your misfortunes.'

"'How can I thank you, my best and only benefactor? from your lips first have I heard the voice of kindness directed towards me; I shall be for ever grateful; and your present humanity assures me of success with those friends whom I am on the point of meeting.'   II.118

"'May I know the names and residence of those friends?'

"I paused. This, I thought, was the moment of decision, which was to rob me of, or bestow happiness on me for ever. I struggled vainly for firmness sufficient to answer him, but the effort destroyed all my remaining strength; I sank on the chair, and sobbed aloud. At that moment I heard the steps of my younger protectors. I had not a moment to lose; but, seizing the hand of the old man, I cried, 'Now is the time!—save and protect me! You and your family are the friends whom I seek. Do not you desert me in the hour of trial!'

"'Great God!' exclaimed the old man, 'who are you?'

II.119   "At that instant the cottage door was opened, and Felix, Safie, and Agatha entered. Who can describe their horror and consternation on beholding me? Agatha fainted; and Safie, unable to attend to her friend, rushed out of the cottage. Felix darted forward, and with supernatural force tore me from his father, to whose knees I clung: in a transport of fury, he dashed me to the ground, and struck me violently with a stick. I could have torn him limb from limb, as the lion rends the antelope. But my heart sunk within me as with bitter sickness, and I refrained. I saw him on the point of repeating his blow, when, overcome by pain and anguish, I quitted the cottage, and in the general tumult escaped unperceived to my hovel.

CHAPTER VIII.

"CURSED, cursed creator! Why did I live? Why, in that instant, did I not extinguish the spark of existence which you had so wantonly bestowed? I know not; despair had not yet taken possession of me; my feelings were those of rage and revenge. I could with pleasure have destroyed the cottage and its inhabitants, and have glutted myself with their shrieks and misery.

"When night came, I quitted my retreat, and wandered in the wood; and now, no longer restrained by the fear of discovery, I gave vent to my anguish in fearful howlings. I was like a wild beast that had broken the toils; destroying the objects that obstructed me, and ranging through the wood with a stag-like swiftness. Oh! what a miserable night I passed! the cold stars shone in mockery, and the bare trees waved their branches above me: now and then the sweet voice of a bird burst forth amidst the universal stillness. All, save I, were at rest or in enjoyment: I, like the arch fiend, bore a hell within me; and, finding myself unsympathized with, wished to tear up the trees, spread havoc and destruction around me, and then to have sat down and enjoyed the ruin.

"But this was a luxury of sensation that could not endure; I became fatigued with excess of bodily exertion, and sank on the damp grass in the sick impotence of despair. There was none among the myriads of men that existed who would pity or assist me; and should I feel kindness towards my enemies? No: from that moment I declared everlasting war against the species, and, more than all, against him who had formed me, and sent me forth to this insupportable misery.

"The sun rose; I heard the voices of men, and knew that it was impossible to return to my retreat during that day. Accordingly I hid myself in some thick underwood, determining to devote the ensuing hours to reflection on my situation.

"The pleasant sunshine, and the pure air of day, restored me to some degree of tranquillity; and when I considered what had passed at the cottage, I could not help believing that I had been too hasty in my conclusions. I had certainly acted imprudently. It was apparent that my conversation had interested the father in my behalf, and I was a fool in having exposed my person to the horror of his children. I ought to have familiarized the old De Lacy to me, and by degrees have discovered myself to the rest of his family, when they should have been prepared for my approach. But I did not believe my errors to be irretrievable; and, after much consideration, I resolved to return to the cottage, seek the old man, and by my representations win him to my party.

"These thoughts calmed me, and in the afternoon I sank into a profound sleep; but the fever of my blood did not allow me to be visited by peaceful dreams. The horrible scene of the preceding day was

II.124 for ever acting before my eyes; the females were flying, and the enraged Felix tearing me from his father's feet. I awoke exhausted; and, finding that it was already night, I crept forth from my hiding-place, and went in search of food.

"When my hunger was appeased, I directed my steps towards the well-known path that conducted to the cottage. All there was at peace. I crept into my hovel, and remained in silent expectation of the accustomed hour when the family arose. That hour past, the sun mounted high in the heavens, but the cottagers did not appear. I trembled violently, apprehending some dreadful misfortune. The inside of the cottage was dark, and I heard no motion; I cannot describe the agony of this suspence.

"Presently two countrymen passed by; but, pausing near the cot-

II.125 tage, they entered into conversation, using violent gesticulations; but I did not understand what they said, as they spoke the language of the country, which differed from that of my protectors.[89] Soon after, however, Felix approached with another man: I was surprised, as I knew that he had not quitted the cottage that morning, and waited anxiously to discover, from his discourse, the meaning of these unusual appearances.

"'Do you consider,' said his companion to him, 'that you will be obliged to pay three months' rent, and to lose the produce of your garden? I do not wish to take any unfair advantage, and I beg therefore that you will take some days to consider of your determination.'

"'It is utterly useless,' replied Felix, 'we can never again inhabit your cottage. The life of my father is in the greatest danger, owing to

II.126 the dreadful circumstance that I have related. My wife and my sister will never recover[90] their horror. I entreat you not to reason with me any more. Take possession of your tenement, and let me fly from this place.'

---

89. I.e., they spoke German, while the Creature has learned French.
90. *Oxford English Dictionary* online s.v. "recover v.," sense 8a, "to get over, get better from" (updated 2009).

"Felix trembled violently as he said this. He and his companion entered the cottage, in which they remained for a few minutes, and then departed. I never saw any of the family of De Lacy more.

"I continued for the remainder of the day in my hovel in a state of utter and stupid[91] despair. My protectors had departed, and had broken the only link that held me to the world. For the first time the feelings of revenge and hatred filled my bosom, and I did not strive to controul them; but, allowing myself to be borne away by the stream, I bent my mind towards injury and death. When I thought of my   II.127 friends, of the mild voice of De Lacy, the gentle eyes of Agatha, and the exquisite beauty of the Arabian, these thoughts vanished, and a gush of tears somewhat soothed me. But again, when I reflected that they had spurned and deserted me, anger returned, a rage of anger; and, unable to injure any thing human, I turned my fury towards inanimate objects. As night advanced, I placed a variety of combustibles around the cottage; and, after having destroyed every vestige of cultivation in the garden, I waited with forced impatience until the moon had sunk to commence my operations.

"As the night advanced, a fierce wind arose from the woods, and quickly dispersed the clouds that had loitered in the heavens: the blast tore along like a mighty avalanche, and produced a kind of in-   II.128 sanity in my spirits, that burst all bounds of reason and reflection. I lighted the dry branch of a tree, and danced with fury around the devoted[92] cottage, my eyes still fixed on the western horizon, the edge of which the moon nearly touched. A part of its orb was at length hid, and I waved my brand; it sunk, and, with a loud scream, I fired the straw, and heath, and bushes, which I had collected. The wind fanned the fire, and the cottage was quickly enveloped by the flames, which clung to it, and licked it with their forked and destroying tongues.

"As soon as I was convinced that no assistance could save any part of the habitation, I quitted the scene, and sought for refuge in the woods.

"And now, with the world before me, whither should I bend my steps?[93] I resolved to fly far from the scene of my misfortunes; but to   II.129 me, hated and despised, every country must be equally horrible. At length the thought of you crossed my mind. I learned from your papers

---

91. Stupefied.
92. *Oxford English Dictionary* online s.v. "devoted adj.," sense 3: consigned to destruction, doomed (updated 1895).
93. Cf. *Paradise Lost*, bk. 12, lines 646–47.

that you were my father, my creator; and to whom could I apply with more fitness than to him who had given me life? Among the lessons that Felix had bestowed upon Safie geography had not been omitted: I had learned from these the relative situations of the different countries of the earth. You had mentioned Geneva as the name of your native town; and towards this place I resolved to proceed.

"But how was I to direct myself? I knew that I must travel in a south-westerly direction to reach my destination; but the sun was my only guide. I did not know the names of the towns that I was to pass through, nor could I ask information from a single human being; but I did not despair. From you only could I hope for succour, although towards you I felt no sentiment but that of hatred. Unfeeling, heartless creator! you had endowed me with perceptions and passions, and then cast me abroad an object for the scorn and horror of mankind. But on you only had I any claim for pity and redress, and from you I determined to seek that justice which I vainly attempted to gain from any other being that wore the human form.

"My travels were long, and the sufferings I endured intense. It was late in autumn when I quitted the district where I had so long resided. I travelled only at night, fearful of encountering the visage of a human being. Nature decayed around me, and the sun became heatless; rain and snow poured around me; mighty rivers were frozen; the surface of the earth was hard, and chill, and bare, and I found no shelter. Oh, earth! how often did I imprecate curses on the cause of my being! The mildness of my nature had fled, and all within me was turned to gall and bitterness. The nearer I approached to your habitation, the more deeply did I feel the spirit of revenge enkindled in my heart. Snow fell, and the waters were hardened, but I rested not. A few incidents now and then directed me, and I possessed a map of the country; but I often wandered wide from my path. The agony of my feelings allowed me no respite: no incident occurred from which my rage and misery could not extract its food; but a circumstance that happened when I arrived on the confines of Switzerland, when the sun had recovered its warmth, and the earth again began to look green, confirmed in an especial manner the bitterness and horror of my feelings.

"I generally rested during the day, and travelled only when I was secured by night from the view of man. One morning, however, finding that my path lay through a deep wood, I ventured to continue my journey after the sun had risen; the day, which was one of the first of spring, cheered even me by the loveliness of its sunshine and the

II.130

II.131

II.132

balminess of the air. I felt emotions of gentleness and pleasure, that had long appeared dead, revive within me. Half surprised by the novelty of these sensations, I allowed myself to be borne away by them; and, forgetting my solitude and deformity, dared to be happy. Soft tears again bedewed my cheeks, and I even raised my humid eyes with thankfulness towards the blessed sun which bestowed such joy upon me. II.133

"I continued to wind among the paths of the wood, until I came to its boundary, which was skirted by a deep and rapid river, into which many of the trees bent their branches, now budding with the fresh spring. Here I paused, not exactly knowing what path to pursue, when I heard the sound of voices, that induced me to conceal myself under the shade of a cypress. I was scarcely hid, when a young girl came running towards the spot where I was concealed, laughing as if she ran from some one in sport. She continued her course along the precipitous sides of the river, when suddenly her foot slipt, and she fell into the rapid stream. I rushed from my hiding place, and, with extreme labour from the force of the current, saved her, and dragged her to shore. She was senseless; and I endeavoured, by every means in my power, to restore animation, when I was suddenly interrupted by the approach of a rustic, who was probably the person from whom she had playfully fled. On seeing me, he darted towards me, and, tearing the girl from my arms, hastened towards the deeper parts of the wood. I followed speedily, I hardly knew why; but when the man saw me draw near, he aimed a gun, which he carried, at my body, and fired. I sunk to the ground, and my injurer, with increased swiftness, escaped into the wood. II.134

"This was then the reward of my benevolence! I had saved a human being from destruction, and, as a recompence, I now writhed under the miserable pain of a wound, which shattered the flesh and bone. The feelings of kindness and gentleness, which I had entertained but a few moments before, gave place to hellish rage and gnashing of teeth. Inflamed by pain, I vowed eternal hatred and vengeance to all mankind. But the agony of my wound overcame me; my pulses paused, and I fainted. II.135

"For some weeks I led a miserable life in the woods, endeavouring to cure the wound which I had received. The ball had entered my shoulder, and I knew not whether it had remained there or passed through; at any rate I had no means of extracting it. My sufferings were augmented also by the oppressive sense of the injustice and ingratitude of their infliction. My daily vows rose for revenge—a deep and deadly revenge, such as would alone compensate for the outrages and anguish I had endured.

II.136   "After some weeks my wound healed, and I continued my journey. The labours I endured were no longer to be alleviated by the bright sun or gentle breezes of spring; all joy was but a mockery, which insulted my desolate state, and made me feel more painfully that I was not made for the enjoyment of pleasure.

"But my toils now drew near a close; and, two months from this time, I reached the environs of Geneva.

"It was evening when I arrived, and I retired to a hiding-place among the fields that surround it, to meditate in what manner I should apply to you. I was oppressed by fatigue and hunger, and far too unhappy to enjoy the gentle breezes of evening, or the prospect of the sun setting behind the stupendous mountains of Jura.

II.137   "At this time a slight sleep relieved me from the pain of reflection, which was disturbed by the approach of a beautiful child, who came running into the recess I had chosen with all the sportiveness of infancy. Suddenly, as I gazed on him, an idea seized me, that this little creature was unprejudiced, and had lived too short a time to have imbibed a horror of deformity. If, therefore, I could seize him, and educate him as my companion and friend, I should not be so desolate in this peopled earth.

"Urged by this impulse, I seized on the boy as he passed, and drew him towards me. As soon as he beheld my form, he placed his hands before his eyes, and uttered a shrill scream: I drew his hand forcibly from his face, and said, 'Child, what is the meaning of this? I do not intend to hurt you; listen to me.'

II.138   "He struggled violently; 'Let me go,' he cried; 'monster! ugly wretch! you wish to eat me, and tear me to pieces—You are an ogre—Let me go, or I will tell my papa.'

"'Boy, you will never see your father again; you must come with me.'

"'Hideous monster! let me go; My papa is a Syndic—he is M. Frankenstein—he would punish you. You dare not keep me.'

"'Frankenstein! you belong then to my enemy—to him towards whom I have sworn eternal revenge; you shall be my first victim.'

"The child still struggled, and loaded me with epithets which carried despair to my heart: I grasped his throat to silence him, and in a moment he lay dead at my feet.

"I gazed on my victim, and my heart swelled with exultation and hellish triumph: clapping my hands, I exclaimed, 'I, too, can create desolation; my enemy is not impregnable; this death will carry despair to him, and a thousand other miseries shall torment and destroy him.' II.139

"As I fixed my eyes on the child, I saw something glittering on his breast. I took it; it was a portrait of a most lovely woman. In spite of my malignity, it softened and attracted me. For a few moments I gazed with delight on her dark eyes, fringed by deep lashes, and her lovely lips; but presently my rage returned: I remembered that I was for ever deprived of the delights that such beautiful creatures could bestow; and that she whose resemblance I contemplated would, in regarding me, have changed that air of divine benignity to one expressive of disgust and affright.

"Can you wonder that such thoughts transported me with rage? I only wonder that at that moment, instead of venting my sensations in exclamations and agony, I did not rush among mankind, and perish in the attempt to destroy them. II.140

"While I was overcome by these feelings, I left the spot where I had committed the murder, and was seeking a more secluded hiding-place, when I perceived a woman passing near me. She was young, not indeed so beautiful as her whose portrait I held, but of an agreeable aspect, and blooming in the loveliness of youth and health. Here, I thought, is one of those whose smiles are bestowed on all but me; she shall not escape: thanks to the lessons of Felix, and the sanguinary laws of man, I have learned how to work mischief. I approached her unperceived, and placed the portrait securely in one of the folds of her dress. II.141

"For some days I haunted the spot where these scenes had taken place; sometimes wishing to see you, sometimes resolved to quit the world and its miseries for ever. At length I wandered towards these mountains, and have ranged through their immense recesses, consumed by a burning passion which you alone can gratify. We may not part until you have promised to comply with my requisition. I am alone, and miserable; man will not associate with me; but one as deformed and horrible as myself would not deny herself to me. My companion must be of the same species, and have the same defects. This being you must create."

CHAPTER IX.

II.142

THE being finished speaking, and fixed his looks upon me in expectation of a reply. But I was bewildered, perplexed, and unable
to arrange my ideas sufficiently to understand the full extent of his
proposition. He continued—

"You must create a female for me, with whom I can live in the interchange of those sympathies necessary for my being. This you alone
can do; and I demand it of you as a right which you must not refuse."

II.143
The latter part of his tale had kindled anew in me the anger that
had died away while he narrated his peaceful life among the cottagers, and, as he said this, I could no longer suppress the rage that
burned within me.

"I do refuse it," I replied; "and no torture shall ever extort a consent
from me. You may render me the most miserable of men, but you
shall never make me base in my own eyes. Shall I create another like
yourself, whose joint wickedness might desolate the world. Begone!
I have answered you; you may torture me, but I will never consent."

"You are in the wrong,'['] replied the fiend; "and, instead of threat-
ening, I am content to reason with you. I am malicious because I am
miserable; am I not shunned and hated by all mankind? You, my creator, would tear me to pieces, and triumph; remember that, and tell
II.144
me why I should pity man more than he pities me? You would not call
it murder, if you could precipitate me into one of those ice-rifts, and
destroy my frame, the work of your own hands. Shall I respect man,
when he contemns[94] me? Let him live with me in the interchange of
kindness, and, instead of injury, I would bestow every benefit upon
him with tears of gratitude at his acceptance. But that cannot be; the
human senses are insurmountable barriers to our union. Yet mine
shall not be the submission of abject slavery. I will revenge my injuries: if I cannot inspire love, I will cause fear; and chiefly towards
you my arch-enemy, because my creator, do I swear inextinguishable
hatred. Have a care: I will work at your destruction, nor finish until I
desolate your heart, so that you curse the hour of your birth."

II.145
A fiendish rage animated him as he said this; his face was wrinkled
into contortions too horrible for human eyes to behold; but presently
he calmed himself, and proceeded—

---

94. Treats with contempt.

"I intended to reason. This passion is detrimental to me; for you do not reflect that you are the cause of its excess. If any being felt emotions of benevolence towards me, I should return them an hundred and an hundred fold; for that one creature's sake, I would make peace with the whole kind! But I now indulge in dreams of bliss that cannot be realized. What I ask of you is reasonable and moderate; I demand a creature of another sex, but as hideous as myself: the gratification is small, but it is all that I can receive, and it shall content me. It is true, we shall be monsters, cut off from all the world; but on that account we shall be more attached to one another. Our lives will not be happy, but they will be harmless, and free from the misery I now feel. Oh! my creator, make me happy; let me feel gratitude towards you for one benefit! Let me see that I excite the sympathy of some existing thing; do not deny me my request!" II.146

I was moved. I shuddered when I thought of the possible consequences of my consent; but I felt that there was some justice in his argument. His tale, and the feelings he now expressed, proved him to be a creature of fine sensations; and did I not, as his maker, owe him all the portion of happiness that it was in my power to bestow? He saw my change of feeling, and continued—

"If you consent, neither you nor any other human being shall ever see us again: I will go to the vast wilds of South America. My food is not that of man; I do not destroy the lamb and the kid, to glut my appetite; acorns and berries afford me sufficient nourishment.[95] My companion will be of the same nature as myself, and will be content with the same fare. We shall make our bed of dried leaves; the sun will shine on us as on man, and will ripen our food. The picture I present to you is peaceful and human, and you must feel that you could deny it only in the wantonness of power and cruelty. Pitiless as you have been towards me, I now see compassion in your eyes: let me seize the favourable moment, and persuade you to promise what I so ardently desire." II.147

"You propose," replied I, "to fly from the habitations of man, to dwell in those wilds where the beasts of the field will be your only companions. How can you, who long for the love and sympathy of man, persevere in this exile? You will return, and again seek their kindness, and you will meet with their detestation; your evil passions will be renewed, and you will then have a companion to aid you in II.148

---

95. PBS was a vegetarian.

the task of destruction. This may not be; cease to argue the point, for I cannot consent."

"How inconstant are your feelings! but a moment ago you were moved by my representations, and why do you again harden yourself to my complaints? I swear to you, by the earth which I inhabit, and by you that made me, that, with the companion you bestow, I will quit the neighbourhood of man, and dwell, as it may chance, in the II.149 most savage of places. My evil passions will have fled, for I shall meet with sympathy; my life will flow quietly away, and, in my dying moments, I shall not curse my maker."

His words had a strange effect upon me. I compassionated him, and sometimes felt a wish to console him; but when I looked upon him, when I saw the filthy mass that moved and talked, my heart sickened, and my feelings were altered to those of horror and hatred. I tried to stifle these sensations; I thought, that as I could not sympathize with him, I had no right to withhold from him the small portion of happiness which was yet in my power to bestow.

"You swear," I said, "to be harmless; but have you not already shewn a degree of malice that should reasonably make me distrust II.150 you? May not even this be a feint that will increase your triumph by affording a wider scope for your revenge?"

"How is this? I thought I had moved your compassion, and yet you still refuse to bestow on me the only benefit that can soften my heart, and render me harmless. If I have no ties and no affections, hatred and vice must be my portion; the love of another will destroy the cause of my crimes, and I shall become a thing, of whose existence every one will be ignorant. My vices are the children of a forced solitude that I abhor; and my virtues will necessarily arise when I live in communion with an equal. I shall feel the affections of a sensitive being, and become linked to the chain of existence and events, from which I am now excluded."

I paused some time to reflect on all he had related, and the vari-II.151 ous arguments which he had employed. I thought of the promise of virtues which he had displayed on the opening of his existence, and the subsequent blight of all kindly feeling by the loathing and scorn which his protectors had manifested towards him. His power and threats were not omitted in my calculations: a creature who could exist in the ice caves of the glaciers, and hide himself from pursuit among the ridges of inaccessible precipices, was a being possessing faculties it would be vain to cope with. After a long pause of reflection, I concluded, that the justice due both to him and my fellow-creatures demanded of me that I should comply with his request. Turning to him, therefore, I said—

"I consent to your demand, on your solemn oath to quit Europe for ever, and every other place in the neighbourhood of man, as soon   II.152 as I shall deliver into your hands a female who will accompany you in your exile."

"I swear," he cried, "by the sun, and by the blue sky of heaven, that if you grant my prayer, while they exist you shall never behold me again. Depart to your home, and commence your labours: I shall watch their progress with unutterable anxiety; and fear not but that when you are ready I shall appear."

Saying this, he suddenly quitted me, fearful, perhaps, of any change in my sentiments. I saw him descend the mountain with greater speed than the flight of an eagle, and quickly lost him among the undulations of the sea of ice.

His tale had occupied the whole day; and the sun was upon the verge of the horizon when he departed. I knew that I ought to hasten   II.153 my descent towards the valley, as I should soon be encompassed in darkness; but my heart was heavy, and my steps slow. The labour of winding among the little paths of the mountains, and fixing my feet firmly as I advanced, perplexed me, occupied as I was by the emotions which the occurrences of the day had produced. Night was far advanced, when I came to the half-way resting-place, and seated myself beside the fountain. The stars shone at intervals, as the clouds passed from over them; the dark pines rose before me, and every here and there a broken tree lay on the ground: it was a scene of wonderful solemnity, and stirred strange thoughts within me. I wept bitterly; and, clasping my hands in agony, I exclaimed, "Oh! stars, and clouds, and winds, ye are all about to mock me: if ye really pity   II.154 me, crush sensation and memory; let me become as nought; but if not, depart, depart and leave me in darkness."

These were wild and miserable thoughts; but I cannot describe to you how the eternal twinkling of the stars weighed upon me, and how I listened to every blast of wind, as if it were a dull ugly siroc[96] on its way to consume me.

Morning dawned before I arrived at the village of Chamounix; but my presence, so haggard and strange, hardly calmed the fears of my family, who had waited the whole night in anxious expectation of my return.

---

96. The sirocco is a wind from Africa.

The following day we returned to Geneva. The intention of my father in coming had been to divert my mind, and to restore me to
my lost tranquillity; but the medicine had been fatal. And, unable
II.155   to account for the excess of misery I appeared to suffer, he hastened
to return home, hoping the quiet and monotony of a domestic life
would by degrees alleviate my sufferings from whatsoever cause they
might spring.

For myself, I was passive in all their arrangements; and the gentle
affection of my beloved Elizabeth was inadequate to draw me from
the depth of my despair. The promise I had made to the dæmon
weighed upon my mind, like Dante's iron cowl on the heads of the
hellish hypocrites.[97] All pleasures of earth and sky passed before me
like a dream, and that thought only had to me the reality of life. Can
you wonder, that sometimes a kind of insanity possessed me, or that
I saw continually about me a multitude of filthy animals inflicting on
me incessant torture, that often extorted screams and bitter groans?

II.156   By degrees, however, these feelings became calmed. I entered
again into the every-day scene of life, if not with interest, at least
with some degree of tranquillity.

---

97. Dante, *Inferno*, canto 23, lines 58ff.

VOLUME III.

CHAPTER I.

DAY after day, week after week, passed away on my return to Geneva; and I could not collect the courage to recommence my work. I feared the vengeance of the disappointed fiend, yet I was unable to overcome my repugnance to the task which was enjoined me. I found that I could not compose a female without again devoting several months to profound study and laborious disquisition.[98] I had heard of some discoveries having been made by an English philosopher, the knowledge of which was material to my success, and I sometimes thought of obtaining my father's consent to visit England for this purpose; but I clung to every pretence of delay, and could not resolve to interrupt my returning tranquillity. My health, which had hitherto declined, was now much restored; and my spirits, when unchecked by the memory of my unhappy promise, rose proportionably. My father saw this change with pleasure, and he turned his thoughts towards the best method of eradicating the remains of my melancholy, which every now and then would return by fits, and with a devouring blackness overcast the approaching sunshine. At these moments I took refuge in the most perfect solitude. I passed whole days on the lake alone in a little boat, watching the clouds, and listening to the rippling of the waves, silent and listless. But the fresh air and bright sun seldom failed to restore me to some degree of composure; and, on my return, I met the salutations of my friends with a readier smile and a more cheerful heart.

It was after my return from one of these rambles that my father, calling me aside, thus addressed me:—

"I am happy to remark, my dear son, that you have resumed your former pleasures, and seem to be returning to yourself. And yet you are still unhappy, and still avoid our society. For some time I was lost in conjecture as to the cause of this; but yesterday an idea struck me, and if it is well founded, I conjure[99] you to avow it. Reserve on such a point would be not only useless, but draw down treble misery on us all."

---

98. Research.
99. Implore.

I trembled violently at this exordium,[100] and my father continued—

"I confess, my son, that I have always looked forward to your marriage with your cousin as the tie of our domestic comfort, and the stay of my declining years. You were attached to each other from your earliest infancy; you studied together, and appeared, in dispositions and tastes, entirely suited to one another. But so blind is the experience of man, that what I conceived to be the best assistants to my plan may have entirely destroyed it. You, perhaps, regard her as your sister, without any wish that she might become your wife. Nay, you may have met with another whom you may love; and, considering yourself as bound in honour to your cousin, this struggle may occasion the poignant misery which you appear to feel."

III.5

"My dear father, re-assure yourself. I love my cousin tenderly and sincerely. I never saw any woman who excited, as Elizabeth does, my warmest admiration and affection. My future hopes and prospects are entirely bound up in the expectation of our union."

"The expression of your sentiments on this subject, my dear Victor, gives me more pleasure than I have for some time experienced. If you feel thus, we shall assuredly be happy, however present events may cast a gloom over us. But it is this gloom, which appears to have taken so strong a hold of your mind, that I wish to dissipate. Tell me, therefore, whether you object to an immediate solemnization of the marriage. We have been unfortunate, and recent events have drawn us from that every-day tranquillity befitting my years and infirmities. You are younger; yet I do not suppose, possessed as you are of a competent fortune, that an early marriage would at all interfere with any future plans of honour and utility that you may have formed. Do not suppose, however, that I wish to dictate happiness to you, or that a delay on your part would cause me any serious uneasiness. Interpret my words with candour, and answer me, I conjure you, with confidence and sincerity."

III.6

I listened to my father in silence, and remained for some time incapable of offering any reply. I revolved rapidly in my mind a multitude of thoughts, and endeavoured to arrive at some conclusion. Alas! to me the idea of an immediate union with my cousin was one of horror and dismay. I was bound by a solemn promise, which I had not yet fulfilled, and dared not break; or, if I did, what manifold miseries might not impend over me and my devoted family! Could I

III.7

---

100. The opening passage in a rhetorical speech.

enter into a festival with this deadly weight yet hanging round my neck, and bowing me to the ground.[101] I must perform my engagement, and let the monster depart with his mate, before I allowed myself to enjoy the delight of an union from which I expected peace.

I remembered also the necessity imposed upon me of either journeying to England, or entering into a long correspondence with those philosophers of that country, whose knowledge and discoveries were of indispensable use to me in my present undertaking. The latter method of obtaining the desired intelligence was dilatory and unsatisfactory: besides, any variation was agreeable to me, and I was III.8 delighted with the idea of spending a year or two in change of scene and variety of occupation, in absence from my family; during which period some event might happen which would restore me to them in peace and happiness: my promise might be fulfilled, and the monster have departed; or some accident might occur to destroy him, and put an end to my slavery for ever.

These feelings dictated my answer to my father. I expressed a wish to visit England; but, concealing the true reasons of this request, I clothed my desires under the guise of wishing to travel and see the world before I sat down for life within the walls of my native town.

I urged my entreaty with earnestness, and my father was easily induced to comply; for a more indulgent and less dictatorial parent III.9 did not exist upon earth. Our plan was soon arranged. I should travel to Strasburgh, where Clerval would join me. Some short time would be spent in the towns of Holland, and our principal stay would be in England. We should return by France; and it was agreed that the tour should occupy the space of two years.

My father pleased himself with the reflection, that my union with Elizabeth should take place immediately on my return to Geneva. "These two years," said he, "will pass swiftly, and it will be the last delay that will oppose itself to your happiness. And, indeed, I earnestly desire that period to arrive, when we shall all be united, and neither hopes or fears arise to disturb our domestic calm."

"I am content," I replied, "with your arrangement. By that time we III.10 shall both have become wiser, and I hope happier, than we at present are." I sighed; but my father kindly forbore to question me further concerning the cause of my dejection. He hoped that new scenes, and the amusement of travelling, would restore my tranquillity.

---

101. Cf. Coleridge, "The Rime of the Ancient Mariner" (1798): "Instead of the Cross the Albatross / About my neck was hung."

I now made arrangements for my journey; but one feeling haunted me, which filled me with fear and agitation. During my absence I should leave my friends unconscious of the existence of their enemy, and unprotected from his attacks, exasperated as he might be by my departure. But he had promised to follow me wherever I might go; and would he not accompany me to England? This imagination was dreadful in itself, but soothing, inasmuch as it supposed the safety of my friends. I was agonized with the idea of the possibility that the reverse of this might happen. But through the whole period during which I was the slave of my creature, I allowed myself to be governed by the impulses of the moment; and my present sensations strongly intimated that the fiend would follow me, and exempt my family from the danger of his machinations.

III.11

It was in the latter end of August that I departed, to pass two years of exile. Elizabeth approved of the reasons of my departure, and only regretted that she had not the same opportunities of enlarging her experience, and cultivating her understanding. She wept, however, as she bade me farewell, and entreated me to return happy and tranquil. "We all," said she, "depend upon you; and if you are miserable, what must be our feelings?"

III.12

I threw myself into the carriage that was to convey me away, hardly knowing whither I was going, and careless of what was passing around. I remembered only, and it was with a bitter anguish that I reflected on it, to order that my chemical instruments should be packed to go with me: for I resolved to fulfil my promise while abroad, and return, if possible, a free man. Filled with dreary imaginations, I passed through many beautiful and majestic scenes; but my eyes were fixed and unobserving. I could only think of the bourne of my travels, and the work which was to occupy me whilst they endured.

After some days spent in listless indolence, during which I traversed many leagues, I arrived at Strasburgh, where I waited two days for Clerval. He came. Alas, how great was the contrast between us! He was alive to every new scene; joyful when he saw the beauties of the setting sun, and more happy when he beheld it rise, and recommence a new day. He pointed out to me the shifting colours of the landscape, and the appearances of the sky. "This is what it is to live;" he cried, "now I enjoy existence! But you, my dear Frankenstein, wherefore are you desponding and sorrowful?" In truth, I was occupied by gloomy thoughts, and neither saw the descent of the evening star, nor the golden sun-rise reflected in the Rhine.—And you, my friend, would be far more amused with the journal of —Clerval,

III.13

who observed the scenery with an eye of feeling and delight, than to listen to my reflections. I, a miserable wretch, haunted by a curse that shut up every avenue to enjoyment.

We had agreed to descend the Rhine in a boat from Strasburgh to III.14
Rotterdam, whence we might take shipping for London. During this voyage, we passed by many willowy islands, and saw several beautiful towns. We staid a day at Manheim, and, on the fifth from our departure from Strasburgh, arrived at Mayence. The course of the Rhine below Mayence becomes much more picturesque. The river descends rapidly, and winds between hills, not high, but steep, and of beautiful forms. We saw many ruined castles standing on the edges of precipices, surrounded by black woods, high and inaccessible. This part of the Rhine, indeed, presents a singularly variegated landscape. In one spot you view rugged hills, ruined castles overlooking tremendous precipices, with the dark Rhine rushing beneath; and, on the sudden turn of a promontory, flourishing vineyards, with green sloping banks, and a meandering river, and populous towns, III.15
occupy the scene.

We travelled at the time of the vintage, and heard the song of the labourers, as we glided down the stream. Even I, depressed in mind, and my spirits continually agitated by gloomy feelings, even I was pleased. I lay at the bottom of the boat, and, as I gazed on the cloudless blue sky, I seemed to drink in a tranquillity to which I had long been a stranger. And if these were my sensations, who can describe those of Henry? He felt as if he had been transported to Fairy-land, and enjoyed a happiness seldom tasted by man. "I have seen," he said, "the most beautiful scenes of my own country; I have visited the lakes of Lucerne and Uri, where the snowy mountains descend almost perpendicularly to the water, casting black and impenetrable III.16
shades, which would cause a gloomy and mournful appearance, were it not for the most verdant islands that relieve the eye by their gay appearance; I have seen this lake agitated by a tempest, when the wind tore up whirlwinds of water, and gave you an idea of what the water-spout must be on the great ocean, and the waves dash with fury the base of the mountain, where the priest and his mistress were overwhelmed by an avalanche, and where their dying voices are still said to be heard amid the pauses of the nightly wind; I have seen the mountains of La Valais, and the Pays de Vaud: but this country, Victor, pleases me more than all those wonders. The mountains of Switzerland are more majestic and strange; but there is a charm in the banks of this divine river, that I never before saw equalled. Look III.17

at that castle which overhangs yon precipice; and that also on the island, almost concealed amongst the foliage of those lovely trees; and now that group of labourers coming from among their vines; and that village half-hid in the recess of the mountain. Oh, surely, the spirit that inhabits and guards this place has a soul more in harmony with man, than those who pile the glacier,[102] or retire to the inaccessible peaks of the mountains of our own country."

Clerval! beloved friend! even now it delights me to record your words, and to dwell on the praise of which you are so eminently deserving. He was a being formed in the "very poetry of nature[103]." His wild and enthusiastic imagination was chastened by the sensibility of his heart. His soul overflowed with ardent affections, and his friendship was of that devoted and wondrous nature that the worldly-minded teach us to look for only in the imagination. But even human sympathies were not sufficient to satisfy his eager mind. The scenery of external nature, which others regard only with admiration, he loved with ardour:

III.18

———————————"The sounding cataract
Haunted *him* like a passion: the tall rock,
The mountain, and the deep and gloomy wood,
Their colours and their forms, were then to him
An appetite; a feeling, and a love,
That had no need of a remoter charm,
By thought supplied, or any interest
Unborrowed from the eye[104]."

III.19

And where does he now exist? Is this gentle and lovely being lost for ever? Has this mind so replete with ideas, imaginations fanciful and magnificent, which formed a world, whose existence depended on the life of its creator; has this mind perished? Does it now only exist in my memory? No, it is not thus; your form so divinely wrought, and beaming with beauty, has decayed, but your spirit still visits and consoles your unhappy friend.

Pardon this gush of sorrow; these ineffectual words are but a slight tribute to the unexampled worth of Henry, but they soothe my heart, overflowing with the anguish which his remembrance creates. I will proceed with my tale.

---

102. Pile up, or heap up, the glaciers.
103. Leigh Hunt's "Rimini." [MWS's note, referring to *The Story of Rimini* (1816)]
104. Wordsworth's "Tintern Abbey." [MWS's note]

Beyond Cologne we descended to the plains of Holland; and we resolved to post[105] the remainder of our way; for the wind was contrary, and the stream of the river was too gentle to aid us.

Our journey here lost the interest arising from beautiful scenery;   III.20
but we arrived in a few days at Rotterdam, whence we proceeded by sea to England. It was on a clear morning, in the latter days of December,[106] that I first saw the white cliffs of Britain. The banks of the Thames presented a new scene; they were flat, but fertile, and almost every town was marked by the remembrance of some story. We saw Tilbury Fort, and remembered the Spanish armada; Gravesend, Woolwich, and Greenwich, places which I had heard of even in my country.

At length we saw the numerous steeples of London, St. Paul's towering above all, and the Tower famed in English history.

---

105. To travel with relays of horses.
106. But see below, p. 127: "We had arrived in England at the beginning of October . . ."

III.21

CHAPTER II.

LONDON was our present point of rest; we determined to remain several months in this wonderful and celebrated city. Clerval desired the intercourse of the men of genius and talent who flourished at this time; but this was with me a secondary object; I was principally occupied with the means of obtaining the information necessary for the completion of my promise, and quickly availed myself of the letters of introduction that I had brought with me, addressed to the most distinguished natural philosophers.

III.22   If this journey had taken place during my days of study and happiness, it would have afforded me inexpressible pleasure. But a blight had come over my existence, and I only visited these people for the sake of the information they might give me on the subject in which my interest was so terribly profound. Company was irksome to me; when alone, I could fill my mind with the sights of heaven and earth; the voice of Henry soothed me, and I could thus cheat myself into a transitory peace. But busy uninteresting joyous faces brought back despair to my heart. I saw an insurmountable barrier placed between me and my fellow-men; this barrier was sealed with the blood of William and Justine; and to reflect on the events connected with those names filled my soul with anguish.

But in Clerval I saw the image of my former self; he was inquisi-
III.23   tive, and anxious to gain experience and instruction. The difference of manners which he observed was to him an inexhaustible source of instruction and amusement. He was for ever busy; and the only check to his enjoyments was my sorrowful and dejected mien. I tried to conceal this as much as possible, that I might not debar him from the pleasures natural to one who was entering on a new scene of life, undisturbed by any care or bitter recollection. I often refused to accompany him, alleging another engagement, that I might remain alone. I now also began to collect the materials necessary for my new creation, and this was to me like the torture of single drops of water continually falling on the head. Every thought that was devoted to it was an extreme anguish, and every word that I spoke in allusion to it
III.24   caused my lips to quiver, and my heart to palpitate.

After passing some months in London, we received a letter from a person in Scotland, who had formerly been our visitor at Geneva. He mentioned the beauties of his native country, and asked us if those were not sufficient allurements to induce us to prolong our journey as far north as Perth, where he resided. Clerval eagerly desired to accept this invitation; and I, although I abhorred society, wished to view again mountains and streams, and all the wondrous works with which Nature adorns her chosen dwelling-places.

We had arrived in England at the beginning of October, and it was now February. We accordingly determined to commence our journey towards the north at the expiration of another month. In this expedition we did not intend to follow the great road to Edinburgh,   III.25
but to visit Windsor, Oxford, Matlock, and the Cumberland lakes, resolving to arrive at the completion of this tour about the end of July. I packed my chemical instruments, and the materials I had collected, resolving to finish my labours in some obscure nook in the northern highlands of Scotland.

We quitted London on the 27th of March, and remained a few days at Windsor, rambling in its beautiful forest. This was a new scene to us mountaineers; the majestic oaks, the quantity of game, and the herds of stately deer, were all novelties to us.

From thence we proceeded to Oxford. As we entered this city, our minds were filled with the remembrance of the events that had been transacted there more than a century and a half before. It was   III.26
here that Charles I. had collected his forces. This city had remained faithful to him, after the whole nation had forsaken his cause to join the standard of parliament and liberty. The memory of that unfortunate king, and his companions, the amiable Falkland, the insolent Gower,[107] his queen, and son, gave a peculiar interest to every part of the city, which they might be supposed to have inhabited. The spirit of elder days found a dwelling here, and we delighted to trace its footsteps. If these feelings had not found an imaginary gratification, the appearance of the city had yet in itself sufficient beauty to obtain our admiration. The colleges are ancient and picturesque; the streets are almost magnificent; and the lovely Isis,[108] which flows beside it through meadows of exquisite verdure, is spread forth into a placid   III.27
expanse of waters, which reflects its majestic assemblage of towers, and spires, and domes, embosomed among aged trees.

I enjoyed this scene; and yet my enjoyment was embittered both by the memory of the past, and the anticipation of the future. I was

---

107. Falkland was a much-admired royalist killed in the Civil War (and a crucial character in Godwin's *Caleb Williams* is named after him). "Gower" is corrected to Goring in 1831—a royalist with a dishonorable reputation.
108. The Thames as it flows through Oxford is called the Isis.

formed for peaceful happiness. During my youthful days discontent never visited my mind; and if I was ever overcome by *ennui*,[109] the sight of what is beautiful in nature, or the study of what is excellent and sublime in the productions of man, could always interest my heart, and communicate elasticity to my spirits. But I am a blasted tree; the bolt[110] has entered my soul; and I felt then that I should survive to exhibit, what I shall soon cease to be—a miserable spectacle of wrecked humanity, pitiable to others, and abhorrent to myself.

III.28   We passed a considerable period at Oxford, rambling among its environs, and endeavouring to identify every spot which might relate to the most animating epoch of English history. Our little voyages of discovery were often prolonged by the successive objects that presented themselves. We visited the tomb of the illustrious Hampden, and the field on which that patriot fell.[111] For a moment my soul was elevated from its debasing and miserable fears to contemplate the divine ideas of liberty and self-sacrifice, of which these sights were the monuments and the remembrancers. For an instant I dared to shake off my chains, and look around me with a free and lofty spirit; but the iron had eaten into my flesh, and I sank again, trembling and hopeless, into my miserable self.

III.29   We left Oxford with regret, and proceeded to Matlock, which was our next place of rest. The country in the neighbourhood of this village resembled, to a greater degree, the scenery of Switzerland; but every thing is on a lower scale, and the green hills want the crown of distant white Alps, which always attend on the piny mountains of my native country. We visited the wondrous cave, and the little cabinets[112] of natural history, where the curiosities are disposed in the same manner as in the collections at Servox and Chamounix. The latter name made me tremble, when pronounced by Henry; and I hastened to quit Matlock, with which that terrible scene was thus associated.

From Derby still journeying northward, we passed two months in Cumberland and Westmoreland. I could now almost fancy myself among the Swiss mountains. The little patches of snow which yet lingered on the northern sides of the mountains, the lakes, and the dashing of the rocky streams, were all familiar and dear sights to

III.30

---

109. Men were supposed to be particularly susceptible to *ennui* or depression, women to hysteria.

110. I.e., the bolt of lightning.

111. Hampden had played a leading role in the opposition to Charles I.

112. A room for holding a display, a museum.

me. Here also we made some acquaintances, who almost contrived to cheat me into happiness. The delight of Clerval was proportionably greater than mine; his mind expanded in the company of men of talent, and he found in his own nature greater capacities and resources than he could have imagined himself to have possessed while he associated with his inferiors. "I could pass my life here," said he to me; "and among these mountains I should scarcely regret Switzerland and the Rhine."

But he found that a traveller's life is one that includes much pain amidst its enjoyments. His feelings are for ever on the stretch; and when he begins to sink into repose, he finds himself obliged to quit   III.31 that on which he rests in pleasure for something new, which again engages his attention, and which also he forsakes for other novelties.

We had scarcely visited the various lakes of Cumberland and Westmoreland, and conceived an affection for some of the inhabitants, when the period of our appointment with our Scotch friend approached, and we left them to travel on. For my own part I was not sorry. I had now neglected my promise for some time, and I feared the effects of the dæmon's disappointment. He might remain in Switzerland, and wreak his vengeance on my relatives. This idea pursued me, and tormented me at every moment from which I might otherwise have snatched repose and peace. I waited for my letters with feverish impatience: if they were delayed, I was miserable, and overcome by a   III.32 thousand fears; and when they arrived, and I saw the superscription of Elizabeth or my father, I hardly dared to read and ascertain my fate. Sometimes I thought that the fiend followed me, and might expedite my remissness by murdering my companion. When these thoughts possessed me, I would not quit Henry for a moment, but followed him as his shadow, to protect him from the fancied rage of his destroyer. I felt as if I had committed some great crime, the consciousness of which haunted me. I was guiltless, but I had indeed drawn down a horrible curse upon my head, as mortal as that of crime.

I visited Edinburgh with languid eyes and mind; and yet that city might have interested the most unfortunate being. Clerval did not like it so well as Oxford; for the antiquity of the latter city was more   III.33 pleasing to him. But the beauty and regularity of the new town of Edinburgh, its romantic castle, and its environs, the most delightful in the world, Arthur's Seat, St. Bernard's Well, and the Pentland Hills, compensated him for the change, and filled him with cheerfulness and admiration. But I was impatient to arrive at the termination of my journey.

We left Edinburgh in a week, passing through Coupar, St. Andrews, and along the banks of the Tay, to Perth, where our friend expected us. But I was in no mood to laugh and talk with strangers, or enter into their feelings or plans with the good humour expected from a guest; and accordingly I told Clerval that I wished to make the

III.34 tour of Scotland alone. "Do you," said I, "enjoy yourself, and let this be our rendezvous. I may be absent a month or two; but do not interfere with my motions, I entreat you: leave me to peace and solitude for a short time; and when I return, I hope it will be with a lighter heart, more congenial to your own temper."

Henry wished to dissuade me; but, seeing me bent on this plan, ceased to remonstrate. He entreated me to write often. "I had rather be with you," he said, "in your solitary rambles, than with these Scotch people, whom I do not know: hasten then, my dear friend, to return, that I may again feel myself somewhat at home, which I cannot do in your absence."

Having parted from my friend, I determined to visit some remote spot of Scotland, and finish my work in solitude. I did not doubt but

III.35 that the monster followed me, and would discover himself to me when I should have finished, that he might receive his companion.

With this resolution I traversed the northern highlands, and fixed on one of the remotest of the Orkneys as the scene [of my] labours. It was a place fitted for such a work, being hardly more than a rock, whose high sides were continually beaten upon by the waves. The soil was barren, scarcely affording pasture for a few miserable cows, and oatmeal for its inhabitants, which consisted of five persons, whose gaunt and scraggy limbs gave tokens of their miserable fare. Vegetables and bread, when they indulged in such luxuries, and even fresh water, was to be procured from the main land, which was about five miles distant.

III.36 On the whole island there were but three miserable huts, and one of these was vacant when I arrived. This I hired. It contained but two rooms, and these exhibited all the squalidness of the most miserable penury. The thatch had fallen in, the walls were unplastered, and the door was off its hinges. I ordered it to be repaired, bought some furniture, and took possession; an incident which would, doubtless, have occasioned some surprise, had not all the senses of the cottagers been benumbed by want and squalid poverty. As it was, I lived ungazed at and unmolested, hardly thanked for the pittance of food and clothes which I gave; so much does suffering blunt even the coarsest sensations of men.

In this retreat I devoted the morning to labour; but in the evening, when the weather permitted, I walked on the stony beach of the sea, to listen to the waves as they roared, and dashed at my feet. It was III.37 a monotonous, yet ever-changing scene. I thought of Switzerland; it was far different from this desolate and appalling landscape. Its hills are covered with vines, and its cottages are scattered thickly in the plains. Its fair lakes reflect a blue and gentle sky; and, when troubled by the winds, their tumult is but as the play of a lively infant, when compared to the roarings of the giant ocean.

In this manner I distributed my occupations when I first arrived; but, as I proceeded in my labour, it became every day more horrible and irksome to me. Sometimes I could not prevail on myself to enter my laboratory for several days; and at other times I toiled day and night in order to complete my work. It was indeed a filthy process in which I was engaged. During my first experiment, a kind of enthu- III.38 siastic frenzy had blinded me to the horror of my employment; my mind was intently fixed on the sequel of my labour, and my eyes were shut to the horror of my proceedings. But now I went to it in cold blood, and my heart often sickened at the work of my hands.

Thus situated, employed in the most detestable occupation, immersed in a solitude where nothing could for an instant call my attention from the actual scene in which I was engaged, my spirits became unequal; I grew restless and nervous. Every moment I feared to meet my persecutor. Sometimes I sat with my eyes fixed on the ground, fearing to raise them lest they should encounter the object which I so much dreaded to behold. I feared to wander from the sight of my fellow-creatures, lest when alone he should come to claim his III.39 companion.

In the mean time I worked on, and my labour was already considerably advanced. I looked towards its completion with a tremulous and eager hope, which I dared not trust myself to question, but which was intermixed with obscure forebodings of evil, that made my heart sicken in my bosom.

CHAPTER III.

I SAT one evening in my laboratory; the sun had set, and the moon
was just rising from the sea; I had not sufficient light for my employment, and I remained idle, in a pause of consideration of whether I
should leave my labour for the night, or hasten its conclusion by an
unremitting attention to it. As I sat, a train of reflection occurred to
me, which led me to consider the effects of what I was now doing.
Three years before I was engaged in the same manner, and had created a fiend whose unparalleled barbarity had desolated my heart,
and filled it for ever with the bitterest remorse. I was now about to
form another being, of whose dispositions I was alike ignorant; she
might become ten thousand times more malignant than her mate,
and delight, for its own sake, in murder and wretchedness. He had
sworn to quit the neighbourhood of man, and hide himself in deserts; but she had not; and she, who in all probability was to become a
thinking and reasoning animal, might refuse to comply with a compact made before her creation. They might even hate each other; the
creature who already lived loathed his own deformity, and might he
not conceive a greater abhorence for it when it came before his eyes
in the female form? She also might turn with disgust from him to the
superior beauty of man; she might quit him, and he be again alone,
exasperated by the fresh provocation of being deserted by one of his
own species.

Even if they were to leave Europe, and inhabit the deserts of the
new world, yet one of the first results of those sympathies for which
the dæmon thirsted would be children, and a race of devils would be
propagated upon the earth, who might make the very existence of the
species of man a condition precarious and full of terror. Had I a right,
for my own benefit, to inflict this curse upon everlasting generations?
I had before been moved by the sophisms of the being I had created;
I had been struck senseless by his fiendish threats: but now, for the
first time, the wickedness of my promise burst upon me; I shuddered
to think that future ages might curse me as their pest, whose selfishness had not hesitated to buy its own peace at the price perhaps of
the existence of the whole human race.

I trembled, and my heart failed within me; when, on looking up, I
saw, by the light of the moon, the dæmon at the casement. A ghastly
grin wrinkled his lips as he gazed on me, where I sat fulfilling the task
which he had allotted to me. Yes, he had followed me in my travels;

he had loitered in forests, hid himself in caves, or taken refuge in wide and desert heaths; and he now came to mark my progress, and claim the fulfilment of my promise.

As I looked on him, his countenance expressed the utmost extent of malice and treachery. I thought with a sensation of madness on my promise of creating another like to him, and, trembling with passion, tore to pieces the thing on which I was engaged. The wretch saw me destroy the creature on whose future existence he depended for happi-   III.44
ness, and, with a howl of devilish despair and revenge, withdrew.

I left the room, and, locking the door, made a solemn vow in my own heart never to resume my labours; and then, with trembling steps, I sought my own apartment. I was alone; none were near me to dissipate the gloom, and relieve me from the sickening oppression of the most terrible reveries.

Several hours past, and I remained near my window gazing on the sea; it was almost motionless, for the winds were hushed, and all nature reposed under the eye of the quiet moon. A few fishing vessels alone specked the water, and now and then the gentle breeze wafted the sound of voices, as the fishermen called to one another. I felt the silence, although I was hardly conscious of its extreme profundity, until my ear was suddenly arrested by the paddling of oars near the   III.45
shore, and a person landed close to my house.

In a few minutes after, I heard the creaking of my door, as if some one endeavoured to open it softly. I trembled from head to foot; I felt a presentiment of who it was, and wished to rouse one of the peasants who dwelt in a cottage not far from mine; but I was overcome by the sensation of helplessness, so often felt in frightful dreams, when you in vain endeavour to fly from an impending danger, and was rooted to the spot.

Presently I heard the sound of footsteps along the passage; the door opened, and the wretch whom I dreaded appeared. Shutting the door, he approached me, and said, in a smothered voice—

"You have destroyed the work which you began; what is it that you   III.46
intend? Do you dare to break your promise? I have endured toil and misery: I left Switzerland with you; I crept along the shores of the Rhine, among its willow islands, and over the summits of its hills. I have dwelt many months in the heaths of England, and among the deserts of Scotland. I have endured incalculable fatigue, and cold, and hunger; do you dare destroy my hopes?"

"Begone! I do break my promise; never will I create another like yourself, equal in deformity and wickedness."

"Slave, I before reasoned with you, but you have proved yourself unworthy of my condescension. Remember that I have power; you believe yourself miserable, but I can make you so wretched that the light of day will be hateful to you. You are my creator, but I am your master;—obey!"

III.47

"The hour of my weakness is past, and the period[113] of your power is arrived. Your threats cannot move me to do an act of wickedness; but they confirm me in a resolution of not creating you a companion in vice. Shall I, in cool blood, set loose upon the earth a dæmon, whose delight is in death and wretchedness. Begone! I am firm, and your words will only exasperate my rage."

The monster saw my determination in my face, and gnashed his teeth in the impotence of anger. "Shall each man," cried he, "find a wife for his bosom, and each beast have his mate, and I be alone? I had feelings of affection, and they were requited by detestation and scorn. Man, you may hate; but beware! Your hours will pass in dread and misery, and soon the bolt will fall which must ravish from you your happiness for ever. Are you to be happy, while I grovel in the intensity of my wretchedness? You can blast my other passions; but revenge remains—revenge, henceforth dearer than light or food! I may die; but first you, my tyrant and tormentor, shall curse the sun that gazes on your misery. Beware; for I am fearless, and therefore powerful. I will watch with the wiliness of a snake, that I may sting with its venom. Man, you shall repent of the injuries you inflict."

III.48

"Devil, cease; and do not poison the air with these sounds of malice. I have declared my resolution to you, and I am no coward to bend beneath words. Leave me; I am inexorable."

"It is well. I go; but remember, I shall be with you on your wedding-night."

III.49

I started forward, and exclaimed, "Villain! before you sign my death-warrant, be sure that you are yourself safe."

I would have seized him; but he eluded me, and quitted the house with precipitation: in a few moments I saw him in his boat, which shot across the waters with an arrowy swiftness, and was soon lost amidst the waves.

All was again silent; but his words rung in my ears. I burned with rage to pursue the murderer of my peace, and precipitate him into the ocean. I walked up and down my room hastily and perturbed,

---

113. End point.

while my imagination conjured up a thousand images to torment and sting me. Why had I not followed him, and closed with him in mortal strife? But I had suffered him to depart, and he had directed his course towards the main land. I shuddered to think who might be the next victim sacrificed to his insatiate revenge. And then I thought again of his words—"*I will be with you on your wedding-night.*" That then was the period fixed for the fulfilment of my destiny. In that hour I should die, and at once satisfy and extinguish his malice. The prospect did not move me to fear; yet when I thought of my beloved Elizabeth,—of her tears and endless sorrow, when she should find her lover so barbarously snatched from her,—tears, the first I had shed for many months, streamed from my eyes, and I resolved not to fall before my enemy without a bitter struggle. III.50

The night passed away, and the sun rose from the ocean; my feelings became calmer, if it may be called calmness, when the violence of rage sinks into the depths of despair. I left the house, the horrid scene of the last night's contention, and walked on the beach of the sea, which I almost regarded as an insuperable barrier between me and my fellow creatures; nay, a wish that such should prove the fact stole across me. I desired that I might pass my life on that barren rock, wearily it is true, but uninterrupted by any sudden shock of misery. If I returned, it was to be sacrificed, or to see those whom I most loved die under the grasp of a dæmon whom I had myself created. III.51

I walked about the isle like a restless spectre, separated from all it loved, and miserable in the separation. When it became noon, and the sun rose higher, I lay down on the grass, and was overpowered by a deep sleep. I had been awake the whole of the preceding night, my nerves were agitated, and my eyes inflamed by watching and misery. The sleep into which I now sunk refreshed me; and when I awoke, I again felt as if I belonged to a race of human beings like myself, and I began to reflect upon what had passed with greater composure; yet still the words of the fiend rung in my ears like a death-knell, they appeared like a dream, yet distinct and oppressive as a reality. III.52

The sun had far descended, and I still sat on the shore, satisfying my appetite, which had become ravenous, with an oaten cake, when I saw a fishing boat land close to me, and one of the men brought me a packet; it contained letters from Geneva, and one from Clerval, entreating me to join him. He said that nearly a year had elapsed since we had quitted Switzerland, and France was yet unvisited. He entreated me, therefore, to leave my solitary isle, and meet him at III.53

Perth, in a week from that time, when we might arrange the plan of our future proceedings. This letter in a degree recalled me to life, and I determined to quit my island at the expiration of two days.

Yet, before I departed, there was a task to perform, on which I shuddered to reflect: I must pack my chemical instruments; and for that purpose I must enter the room which had been the scene of my odious work, and I must handle those utensils, the sight of which was sickening to me. The next morning, at day-break, I summoned suffi-cient courage, and unlocked the door of my laboratory. The remains of the half-finished creature, whom I had destroyed, lay scattered on III.54   the floor, and I almost felt as if I had mangled the living flesh of a hu-man being. I paused to collect myself, and then entered the chamber. With trembling hand I conveyed the instruments out of the room; but I reflected that I ought not to leave the relics of my work to excite the horror and suspicion of the peasants, and I accordingly put them into a basket, with a great quantity of stones, and laying them up, determined to throw them into the sea that very night; and in the mean time I sat upon the beach, employed in cleaning and arranging my chemical apparatus.

Nothing could be more complete than the alteration that had taken place in my feelings since the night of the appearance of the dæmon. I had before regarded my promise with a gloomy despair, as a thing that, with whatever consequences, must be fulfilled; but I III.55   now felt as if a film had been taken from before my eyes, and that I, for the first time, saw clearly. The idea of renewing my labours did not for one instant occur to me; the threat I had heard weighed on my thoughts, but I did not reflect that a voluntary act of mine could avert it. I had resolved in my own mind, that to create another like the fiend I had first made would be an act of the basest and most atrocious selfishness; and I banished from my mind every thought that could lead to a different conclusion.

Between two and three in the morning the moon rose; and I then, putting my basket aboard a little skiff, sailed out about four miles from the shore. The scene was perfectly solitary: a few boats were returning towards land, but I sailed away from them. I felt as if I was about the commission of a dreadful crime, and avoided with shud-III.56   dering anxiety any encounter with my fellow-creatures. At one time the moon, which had before been clear, was suddenly overspread by a thick cloud, and I took advantage of the moment of darkness, and cast my basket into the sea; I listened to the gurgling sound as it sunk, and then sailed away from the spot. The sky became clouded;

but the air was pure, although chilled by the north-east breeze that was then rising. But it refreshed me, and filled me with such agreeable sensations, that I resolved to prolong my stay on the water, and fixing the rudder in a direct position, stretched myself at the bottom of the boat. Clouds hid the moon, every thing was obscure, and I heard only the sound of the boat, as its keel cut through the waves; the murmur lulled me, and in a short time I slept soundly.

I do not know how long I remained in this situation, but when I III.57 awoke I found that the sun had already mounted considerably. The wind was high, and the waves continually threatened the safety of my little skiff. I found that the wind was north-east, and must have driven me far from the coast from which I had embarked. I endeavoured to change my course, but quickly found that if I again made the attempt the boat would be instantly filled with water. Thus situated, my only resource was to drive before the wind. I confess that I felt a few sensations of terror. I had no compass with me, and was so little acquainted with the geography of this part of the world that the sun was of little benefit to me. I might be driven into the wide Atlantic, and feel all the tortures of starvation, or be swallowed up in the immeasurable waters that roared and buffeted around me. I had al- III.58 ready been out many hours, and felt the torment of a burning thirst, a prelude to my other sufferings. I looked on the heavens, which were covered by clouds that flew before the wind only to be replaced by others: I looked upon the sea, it was to be my grave. "Fiend," I exclaimed, "your task is already fulfilled!" I thought of Elizabeth, of my father, and of Clerval; and sunk into a reverie, so despairing and frightful, that even now, when the scene is on the point of closing before me for ever, I shudder to reflect on it.

Some hours passed thus; but by degrees, as the sun declined towards the horizon, the wind died away into a gentle breeze, and the sea became free from breakers. But these gave place to a heavy swell; I felt sick, and hardly able to hold the rudder, when suddenly I saw a III.59 line of high land towards the south.

Almost spent, as I was, by fatigue, and the dreadful suspense I endured for several hours, this sudden certainty of life rushed like a flood of warm joy to my heart, and tears gushed from my eyes.

How mutable are our feelings, and how strange is that clinging love we have of life even in the excess of misery! I constructed another sail with a part of my dress, and eagerly steered my course towards the land. It had a wild and rocky appearance; but as I approached nearer, I easily perceived the traces of cultivation. I saw vessels near the shore, and found myself suddenly transported back to the neighbourhood of civilized man. I eagerly traced the windings of the land, and hailed a steeple which I at length saw issuing from behind a small promontory. As I was in a state of extreme debility, I resolved to sail directly towards the town as a place where I could most easily procure nourishment. Fortunately I had money with me. As I turned the promontory, I perceived a small neat town and a good harbour, which I entered, my heart bounding with joy at my unexpected escape.

As I was occupied in fixing the boat and arranging the sails, several people crowded towards the spot. They seemed very much surprised at my appearance; but, instead of offering me any assistance, whispered together with gestures that at any other time might have produced in me a slight sensation of alarm. As it was, I merely remarked that they spoke English; and I therefore addressed them in that language: "My good friends," said I, "will you be so kind as to tell me the name of this town, and inform me where I am?"

"You will know that soon enough," replied a man with a gruff voice. "May be you are come to a place that will not prove much to your taste; but you will not be consulted as to your quarters, I promise you."

I was exceedingly surprised on receiving so rude an answer from a stranger; and I was also disconcerted on perceiving the frowning and angry countenances of his companions. "Why do you answer me so roughly?" I replied: "surely it is not the custom of Englishmen to receive strangers so inhospitably."

"I do not know," said the man, "what the custom of the English may be; but it is the custom of the Irish to hate villains."

While this strange dialogue continued, I perceived the crowd rapidly increase. Their faces expressed a mixture of curiosity and anger, which annoyed, and in some degree alarmed me. I inquired the way to the inn; but no one replied. I then moved forward, and a murmuring sound arose from the crowd as they followed and surrounded me; when an ill-looking man approaching, tapped me on the shoulder, and said, "Come, Sir, you must follow me to Mr. Kirwin's, to give an account of yourself."

"Who is Mr. Kirwin? Why am I to give an account of myself? Is not this a free country?"

"Aye, Sir, free enough for honest folks. Mr. Kirwin is a magistrate; and you are to give an account of the death of a gentleman who was found murdered here last night."

III.60

III.61

III.62

This answer startled me; but I presently recovered myself. I was III.63 innocent; that could easily be proved: accordingly I followed my conductor in silence, and was led to one of the best houses in the town. I was ready to sink from fatigue and hunger; but, being surrounded by a crowd, I thought it politic to rouse all my strength, that no physical debility might be construed into apprehension or conscious guilt. Little did I then expect the calamity that was in a few moments to overwhelm me, and extinguish in horror and despair all fear of ignominy or death.

I must pause here; for it requires all my fortitude to recall the memory of the frightful events which I am about to relate, in proper detail, to my recollection.

CHAPTER IV.

III.64

I WAS soon introduced into the presence of the magistrate, an old benevolent man, with calm and mild manners. He looked upon me, however, with some degree of severity; and then, turning towards my conductors, he asked who appeared as witnesses on this occasion.

About half a dozen men came forward; and one being selected by the magistrate, he deposed, that he had been out fishing the night before with his son and brother-in-law, Daniel Nugent, when, about ten o'clock, they observed a strong northerly blast rising, and they accordingly put in for port. It was a very dark night, as the moon had not yet risen; they did not land at the harbour, but, as they had been accustomed, at a creek about two miles below. He walked on first, carrying a part of the fishing tackle, and his companions followed him at some distance. As he was proceeding along the sands, he struck his foot against something, and fell all his length on the ground. His companions came up to assist him; and, by the light of their lantern, they found that he had fallen on the body of a man, who was to all appearance dead. Their first supposition was, that it was the corpse of some person who had been drowned, and was thrown on shore by the waves; but, upon examination, they found that the clothes were not wet, and even that the body was not then cold. They instantly carried it to the cottage of an old woman near the spot, and endeavoured, but in vain, to restore it to life. He appeared to be a handsome young man, about five and twenty years of age. He had apparently been strangled; for there was no sign of any violence, except the black mark of fingers on his neck.

The first part of this deposition did not in the least interest me; but when the mark of the fingers was mentioned, I remembered the murder of my brother, and felt myself extremely agitated; my limbs trembled, and a mist came over my eyes, which obliged me to lean on a chair for support. The magistrate observed me with a keen eye, and of course drew an unfavourable augury from my manner.

The son confirmed his father's account: but when Daniel Nugent was called, he swore positively that, just before the fall of his companion, he saw a boat, with a single man in it, at a short distance from the shore; and, as far as he could judge by the light of a few stars, it was the same boat in which I had just landed.

A woman deposed, that she lived near the beach, and was standing at the door of her cottage, waiting for the return of the fishermen,

III.65

III.66

III.67

about an hour before she heard of the discovery of the body, when she saw a boat, with only one man in it, push off from that part of the shore where the corpse was afterwards found.

Another woman confirmed the account of the fishermen having brought the body into her house; it was not cold. They put it into a bed, and rubbed it; and Daniel went to the town for an apothecary, but life was quite gone. III.68

Several other men were examined concerning my landing; and they agreed, that, with the strong north wind that had arisen during the night, it was very probable that I had beaten about for many hours, and had been obliged to return nearly to the same spot from which I had departed. Besides, they observed that it appeared that I had brought the body from another place, and it was likely, that as I did not appear to know the shore, I might have put into the harbour ignorant of the distance of the town of ———— from the place where I had deposited the corpse.

Mr. Kirwin, on hearing this evidence, desired that I should be taken into the room where the body lay for interment, that it might be observed what effect the sight of it would produce upon me. This III.69 idea was probably suggested by the extreme agitation I had exhibited when the mode of the murder had been described. I was accordingly conducted, by the magistrate and several other persons, to the inn. I could not help being struck by the strange coincidences that had taken place during this eventful night; but, knowing that I had been conversing with several persons in the island I had inhabited about the time that the body had been found, I was perfectly tranquil as to the consequences of the affair.

I entered the room where the corpse lay, and was led up to the coffin. How can I describe my sensations on beholding it? I feel yet parched with horror, nor can I reflect on that terrible moment without shuddering and agony, that faintly reminds me of the anguish III.70 of the recognition. The trial, the presence of the magistrate and witnesses, passed like a dream from my memory, when I saw the lifeless form of Henry Clerval stretched before me. I gasped for breath; and, throwing myself on the body, I exclaimed, "Have my murderous machinations deprived you also, my dearest Henry, of life? Two I have already destroyed; other victims await their destiny: but you, Clerval, my friend, my benefactor"——

The human frame could no longer support the agonizing suffering that I endured, and I was carried out of the room in strong convulsions.

A fever succeeded to this. I lay for two months on the point of death: my ravings, as I afterwards heard, were frightful; I called myself the murderer of William, of Justine, and of Clerval. Sometimes I entreated my attendants to assist me in the destruction of the fiend by whom I was tormented; and, at others, I felt the fingers of the monster already grasping my neck, and screamed aloud with agony and terror. Fortunately, as I spoke my native language, Mr. Kirwin alone understood me; but my gestures and bitter cries were sufficient to affright the other witnesses.

III.71

Why did I not die? More miserable than man ever was before, why did I not sink into forgetfulness and rest? Death snatches away many blooming children, the only hopes of their doating parents: how many brides and youthful lovers have been one day in the bloom of health and hope, and the next a prey for worms and the decay of the tomb! Of what materials was I made, that I could thus resist so many shocks, which, like the turning of the wheel, continually renewed the torture.

III.72

But I was doomed to live; and, in two months, found myself as awaking from a dream, in a prison, stretched on a wretched bed, surrounded by gaolers, turnkeys, bolts, and all the miserable apparatus of a dungeon. It was morning, I remember, when I thus awoke to understanding: I had forgotten the particulars of what had happened, and only felt as if some great misfortune had suddenly overwhelmed me; but when I looked around, and saw the barred windows, and the squalidness of the room in which I was, all flashed across my memory, and I groaned bitterly.

This sound disturbed an old woman who was sleeping in a chair beside me. She was a hired nurse, the wife of one of the turnkeys, and her countenance expressed all those bad qualities which often characterize that class. The lines of her face were hard and rude, like that of persons accustomed to see without sympathizing in sights of misery. Her tone expressed her entire indifference; she addressed me in English, and the voice struck me as one that I had heard during my sufferings:

III.73

"Are you better now, Sir?" said she.

I replied in the same language, with a feeble voice, "I believe I am; but if it be all true, if indeed I did not dream, I am sorry that I am still alive to feel this misery and horror."

"For that matter," replied the old woman, "if you mean about the gentleman you murdered, I believe that it were better for you if you were dead, for I fancy it will go hard with you; but you will be hung

III.74

when the next sessions come on. However, that's none of my business, I am sent to nurse you, and get you well; I do my duty with a safe conscience, it were well if every body did the same."

I turned with loathing from the woman who could utter so unfeeling a speech to a person just saved, on the very edge of death; but I felt languid, and unable to reflect on all that had passed. The whole series of my life appeared to me as a dream; I sometimes doubted if indeed it were all true, for it never presented itself to my mind with the force of reality.

As the images that floated before me became more distinct, I grew feverish; a darkness pressed around me; no one was near me who soothed me with the gentle voice of love; no dear hand supported me. III.75 The physician came and prescribed medicines, and the old woman prepared them for me; but utter carelessness was visible in the first, and the expression of brutality was strongly marked in the visage of the second. Who could be interested in the fate of a murderer, but the hangman who would gain his fee?

These were my first reflections; but I soon learned that Mr. Kirwin had shewn me extreme kindness. He had caused the best room in the prison to be prepared for me (wretched indeed was the best); and it was he who had provided a physician and a nurse. It is true, he seldom came to see me; for, although he ardently desired to relieve the sufferings of every human creature, he did not wish to be present at the agonies and miserable ravings of a murderer. He came, therefore, sometimes to see that I was not neglected; but his visits were III.76 short, and at long intervals.

One day, when I was gradually recovering, I was seated in a chair, my eyes half open, and my cheeks livid like those in death, I was overcome by gloom and misery, and often reflected I had better seek death than remain miserably pent up only to be let loose in a world replete with wretchedness. At one time I considered whether I should not declare myself guilty, and suffer the penalty of the law, less innocent than poor Justine had been. Such were my thoughts, when the door of my apartment was opened, and Mr. Kirwin entered. His countenance expressed sympathy and compassion; he drew a chair close to mine, and addressed me in French—

"I fear that this place is very shocking to you; can I do any thing to III.77 make you more comfortable?"

"I thank you; but all that you mention is nothing to me: on the whole earth there is no comfort which I am capable of receiving."

"I know that the sympathy of a stranger can be but of little relief to one borne down as you are by so strange a misfortune. But you will, I hope, soon quit this melancholy abode; for, doubtless, evidence can easily be brought to free you from the criminal charge."

"That is my least concern: I am, by a course of strange events, become the most miserable of mortals. Persecuted and tortured as I am and have been, can death be any evil to me?"

III.78 "Nothing indeed could be more unfortunate and agonizing than the strange chances that have lately occurred. You were thrown, by some surprising accident, on this shore, renowned for its hospitality: seized immediately, and charged with murder. The first sight that was presented to your eyes was the body of your friend, murdered in so unaccountable a manner, and placed, as it were, by some fiend across your path."

As Mr. Kirwin said this, notwithstanding the agitation I endured on this retrospect of my sufferings, I also felt considerable surprise at the knowledge he seemed to possess concerning me. I suppose some astonishment was exhibited in my countenance; for Mr. Kirwin hastened to say—

"It was not until a day or two after your illness that I thought of examining your dress, that I might discover some trace by which I could
III.79 send to your relations an account of your misfortune and illness. I found several letters, and, among others, one which I discovered from its commencement to be from your father. I instantly wrote to Geneva: nearly two months have elapsed since the departure of my letter.—But you are ill; even now you tremble: you are unfit for agitation of any kind."

"This suspense is a thousand times worse than the most horrible event: tell me what new scene of death has been acted, and whose murder I am now to lament."

"Your family is perfectly well," said Mr. Kirwin, with gentleness; "and some one, a friend, is come to visit you."

I know not by what chain of thought the idea presented itself, but it instantly darted into my mind that the murderer had come to mock
III.80 at my misery, and taunt me with the death of Clerval, as a new incitement for me to comply with his hellish desires. I put my hand before my eyes, and cried out in agony—

"Oh! take him away! I cannot see him; for God's sake, do not let him enter!"

Mr. Kirwin regarded me with a troubled countenance. He could not help regarding my exclamation as a presumption of my guilt, and said, in rather a severe tone—

"I should have thought, young man, that the presence of your father would have been welcome, instead of inspiring such violent repugnance."

"My father!" cried I, while every feature and every muscle was relaxed from anguish to pleasure. "Is my father, indeed, come? How kind, how very kind. But where is he, why does he not hasten to me?"

My change of manner surprised and pleased the magistrate; III.81 perhaps he thought that my former exclamation was a momentary return of delirium, and now he instantly resumed his former benevolence. He rose, and quitted the room with my nurse, and in a moment my father entered it.

Nothing, at this moment, could have given me greater pleasure than the arrival of my father. I stretched out my hand to him, and cried—

"Are you then safe—and Elizabeth—and Ernest?"

My father calmed me with assurances of their welfare, and endeavoured, by dwelling on these subjects so interesting to my heart, to raise my desponding spirits; but he soon felt that a prison cannot be the abode of cheerfulness. "What a place is this that you inhabit, my son!" said he, looking mournfully at the barred windows, and wretched appearance of the room. "You travelled to seek happiness, III.82 but a fatality seems to pursue you. And poor Clerval—"

The name of my unfortunate and murdered friend was an agitation too great to be endured in my weak state; I shed tears.

"Alas! yes, my father," replied I; "some destiny of the most horrible kind hangs over me, and I must live to fulfil it, or surely I should have died on the coffin of Henry."

We were not allowed to converse for any length of time, for the precarious state of my health rendered every precaution necessary that could insure tranquillity. Mr. Kirwin came in, and insisted that my strength should not be exhausted by too much exertion. But the appearance of my father was to me like that of my good angel, and I gradually recovered my health.

As my sickness quitted me, I was absorbed by a gloomy and black III.83 melancholy, that nothing could dissipate. The image of Clerval was for ever before me, ghastly and murdered. More than once the agitation into which these reflections threw me made my friends dread a dangerous relapse. Alas! why did they preserve so miserable and detested a life? It was surely that I might fulfil my destiny, which is now drawing to a close. Soon, oh, very soon, will death extinguish these throbbings, and relieve me from the mighty weight of anguish that bears me to the dust; and, in executing the award of justice, I shall also sink to rest. Then the appearance of death was distant, although the wish was ever present to my thoughts; and I often sat for hours motionless and speechless, wishing for some mighty revolution that

III.84   might bury me and my destroyer in its ruins.

The season of the assizes approached. I had already been three months in prison; and although I was still weak, and in continual danger of a relapse, I was obliged to travel nearly a hundred miles to the county-town, where the court was held. Mr. Kirwin charged himself with every care of collecting witnesses, and arranging my defence. I was spared the disgrace of appearing publicly as a criminal, as the case was not brought before the court that decides on life and death. The grand jury rejected the bill, on its being proved that I was on the Orkney Islands at the hour the body of my friend was found, and a fortnight after my removal I was liberated from prison.

My father was enraptured on finding me freed from the vexa-
III.85   tions of a criminal charge, that I was again allowed to breathe the fresh atmosphere, and allowed to return to my native country. I did not participate in these feelings; for to me the walls of a dungeon or a palace were alike hateful. The cup of life was poisoned for ever; and although the sun shone upon me, as upon the happy and gay of heart, I saw around me nothing but a dense and frightful darkness, penetrated by no light but the glimmer of two eyes that glared upon me. Sometimes they were the expressive eyes of Henry, languishing in death, the dark orbs nearly covered by the lids, and the long black lashes that fringed them; sometimes it was the watery clouded eyes of the monster, as I first saw them in my chamber at Ingolstadt.

My father tried to awaken in me the feelings of affection. He
III.86   talked of Geneva, which I should soon visit—of Elizabeth, and Ernest; but these words only drew deep groans from me. Sometimes, indeed, I felt a wish for happiness; and thought, with melancholy delight, of my beloved cousin; or longed, with a devouring *maladie du pays*,[114] to see once more the blue lake and rapid Rhone, that had been so dear to me in early childhood: but my general state of feeling was a torpor, in which a prison was as welcome a residence as the

---

114. Homesickness, thought at this time to be a serious illness that could result in death.

divinest scene in nature; and these fits were seldom interrupted, but by paroxysms of anguish and despair. At these moments I often endeavoured to put an end to the existence I loathed; and it required unceasing attendance and vigilance to restrain me from committing some dreadful act of violence.

I remember, as I quitted the prison, I heard one of the men say,   III.87 "He may be innocent of the murder, but he has certainly a bad conscience." These words struck me. A bad conscience! yes, surely I had one. William, Justine, and Clerval, had died through my infernal machinations; "And whose death," cried I, "is to finish the tragedy? Ah! my father, do not remain in this wretched country; take me where I may forget myself, my existence, and all the world."

My father easily acceded to my desire; and, after having taken leave of Mr. Kirwin, we hastened to Dublin. I felt as if I was relieved from a heavy weight, when the packet[115] sailed with a fair wind from Ireland, and I had quitted for ever the country which had been to me the scene of so much misery.

It was midnight. My father slept in the cabin; and I lay on the   III.88 deck, looking at the stars, and listening to the dashing of the waves. I hailed the darkness that shut Ireland from my sight, and my pulse beat with a feverish joy, when I reflected that I should soon see Geneva. The past appeared to me in the light of a frightful dream; yet the vessel in which I was, the wind that blew me from the detested shore of Ireland, and the sea which surrounded me, told me too forcibly that I was deceived by no vision, and that Clerval, my friend and dearest companion, had fallen a victim to me and the monster of my creation. I repassed, in my memory, my whole life; my quiet happiness while residing with my family in Geneva, the death of my mother, and my departure for Ingolstadt. I remembered shuddering at the mad enthusiasm that hurried me on to the creation of my hideous enemy, and I called to mind the   III.89 night during which he first lived. I was unable to pursue the train of thought; a thousand feelings pressed upon me, and I wept bitterly.

Ever since my recovery from the fever I had been in the custom of taking every night a small quantity of laudanum;[116] for it was by means of this drug only that I was enabled to gain the rest necessary for the preservation of life. Oppressed by the recollection of my

---

115. The packet-boat, or boat carrying mail.
116. Opium dissolved in alcohol—widely used in this period.

various misfortunes, I now took a double dose, and soon slept profoundly. But sleep did not afford me respite from thought and misery; my dreams presented a thousand objects that scared me. Towards morning I was possessed by a kind of night-mare;[117] I felt the fiend's grasp in my neck, and could not free myself from it; groans and cries rung in my ears. My father, who was watching over me, perceiving my restlessness, awoke me, and pointed to the port of Holyhead, which we were now entering.

III.90

117. In the sense of "a female spirit or monster supposed to settle on and produce a feeling of suffocation in a sleeping person or animal" (*Oxford English Dictionary* online, s.v. "nightmare n. and adj.," sense 1 [updated 2003]).

CHAPTER V.

WE had resolved not to go to London, but to cross the country to Portsmouth, and thence to embark for Havre. I preferred this plan principally because I dreaded to see again those places in which I had enjoyed a few moments of tranquillity with my beloved Clerval. I thought with horror of seeing again those persons whom we had been accustomed to visit together, and who might make inquiries concerning an event, the very remembrance of which made me again feel the pang I endured when I gazed on his lifeless form in the inn
at————.

As for my father, his desires and exertions were bounded to the again seeing me restored to health and peace of mind. His tenderness and attentions were unremitting; my grief and gloom was obstinate, but he would not despair. Sometimes he thought that I felt deeply the degradation of being obliged to answer a charge of murder, and he endeavoured to prove to me the futility of pride.

"Alas! my father," said I, "how little do you know me. Human beings, their feelings and passions, would indeed be degraded, if such a wretch as I felt pride. Justine, poor unhappy Justine, was as innocent as I, and she suffered the same charge; she died for it; and I am the cause of this—I murdered her. William, Justine, and Henry—they all
died by my hands."

My father had often, during my imprisonment, heard me make the same assertion; when I thus accused myself, he sometimes seemed to desire an explanation, and at others he appeared to consider it as caused by delirium, and that, during my illness, some idea of this kind had presented itself to my imagination, the remembrance of which I preserved in my convalescence. I avoided explanation, and maintained a continual silence concerning the wretch I had created. I had a feeling that I should be supposed mad, and this for ever chained my tongue, when I would have given the whole world to have confided the fatal secret.

Upon this occasion my father said, with an expression of unbounded wonder, "What do you mean, Victor? are you mad? My dear son, I
entreat you never to make such an assertion again."

"I am not mad," I cried energetically; "the sun and the heavens, who have viewed my operations, can bear witness of my truth. I am the assassin of those most innocent victims; they died by my machinations. A thousand times would I have shed my own blood, drop by drop, to have saved their lives; but I could not, my father, indeed I could not sacrifice the whole human race."

The conclusion of this speech convinced my father that my ideas were deranged, and he instantly changed the subject of our conversation, and endeavoured to alter the course of my thoughts. He wished as much as possible to obliterate the memory of the scenes that had III.95   taken place in Ireland, and never alluded to them, or suffered me to speak of my misfortunes.

As time passed away I became more calm: misery had her dwelling in my heart, but I no longer talked in the same incoherent manner of my own crimes; sufficient for me was the consciousness of them. By the utmost self-violence, I curbed the imperious voice of wretchedness, which sometimes desired to declare itself to the whole world; and my manners were calmer and more composed than they had ever been since my journey to the sea of ice.

We arrived at Havre on the 8th of May, and instantly proceeded to Paris, where my father had some business which detained us a few weeks. In this city, I received the following letter from Elizabeth:—

III.96   "*To* VICTOR FRANKENSTEIN.

"MY DEAREST FRIEND,

"It gave me the greatest pleasure to receive a letter from my uncle dated at Paris; you are no longer at a formidable distance, and I may hope to see you in less than a fortnight. My poor cousin, how much you must have suffered! I expect to see you looking even more ill than when you quitted Geneva. This winter has been passed most miserably, tortured as I have been by anxious suspense; yet I hope to see peace in your countenance, and to find that your heart is not totally devoid of comfort and tranquillity.

"Yet I fear that the same feelings now exist that made you so mis- III.97   erable a year ago, even perhaps augmented by time. I would not disturb you at this period, when so many misfortunes weigh upon you; but a conversation that I had with my uncle previous to his departure renders some explanation necessary before we meet.

"Explanation! you may possibly say; what can Elizabeth have to explain? If you really say this, my questions are answered, and I have no more to do than to sign myself your affectionate cousin. But you are distant from me, and it is possible that you may dread, and yet be pleased with this explanation; and, in a probability of this being the case, I dare not any longer postpone writing what, during your absence, I have often wished to express to you, but have never had the courage to begin.

"You well know, Victor, that our union had been the favourite plan of your parents ever since our infancy. We were told this when young, and taught to look forward to it as an event that would certainly take place. We were affectionate playfellows during childhood, and, I believe, dear and valued friends to one another as we grew older. But as brother and sister often entertain a lively affection towards each other, without desiring a more intimate union, may not such also be our case? Tell me, dearest Victor. Answer me, I conjure you, by our mutual happiness, with simple truth—Do you not love another? III.98

"You have travelled; you have spent several years of your life at Ingolstadt; and I confess to you, my friend, that when I saw you last autumn so unhappy, flying to solitude, from the society of every creature, I could not help supposing that you might regret our III.99 connexion, and believe yourself bound in honour to fulfil the wishes of your parents, although they opposed themselves to your inclinations. But this is false reasoning. I confess to you, my cousin, that I love you, and that in my airy dreams of futurity you have been my constant friend and companion. But it is your happiness I desire as well as my own, when I declare to you, that our marriage would render me eternally miserable, unless it were the dictate of your own free choice. Even now I weep to think, that, borne down as you are by the cruelest misfortunes, you may stifle, by the word *honour*, all hope of that love and happiness which would alone restore you to yourself. I, who have so interested an affection for you, may increase your miseries ten-fold, by being an obstacle to your wishes. Ah, Victor, be assured that your cousin and playmate has too sincere a love III.100 for you not to be made miserable by this supposition. Be happy, my friend; and if you obey me in this one request, remain satisfied that nothing on earth will have the power to interrupt my tranquillity.

"Do not let this letter disturb you; do not answer it to-morrow, or the next day, or even until you come, if it will give you pain. My uncle will send me news of your health; and if I see but one smile on your lips when we meet, occasioned by this or any other exertion of mine, I shall need no other happiness.

"ELIZABETH LAVENZA.

"Geneva, May 18th, 17—."

This letter revived in my memory what I had before forgotten, the threat of the fiend—"*I will be with you on your wedding-night!*" III.101

Such was my sentence, and on that night would the dæmon employ every art to destroy me, and tear me from the glimpse of happiness which promised partly to console my sufferings. On that night he had determined to consummate his crimes by my death. Well, be it so; a deadly struggle would then assuredly take place, in which if he was victorious, I should be at peace, and his power over me be at an end. If he were vanquished, I should be a free man. Alas! what freedom? such as the peasant enjoys when his family have been massacred before his eyes, his cottage burnt, his lands laid waste, and he is turned adrift, homeless, pennyless, and alone, but free. Such would be my liberty, except that in my Elizabeth I possessed a treasure; alas! III.102   balanced by those horrors of remorse and guilt, which would pursue me until death.

Sweet and beloved Elizabeth! I read and re-read her letter, and some softened feelings stole into my heart, and dared to whisper paradisaical dreams of love and joy; but the apple was already eaten, and the angel's arm bared to drive me from all hope. Yet I would die to make her happy. If the monster executed his threat, death was inevitable; yet, again, I considered whether my marriage would hasten my fate. My destruction might indeed arrive a few months sooner; but if my torturer should suspect that I postponed it, influenced by his menaces, he would surely find other, and perhaps more dreadful means of revenge. He had vowed *to be with me on my wedding-night*, yet he III.103   did not consider that threat as binding him to peace in the mean time; for, as if to shew me that he was not yet satiated with blood, he had murdered Clerval immediately after the enunciation of his threats. I resolved, therefore, that if my immediate union with my cousin would conduce either to her's or my father's happiness, my adversary's designs against my life should not retard it a single hour.

In this state of mind I wrote to Elizabeth. My letter was calm and affectionate. "I fear, my beloved girl," I said, "little happiness remains for us on earth; yet all that I may one day enjoy is concentered in you. Chase away your idle fears; to you alone do I consecrate my life, and my endeavours for contentment. I have one secret, Elizabeth, a dreadful one; when revealed to you, it will chill your frame with horror, and then, far from being surprised at my misery, you will only III.104   wonder that I survive what I have endured. I will confide this tale of misery and terror to you the day after our marriage shall take place; for, my sweet cousin, there must be perfect confidence between us. But until then, I conjure you, do not mention or allude to it. This I most earnestly entreat, and I know you will comply."

In about a week after the arrival of Elizabeth's letter, we returned to Geneva. My cousin welcomed me with warm affection; yet tears were in her eyes, as she beheld my emaciated frame and feverish cheeks. I saw a change in her also. She was thinner, and had lost much of that heavenly vivacity that had before charmed me; but her gentleness, and soft looks of compassion, made her a more fit companion for one blasted and miserable as I was.

The tranquillity which I now enjoyed did not endure. Memory III.105 brought madness with it; and when I thought on what had passed, a real insanity possessed me; sometimes I was furious, and burnt with rage, sometimes low and despondent. I neither spoke or looked, but sat motionless, bewildered by the multitude of miseries that overcame me.

Elizabeth alone had the power to draw me from these fits; her gentle voice would soothe me when transported by passion, and inspire me with human feelings when sunk in torpor. She wept with me, and for me. When reason returned, she would remonstrate, and endeavour to inspire me with resignation. Ah! it is well for the unfortunate to be resigned, but for the guilty there is no peace. The agonies of remorse poison the luxury there is otherwise sometimes found in in- III.106 dulging the excess of grief.

Soon after my arrival my father spoke of my immediate marriage with my cousin. I remained silent.

"Have you, then, some other attachment?"

"None on earth. I love Elizabeth, and look forward to our union with delight. Let the day therefore be fixed; and on it I will consecrate myself, in life or death, to the happiness of my cousin."

"My dear Victor, do not speak thus. Heavy misfortunes have befallen us; but let us only cling closer to what remains, and transfer our love for those whom we have lost to those who yet live. Our circle will be small, but bound close by the ties of affection and mutual misfortune. And when time shall have softened your despair, new and III.107 dear objects of care will be born to replace those of whom we have been so cruelly deprived."

Such were the lessons of my father. But to me the remembrance of the threat returned: nor can you wonder, that, omnipotent as the fiend had yet been in his deeds of blood, I should almost regard him as invincible; and that when he had pronounced the words, "*I shall be with you on your wedding-night,*" I should regard the threatened fate as unavoidable. But death was no evil to me, if the loss of

Elizabeth were balanced with it; and I therefore, with a contented and even cheerful countenance, agreed with my father, that if my cousin would consent, the ceremony should take place in ten days, and thus put, as I imagined, the seal to my fate.

III.108 Great God! if for one instant I had thought what might be the hellish intention of my fiendish adversary, I would rather have banished myself for ever from my native country, and wandered a friendless outcast over the earth, than have consented to this miserable marriage. But, as if possessed of magic powers, the monster had blinded me to his real intentions; and when I thought that I prepared only my own death, I hastened that of a far dearer victim.

As the period fixed for our marriage drew nearer, whether from cowardice or a prophetic feeling, I felt my heart sink within me. But I concealed my feelings by an appearance of hilarity, that brought smiles and joy to the countenance of my father, but hardly deceived the ever-watchful and nicer[118] eye of Elizabeth. She looked forward to
III.109 our union with placid contentment, not unmingled with a little fear, which past misfortunes had impressed, that what now appeared certain and tangible happiness, might soon dissipate into an airy dream, and leave no trace but deep and everlasting regret.

Preparations were made for the event; congratulatory visits were received; and all wore a smiling appearance. I shut up, as well as I could, in my own heart the anxiety that preyed there, and entered with seeming earnestness into the plans of my father, although they might only serve as the decorations of my tragedy. A house was purchased for us near Cologny, by which we should enjoy the pleasures of the country, and yet be so near Geneva as to see my father every day; who would still reside within the walls, for the benefit of Ernest, that he might follow his studies at the schools.

III.110 In the mean time I took every precaution to defend my person, in case the fiend should openly attack me. I carried pistols and a dagger constantly about me, and was ever on the watch to prevent artifice; and by these means gained a greater degree of tranquillity. Indeed, as the period approached, the threat appeared more as a delusion, not to be regarded as worthy to disturb my peace, while the happiness I hoped for in my marriage wore a greater appearance of certainty, as the day fixed for its solemnization drew nearer, and I heard it continually spoken of as an occurrence which no accident could possibly prevent.

---

118. More perceptive.

Elizabeth seemed happy; my tranquil demeanour contributed greatly to calm her mind. But on the day that was to fulfil my wish- III.111 es and my destiny, she was melancholy, and a presentiment of evil pervaded her; and perhaps also she thought of the dreadful secret, which I had promised to reveal to her the following day. My father was in the mean time overjoyed, and, in the bustle of preparation, only observed in the melancholy of his niece the diffidence of a bride.

After the ceremony was performed, a large party assembled at my father's; but it was agreed that Elizabeth and I should pass the afternoon and night at Evian, and return to Cologny the next morn- ing. As the day was fair, and the wind favourable, we resolved to go by water.

Those were the last moments of my life during which I enjoyed the feeling of happiness. We passed rapidly along: the sun was hot, but we were sheltered from its rays by a kind of canopy, while we enjoyed the beauty of the scene, sometimes on one side of the lake, III.112 where we saw Mont Salêve, the pleasant banks of Montalêgre, and at a distance, surmounting all, the beautiful Mont Blânc, and the as- semblage of snowy mountains that in vain endeavour to emulate her; sometimes coasting the opposite banks, we saw the mighty Jura op- posing its dark side to the ambition that would quit its native coun- try, and an almost insurmountable barrier to the invader who should wish to enslave it.

I took the hand of Elizabeth: "You are sorrowful, my love. Ah! if you knew what I have suffered, and what I may yet endure, you would endeavour to let me taste the quiet, and freedom from despair, that this one day at least permits me to enjoy."

"Be happy, my dear Victor," replied Elizabeth; "there is, I hope, nothing to distress you; and be assured that if a lively joy is not paint- III.113 ed in my face, my heart is contented. Something whispers to me not to depend too much on the prospect that is opened before us; but I will not listen to such a sinister voice. Observe how fast we move along, and how the clouds which sometimes obscure, and sometimes rise above the dome of Mont Blânc, render this scene of beauty still more interesting. Look also at the innumerable fish that are swim- ming in the clear waters, where we can distinguish every pebble that lies at the bottom. What a divine day! how happy and serene all na- ture appears!"

Thus Elizabeth endeavoured to divert her thoughts and mine from all reflection upon melancholy subjects. But her temper was

III.114   fluctuating; joy for a few instants shone in her eyes, but it continually gave place to distraction and reverie.

The sun sunk lower in the heavens; we passed the river Drance, and observed its path through the chasms of the higher, and the glens of the lower hills. The Alps here come closer to the lake, and we approached the amphitheatre of mountains which forms its eastern boundary. The spire of Evian shone under the woods that surrounded it, and the range of mountain above mountain by which it was overhung.

The wind, which had hitherto carried us along with amazing rapidity, sunk at sunset to a light breeze; the soft air just ruffled the water, and caused a pleasant motion among the trees as we approached the shore, from which it wafted the most delightful scent of flowers

III.115   and hay. The sun sunk beneath the horizon as we landed; and as I touched the shore, I felt those cares and fears revive, which soon were to clasp me, and cling to me for ever.

CHAPTER VI.

III.116

IT was eight o'clock when we landed; we walked for a short time on the shore, enjoying the transitory light, and then retired to the inn, and contemplated the lovely scene of waters, woods, and mountains, obscured in darkness, yet still displaying their black outlines.

The wind, which had fallen in the south, now rose with great violence in the west. The moon had reached her summit in the heavens, and was beginning to descend; the clouds swept across it swifter than the flight of the vulture, and dimmed her rays, while the lake reflected the III.117 scene of the busy heavens, rendered still busier by the restless waves that were beginning to rise. Suddenly a heavy storm of rain descended.

I had been calm during the day; but so soon as night obscured the shapes of objects, a thousand fears arose in my mind. I was anxious and watchful, while my right hand grasped a pistol which was hidden in my bosom; every sound terrified me; but I resolved that I would sell my life dearly, and not relax the impending conflict until my own life, or that of my adversary, were extinguished.

Elizabeth observed my agitation for some time in timid and fearful silence; at length she said, "What is it that agitates you, my dear Victor? What is it you fear?"

"Oh! peace, peace, my love," replied I, "this night, and all will be III.118 safe: but this night is dreadful, very dreadful."

I passed an hour in this state of mind, when suddenly I reflected how dreadful the combat which I momentarily expected would be to my wife, and I earnestly entreated her to retire, resolving not to join her until I had obtained some knowledge as to the situation of my enemy.

She left me, and I continued some time walking up and down the passages of the house, and inspecting every corner that might afford a retreat to my adversary. But I discovered no trace of him, and was beginning to conjecture that some fortunate chance had intervened to prevent the execution of his menaces; when suddenly I heard a shrill and dreadful scream. It came from the room into which Elizabeth had retired. As I heard it, the whole truth rushed into my III.119 mind, my arms dropped, the motion of every muscle and fibre was suspended; I could feel the blood trickling in my veins, and tingling in the extremities of my limbs. This state lasted but for an instant; the scream was repeated, and I rushed into the room.

Great God! why did I not then expire! Why am I here to relate the destruction of the best hope, and the purest creature of earth. She was there, lifeless and inanimate, thrown across the bed, her head hanging down, and her pale and distorted features half covered by her hair. Every where I turn I see the same figure—her bloodless arms and relaxed form flung by the murderer on its bridal bier. Could I behold this, and live? Alas! life is obstinate, and clings closest where III.120   it is most hated. For a moment only did I lose recollection; I fainted.

When I recovered, I found myself surrounded by the people of the inn; their countenances expressed a breathless terror: but the horror of others appeared only as a mockery, a shadow of the feelings that oppressed me. I escaped from them to the room where lay the body of Elizabeth, my love, my wife, so lately living, so dear, so worthy. She had been moved from the posture in which I had first beheld her; and now, as she lay, her head upon her arm, and a handkerchief thrown across her face and neck, I might have supposed her asleep. I rushed towards her, and embraced her with ardour; but the deathly languor and coldness of the limbs told me, that what I now held in my arms had ceased to be the Elizabeth whom I had loved and cher-
III.121   ished. The murderous mark of the fiend's grasp was on her neck, and the breath had ceased to issue from her lips.

While I still hung over her in the agony of despair, I happened to look up. The windows of the room had before been darkened; and I felt a kind of panic on seeing the pale yellow light of the moon illuminate the chamber. The shutters had been thrown back; and, with a sensation of horror not to be described, I saw at the open window a figure the most hideous and abhorred. A grin was on the face of the monster; he seemed to jeer, as with his fiendish finger he pointed towards the corpse of my wife. I rushed towards the window, and drawing a pistol from my bosom, shot; but he eluded me, leaped from his station, and, running with the swiftness of lightning, plunged into the lake.

III.122   The report of the pistol brought a crowd into the room. I pointed to the spot where he had disappeared, and we followed the track with boats; nets were cast, but in vain. After passing several hours, we returned hopeless, most of my companions believing it to have been a form conjured by my fancy. After having landed, they proceeded to search the country, parties going in different directions among the woods and vines.

I did not accompany them; I was exhausted: a film covered my eyes, and my skin was parched with the heat of fever. In this state I lay on a bed, hardly conscious of what had happened; my eyes wandered round the room, as if to seek something that I had lost.

At length I remembered that my father would anxiously expect the return of Elizabeth and myself, and that I must return alone. This III.123 reflection brought tears into my eyes, and I wept for a long time; but my thoughts rambled to various subjects, reflecting on my misfortunes, and their cause. I was bewildered in a cloud of wonder and horror. The death of William, the execution of Justine, the murder of Clerval, and lastly of my wife; even at that moment I knew not that my only remaining friends were safe from the malignity of the fiend; my father even now might be writhing under his grasp, and Ernest might be dead at his feet. This idea made me shudder, and recalled me to action. I started up, and resolved to return to Geneva with all possible speed.

There were no horses to be procured, and I must return by the lake; but the wind was unfavourable, and the rain fell in torrents. III.124 However, it was hardly morning, and I might reasonably hope to arrive by night. I hired men to row, and took an oar myself, for I had always experienced relief from mental torment in bodily exercise. But the overflowing misery I now felt, and the excess of agitation that I endured, rendered me incapable of any exertion. I threw down the oar; and, leaning my head upon my hands, gave way to every gloomy idea that arose. If I looked up, I saw the scenes which were familiar to me in my happier time, and which I had contemplated but the day before in the company of her who was now but a shadow and a recollection. Tears streamed from my eyes. The rain had ceased for a moment, and I saw the fish play in the waters as they had done a few hours before; they had then been observed by Elizabeth. Nothing is III.125 so painful to the human mind as a great and sudden change. The sun might shine, or the clouds might lour; but nothing could appear to me as it had done the day before. A fiend had snatched from me every hope of future happiness: no creature had ever been so miserable as I was; so frightful an event is single in the history of man.

But why should I dwell upon the incidents that followed this last overwhelming event. Mine has been a tale of horrors; I have reached their *acme*, and what I must now relate can but be tedious to you. Know that, one by one, my friends were snatched away; I was left desolate. My own strength is exhausted; and I must tell, in a few words, what remains of my hideous narration.

I arrived at Geneva. My father and Ernest yet lived; but the for- III.126 mer sunk under the tidings that I bore. I see him now, excellent and venerable old man! his eyes wandered in vacancy, for they had lost their charm and their delight—his niece, his more than daughter, whom he doated on with all that affection which a man feels, who, in the decline of life, having few affections, clings more earnestly to those that remain. Cursed, cursed be the fiend that brought misery on his grey hairs, and doomed him to waste in wretchedness! He could not live under the horrors that were accumulated around him; an apoplectic fit was brought on, and in a few days he died in my arms.

III.127

What then became of me? I know not; I lost sensation, and chains and darkness were the only objects that pressed upon me. Sometimes, indeed, I dreamt that I wandered in flowery meadows and pleasant vales with the friends of my youth; but awoke, and found myself in a dungeon. Melancholy followed, but by degrees I gained a clear conception of my miseries and situation, and was then released from my prison. For they had called me mad; and during many months, as I understood, a solitary cell had been my habitation.

III.128

But liberty had been a useless gift to me had I not, as I awakened to reason, at the same time awakened to revenge. As the memory of past misfortunes pressed upon me, I began to reflect on their cause—the monster whom I had created, the miserable dæmon whom I had sent abroad into the world for my destruction. I was possessed by a maddening rage when I thought of him, and desired and ardently prayed that I might have him within my grasp to wreak a great and signal revenge on his cursed head.

Nor did my hate long confine itself to useless wishes; I began to reflect on the best means of securing him; and for this purpose, about a month after my release, I repaired to a criminal judge in the town, and told him that I had an accusation to make; that I knew the destroyer of my family; and that I required him to exert his whole authority for the apprehension of the murderer.

The magistrate listened to me with attention and kindness: "Be assured, sir," said he, "no pains or exertions on my part shall be spared to discover the villain."

III.129

"I thank you," replied I; "listen, therefore, to the deposition that I have to make. It is indeed a tale so strange, that I should fear you would not credit it, were there not something in truth which, however wonderful, forces conviction. The story is too connected to be mistaken for a dream, and I have no motive for falsehood." My manner, as I thus addressed him, was impressive, but calm; I had formed in my own heart a resolution to pursue my destroyer to death; and this purpose quieted my agony, and provisionally reconciled me to life.

I now related my history briefly, but with firmness and precision, marking the dates with accuracy, and never deviating into invective or exclamation.

The magistrate appeared at first perfectly incredulous, but as I continued he became more attentive and interested; I saw him sometimes shudder with horror, at others a lively surprise, unmingled with disbelief, was painted on his countenance.

When I had concluded my narration, I said, "This is the being III.130 whom I accuse, and for whose detection and punishment I call upon you to exert your whole power. It is your duty as a magistrate, and I believe and hope that your feelings as a man will not revolt from the execution of those functions on this occasion."

This address caused a considerable change in the physiognomy of my auditor. He had heard my story with that half kind of belief that is given to a tale of spirits and supernatural events; but when he was called upon to act officially in consequence, the whole tide of his incredulity returned. He, however, answered mildly, "I would willingly afford you every aid in your pursuit; but the creature of whom you speak appears to have powers which would put all my exertions to defiance. Who can follow an animal which can traverse the sea of III.131 ice, and inhabit caves and dens, where no man would venture to intrude? Besides, some months have elapsed since the commission of his crimes, and no one can conjecture to what place he has wandered, or what region he may now inhabit."

"I do not doubt that he hovers near the spot which I inhabit; and if he has indeed taken refuge in the Alps, he may be hunted like the chamois,[119] and destroyed as a beast of prey. But I perceive your thoughts: you do not credit my narrative, and do not intend to pursue my enemy with the punishment which is his desert."

As I spoke, rage sparkled in my eyes; the magistrate was intimidated; "You are mistaken," said he, "I will exert myself; and if it is in III.132 my power to seize the monster, be assured that he shall suffer punishment proportionate to his crimes. But I fear, from what you have yourself described to be his properties, that this will prove impracticable, and that, while every proper measure is pursued, you should endeavour to make up your mind to disappointment."

"That cannot be; but all that I can say will be of little avail. My revenge is of no moment to you; yet, while I allow it to be a vice, I confess that it is the devouring and only passion of my soul. My

---

119. The only species of antelope found in Europe.

rage is unspeakable, when I reflect that the murderer, whom I have turned loose upon society, still exists. You refuse my just demand: I have but one resource; and I devote myself, either in my life or death, to his destruction."

III.133   I trembled with excess of agitation as I said this; there was a phrenzy in my manner, and something, I doubt not, of that haughty fierceness, which the martyrs of old are said to have possessed. But to a Genevan magistrate, whose mind was occupied by far other ideas than those of devotion and heroism, this elevation of mind had much the appearance of madness. He endeavoured to soothe me as a nurse does a child, and reverted to[120] my tale as the effects of delirium.

"Man," I cried, "how ignorant art thou in thy pride of wisdom! Cease; you know not what it is you say."

I broke from the house angry and disturbed, and retired to meditate on some other mode of action.

---

120. Returned to regarding . . .

CHAPTER VII.

MY present situation was one in which all voluntary thought was swallowed up and lost. I was hurried away by fury; revenge alone endowed me with strength and composure; it modelled my feelings, and allowed me to be calculating and calm, at periods when otherwise delirium or death would have been my portion.

My first resolution was to quit Geneva for ever; my country, which, when I was happy and beloved, was dear to me, now, in my adversity, became hateful. I provided myself with a sum of money, together III.135 with a few jewels which had belonged to my mother, and departed.

And now my wanderings began, which are to cease but with life. I have traversed a vast portion of the earth, and have endured all the hardships which travellers, in deserts and barbarous countries, are wont to meet. How I have lived I hardly know; many times have I stretched my failing limbs upon the sandy plain, and prayed for death. But revenge kept me alive; I dared not die, and leave my adversary in being.

When I quitted Geneva, my first labour was to gain some clue by which I might trace the steps of my fiendish enemy. But my plan was unsettled; and I wandered many hours around the confines of the town, uncertain what path I should pursue. As night approached, I III.136 found myself at the entrance of the cemetery where William, Elizabeth, and my father, reposed. I entered it, and approached the tomb which marked their graves. Every thing was silent, except the leaves of the trees, which were gently agitated by the wind; the night was nearly dark; and the scene would have been solemn and affecting even to an uninterested observer. The spirits of the departed seemed to flit around, and to cast a shadow, which was felt but seen not, around the head of the mourner.

The deep grief which this scene had at first excited quickly gave way to rage and despair. They were dead, and I lived; their murderer also lived, and to destroy him I must drag out my weary existence. I knelt on the grass, and kissed the earth, and with quivering lips ex- III.137 claimed, "By the sacred earth on which I kneel, by the shades[121] that wander near me, by the deep and eternal grief that I feel, I swear; and by thee, O Night, and by the spirits that preside over thee, I swear to pursue the dæmon, who caused this misery, until he or I shall perish

---

121. Spirits of the dead.

in mortal conflict. For this purpose I will preserve my life: to execute this dear revenge, will I again behold the sun, and tread the green herbage of earth, which otherwise should vanish from my eyes for ever. And I call on you, spirits of the dead; and on you, wandering ministers of vengeance, to aid and conduct me in my work. Let the cursed and hellish monster drink deep of agony; let him feel the despair that now torments me."

III.138   I had begun my adjuration with solemnity, and an awe which almost assured me that the shades of my murdered friends heard and approved my devotion; but the furies[122] possessed me as I concluded, and rage choked my utterance.

I was answered through the stillness of night by a loud and fiendish laugh. It rung on my ears long and heavily; the mountains reechoed it, and I felt as if all hell surrounded me with mockery and laughter. Surely in that moment I should have been possessed by phrenzy, and have destroyed my miserable existence, but that my vow was heard, and that I was reserved for vengeance. The laughter died away; when a well-known and abhorred voice, apparently close to my ear, addressed me in an audible whisper—"I am satisfied: miserable wretch! you have determined to live, and I am satisfied."

III.139   I darted towards the spot from which the sound proceeded; but the devil eluded my grasp. Suddenly the broad disk of the moon arose, and shone full upon his ghastly and distorted shape, as he fled with more than mortal speed.

I pursued him; and for many months this has been my task. Guided by a slight clue, I followed the windings of the Rhone, but vainly. The blue Mediterranean appeared; and, by a strange chance, I saw the fiend enter by night, and hide himself in a vessel bound for the Black Sea. I took my passage in the same ship; but he escaped, I know not how.

Amidst the wilds of Tartary and Russia, although he still evaded me, I have ever followed in his track. Sometimes the peasants, scared by this horrid apparition, informed me of his path; sometimes
III.140   he himself, who feared that if I lost all trace I should despair and die, often left some mark to guide me. The snows descended on my head, and I saw the print of his huge step on the white plain. To you first entering on life, to whom care is new, and agony unknown, how can you understand what I have felt, and still feel? Cold, want, and fatigue, were the least pains which I was destined to endure; I was

---

122. The Eumenides, spirits of vengeance in Greek mythology.

cursed by some devil, and carried about with me my eternal hell; yet still a spirit of good followed and directed my steps, and, when I most murmured, would suddenly extricate me from seemingly insurmountable difficulties. Sometimes, when nature, overcome by hunger, sunk under the exhaustion, a repast was prepared for me in the desert, that restored and inspirited me. The fare was indeed coarse, such as the peasants of the country ate; but I may not doubt III.141 that it was set there by the spirits that I had invoked to aid me. Often, when all was dry, the heavens cloudless, and I was parched by thirst, a slight cloud would bedim the sky, shed the few drops that revived me, and vanish.

I followed, when I could, the courses of the rivers; but the dæmon generally avoided these, as it was here that the population of the country chiefly collected. In other places human beings were seldom seen; and I generally subsisted on the wild animals that crossed my path. I had money with me, and gained the friendship of the villagers by distributing it, or bringing with me some food that I had killed, which, after taking a small part, I always presented to those who had provided me with fire and utensils for cooking.

My life, as it passed thus, was indeed hateful to me, and it was III.142 during sleep alone that I could taste joy. O blessed sleep! often, when most miserable, I sank to repose, and my dreams lulled me even to rapture. The spirits that guarded me had provided these moments, or rather hours, of happiness, that I might retain strength to fulfil my pilgrimage. Deprived of this respite, I should have sunk under my hardships. During the day I was sustained and inspirited by the hope of night: for in sleep I saw my friends, my wife, and my beloved country; again I saw the benevolent countenance of my father, heard the silver tones of my Elizabeth's voice, and beheld Clerval enjoying health and youth. Often, when wearied by a toilsome march, I persuaded myself that I was dreaming until night should come, and that III.143 I should then enjoy reality in the arms of my dearest friends. What agonizing fondness did I feel for them! how did I cling to their dear forms, as sometimes they haunted even my waking hours, and persuade myself that they still lived! At such moments vengeance, that burned within me, died in my heart, and I pursued my path towards the destruction of the dæmon, more as a task enjoined by heaven, as the mechanical impulse of some power of which I was unconscious, than as the ardent desire of my soul.

What his feelings were whom I pursued, I cannot know. Sometimes, indeed, he left marks in writing on the barks of the trees, or

III.144

cut in stone, that guided me, and instigated my fury. "My reign is not yet over," (these words were legible in one of these inscriptions); "you live, and my power is complete. Follow me; I seek the everlasting ices of the north, where you will feel the misery of cold and frost, to which I am impassive. You will find near this place, if you follow not too tardily, a dead hare; eat, and be refreshed. Come on, my enemy; we have yet to wrestle for our lives; but many hard and miserable hours must you endure, until that period shall arrive."

Scoffing devil! Again do I vow vengeance; again do I devote thee, miserable fiend, to torture and death. Never will I omit my search, until he or I perish; and then with what ecstacy shall I join my Elizabeth, and those who even now prepare for me the reward of my tedious toil and horrible pilgrimage.

III.145

As I still pursued my journey to the northward, the snows thickened, and the cold increased in a degree almost too severe to support. The peasants were shut up in their hovels, and only a few of the most hardy ventured forth to seize the animals whom starvation had forced from their hiding-places to seek for prey. The rivers were covered with ice, and no fish could be procured; and thus I was cut off from my chief article of maintenance.

The triumph of my enemy increased with the difficulty of my labours. One inscription that he left was in these words: "Prepare! your toils only begin: wrap yourself in furs, and provide food, for we shall soon enter upon a journey where your sufferings will satisfy my everlasting hatred."

III.146

My courage and perseverance were invigorated by these scoffing words; I resolved not to fail in my purpose; and, calling on heaven to support me, I continued with unabated fervour to traverse immense deserts, until the ocean appeared at a distance, and formed the utmost boundary of the horizon. Oh! how unlike it was to the blue seas of the south! Covered with ice, it was only to be distinguished from land by its superior wildness and ruggedness. The Greeks wept for joy when they beheld the Mediterranean from the hills of Asia, and hailed with rapture the boundary of their toils.[123] I did not weep; but I knelt down, and, with a full heart, thanked my guiding spirit for conducting me in safety to the place where I hoped, notwithstanding my adversary's gibe, to meet and grapple with him.

Some weeks before this period I had procured a sledge and dogs, and thus traversed the snows with inconceivable speed. I know not

---

123. Xenophon, *Anabasis*, reporting the retreat of the Greek army in 401 BCE.

whether the fiend possessed the same advantages; but I found that, as before I had daily lost ground in the pursuit, I now gained on him; III.147 so much so, that when I first saw the ocean, he was but one day's journey in advance, and I hoped to intercept him before he should reach the beach. With new courage, therefore, I pressed on, and in two days arrived at a wretched hamlet on the seashore. I inquired of the inhabitants concerning the fiend, and gained accurate information. A gigantic monster, they said, had arrived the night before, armed with a gun and many pistols; putting to flight the inhabitants of a solitary cottage, through fear of his terrific appearance. He had carried off their store of winter food, and, placing it in a sledge, to draw which he had seized on a numerous drove of trained dogs, he had harnessed them, and the same night, to the joy of the horror-struck villagers, had pursued his journey across the sea in a direction that led to no III.148 land; and they conjectured that he must speedily be destroyed by the breaking of the ice, or frozen by the eternal frosts.

On hearing this information, I suffered a temporary access of despair. He had escaped me; and I must commence a destructive and almost endless journey across the mountainous ices of the ocean,—amidst cold that few of the inhabitants could long endure, and which I, the native of a genial and sunny climate, could not hope to survive. Yet at the idea that the fiend should live and be triumphant, my rage and vengeance returned, and, like a mighty tide, overwhelmed every other feeling. After a slight repose, during which the spirits of the dead hovered round, and instigated me to toil and revenge, I prepared for my journey.

I exchanged my land sledge for one fashioned for the inequalities III.149 of the frozen ocean; and, purchasing a plentiful stock of provisions, I departed from land.

I cannot guess how many days have passed since then; but I have endured misery, which nothing but the eternal sentiment of a just retribution burning within my heart could have enabled me to support. Immense and rugged mountains of ice often barred up my passage, and I often heard the thunder of the ground sea, which threatened my destruction. But again the frost came, and made the paths of the sea secure.

By the quantity of provision which I had consumed I should guess that I had passed three weeks in this journey; and the continual protraction of hope, returning back upon the heart, often wrung bitter III.150 drops of despondency and grief from my eyes. Despair had indeed almost secured her prey, and I should soon have sunk beneath this misery; when once, after the poor animals that carried me had with incredible toil gained the summit of a sloping ice mountain, and one sinking under his fatigue died, I viewed the expanse before me with anguish, when suddenly my eye caught a dark speck upon the dusky plain. I strained my sight to discover what it could be, and uttered a wild cry of ecstacy when I distinguished a sledge, and the distorted proportions of a well-known form within. Oh! with what a burning gush did hope revisit my heart! warm tears filled my eyes, which I hastily wiped away, that they might not intercept the view I had of

III.151   the dæmon; but still my sight was dimmed by the burning drops, until, giving way to the emotions that oppressed me, I wept aloud.

But this was not the time for delay; I disencumbered the dogs of their dead companion, gave them a plentiful portion of food; and, after an hour's rest, which was absolutely necessary, and yet which was bitterly irksome to me, I continued my route. The sledge was still visible; nor did I again lose sight of it, except at the moments when for a short time some ice rock concealed it with its intervening crags. I indeed perceptibly gained on it; and when, after nearly two days' journey, I beheld my enemy at no more than a mile distant, my heart bounded within me.

But now, when I appeared almost within grasp of my enemy, my hopes were suddenly extinguished, and I lost all trace of him more

III.152   utterly than I had ever done before. A ground sea was heard; the thunder of its progress, as the waters rolled and swelled beneath me, became every moment more ominous and terrific. I pressed on, but in vain. The wind arose; the sea roared; and, as with the mighty shock of an earthquake, it split, and cracked with a tremendous and overwhelming sound. The work was soon finished: in a few minutes a tumultuous sea rolled between me and my enemy, and I was left drifting on a scattered piece of ice, that was continually lessening, and thus preparing for me a hideous death.

In this manner many appalling hours passed; several of my dogs died; and I myself was about to sink under the accumulation of distress, when I saw your vessel riding at anchor, and holding forth to me hopes of succour and life. I had no conception that vessels ever came

III.153   so far north, and was astounded at the sight. I quickly destroyed part of my sledge to construct oars; and by these means was enabled, with infinite fatigue, to move my ice-raft in the direction of your ship. I had determined, if you were going southward, still to trust myself to the mercy of the seas, rather than abandon my purpose. I hoped to induce you to grant me a boat with which I could still pursue my enemy. But your direction was northward. You took me on board when my vigour was exhausted, and I should soon have sunk under my multiplied hardships into a death, which I still dread,—for my task is unfulfilled.

Oh! when will my guiding spirit, in conducting me to the dæmon, allow me the rest I so much desire; or must I die, and he yet live? If I do, swear to me, Walton, that he shall not escape; that you will seek him, and satisfy my vengeance in his death. Yet, do I dare ask you to undertake my pilgrimage, to endure the hardships that I have undergone? III.154
No; I am not so selfish. Yet, when I am dead, if he should appear; if the ministers of vengeance should conduct him to you, swear that he shall not live—swear that he shall not triumph over my accumulated woes, and live to make another such a wretch as I am. He is eloquent and persuasive; and once his words had even power over my heart: but trust him not. His soul is as hellish as his form, full of treachery and fiend-like malice. Hear him not; call on the manes[124] of William, Justine, Clerval, Elizabeth, my father, and of the wretched Victor, and thrust your sword into his heart. I will hover near, and direct the steel aright.

WALTON, *in continuation.*   III.155

August 26th, 17—.

YOU have read this strange and terrific story, Margaret; and do you not feel your blood congealed with horror, like that which even now curdles mine? Sometimes, seized with sudden agony, he could not continue his tale; at others, his voice broken, yet piercing, uttered with difficulty the words so replete with agony. His fine and lovely eyes were now lighted up with indignation, now subdued to downcast sorrow, and quenched in infinite wretchedness. Sometimes he commanded his countenance and tones, and related the most horrible incidents with a tranquil voice, suppressing every mark of agitation; then, like a volcano bursting forth, his face would suddenly III.156
change to an expression of the wildest rage, as he shrieked out imprecations on his persecutor.

His tale is connected,[125] and told with an appearance of the simplest truth; yet I own to you that the letters of Felix and Safie, which he shewed me, and the apparition of the monster, seen from our ship, brought to me a greater conviction of the truth of his narrative than his asseverations, however earnest and connected. Such a monster has then really existence; I cannot doubt it; yet I am lost in surprise and admiration. Sometimes I endeavoured to gain from

---

124. Spirits of the dead.
125. Coherent.

Frankenstein the particulars of his creature's formation; but on this
point he was impenetrable.

III.157 "Are you mad, my friend?" said he, "or whither does your senseless
curiosity lead you? Would you also create for yourself and the world
a demoniacal enemy? Or to what do your questions tend? Peace,
peace! learn my miseries, and do not seek to increase your own."

Frankenstein discovered that I made notes concerning his history:
he asked to see them, and then himself corrected and augmented
them in many places; but principally in giving the life and spirit to
the conversations he held with his enemy. "Since you have preserved
my narration," said he, "I would not that a mutilated one should go
down to posterity."

Thus has a week passed away, while I have listened to the strangest
tale that ever imagination formed. My thoughts, and every feeling of
my soul, have been drunk up by the interest for my guest, which this
III.158 tale, and his own elevated and gentle manners have created. I wish
to soothe him; yet can I counsel one so infinitely miserable, so destitute of every hope of consolation, to live? Oh, no! the only joy that
he can now know will be when he composes his shattered feelings to
peace and death. Yet he enjoys one comfort, the offspring of solitude
and delirium: he believes, that, when in dreams he holds converse
with his friends, and derives from that communion consolation for
his miseries, or excitements to his vengeance, that they are not the
creations of his fancy, but the real beings who visit him from the regions of a remote world. This faith gives a solemnity to his reveries
that render them to me almost as imposing and interesting as truth.

Our conversations are not always confined to his own history and
III.159 misfortunes. On every point of general literature he displays unbounded knowledge, and a quick and piercing apprehension. His eloquence is forcible and touching; nor can I hear him, when he relates
a pathetic incident, or endeavours to move the passions of pity or
love, without tears. What a glorious creature must he have been in
the days of his prosperity, when he is thus noble and godlike in ruin.
He seems to feel his own worth, and the greatness of his fall.

"When younger," said he, "I felt as if I were destined for some great
enterprise. My feelings are profound; but I possessed a coolness of
judgment that fitted me for illustrious achievements. This sentiment
of the worth of my nature supported me, when others would have
been oppressed; for I deemed it criminal to throw away in useless
III.160 grief those talents that might be useful to my fellow-creatures. When I

reflected on the work I had completed, no less a one than the creation of a sensitive and rational animal, I could not rank myself with the herd of common projectors.[126] But this feeling, which supported me in the commencement of my career, now serves only to plunge me lower in the dust. All my speculations and hopes are as nothing; and, like the archangel who aspired to omnipotence, I am chained in an eternal hell. My imagination was vivid, yet my powers of analysis and application were intense; by the union of these qualities I conceived the idea, and executed the creation of a man. Even now I cannot recollect, without passion, my reveries while the work was incomplete. I trod heaven in my thoughts, now exulting in my powers, now burning with the idea of their effects. From my infancy I was imbued with high hopes and a lofty ambition; but how am I sunk! Oh! my friend, if you had known me as I once was, you would not recognize me in this state of degradation. Despondency rarely visited my heart; a high destiny seemed to bear me on, until I fell, never, never again to rise." III.161

Must I then lose this admirable being? I have longed for a friend; I have sought one who would sympathize with and love me. Behold, on these desert seas I have found such a one; but, I fear, I have gained him only to know his value, and lose him. I would reconcile him to life, but he repulses the idea.

"I thank you, Walton," he said, "for your kind intentions towards so miserable a wretch; but when you speak of new ties, and fresh affections, think you that any can replace those who are gone? Can any man be to me as Clerval was; or any woman another Elizabeth? Even where the affections are not strongly moved by any superior excellence, the companions of our childhood always possess a certain power over our minds, which hardly any later friend can obtain. They know our infantine dispositions, which, however they may be afterwards modified, are never eradicated; and they can judge of our actions with more certain conclusions as to the integrity of our motives. A sister or a brother can never, unless indeed such symptoms have been shewn early, suspect the other of fraud or false dealing, when another friend, however strongly he may be attached, may, in spite of himself, be invaded with suspicion. But I enjoyed friends, dear not only through habit and association, but from their own merits; and, wherever I am, the soothing voice of my Elizabeth, and the conversation of Clerval, will be ever whispered in my ear. They are dead; and but one feeling in such III.162 III.163

126. A projector is someone who proposes a novel project, often a crank or cheat.

a solitude can persuade me to preserve my life. If I were engaged in any high undertaking or design, fraught with extensive utility to my fellow-creatures, then could I live to fulfil it. But such is not my destiny; I must pursue and destroy the being to whom I gave existence; then my lot on earth will be fulfilled, and I may die."

September 2d.

MY BELOVED SISTER,

I write to you, encompassed by peril, and ignorant whether I am ever doomed to see again dear England, and the dearer friends that
III.164 inhabit it. I am surrounded by mountains of ice, which admit of no escape, and threaten every moment to crush my vessel. The brave fellows, whom I have persuaded to be my companions, look towards me for aid; but I have none to bestow. There is something terribly appalling in our situation, yet my courage and hopes do not desert me. We may survive; and if we do not, I will repeat the lessons of my Seneca,[127] and die with a good heart.

Yet what, Margaret, will be the state of your mind? You will not hear of my destruction, and you will anxiously await my return. Years will pass, and you will have visitings of despair, and yet be tortured by hope. Oh! my beloved sister, the sickening failings of your heart-felt expectations are, in prospect, more terrible to me than my
III.165 own death. But you have a husband, and lovely children; you may be happy: heaven bless you, and make you so!

My unfortunate guest regards me with the tenderest compassion. He endeavours to fill me with hope; and talks as if life were a possession which he valued. He reminds me how often the same accidents have happened to other navigators, who have attempted this sea, and, in spite of myself, he fills me with cheerful auguries. Even the sailors feel the power of his eloquence: when he speaks, they no longer despair; he rouses their energies, and, while they hear his voice, they believe these vast mountains of ice are mole-hills, which will vanish before the resolutions of man. These feelings are transitory; each day's expectation delayed fills them with fear, and I almost dread a mutiny caused by this despair.

---

127. Seneca was a Roman politician, philosopher, and playwright. He advocated stoicism—arguing that philosophers should be unmoved by pain and suffering. Ordered by Nero to kill himself he did so without complaint.

September 5th.   III.166

A scene has just passed of such uncommon interest, that although it is highly probable that these papers may never reach you, yet I cannot forbear recording it.

We are still surrounded by mountains of ice, still in imminent danger of being crushed in their conflict. The cold is excessive, and many of my unfortunate comrades have already found a grave amidst this scene of desolation. Frankenstein has daily declined in health: a feverish fire still glimmers in his eyes; but he is exhausted, and, when suddenly roused to any exertion, he speedily sinks again into apparent lifelessness.

I mentioned in my last letter the fears I entertained of a mutiny. This morning, as I sat watching the wan countenance of my friend— his eyes half closed, and his limbs hanging listlessly,—I was roused   III.167 by half a dozen of the sailors, who desired admission into the cabin. They entered; and their leader addressed me. He told me that he and his companions had been chosen by the other sailors to come in deputation to me, to make me a demand, which, in justice, I could not refuse. We were immured in ice, and should probably never escape; but they feared that if, as was possible, the ice should dissipate, and a free passage be opened, I should be rash enough to continue my voyage, and lead them into fresh dangers, after they might happily have surmounted this. They desired, therefore, that I should engage with a solemn promise, that if the vessel should be freed, I would instantly direct my course southward.

This speech troubled me. I had not despaired; nor had I yet conceived the idea of returning, if set free. Yet could I, in justice, or even   III.168 in possibility, refuse this demand? I hesitated before I answered; when Frankenstein, who had at first been silent, and, indeed, appeared hardly to have force enough to attend, now roused himself; his eyes sparkled, and his cheeks flushed with momentary vigour. Turning towards the men, he said—

"What do you mean? What do you demand of your captain? Are you then so easily turned from your design? Did you not call this a glorious expedition? and wherefore was it glorious? Not because the way was smooth and placid as a southern sea, but because it was full of dangers and terror; because, at every new incident, your fortitude was to be called forth, and your courage exhibited; because danger and death surrounded, and these dangers you were to brave   III.169 and overcome. For this was it a glorious, for this was it an honourable undertaking. You were hereafter to be hailed as the benefactors of your species; your name adored, as belonging to brave men who encountered death for honour and the benefit of mankind. And now, behold, with the first imagination of danger, or, if you will, the first mighty and terrific trial of your courage, you shrink away, and are content to be handed down as men who had not strength enough to endure cold and peril; and so, poor souls, they were chilly, and returned to their warm fire-sides. Why, that requires not this preparation; ye need not have come thus far, and dragged your captain to the shame of a defeat, merely to prove yourselves cowards. Oh! be

III.170   men, or be more than men. Be steady to your purposes, and firm as a rock. This ice is not made of such stuff as your hearts might be; it is mutable, cannot withstand you, if you say that it shall not. Do not return to your families with the stigma of disgrace marked on your brows.[128] Return as heroes who have fought and conquered, and who know not what it is to turn their backs on the foe."

He spoke this with a voice so modulated to the different feelings expressed in his speech, with an eye so full of lofty design and heroism, that can you wonder that these men were moved. They looked at one another, and were unable to reply. I spoke; I told them to retire, and consider of what had been said: that I would not lead them further north, if they strenuously desired the contrary; but that I hoped

III.171   that, with reflection, their courage would return.

They retired, and I turned towards my friend; but he was sunk in languor, and almost deprived of life.

How all this will terminate, I know not; but I had rather die, than return shamefully,—my purpose unfulfilled. Yet I fear such will be my fate; the men, unsupported by ideas of glory and honour, can never willingly continue to endure their present hardships.

September 7th.

The die is cast;[129] I have consented to return, if we are not destroyed. Thus are my hopes blasted by cowardice and indecision; I come back ignorant and disappointed. It requires more philosophy than I possess, to bear this injustice with patience.

III.172

September 12th.

It is past; I am returning to England. I have lost my hopes of utility and glory;—I have lost my friend. But I will endeavour to detail these

128. A reference to the mark of Cain (Genesis 4:15).
129. *Alea iacta est*: Caesar said this as he crossed the Rubicon in 49 BCE to invade Italy.

bitter circumstances to you, my dear sister; and, while I am wafted towards England, and towards you, I will not despond.

September 19th,[130] the ice began to move, and roarings like thunder were heard at a distance, as the islands split and cracked in every direction. We were in the most imminent peril; but, as we could only remain passive, my chief attention was occupied by my unfortunate guest, whose illness increased in such a degree, that he was entirely confined to his bed. The ice cracked behind us, and was driven with force towards the north; a breeze sprung from the west, and on the 11th the passage towards the south became perfectly free. When the III.173 sailors saw this, and that their return to their native country was apparently assured, a shout of tumultuous joy broke from them, loud and long-continued. Frankenstein, who was dozing, awoke, and asked the cause of the tumult. "They shout," I said, "because they will soon return to England."

"Do you then really return?"

"Alas! yes; I cannot withstand their demands. I cannot lead them unwillingly to danger, and I must return."

"Do so, if you will; but I will not. You may give up your purpose; but mine is assigned to me by heaven, and I dare not. I am weak; but surely the spirits who assist my vengeance will endow me with sufficient strength." Saying this, he endeavoured to spring from the bed, but the exertion was too great for him; he fell back, and fainted. III.174

It was long before he was restored; and I often thought that life was entirely extinct. At length he opened his eyes, but he breathed with difficulty, and was unable to speak. The surgeon gave him a composing draught,[131] and ordered us to leave him undisturbed. In the mean time he told me, that my friend had certainly not many hours to live.

His sentence was pronounced; and I could only grieve, and be patient. I sat by his bed watching him; his eyes were closed, and I thought he slept; but presently he called to me in a feeble voice, and, bidding me come near, said—"Alas! the strength I relied on is gone; I feel that I shall soon die, and he, my enemy and persecutor, may still be in being. Think not, Walton, that in the last moments of my existence I feel that III.175 burning hatred, and ardent desire of revenge, I once expressed, but I feel myself justified in desiring the death of my adversary. During these last days I have been occupied in examining my past conduct;

---

130. An error for September 9th.
131. A liquid sedative.

nor do I find it blameable. In a fit of enthusiastic madness I created
a rational creature, and was bound towards him, to assure, as far as
was in my power, his happiness and well-being. This was my duty;
but there was another still paramount to that. My duties towards my
fellow-creatures had greater claims to my attention, because they
included a greater proportion of happiness or misery. Urged by this
view, I refused, and I did right in refusing, to create a companion for
the first creature. He shewed unparalleled malignity and selfishness,
III.176   in evil: he destroyed my friends; he devoted to destruction beings who
possessed exquisite sensations, happiness, and wisdom; nor do I know
where this thirst for vengeance may end. Miserable himself, that he
may render no other wretched, he ought to die. The task of his destruction was mine, but I have failed. When actuated by selfish and vicious
motives, I asked you to undertake my unfinished work; and I renew
this request now, when I am only induced by reason and virtue.

"Yet I cannot ask you to renounce your country and friends, to
fulfil this task; and now, that you are returning to England, you will
have little chance of meeting with him. But the consideration of these
points, and the well-balancing of what you may esteem your duties,
III.177   I leave to you; my judgment and ideas are already disturbed by the
near approach of death. I dare not ask you to do what I think right,
for I may still be misled by passion.

"That he should live to be an instrument of mischief disturbs me;
in other respects this hour, when I momentarily expect my release,
is the only happy one which I have enjoyed for several years. The
forms of the beloved dead flit before me, and I hasten to their arms.
Farewell, Walton! Seek happiness in tranquillity, and avoid ambition, even if it be only the apparently innocent one of distinguishing
yourself in science and discoveries. Yet why do I say this? I have myself been blasted in these hopes, yet another may succeed."

His voice became fainter as he spoke; and at length, exhausted by
III.178   his effort, he sunk into silence. About half an hour afterwards he attempted again to speak, but was unable; he pressed my hand feebly,
and his eyes closed for ever, while the irradiation of a gentle smile
passed away from his lips.

Margaret, what comment can I make on the untimely extinction
of this glorious spirit? What can I say, that will enable you to understand the depth of my sorrow? All that I should express would be
inadequate and feeble. My tears flow; my mind is overshadowed by a
cloud of disappointment. But I journey towards England, and I may
there find consolation.

I am interrupted. What do these sounds portend? It is midnight;
the breeze blows fairly, and the watch on deck scarcely stir. Again;
there is a sound as of a human voice, but hoarser; it comes from the   III.179
cabin where the remains of Frankenstein still lie. I must arise, and
examine. Good night, my sister.

Great God! what a scene has just taken place! I am yet dizzy with
the remembrance of it. I hardly know whether I shall have the power
to detail it; yet the tale which I have recorded would be incomplete
without this final and wonderful catastrophe.

I entered the cabin, where lay the remains of my ill-fated and admirable friend. Over him hung a form which I cannot find words to
describe; gigantic in stature, yet uncouth and distorted in its proportions. As he hung over the coffin, his face was concealed by long locks
of ragged hair; but one vast hand was extended, in colour and apparent texture like that of a mummy. When he heard the sound of my
approach, he ceased to utter exclamations of grief and horror, and   III.180
sprung towards the window. Never did I behold a vision so horrible
as his face, of such loathsome, yet appalling hideousness. I shut my
eyes involuntarily, and endeavoured to recollect what were my duties
with regard to this destroyer. I called on him to stay.

He paused, looking on me with wonder; and, again turning towards the lifeless form of his creator, he seemed to forget my presence, and every feature and gesture seemed instigated by the wildest
rage of some uncontrollable passion.

"That is also my victim!" he exclaimed; "in his murder my crimes
are consummated; the miserable series of my being is wound to its
close! Oh, Frankenstein! generous and self-devoted[132] being! what
does it avail that I now ask thee to pardon me? I, who irretrievably   III.181
destroyed thee by destroying all thou lovedst. Alas! he is cold; he may
not answer me."

His voice seemed suffocated; and my first impulses, which had
suggested to me the duty of obeying the dying request of my friend, in
destroying his enemy, were now suspended by a mixture of curiosity
and compassion. I approached this tremendous being; I dared not
again raise my looks upon his face, there was something so scaring
and unearthly in his ugliness. I attempted to speak, but the words died
away on my lips. The monster continued to utter wild and incoherent
self-reproaches. At length I gathered resolution to address him, in
a pause of the tempest of his passion: "Your repentance," I said, "is

---

132. Meaning someone who has devoted themselves to a noble cause.

III.182   now superfluous. If you had listened to the voice of conscience, and heeded the stings of remorse, before you had urged your diabolical vengeance to this extremity, Frankenstein would yet have lived."

"And do you dream?" said the dæmon; "do you think that I was then dead to agony and remorse?—He," he continued, pointing to the corpse, "he suffered not more in the consummation of the deed;—oh! not the ten-thousandth portion of the anguish that was mine during the lingering detail of its execution. A frightful selfishness hurried me on, while my heart was poisoned with remorse. Think ye that the groans of Clerval were music to my ears? My heart was fashioned to be susceptible of love and sympathy; and, when wrenched by misery to vice and hatred, it did not endure the violence of the change without torture, such as you cannot even imagine.

III.183   "After the murder of Clerval, I returned to Switzerland, heart-broken and overcome. I pitied Frankenstein; my pity amounted to horror: I abhorred myself. But when I discovered that he, the author at once of my existence and of its unspeakable torments, dared to hope for happiness; that while he accumulated wretchedness and despair upon me, he sought his own enjoyment in feelings and passions from the indulgence of which I was for ever barred, then impotent envy and bitter indignation filled me with an insatiable thirst for vengeance. I recollected my threat, and resolved that it should be accomplished. I knew that I was preparing for myself a deadly torture; but I was the slave, not the master of an impulse, which I detested, yet could not disobey. Yet when she died!—nay, then I was not misera-

III.184   ble. I had cast off all feeling, subdued all anguish to riot in the excess of my despair. Evil thenceforth became my good.[133] Urged thus far, I had no choice but to adapt my nature to an element which I had willingly chosen. The completion of my demoniacal design became an insatiable passion. And now it is ended; there is my last victim!"

I was at first touched by the expressions of his misery; yet when I called to mind what Frankenstein had said of his powers of eloquence and persuasion, and when I again cast my eyes on the lifeless form of my friend, indignation was re-kindled within me. "Wretch!" I said, "it is well that you come here to whine over the desolation that you have made. You throw a torch[134] into a pile of buildings, and when they are consumed you sit among the ruins, and lament the

III.185   fall. Hypocritical fiend! if he whom you mourn still lived, still would

---

133. Cf. Satan, in Milton's *Paradise Lost*, bk. 4, line 110: "Evil be thou my good."
134. I.e., a naked flame.

he be the object, again would he become the prey of your accursed vengeance. It is not pity that you feel; you lament only because the victim of your malignity is withdrawn from your power."

"Oh, it is not thus—not thus," interrupted the being; "yet such must be the impression conveyed to you by what appears to be the purport of my actions. Yet I seek not a fellow-feeling in my misery. No sympathy may I ever find. When I first sought it, it was the love of virtue, the feelings of happiness and affection with which my whole being overflowed, that I wished to be participated. But now, that virtue has become to me a shadow, and that happiness and affection are turned into bitter and loathing despair, in what should I seek for sympathy? III.186 I am content to suffer alone, while my sufferings shall endure: when I die, I am well satisfied that abhorrence and opprobrium should load my memory. Once my fancy was soothed with dreams of virtue, of fame, and of enjoyment. Once I falsely hoped to meet with beings, who, pardoning my outward form, would love me for the excellent qualities which I was capable of bringing forth. I was nourished with high thoughts of honour and devotion. But now vice has degraded me beneath the meanest animal. No crime, no mischief, no malignity, no misery, can be found comparable to mine. When I call over the frightful catalogue of my deeds, I cannot believe that I am he whose thoughts were once filled with sublime and transcendant visions of the beauty and the majesty of goodness. But it is even so; the fallen III.187 angel becomes a malignant devil. Yet even that enemy of God and man had friends and associates in his desolation; I am quite alone.

"You, who call Frankenstein your friend, seem to have a knowledge of my crimes and his misfortunes. But, in the detail which he gave you of them, he could not sum up the hours and months of misery which I endured, wasting in impotent passions. For whilst I destroyed his hopes, I did not satisfy my own desires. They were for ever ardent and craving; still I desired love and fellowship, and I was still spurned. Was there no injustice in this? Am I to be thought the only criminal, when all human kind sinned against me? Why do you not hate Felix, who drove his friend from his door with contumely? Why do you not execrate the rustic who sought to destroy the saviour III.188 of his child? Nay, these are virtuous and immaculate beings! I, the miserable and the abandoned, am an abortion, to be spurned at, and kicked, and trampled on. Even now my blood boils at the recollection of this injustice.

"But it is true that I am a wretch. I have murdered the lovely and the helpless; I have strangled the innocent as they slept, and grasped to death his throat who never injured me or any other living thing. I have devoted my creator, the select specimen of all that is worthy of love and admiration among men, to misery; I have pursued him even to that irremediable ruin. There he lies, white and cold in death. You hate me; but your abhorrence cannot equal that with which I regard myself. I look on the hands which executed the deed; I think

III.189   on the heart in which the imagination of it was conceived, and long for the moment when they will meet my eyes, when it will haunt my thoughts, no more.

"Fear not that I shall be the instrument of future mischief. My work is nearly complete. Neither your's nor any man's death is needed to consummate the series of my being, and accomplish that which must be done; but it requires my own. Do not think that I shall be slow to perform this sacrifice. I shall quit your vessel on the ice-raft which brought me hither, and shall seek the most northern extremity of the globe; I shall collect my funeral pile, and consume to ashes this miserable frame, that its remains may afford no light to any curious and unhallowed wretch, who would create such another as I

III.190   have been. I shall die. I shall no longer feel the agonies which now consume me, or be the prey of feelings unsatisfied, yet unquenched. He is dead who called me into being; and when I shall be no more, the very remembrance of us both will speedily vanish. I shall no longer see the sun or stars, or feel the winds play on my cheeks. Light, feeling, and sense, will pass away; and in this condition must I find my happiness. Some years ago, when the images which this world affords first opened upon me, when I felt the cheering warmth of summer, and heard the rustling of the leaves and the chirping of the birds, and these were all to me, I should have wept to die; now it is my only consolation. Polluted by crimes, and torn by the bitterest remorse, where can I find rest but in death?

III.191   "Farewell! I leave you, and in you the last of human kind whom these eyes will ever behold. Farewell, Frankenstein! If thou wert yet alive, and yet cherished a desire of revenge against me, it would be better satiated in my life than in my destruction. But it was not so; thou didst seek my extinction, that I might not cause greater wretchedness; and if yet, in some mode unknown to me, thou hast not yet ceased to think and feel, thou desirest not my life for my own misery. Blasted as thou wert, my agony was still superior to thine; for the bitter sting of remorse may not cease to rankle in my wounds until death shall close them for ever.

"But soon," he cried, with sad and solemn enthusiasm, "I shall die, and what I now feel be no longer felt. Soon these burning miseries will be extinct. I shall ascend my funeral pile triumphantly, and exult   III.192 in the agony of the torturing flames. The light of that conflagration will fade away; my ashes will be swept into the sea by the winds. My spirit will sleep in peace; or if it thinks, it will not surely think thus. Farewell."

He sprung from the cabin-window, as he said this, upon the ice-raft which lay close to the vessel. He was soon borne away by the waves, and lost in darkness and distance.

THE END.

Related Texts

1. *Frankenstein*: The Introduction to the 1831 edition

[The 1831 edition of Frankenstein *contained a new Introduction written by Mary Shelley, replacing the 1818 Preface written by Percy.]*

The Publishers of the Standard Novels, in selecting "Frankenstein" for one of their series, expressed a wish that I should furnish them with some account of the origin of the story. I am the more willing to comply, because I shall thus give a general answer to the question, so very frequently asked me—"How I, then a young girl, came to think of, and to dilate upon, so very hideous an idea?" It is true that I am very averse to bringing myself forward in print; but as my account will only appear as an appendage to a former production, and as it will be confined to such topics as have connection with my authorship alone, I can scarcely accuse myself of a personal intrusion.

It is not singular that, as the daughter of two persons of distinguished literary celebrity, I should very early in life have thought of writing. As a child I scribbled; and my favourite pastime, during the hours given me for recreation, was to "write stories." Still I had a dearer pleasure than this, which was the formation of castles in the air—the indulging in waking dreams—the following up trains of thought, which had for their subject the formation of a succession of imaginary incidents. My dreams were at once more fantastic and agreeable than my writings. In the latter I was a close imitator—rather doing as others had done, than putting down the suggestions of my own mind. What I wrote was intended at least for one other eye—my childhood's companion and friend; but my dreams were all my own; I accounted for them to nobody; they were my refuge when annoyed—my dearest pleasure when free.

I lived principally in the country as a girl,[1] and passed a considerable time in Scotland. I made occasional visits to the more picturesque parts; but my

---

1. [Not strictly true: see above p. ix.]

habitual residence was on the blank and dreary northern shores of the Tay, near Dundee. Blank and dreary on retrospection I call them; they were not so to me then. They were the eyry[2] of freedom, and the pleasant region where unheeded I could commune with the creatures of my fancy. I wrote then— but in a most common-place style. It was beneath the trees of the grounds belonging to our house, or on the bleak sides of the woodless mountains near, that my true compositions, the airy flights of my imagination, were born and fostered. I did not make myself the heroine of my tales. Life appeared to me too common-place an affair as regarded myself. I could not figure to myself that romantic woes or wonderful events would ever be my lot; but I was not confined to my own identity, and I could people the hours with creations far more interesting to me at that age, than my own sensations.

After this my life became busier, and reality stood in place of fiction. My husband, however, was from the first, very anxious that I should prove myself worthy of my parentage, and enrol myself on the page of fame. He was for ever inciting me to obtain literary reputation, which even on my own part I cared for then, though since I have become infinitely indifferent to it. At this time he desired that I should write, not so much with the idea that I could produce any thing worthy of notice, but that he might himself judge how far I possessed the promise of better things hereafter. Still I did nothing. Travelling, and the cares of a family, occupied my time; and study, in the way of reading, or improving my ideas in communication with his far more cultivated mind, was all of literary employment that engaged my attention.

In the summer of 1816, we visited Switzerland, and became the neighbours of Lord Byron. At first we spent our pleasant hours on the lake, or wandering on its shores; and Lord Byron, who was writing the third canto of Childe Harold, was the only one among us who put his thoughts upon paper. These, as he brought them successively to us, clothed in all the light and harmony of poetry, seemed to stamp as divine the glories of heaven and earth, whose influences we partook with him.

But it proved a wet, ungenial summer, and incessant rain often confined us for days to the house. Some volumes of ghost stories, translated from the German into French, fell into our hands. There was the History of the Inconstant Lover, who, when he thought to clasp the bride to whom he had pledged his vows, found himself in the arms of the pale ghost of her whom he had deserted. There was the tale of the sinful founder of his race, whose miserable doom it was to bestow the kiss of death on all the younger sons of his fated house, just when they reached the age of promise. His gigantic,

---

2. [An eagle's nest.]

shadowy form, clothed like the ghost in Hamlet, in complete armour, but with the beaver[3] up, was seen at midnight, by the moon's fitful beams, to advance slowly along the gloomy avenue. The shape was lost beneath the shadow of the castle walls; but soon a gate swung back, a step was heard, the door of the chamber opened, and he advanced to the couch of the blooming youths, cradled in healthy sleep. Eternal sorrow sat upon his face as he bent down and kissed the forehead of the boys, who from that hour withered like flowers snapt upon the stalk. I have not seen these stories since then; but their incidents are as fresh in my mind as if I had read them yesterday.

"We will each write a ghost story," said Lord Byron; and his proposition was acceded to. There were four of us. The noble author began a tale, a fragment of which he printed at the end of his poem of Mazeppa. Shelley, more apt to embody ideas and sentiments in the radiance of brilliant imagery, and in the music of the most melodious verse that adorns our language, than to invent the machinery of a story, commenced one founded on the experiences of his early life. Poor Polidori had some terrible idea about a skull-headed lady, who was so punished for peeping through a key-hole—what to see I forget—something very shocking and wrong of course; but when she was reduced to a worse condition than the renowned Tom of Coventry, he did not know what to do with her, and was obliged to despatch her to the tomb of the Capulets, the only place for which she was fitted.[4] The illustrious poets also, annoyed by the platitude of prose, speedily relinquished their uncongenial task.

I busied myself *to think of a story*,—a story to rival those which had excited us to this task. One which would speak to the mysterious fears of our nature, and awaken thrilling horror—one to make the reader dread to look round, to curdle the blood, and quicken the beatings of the heart. If I did not accomplish these things, my ghost story would be unworthy of its name. I thought and pondered—vainly. I felt that blank incapability of invention which is the greatest misery of authorship, when dull Nothing replies to our anxious invocations. *Have you thought of a story?* I was asked each morning, and each morning I was forced to reply with a mortifying negative.

Every thing must have a beginning, to speak in Sanchean[5] phrase; and that beginning must be linked to something that went before. The Hindoos give the world an elephant to support it, but they make the elephant stand upon a tortoise. Invention, it must be humbly admitted, does not

---

3. [The visor.]

4. [Tom of Coventry looked (in the traditional story) at Lady Godiva as she rode naked through the streets of Coventry. In Shakespeare's *Romeo and Juliet* the two protagonists end their lives in Juliet's family tomb.]

5. [Sancho Panza, the squire to Don Quixote in Cervantes's novel.]

consist in creating out of void, but out of chaos; the materials must, in the first place, be afforded: it can give form to dark, shapeless substances, but cannot bring into being the substance itself. In all matters of discovery and invention, even of those that appertain to the imagination, we are continually reminded of the story of Columbus and his egg.[6] Invention consists in the capacity of seizing on the capabilities of a subject, and in the power of moulding and fashioning ideas suggested to it.

Many and long were the conversations between Lord Byron and Shelley, to which I was a devout but nearly silent listener. During one of these, various philosophical doctrines were discussed, and among others the nature of the principle of life, and whether there was any probability of its ever being discovered and communicated. They talked of the experiments of Dr. Darwin, (I speak not of what the Doctor really did, or said that he did, but, as more to my purpose, of what was then spoken of as having been done by him,) who preserved a piece of vermicelli in a glass case, till by some extraordinary means it began to move with voluntary motion.[7] Not thus, after all, would life be given. Perhaps a corpse would be re-animated; galvanism had given token of such things:[8] perhaps the component parts of a creature might be manufactured, brought together, and endued with vital warmth.

Night waned upon this talk, and even the witching hour[9] had gone by, before we retired to rest. When I placed my head on my pillow, I did not sleep, nor could I be said to think. My imagination, unbidden, possessed and guided me, gifting the successive images that arose in my mind with a vividness far beyond the usual bounds of reverie. I saw—with shut eyes, but acute mental vision,—I saw the pale student of unhallowed arts kneeling beside the thing he had put together. I saw the hideous phantasm of a man stretched out, and then, on the working of some powerful engine, show signs of life, and stir with an uneasy, half vital motion. Frightful must it be; for supremely frightful would be the effect of any human endeavour to mock the stupendous mechanism of the Creator of the world. His success would terrify the artist; he would rush away from his odious handywork, horror-stricken. He would hope that, left to itself, the slight spark of life which he had communicated would fade; that this thing, which had

---

6. [Columbus when told that anyone could have discovered the New World challenged those present to stand an egg on end. When all failed, he crushed one end and stood the egg on it. The moral is that what seems impossible is easy, once one has been shown how to do it.]

7. [MWS is reporting a garbled account of a passage in Darwin: see below, p. 233.]

8. [See below, pp. 235 –44.]

9. [Midnight—when witches were supposed to be active.]

received such imperfect animation, would subside into dead matter; and he might sleep in the belief that the silence of the grave would quench for ever the transient existence of the hideous corpse which he had looked upon as the cradle of life. He sleeps; but he is awakened; he opens his eyes; behold the horrid thing stands at his bedside, opening his curtains, and looking on him with yellow, watery, but speculative eyes.

I opened mine in terror. The idea so possessed my mind, that a thrill of fear ran through me, and I wished to exchange the ghastly image of my fancy for the realities around. I see them still; the very room, the dark *parquet*, the closed shutters, with the moonlight struggling through, and the sense I had that the glassy lake and white high Alps were beyond. I could not so easily get rid of my hideous phantom; still it haunted me. I must try to think of something else. I recurred to my ghost story,—my tiresome unlucky ghost story! O! if I could only contrive one which would frighten my reader as I myself had been frightened that night!

Swift as light and as cheering was the idea that broke in upon me. "I have found it! What terrified me will terrify others; and I need only describe the spectre which had haunted my midnight pillow." On the morrow I announced that I had *thought of a story*. I began that day with the words, *It was on a dreary night of November*, making only a transcript of the grim terrors of my waking dream.

At first I thought but of a few pages—of a short tale; but Shelley urged me to develope the idea at greater length. I certainly did not owe the suggestion of one incident, nor scarcely of one train of feeling, to my husband, and yet but for his incitement, it would never have taken the form in which it was presented to the world. From this declaration I must except the preface. As far as I can recollect, it was entirely written by him.

And now, once again, I bid my hideous progeny go forth and prosper. I have an affection for it, for it was the offspring of happy days, when death and grief were but words, which found no true echo in my heart. Its several pages speak of many a walk, many a drive, and many a conversation, when I was not alone; and my companion was one who, in this world, I shall never see more. But this is for myself; my readers have nothing to do with these associations.

I will add but one word as to the alterations I have made. They are principally those of style. I have changed no portion of the story, nor introduced any new ideas or circumstances. I have mended the language where it was so bald as to interfere with the interest of the narrative; and these changes occur almost exclusively in the beginning of the first volume. Throughout they are entirely confined to such parts as are mere adjuncts to the story, leaving the core and substance of it untouched.

M. W. S.

London, October 15. 1831.

2. Percy Shelley to Thomas Love Peacock, from Mary W. Shelley and Percy B. Shelley, *A History of a Six Weeks' Tour* (1817)

[A History of a Six Weeks' Tour *was published anonymously. Mary Shelley added to her and Percy's journal of their 1814 travels in France and Switzerland two of her own letters, perhaps originally addressed to Fanny Imlay, dating from early in her 1816 stay near Geneva (Mary Wollstonecraft Shelley,* The Letters of Mary Wollstonecraft Shelley, *ed. Betty T. Bennett, 3 vols. [Baltimore: Johns Hopkins University Press, 1980–1988], 1:16–22), signed M, along with two further letters signed S, and Percy Shelley's poem "Mont Blanc." The selection reproduced here is from a letter from Percy to Thomas Love Peacock (Thomas Love Peacock,* Peacock's Memoirs of Shelley, with Shelley's Letters to Peacock, *ed. Herbert Francis Brett Brett-Smith [London: Henry Frowde, 1909], 111–21); its description of the landscape, particularly the Sea of Ice, closely corresponds to passages in* Frankenstein.]

Hôtel de Londres, Chamouni, July 22d 1816

. . .

From Servoz three leagues remain to Chamouni.—Mont Blanc was before us—the Alps, with their innumerable glaciers on high all around, closing in the complicated windings of the single vale—forests inexpressibly beautiful, but majestic in their beauty—intermingled beech and pine, and oak, overshadowed our road, or receded, whilst lawns of such verdure as I have never seen before occupied these openings, and gradually became darker in their recesses. Mont Blanc was before us, but it was covered with cloud; its base, furrowed with dreadful gaps, was seen above. Pinnacles of snow intolerably bright, part of the chain connected with Mont Blanc, shone through the clouds at intervals on high. I never knew—I never imagined what mountains were before. The immensity of these aerial summits excited, when they suddenly burst upon the sight, a sentiment of extatic wonder, not unallied to madness. And remember this was all one scene, it all pressed home to our regard and our imagination. Though it embraced a vast extent of space, the snowy pyramids which shot into the bright blue sky seemed to overhang our path; the ravine, clothed with gigantic pines, and black with its depth below, so deep that the very roaring of the untameable Arve, which rolled through it, could not be heard above—all was as much our own, as if we had been the creators of such impressions in the minds of others as now occupied our own. Nature was the poet, whose harmony held our spirits more breathless than that of the divinest.

As we entered the valley of Chamouni (which in fact may be considered as a continuation of those which we have followed from Bonneville and Cluses) clouds hung upon the mountains at the distance perhaps of 6000 feet from the earth, but so as effectually to conceal not only Mont Blanc, but the other *aiguilles*, as they call them here, attached and subordinate to it. We were travelling along the valley, when suddenly we heard a sound as of the burst of smothered thunder rolling above; yet there was something earthly in the sound, that told us it could not be thunder. Our guide hastily pointed out to us a part, of the mountain opposite, from whence the sound came. It was an avalanche. We saw the smoke of its path among the rocks, and continued to hear at intervals the bursting of its fall. It fell on the bed of a torrent, which it displaced, and presently we saw its tawny-coloured waters also spread themselves over the ravine, which was their couch.

We did not, as we intended, visit the *Glacier de Boisson* to-day, although it descends within a few minutes' walk of the road, wishing to survey it at least when unfatigued. We saw this glacier which comes close to the fertile plain, as we passed, its surface was broken into a thousand unaccountable figures: conical and pyramidical crystalizations, more than fifty feet in height, rise from its surface, and precipices of ice, of dazzling splendour, overhang the woods and meadows of the vale. This glacier winds upwards from the valley, until it joins the masses of frost from which it was produced above, winding through its own ravine like a bright belt flung over the black region of pines. There is more in all these scenes than mere magnitude of proportion: there is a majesty of outline; there is an awful grace in the very colours which invest these wonderful shapes—a charm which is peculiar to them, quite distinct even from the reality of their unutterable greatness.

July 24.

Yesterday morning we went to the source of the Arveiron. It is about a league from this village; the river rolls forth impetuously from an arch of ice, and spreads itself in many streams over a vast space of the valley, ravaged and laid bare by its inundations. The glacier by which its waters are nourished, overhangs this cavern and the plain, and the forests of pine which surround it, with terrible precipices of solid ice. On the other side rises the immense glacier of Montanvert, fifty miles in extent, occupying a chasm among mountains of inconceivable height, and of forms so pointed and abrupt, that they seem to pierce the sky. From this glacier we saw as we sat on a rock, close to one of the streams of the Arveiron, masses of ice detach themselves from on high, and rush with a loud dull noise into the vale. The violence of their fall turned them into powder, which flowed over the rocks in imitation of waterfalls, whose ravines they usurped and filled.

In the evening I went with Ducrée, my guide, the only tolerable person I have seen in this country, to visit the glacier of Boisson. This glacier, like that of Montanvert, comes close to the vale, overhanging the green meadows and the dark woods with the dazzling whiteness of its precipices and pinnacles, which are like spires of radiant crystal, covered with a net-work of frosted silver. These glaciers flow perpetually into the valley, ravaging in their slow but irresistible progress the pastures and the forests which surround them, performing a work of desolation in ages, which a river of lava might accomplish in an hour, but far more irretrievably; for where the ice has once descended, the hardiest plant refuses to grow; if even, as in some extraordinary instances, it should recede after its progress has once commenced. The glaciers perpetually move onward, at the rate of a foot each day, with a motion that commences at the spot where, on the boundaries of perpetual congelation, they are produced by the freezing of the waters which arise from the partial melting of the eternal snows. They drag with them from the regions whence they derive their origin, all the ruins of the mountain, enormous rocks, and immense accumulations of sand and stones. These are driven onwards by the irresistible stream of solid ice; and when they arrive at a declivity of the mountain, sufficiently rapid, roll down, scattering ruin. I saw one of these rocks which had descended in the spring, (winter here is the season of silence and safety) which measured forty feet in every direction.

The verge of a glacier, like that of Boisson, presents the most vivid image of desolation that it is possible to conceive. No one dares to approach it; for the enormous pinnacles of ice which perpetually fall, are perpetually reproduced. The pines of the forest, which bound it at one extremity, are overthrown and shattered to a wide extent at its base. There is something inexpressibly dreadful in the aspect of the few branchless trunks, which, nearest to the ice rifts, still stand in the uprooted soil. The meadows perish, overwhelmed with sand and stones. Within this last year, these glaciers have advanced three hundred feet into the valley. Saussure, the naturalist, says, that they have their periods of increase and decay: the people of the country hold an opinion entirely different; but as I judge, more probable. It is agreed by all, that the snow on the summit of Mont Blanc and the neighbouring mountains perpetually augments, and that ice, in the form of glaciers, subsists without melting in the valley of Chamouni during its transient and variable summer. If the snow which produces this glacier must augment, and the heat of the valley is no obstacle to the perpetual existence of such masses of ice as have already descended into it, the consequence is obvious; the glaciers must augment and will subsist, at least until they have overflowed this vale.

I will not pursue Buffon's[10] sublime but gloomy theory—that this globe which we inhabit will at some future period be changed into a mass of frost by the encroachments of the polar ice, and of that produced on the most elevated points of the earth. Do you, who assert the supremacy of Ahriman,[11] imagine him throned among these desolating snows, among these palaces of death and frost, so sculptured in this their terrible magnificence by the adamantine hand of necessity, and that he casts around him, as the first essays of his final usurpation, avalanches, torrents, rocks, and thunders, and above all these deadly glaciers, at once the proof and symbols of his reign;—add to this, the degradation of the human specks—who in these regions are half deformed or idiotic, and most of whom are deprived of any thing that can excite interest or admiration. This is a part of the subject more mournful and less sublime; but such as neither the poet nor the philosopher should disdain to regard.

This morning we departed, on the promise of a fine day, to visit the glacier of Montanvert. In that part where it fills a slanting valley, it is called the Sea of Ice, This valley is 950 toises, or 7600 feet above the level of the sea. We had not proceeded far before the rain began to fall, but we persisted until we had accomplished more than half of our journey, when we returned, wet through.

Chamouni, July 25th.

We have returned from visiting the glacier of Montanvert, or as it is called, the Sea of Ice, a scene in truth of dizzying wonder. The path that winds to it along the side of a mountain, now clothed with pines, now intersected with snowy hollows, is wide and steep. The cabin of Montanvert is three leagues from Chamouni, half of which distance is performed on mules, not so sure footed, but that on the first day the one which I rode fell in what the guides call a *mauvais pas*, so that I narrowly escaped being precipitated down the mountain. We passed over a hollow covered with snow, down which vast stones are accustomed to roll. One had fallen the preceding day, a little time after we had returned: our guides desired us to pass quickly, for it is said that sometimes the least sound will accelerate their descent. We arrived at Montanvert, however, safe.

On all sides precipitous mountains, the abodes of unrelenting frost, surround this vale: their sides are banked up with ice and snow, broken, heaped high, and exhibiting terrific chasms. The summits are sharp and naked pinnacles, whose overhanging steepness will not even permit snow

---

10. [Georges-Louis Leclerc, comte de Buffon (1707–1788), the great naturalist.]
11. [The spirit of destruction in Zoroastrianism.]

to rest upon them. Lines of dazzling ice occupy here and there their per-pendicular rifts, and shine through the driving vapours with inexpressible brilliance: they pierce the clouds like things not belonging to this earth. The vale itself is filled with a mass of undulating ice, and has an ascent sufficiently gradual even to the remotest abysses of these horrible desarts. It is only half a league (about two miles) in breadth, and seems much less. It exhibits an appearance as if frost had suddenly bound up the waves and whirlpools of a mighty torrent. We walked some distance upon its surface. The waves are elevated about 12 or 15 feet from the surface of the mass, which is intersected by long gaps of unfathomable depth, the ice of whose sides is more beautifully azure than the sky. In these regions every thing changes, and is in motion. This vast mass of ice has one general progress, which ceases neither day nor night; it breaks and bursts for ever: some undulations sink while others rise; it is never the same. The echo of rocks, or of the ice and snow which fall from their overhanging precipices, or roll from their aerial summits, scarcely ceases for one moment. One would think that Mont Blanc, like the god of the Stoics, was a vast ani-mal, and that the frozen blood for ever circulated through his stony veins.

We dined (Mary, Claire, and I) on the grass, in the open air, surrounded by this scene. The air is piercing and clear. We returned down the moun-tain, sometimes encompassed by the driving vapours, sometimes cheered by the sunbeams, and arrived at our inn by seven o'clock.

3. Polidori's diary for the period he was in contact with Mary Godwin/Shelley

[From John William Polidori, The Diary of Dr. John William Polidori, 1816: Relating to Byron, Shelley, Etc., *ed. W. M. Rossetti (London: Elkin Mathews, 1911)]*

May 27.—Got up; went about a boat; got one for 3 fr. a day; rowed to Sécheron. Breakfasted. Got into a carriage. Went to Banker's, who changed our money, and afterwards left his card. To Pictet—not at home. Home, and looked at accounts: bad temper on my side. Went into the boat, rowed across to Diodati; cannot have it for three years;[12] English

---

12. [Polidori is searching for accommodation for Byron; they do, in fact, end up at Villa Diodati.]

family. Crossed again; I went; L[ord] B[yron] back. Getting out, L[ord] B[yron] met M[ary] Wollstonecraft Godwin, her sister, and Percy Shelley. I got into the boat into the middle of Leman Lake, and there lay my length, letting the boat go its way.

Found letter from De Roche inviting me to breakfast to-morrow; curious with regard to L[ord] B[yron]. Dined; P[ercy] S[helley], the author of *Queen Mab*, came; bashful, shy, consumptive; twenty-six;[13] separated from his wife; keeps the two daughters of Godwin, who practise his theories;[14] one L[ord] B[yron]'s.[15]

Into the calèche; horloger's at Geneva; L[ord] B[yron] paid 15 nap. towards a watch;[16] I, 13: repeater and minute-hand; foolish watch.

Went to see the house of Madame Necker, 100 a half-year; came home, etc.

May 28.—Went to Geneva, to breakfast with Dr. De Roche; acute, sensible, a listener to himself; good clear head. Told me that armies on their march induce a fever (by their accumulation of animal dirt, irregular regimen) of the most malignant typhoid kind; it is epidemic. There was a whole feverish line from Moscow to Metz, and it spread at Geneva the only almost epidemic typhus for many years. He is occupied in the erection of Lancaster schools, which he says succeed well. He is a Louis Bourbonist. He told me my fever was not an uncommon one among travellers. He came home with me, and we had a chat with L[ord] B[yron]; chiefly politics, where of course we differed. He had a system well worked out, but I hope only hypothetical, about liberty of the French being Machiavellianly not desirable by Europe. He pointed out Dumont in the court, the rédacteur of Bentham.

Found a letter from Necker to the hotel-master, asking 100 nap. for three months; and another from Pictet inviting L[ord] B[yron] and any friend to go with him at 8 to Madame Einard, a connection of his. We then, ascending our car, went to see some other houses, none suiting.

When we returned home, Mr. Percy Shelley came in to ask us to dinner; declined; engaged for tomorrow. We walked with him, and got into his boat, though the wind raised a little sea upon the lake. Dined at four. Mr. Hentsch, the banker, came in; very polite; told L[ord] B[yron] that, when

---

13. [Actually twenty-three.]

14. [I.e., they believe in "free love."]

15. [I.e., one of these daughters is involved with Byron.]

16. [I.e., Byron contributed fifteen napoleons (a considerable sum of money—two weeks' rent on a large villa) toward the cost of a watch for Polidori.]

he saw him yesterday, he had not an idea that he was speaking to one of the most famous lords of England.

Dressed and went to Pictet's: an oldish man, about forty-six, tall, well-looking, speaks English well. His daughter showed us a picture, by a young female artist, of Madame Lavallière in the chapel; well executed in pencil—good lights and a lusciously grieving expression.

Went to Madame Einard. Introduced to a room where about 8 (afterwards 20), 2 ladies (1 more). L[ord] B[yron]'s name was alone mentioned; mine, like a star in the halo of the moon, invisible. L[ord] B[yron] not speaking French, M. Einard spoke bad Italian. A Signor Rossi came in, who had joined Murat at Bologna. Manly in thought; admired Dante as a poet more than Ariosto, and a discussion about manliness in a language. Told me Geneva women amazingly chaste even in thoughts. Saw the Lavallière artist. A bonny, rosy, seventy-yeared man, called Bonstetten, the beloved of Gray and the correspondent of Mathison.

Madame Einard made tea, and left all to take sugar with the fingers. Madame Einard showed some historical pieces of her doing in acquerella,[17] really good, a little too French-gracish. Obliged to leave before ten for the gates shut.[18] Came home, went to bed.

Was introduced by Shelley to Mary Wollstonecraft Godwin, called here Mrs. Shelley. Saw picture by Madame Einard of a cave in the Jura where in winter there is no ice, in summer plenty. No names announced, no ceremony—each speaks to whom he pleases. Saw the bust of Jean Jacques[19] erected upon the spot where the Geneva magistrates were shot.[20] L[ord] B[yron] said it was probably built of some of the stones with which they pelted him.[21] The walk is deserted. They are now mending their roads. Formerly they could not, because the municipal money always went to the public box.

May 29.—Went with Mr. Hentsch to see some houses along the valley in which runs the Rhone: nothing. Dined with Mr. and Mrs. Percy Shelley and Wollstonecraft Godwin. Hentsch told us that the English last year exported corn to Italy to a great amount.

May 30.—Got up late. Went to Mr. and Mrs. Shelley; breakfasted with them; rowed out to see a house together. S[helley] went from Lucerne with

---

17. [I.e., watercolor.]
18. [The gates of Geneva were shut every evening and reopened the next day.]
19. [Rousseau.]
20. [In the Revolution of 1792.]
21. [This did not happen at Geneva but rather at Môtiers in 1765.]

the two, with merely £26, to England along the Rhine in bateaux.[22] Gone through much misery, thinking he was dying; married a girl for the mere sake of letting her have the jointure that would accrue to her; recovered; found he could not agree; separated; paid Godwin's debts, and seduced his daughter; then wondered that he would not see him. The sister left the father to go with the other. Got a child.[23] All clever, and no meretricious appearance. He is very clever; the more I read his *Queen Mab*, the more beauties I find. Published at fourteen a novel;[24] got £30 for it; by his second work £100. *Mab* not published.[25]—Went in calèche with L[ord] B[yron] to see a house; again after dinner to leave cards; then on lake with L[ord] B[yron]. I, Mrs. S[helley], and Miss G[odwin], on to the lake till nine. Drank tea, and came away at 11 after confabbing. The batelier went to Shelley, and asked him as a favour not to tell L[ord] B[yron] what he gave for his boat, as he thought it quite fit that Milord's payment be double; we sent Berger to say we did not wish for the boat.

May 31.—Breakfasted with Shelley; read Italian with Mrs. S[helley]; dined; went into a boat with Mrs. S[helley], and rowed all night till 9; tea'd together; chatted, etc.

June 1.—Breakfasted with S[helley]; entered a calèche; took Necker's house for 100 louis for 8 or 365 days. Saw several houses for Shelley; one good. Dined; went in the boat; all tea'd together.

Rogers[26] the subject: L[or]d B[yron] thinks good poet; malicious. Marquis of Lansdowne being praised by a whole company as a happy man, having all good, R[ogers] said, "But how horridly he carves turbot!" Ward[27] having reviewed his poems in the *Quarterly*, having a bad heart and being accused of learning his speeches, L[ord] B[yron], upon malignantly hinting to him [Rogers] how he had been carved, heard him say: "I stopped his speaking though by my epigram, which is—

"'Ward has no heart, they say, but I deny it;

He has a heart, and gets his speeches by it.'"

On L[ord] B[yron's] writing a poem to his sister wherein he says, "And when friends e'en paused and love," etc., Rogers, going to some one, said:

---

22. [A reference to the Six Weeks' Tour.]
23. [I.e., Mary and Percy's daughter, Clara, who died in infancy.]
24. [*Zastrozzi*; he was seventeen or eighteen.]
25. [*Queen Mab* was privately printed in 1813, but not put on public sale. Polidori was presumably reading one of these copies, which were printed but not published.]
26. [Byron's friend Samuel Rogers.]
27. [John William Ward, later Earl of Dudley.]

"I don't know what L[ord] B[yron] means by *pausing*; I called upon him every day." He did this regularly, telling L[ord] B[yron] all the bad news with a malignant grin. When L[ord] B[yron] wrote "Weep, daughter of a royal line," Rogers came to him one day, and, taking up the *Courier*, said: "I am sure now you're attacked there; now don't mind them"; and began reading, looking every now and then at L[ord] B[yron] with an anxious searching eye, till he came to "that little poet and disagreeable person, Mr. Samuel—" when he tore the paper, and said: "Now this must be that fellow Croker,"[28] and wished L[ord] B[yron] to challenge him. He talked of going to Cumberland with L[ord] B[yron], and, asking him how he meant to travel, L[ord] B[yron] said "With four horses." Rogers went to company, and said: "It is strange to hear a man talking of four horses who seals his letters with a tallow candle."[29]

Shelley is another instance of wealth inducing relations to confine for madness, and was only saved by his physician being honest. He was betrothed from a boy to his cousin, for age;[30] another came who had as much as he *would* have, and she left him "because he was an atheist." When starving, a friend to whom he had given £2000, though he knew it, would not come near him. Heard Mrs. Shelley repeat Coleridge on Pitt,[31] which persuades me he is a poet.

A young girl of eighteen, handsome, died within half-an-hour yesterday: buried to-day. Geneva is fortified—legumes growing in the fosses.[32]— Went about linen and plate.[33]

June 2.—Breakfasted with Shelley. Read Tasso with Mrs. Shelley. Took child for vaccination.

Found gates shut because of church-service. Went in search of Rossi. Saw a village where lads and lasses, soubrettes and soldiers, were dancing, to a tabor and drum, waltzes, cotillions, etc. Dr. R[ossi] not at home.

Dined with S[helley]; went to the lake with them and L[ord] B[yron]. Saw their house; fine. Coming back, the sunset, the mountains on one side, a dark mass of outline on the other, trees, houses hardly visible, just distinguishable; a white light mist, resting on the hills around, formed the blue into a circular dome bespangled with stars only and lighted by the moon which gilt the lake. The dome of heaven seemed oval. At 10 landed and drank tea. Madness, Grattan, Curran, etc., subjects.

---

28. [Presumably the same John Wilson Croker who reviewed *Frankenstein*.]
29. [Tallow candles, made from sheep's fat, were cheap, unlike beeswax candles.]
30. [The legal age for marriage with parental consent in England was 14 for boys, 12 for girls.]
31. [From Coleridge's poem "Fire, Famine, and Slaughter."]
32. [I.e., vegetables growing in the ditches below the ramparts.]
33. [Linen (for bedding) and silverware to set up house.]

June 3.—Went to Pictet's on English day.

June 4.—Went about Diodati's house. Then to see Shelley, who, with Mrs. Shelley, came over. Went in the evening to a musical society of about ten members at M. Odier's; who read a very interesting memoir upon the subject of whether a physician should in any case tell a lover the health [of the lady of his affections], or anything that, from being her physician, comes to his knowledge. Afterwards had tea and politics. Saw there a Dr. Gardner, whom I carried home in the calèche. Odier invited me for every Wednesday.

Came home. Went on the lake with Shelley and Lord Byron, who quarrelled with me.

June 5.—At 12 went to Hentsch about Diodati; thence to Shelley's. Read Tasso. Home in calèche. Dined with them in the public room: walked in the garden. Then dressed, and to Odier's, who talked with me about somnambulism.[34] Was at last seated, and conversed with some Génevoises: so so—too fine. Quantities of English; speaking amongst themselves, arms by their sides, mouths open and eyes glowing; might as well make a tour of the Isle of Dogs. Odier gave me yesterday many articles of *Bibliothèque* [illegible]—translated and *rédigés* by himself, and to-day a manuscript on somnambulism.

June 6.—At 1 up—breakfasted. With Lord Byron in the calèche to Hentsch, where we got the paper making us masters of Diodati for six months to November 1 for 125 louis.

Thence to Shelley: back: dinner. To Shelley in boat: driven on shore: home. Looked over inventory and Berger's accounts. Bed.

June 7.—Up at——. Pains in my loins and languor in my bones. Breakfasted—looked over inventory.

Saw L[ord] B[yron] at dinner; wrote to my father and Shelley; went in the boat with L[ord] B[yron]; agreed with boatman for English boat. Told us Napoleon had caused him to get his children. Saw Shelley over again.

June 8.—Up at 9; went to Geneva on horseback, and then to Diodati to see Shelley; back; dined; into the new boat—Shelley's,—and talked, till the ladies' brains whizzed with giddiness, about idealism. Back; rain; puffs of wind. Mistake.

---

34. [Polidori had written a dissertation on somnambulism.]

June 9.—Up by 1: breakfasted. Read Lucian. Dined. Did the same: tea'd. Went to Hentsch: came home. Looked at the moon, and ordered packing-up.

June 10.—Up at 9. Got things ready for going to Diodati; settled accounts, etc. Left at 3; went to Diodati; went back to dinner, and then returned. Shelley etc. came to tea, and we sat talking till 11. My rooms are so:

Picture-gallery.	
Bedroom	

June 11.—Wrote home and to Pryse Gordon. Read Lucian. Went to Shelley's; dined; Shelley in the evening with us.

June 12.—Rode to town. Subscribed to a circulating library, and went in the evening to Madame Odier. Found no one. Miss O[dier], to make time pass, played the Ranz des Vaches[35]—plaintive and war-like. People arrived. Had a confab with Dr. O. about perpanism,[36] etc. Began dancing: waltzes, cotillons, French country-dances and English ones: first time I shook my feet to French measure. Ladies all waltzed except the English: *they* looked on frowning. Introduced to Mrs. Slaney: invited me for next night. You ask without introduction; the girls refuse those they dislike. Till 12. Went and slept at the Balance.[37]

June 13.—Rode home, and to town again. Went to Mrs. Slaney: a ball. Danced and played at chess. Walked home in thunder and lightning: lost my way. Went back in search of some one—fell upon the police. Slept at the Balance.

June 14.—Rode home—rode almost all day. Dined with Rossi, who came to us; shrewd, quick, manly-minded fellow; like him very much. Shelley etc. fell in in the evening.

June 15.—Up late; began my letters. Went to Shelley's. After dinner, jumping a wall my foot slipped and I strained my left ankle. Shelley etc. came in the evening; talked of my play etc., which all agreed was worth

---

35. [A Swiss tune sung or played on an alpenhorn to call cattle from pasture.]
36. [No one knows what this word is intended to be.]
37. [An inn in Geneva, the gates being locked.]

nothing. Afterwards Shelley and I had a conversation about principles,— whether man was to be thought merely an instrument.[38]

June 16.—Laid up. Shelley came, and dined and slept here, with Mrs. S[helley] and Miss Clare Clairmont. Wrote another letter.

June 17.—Went into the town; dined with Shelley etc. here. Went after dinner to a ball at Madame Odier's; where I was introduced to Princess Something and Countess Potocka, Poles, and had with them a long confab. Attempted to dance, but felt such horrid pain was forced to stop. The ghost-stories are begun by all but me.[39]

June 18.—My leg much worse. Shelley and party here. Mrs. S[helley] called me her brother (younger). Began my ghost-story after tea. Twelve o'clock, really began to talk ghostly. L[ord] B[yron] repeated some verses of Coleridge's *Christabel*, of the witch's breast; when silence ensued, and Shelley, suddenly shrieking and putting his hands to his head, ran out of the room with a candle. Threw water in his face, and after gave him ether. He was looking at Mrs. S[helley], and suddenly thought of a woman he had heard of who had eyes instead of nipples, which, taking hold of his mind, horrified him.—He married; and, a friend of his liking his wife, he tried all he could to induce her to love him in turn.[40] He is surrounded by friends who feed upon him, and draw upon him as their banker.[41] Once, having hired a house, a man wanted to make him pay more, and came trying to bully him, and at last challenged him. Shelley refused, and was knocked down; coolly said that would not gain him his object, and was knocked down again.—Slaney called.

June 19.—Leg worse; began my ghost-story. Mr. S[helley?] etc. forth here. Bonstetten and Rossi called. B[onstetten] told me a story of the religious feuds in Appenzel; a civil war between Catholics and Protestants. Battle arranged; chief advances; calls the other. Calls himself and other fools, for battles will not persuade of his being wrong. Other agreed, and persuaded them to take the boundary rivulet; they did. Bed at 3 as usual.

---

38. [Perhaps a discussion about the principle of life, and whether human beings are merely machines.]
39. [See above, p. 185.]
40. [Shelley tried to persuade both his first wife and MWS (before their marriage) to sleep with his friend Thomas Jefferson Hogg.]
41. [Surely a reference to William Godwin.]

June 20.—My leg kept me at home. Shelley etc. here.

June 21.—Same.

June 22.—L[ord] B[yron] and Shelley went to Vevay; Mrs. S[helley] and Miss Clare Clairmont to town. Went to Rossi's—had tired his patience. Called on Odier; Miss [Clairmont?] reading Byron.

June 23.—Went to town; apologized to Rossi. Called on Dr. Slaney etc. Walked to Mrs. Shelley. Pictet, Odier, Slaney, dined with me. Went down to Mrs. S[helley] for the evening. Odier mentioned the cases of two gentlemen who, on taking the nitrate of silver, some time after had a blacker face. Pictet confirmed it.

June 24.—Up at 12. Dined down with Mrs. S[helley] and Miss C[lare] C[lairmont].

June 26.—Up. Mounted on horseback: went to town. Saw Mrs. Shelley: dined. To Dr. Rossi's party of physicians: after at Mrs. S[helley's].

June 27.—Up at Mrs. Shelley's: dined. No calèche arrived: walked to G[eneva]. No horses: ordered saddle-horse. Walked to Rossi's—gone. Went to the gate: found him. Obliged to break off the appointment. Went to Odier's. Met with Mr. ——, a friend of Lord Byron's father. Invited me to his house: been a long time on the Continent. Music, ranz des vaches, beautiful. Rode two hours; went to Mrs. S[helley]; Miss C[lairmont] talked of a soliloquy.

June 28.—All day at Mrs. S[helley's].

June 29.—Up at 1; studied; down at Mrs. S[helley's].

June 30.—Same.

July 1.—Went in calèche to town with Mrs. S[helley] and C[lare] for a ride, and to mass (which we did not go to, being begun). Dined at 1. Went to town to Rossi. Introduced to Marchese Saporati; together to Mr. Saladin of Vaugeron, Countess Breuss, Calpnafur; and then to a party of ladies.
Found Lord Byron and Shelley returned.

July 2.—Rain all day. In the evening to Mrs. S[helley].

September 5.—Not written my Journal till now through neglect and dissipation. Had a long explanation with S[helley] and L[ord] B[yron] about my conduct to L[ord] B[yron]; threatened to shoot S[helley] one day on the water. Horses been a subject of quarrel twice, Berger having accused me of laming one.

4. "Prometheus," from Edward Baldwin [i.e., William Godwin], *The Pantheon* (1806)

Prometheus was, like the rest of his family [the Titans, the pre-Olympian deities overthrown by Jupiter], an enemy to the progeny of Saturn [Jupiter's father]: a dispute is said to have arisen, as to what part of the sacrifices offered by the subjects of Jupiter was to be considered as appropriated to the God at whose altar it was slain; for from the first institution of sacrifices, it was the custom for the victim to be amicably shared, according to a fixed rule, between the God and his worshipper.

Prometheus offered himself as umpire in this dispute: he was always regarded as the wisest, or rather as the craftiest and most wily, of the heavenly race: he killed two bulls, and skilfully divided the flesh, the fat, the offal and the bones: he sewed up the flesh very neatly in the skin of one of the bulls, and the bones, inclosed in an envelop of fat, in the other: he then called upon Jupiter to look on the parcels, and to say which of them he chose for his own share: Jupiter, deceived by the fair appearance of the fat which peeped here and there through the apertures of the skin, chose that parcel, in preference to the other which contained all that was most wholesome and valuable of the two animals: this is an ugly story; and the part assigned in it to Jupiter is wholly unworthy of our idea of a God.

From this moment Jupiter became the bitter enemy of Prometheus, and to punish him and his race withheld from them the use of the celestial element of fire: Prometheus, who surpassed the whole universe in mechanical skill and contrivance, formed a man of clay of such exquisite workmanship, that he wanted nothing but a living soul to cause him to be acknowledged the paragon of creation: Minerva, the Goddess of arts, beheld the performance of Prometheus with approbation, and offered him any assistance in her power to complete his work: she conducted him to Heaven, where he watched his opportunity to carry off at the tip of his wand a portion of celestial fire, from the chariot of the sun: with this he animated his image: and the man of Prometheus immediately moved, and thought, and spoke, and became every thing that the fondest wishes of his creator could ask.

Jupiter became still more exasperated than ever with this new specimen of Prometheus's ability and artifice: he ordered Vulcan, the great artificer of Heaven, to make a woman of clay, that should be still more consummate and beautiful of structure than Prometheus's man: with this alluring present Jupiter determined to tempt Prometheus to his ruin: all the Gods of the Saturnian race, eager to abet the project of their chief, gave her each one a several gift, from which circumstance she obtained the name of Pandora, *all gifts*: Venus gave her the power to charm; the Graces bestowed upon her symmetry of limb and elegance of motion; Apollo the accomplishments of vocal and instrumental music; Mercury the art of persuasive speech; June a multitude of rich and gorgeous ornaments; and Minerva the management of the loom and the needle: last of all, Jupiter presented her with a sealed box, which she was to bestow on whoever became her husband: thus prepared, he sent her to Prometheus by Mercury, as if he had intended him a compliment upon the wonders of his own performance: Prometheus however saw through the deceit, and rejected her: Mercury then presented her to Epimetheus, Prometheus's brother, who was less on his guard, received the seemingly angelic creature with delight, and eagerly opened the box she brought him: the lid was no sooner unclosed than a multitude of calamities and evils of all imaginable sorts flew out, which dispersed themselves over the world, and from that fatal moment have never ceased to afflict the human race: Hope only remained at the bottom, being all that is left us to relieve our sorrows, and render the labours and troubles of life capable of being endured.

Jupiter thus constantly failing in every indirect attempt of retaliation upon his redoubtable adversary Prometheus, at last proceeded to a more open hostility: he sent Vulcan and Mercury, who seizing upon this extraordinary personage, conveyed him by main force to Mount Caucasus, where, being chained to the rock, a vulture commissioned by Jupiter cowered upon his breast, continually preying upon his liver, which grew again as fast as it was devoured: how the unfortunate Prometheus was delivered from this punishment I shall have occasion to mention hereafter.[42]

The fable of Prometheus's man, and Pandora, the first woman, was intended to convey an allegorical sense: the ancients saw to how many evils the human race is exposed, how many years of misery many of them

---

42. [Godwin later reports that Hercules shot the vulture that was eating Prometheus's liver.]

endure, with what a variety of diseases they are afflicted, how the great majority is condemned to perpetual labour, poverty and ignorance, and how many vices are contracted by men, in consequence of which they afflict each other with a thousand additional evils, perfidy, tyranny, cruel tortures, murder and war: the views of the early ancients, in times of savage rudeness, and before the refinements of society were invented, were more melancholy respecting the lot of man than ours have been since: they could not therefore admit that he was the creature of Jupiter: they were rather prone to believe that Jupiter was from the first his enemy: the same views led them to revile and speak evil of the female sex: Hesiod, who together with Homer are the two oldest Grecian poets, and who has related this story of Prometheus at length, says "that the men are like industrious bees who by their labours procure all the honey, and that the women are the idle drones who fatten upon the good things which their more assiduous fellows have accumulated:" it is impossible not to remark a considerable resemblance between the story of Pandora's box, and that of the apple with which Eve in the Bible *tempted* her husband, *and he did eat.*

There is a further story that has been told of Prometheus, which for its strangeness it may seem worthwhile to relate: some of the first race of mankind proved ungrateful to their former [i.e., maker], and gave a perfidious information to Jupiter against him: Jupiter rewarded the informers with the gift of immortal life, for all men were hitherto mortal: he packed the gift however upon the back of an ass: the ass had already travelled a long way, and was exceedingly weary, and troubled with a tormenting thirst: he at length came to a river, but a water-serpent guarded the stream, and would not suffer him to drink: the wily serpent would yield upon no other terms than that the ass should surrender to him the invaluable burthen he bore, in exchange for his draught: the ass accepted the bargain: thus the serpent obtained the gift of immortal life, in consequence of which every year he casts his slough, and comes forth as young and vigorous as ever, while the unworthy mortals for whom Jupiter destined it, lost the reward of their treachery.

The story of the creation of man by the hands of Prometheus was not however universally received in the religion of the Greeks; many deemed it more decent and just to ascribe this event to the power of Jupiter.

5. Humphry Davy, "Historical View of the Progress of Chemistry" from *Elements of Chemical Philosophy* (1812)

[Sir Humphry Davy (1778–1829) was one of the most important chemists of the early nineteenth century, and a founder of modern chemistry. Mary Shelley read this text with care.[43] This is the complete text of the "Historical View," except for the omission of some footnote references, especially to works in foreign languages. The remaining notes are Davy's.]

Most of the substances belonging to our globe are constantly undergoing alterations in sensible qualities, and one variety of matter becomes as it were transmuted into another.

Such changes, whether natural or artificial, whether slowly or rapidly performed, are called chemical; thus the gradual and almost imperceptible decay of the leaves and branches of a fallen tree exposed to the atmosphere, and the rapid combustion of wood in our fires, are both chemical operations.

The object of Chemical Philosophy is to ascertain the causes of all phænomena of this kind, and to discover the laws by which they are governed.

The ends of this branch of knowledge are the application of natural substances to new uses, for increasing the comforts and enjoyments of man, and the demonstration of the order, harmony, and intelligent design of the system of the earth.

The foundations of chemical philosophy, are observation, experiment, and analogy. By observation, facts are distinctly and minutely impressed on the mind. By analogy, similar facts are connected. By experiment, new facts are discovered; and, in the progression of knowledge, observation, guided by analogy, leads to experiment, and analogy confirmed by experiment, becomes scientific truth.

To give an instance.—Whoever will consider with attention the slender green vegetable filaments (*Conferva rivularis*) which in the summer exist in almost all streams, likes, or pools, under the different circumstances of shade and sunshine, will discover globules of air upon the filaments exposed under water to the sun, but no air on the filaments that are shaded. He will find that the effect is owing to the presence of light. This is an *observation*; but it gives no information respecting the nature of the air.

---

43. [See above, p. xxv, n. 61.]

Let a wine glass filled with water be inverted over the Conferva, the air will collect in the upper part of the glass, and when the glass is filled with air, it may be closed by the hand, placed in its usual position, and an inflamed taper introduced into it; the taper will burn with more brilliancy than in the atmosphere. This is an *experiment*. If the phenomena are reasoned upon, and the question is put, whether all vegetables of this kind, in fresh or in salt water, do not produce such air under like circumstance, the enquirer is guided by *analogy*: and when this is determined to be the case by new trials, a *general scientific truth* is established—That all Confervæ in the sunshine produce a species of air that supports flame in a superior degree; which has been shown to be the case by various minute investigations.

These principles of research, and combinations of methods, have been little applied, except in late times. A transient view of the progress of chemical philosophy will prove that the most brilliant discoveries, and the happiest theoretical arrangements belonging to it are of very recent origin; and a few historical details and general observations upon the progress and effects of the science will form, perhaps, no improper introduction to the elements of this branch of knowledge.

The only processes which can be called chemical, known to the civilized nations of antiquity, belonged to certain arts, such as metallurgy, dyeing, and the manufacture of glass or porcelain; but these processes appear to have been independent of each other, pursued in the workshop alone, and unconnected with general knowledge.

In the early mythological systems of the Egyptian priests, and the Bramins of Hindostan, some views respecting the chemical changes of the elements seem to have been developed, which passed, under new modifications, into the theories of the Greeks; but as the most refined doctrines of this enlightened people, concerning natural causes, in their best times, were little more than a collection of vague speculations, rather poetical than philosophical, it cannot well be supposed that in earlier ages, and amongst nations less advanced in cultivation, there were any traces of genuine science.

The inhabitants of Lower Egypt, where the overflowing of the Nile covered a sandy desert with vegetation and life, might easily adopt the notion, that water, in different modifications, produced all the varieties of inanimate and organized matter; and this dogma characterized the earliest school of Greece.

To generalize upon the great forms or powers of nature, as elements, requires only very superficial observation; and hence the theories seem to have originated, which have been attributed to Anaximander, and others of the early Greek philosophers, concerning air, earth, water, and fire.

As geometry and the mathematical sciences became improved, mechanical solutions of the changes of bodies were natural consequences, such as the atomic philosophy of the Ionian sect, and the five regular solids assumed by the Pythagoreans as the materials of the universe.

In the beginning of the Macedonian dynasty, the school of Aristotle gave a transient attention to the objects of natural science, but the great founder attempted too many subjects to be able to offer correct views of any one series.—And his erroneous practice, that of advancing general principles, and applying them to particular instances, so fatal to truth in all sciences, more particularly opposed itself to the progress of one founded upon a minute examination of obscure and hidden properties of natural bodies.

Theophrastus, the successor of Aristotle, did not, it appears, adopt the sublime, though purely speculative doctrine of his master, the identity of matter, and its diversity of form;—for he says, in the beginning of his book concerning fossils, 'stones are produced from earth, metals from water.'—How such a notion as the last could have been formed, it is difficult to discover; yet, Theophrastus is perhaps the best observer amongst the ancients, whose works are in our possession, and the theories of this distinguished teacher, who is said to have had a class of 2000 pupils, cannot be considered as an unfavourable specimen of the theoretical physics of the age.

In all pursuits which required only the native powers of the intellect, or the refinements of taste, the Greeks were pre-eminent;—their literature, their works of art, offer models which have never been excelled. They possessed, as if instinctively, the perception of every thing beautiful, grand, and decorous. As philosophers, they failed not from a want of genius, or even of application, but merely because they pursued a false path,—because they reasoned more upon an imaginary system of nature, than upon the visible and tangible universe.

It will be in vain to look in the annals of Rome for science, that did not exist in Greece. The conquerors became the pupils of the conquered; and the Romans did little more than clothe the systems of their masters in a new dress, and adapt them to a new people.

The grand, but unequal poem of Lucretius, contains the abstract of the opinions of Epicurus, compared with those of other celebrated teachers. The Natural History of Pliny, is a collection from all sources, but principally from Theophrastus and Aristotle. The details from his own observation are more interesting when they relate to artificial, than when they refer to natural operations; the speculative notions are of the rudest kind. The earlier philosophical work of the Romans, as if indicative of the youth of the people, is marked by power and genius, by boldness and incorrectness; the later, as if it belonged to their old age, by garrulity, copious and amusing anecdote, superstitious notions, and vulgar prejudices.

Some of the historians of this science,[44] in their zeal for the honour of its antiquity, have indeed endeavoured to find instances of an acquaintance with some doctrines of practical chemistry, at least, amongst the ancients.—Thus Democritus is quoted by Laertius as having employed himself in processes for imitating gems, and for softening and working ivory. Caligula is said to have made experiments with the view of extracting gold from orpiment.—Dioscorides, who is supposed to have been physician to the celebrated Cleopatra, has described the process of subliming mercury from its ores.—Even Cleopatra herself, on the evidence of such circumstances, might be considered as an experimenter, because, in the madness of profusion, she dissolved a pearl in vinegar, and made a nauseous draught of a costly and beautiful substance; but it is idle to relate such circumstances as indications of *science*. If chemical operations had been known to any extent, beyond their mere relations to the arts, some mention of them might have been expected in the medical writings of those times; but not even distillation is noticed in the works of Hippocrates or Galen; and the same Dioscorides who has just been alluded to, and who probably possessed whatever knowledge was at that time extant in Egypt, recommends the use of a fleece of wool or a sponge, for collecting the products from boiling or burning substances.

The origin of chemistry, as a science of experiment, cannot be dated farther back than the seventh or eighth century of the Christian era, and it seems to have been coeval with the short period in which cultivation and improvements were promoted by the Arabians.

The early Mahometans endeavoured to destroy all the records of the former progress of the human mind; and, as if to make compensation for this barbarian spirit, the same people were destined, in a more advanced period, to rekindle the light of letters, and to become the inventors and cultivators of a new science.

The early nomenclature of chemistry demonstrates how much it owes to the Arabians.—The words alcohol, alkahest, aludel, alembic, alkali, require no comment.

The first Arabian systematic works on chemistry are said to have been composed by Geber in the reigns of the caliphs Almainon and Almanzor. The preparation of medicines seems to have been the primary object in this

---

44. Many of the alchemical writers derive alchemy from Tubal Cain; others from Hermes Trismegistus, the Mercury of the Greeks. The first writing specifically on a chemical subject, is a manuscript supposed to be of the fifth century, by Zosimus, on the art of making gold and silver; which was in the king's library at Paris. Suidas, who wrote in the ninth or tenth century, mentions Diocletian as having burnt the books of the Egyptians concerning the chemistry of silver and gold.

study; and Rhases, Avicenna, and Avenzoar, who have described various chemical operations in their works, were the celebrated physicians of the age.

Amongst a people of conquerors, disposed to sensuality and luxury even from the spirit of their religion, and romantic and magnificent in their views of power, it was not to be expected that any new knowledge should be followed in a rational and philosophical manner; and the early chemical discoveries led to the pursuit of alchemy, the objects of which were to produce a substance capable of converting all other metals into gold; and an universal remedy calculated indefinitely to prolong the period of human life.

Reasonings upon the nature of the metals, and the composition of the philosopher's stone, form a principal part of the treatises ascribed to Geber;[45] and the disciples of the School of Bagdat seem to have been the first professed alchemists.

It required strong motives to induce men to pursue the tedious and disgusting processes of the furnace; but labourers could hardly be wanting, when prospects so brilliant and magnificent were offered to them; the means of procuring unbounded wealth; of forming a paradise on earth; and of enjoying an immortality depending on their own powers.

The processes supposed to relate to the transmutation of metals, and the elixir of life, were probably first made known to the Europeans during the time of the crusades—and many of the warriors who, animated with visionary plans of conquest, fought the battles of their religion in the plains of Palestine, seemed to have returned to their native countries under the influence of a new delusion.

The public spirit in the West, was calculated to assist the progress of all pursuits that carried with them an air of mysticism. Warm with the ardor of an extending and exalted religion, men were much more disposed to believe than to reason;—the love of knowledge and power is instinctive in the human mind; in darkness it desires light, and follows it with enthusiasm even when appearing merely in delusive glimmerings.

---

45. The library of the British Museum contains several works bearing the name of Geber: amongst them are De Alchemia argentea, Speculum Alchemiae, et de Inventione perfectionis: but they appear to be compilations formed by alchemists of the 15th and 16th centuries. Arsenic, mercury, and sulphur, are considered in them as elements of the metals; distillation is distinctly described. Alcohol, corrosive sublimate, and different saline combinations of iron, tin, copper, and lead, are mentioned in them; but they abound in obscure descriptions of mysterious processes, and contain an account of some impracticable experiments.—The Liber Fornacum is the most intelligible part of the works ascribed to Geber; it contains a description of several metallurgical operations, and of the common apparatus of the assayer.

The records of the middle ages contain a great variety of anecdotes relating to the transmutation of metals, and the views or pretensions of persons considered as adepts in alchemy: these early periods constitute what may be regarded as the heroic or fabulous ages of chemistry. Some of the alchemists were low imposters, whose object was to delude the credulous and the ignorant; others seemed to have deceived themselves with vain hopes; but all followed the pursuit as a secret and mysterious study. The processes were communicated only to chosen disciples, and being veiled in the most enigmatic and obscure language, their importance was enhanced by the concealment. In all times men are governed more by what they desire or fear, than by what they know; and in this age it was peculiarly easy to deceive, but difficult to enlighten, the public mind; truths were discovered, but they were blended with the false and the marvellous; and another era was required to separate them from absurdities, and to demonstrate their importance and uses.

Arnald of Villa Nova, who is said to have died in 1250, was one of the earliest European Enquirers who attended to chemical operations. In the edition of the works ascribed to him, published at Leyden in 1509, there are several treatises on alchemical subjects, which shew that he firmly believed in the transmutation of metals; the same opinions are attributed to him and to Geber; and he seems to have followed the study with no other views than those of preparing medicines, and attempting the composition of the philosopher's stone.

Raymund Lully of Majorca is said to have been a disciple of Arnald, and applied himself much more than his instructor to philosophy; but the works on general science, ascribed to him, are more abundant in abstract metaphysical propositions, than in facts; he followed, in his physical views, the plan of Aristotle, and our opinion of his chemical talents cannot be very exalted, if the alchemical treatises bearing his name be regarded as genuine documents.

Arnald and Lully are both celebrated by the vindicators of alchemy, as having been certainly possessed of the secret of transmutation. Arnald is said to have converted iron into gold at Rome; and it is pretended that Lully performed a similar operation before Edward I. in London, of which gold nobles were said to have been made.

That the delusions of alchemy were ardently pursued at this time may be learned from a reference to the public acts of these periods. Pope John the 22d, who was raised to the pontificate in the year 1316, openly condemned the alchemists as impostors, and the bull begins by stating, that "they promise what they do not perform;" and in England an act of Parliament was passed in the fifth year of the reign of Henry IV. prohibiting the attempts at transmutation, and making them felonious.[46]

---

46. Lord Coke calls this act the shortest he ever met with.

Even in these times, however, there were some few efforts to form scientific views. In the beginning of the thirteenth century, Roger Bacon of Oxford applied himself to experiment, and his works offer proofs of talents, industry, and sagacity. He was a man of a truly philosophical turn, desirous of investigating nature, and of extending the resources of art, and his inquiries offered some very extraordinary combinations; but neither his labours, nor those of Albert of Cologne, his contemporary, who appears to have been a genius of a kindred character, had any considerable influence on the improvement of their age. The wonders performed by the experimental art were attributed by the vulgar to magic; and at a time when knowledge belonged only to the cloister, any new philosophy was of course regarded even by the learned with a jealous eye.

It would be a labour of little profit to dwell upon the works of the professed alchemists of the fourteenth and fifteenth centuries, of Richard and Ripley in England, Isac in Holland, Pico of Mirandula and Koffsky, in Poland. The works attributed to these persons are of similar stamp, and contain nothing which can either instruct or amuse an intelligent reader. Basil Valentine of Erfurt deserves to be separated from the rest of the enquirers of this age, on account of the novelty and variety of his experiments on metallic preparations, particularly antimony: in his *Currus triumphalis Antimonii* he has described a number of the combinations of this metal. He used the mineral acids for solutions, and seems to have been one of the first persons who observed the production of ether from alcohol. He flourished about the year 1413.

Cornelius Agrippa, who was born at Cologne in 1486, openly professed magic, and endeavoured to connect together judicial astrology, the hermetic art, and metaphysical philosophy; and he was followed by Paracelsus, in Switzerland, and Digby, Kelly, and Dee, in England.

The first Arabian Alchemists seem to have adopted the idea, that the elements were under the dominion of spiritual beings, who might be submitted to human power; and the notions of fairies and of genii, which have been depicted with so much vividness of fancy and liveliness of description in the Thousand and One Nights, seem to have been connected with the pursuit of the science of transmutation, and the production of the elixir of life. The speculative ideas of the Arabians were more or less adopted by their European disciples. The Rosicrucian philosophy, in which gnomes, sylphs, salamanders, and nymphs were the spiritual agents, supposed capable of being governed or enslaved by man, seems to have originated with the Alchemists of this period; and Agrippa, Paracelsus, and their followers, above mentioned, all professed to believe in supernatural powers, in an art above experiment, in a system of knowledge not derived from the senses.

It would be a tedious and useless task, to describe all the absurdities in the opinions and practices of this school. Paracelsus alone deserves particular notice, from the circumstance of his being the first public lecturer on chemistry in Europe, and from the more important circumstance of his application of mercurial preparations to the cure of diseases. The Magistrates of Basle established a professor's chair for their countryman, but he soon quitted an occupation in which regularity was necessary, and spent his days in wandering from place to place, searching for, and revealing secrets. He pretended to confer immortality, by his medicines, and yet died at the age of 49, at Saltsburg, in the year 1541.

The enthusiasm of this man almost supplied his want of genius. He formed a number of new preparations of the metals, which were studied and applied by his disciples; his exaggerated censure of the methods of the ancients, and of the systems of his day, had an effect in diminishing their popularity; one error was expelled by another; and it is a great step towards improvement, that men should know they have been in delusion.

Van Helmont, of Brussels, born in 1588, was formed in the school of Alchemy, and his mind was tinctured with its prejudices: but his views concerning nature and the elements were distinguished by much more philosophical acuteness, and more sagacity, than those of any former writer. He is the first person who seems to have had any idea respecting elastic fluids, different from the air of the atmosphere; and he has distinctly mentioned three of these substances, to which he applied the term gases: namely, aqueous gas or steam, unctuous or inflammable gas, and gas from wood or carbonic acid gas. Van Helmont developed some accurate views respecting the permanent elasticity of air, and the operation of heat upon it; and a sketch of a curious instrument very similar to the differential thermometer, is to be found in his works.

Van Helmont has used a term not so applicable or intelligible as gas, namely, Blas; which he supposed to be an influence derived from the heavenly bodies, of a most subtile and etherial nature; and on the idea of its operations in our terrestrial system, he has endeavoured to found the vindication of astrology.

At this period there was no taste in the public mind to restrain vague imaginations. There were no severe critics to correct the wanderings of genius. The systems of logic, adopted in the schools were founded rather upon the analogies of words, than upon the relations of things; and they were more calculated to conceal error, than to discover truth.—Till the revival of literature in Europe, there was no attempt at philosophical discussion in any of the sciences; the diffusion of letters gradually brought the opinions of men to the standard of nature and truth; failures in the experimental arts produced caution, and the detection of imposture created rational scepticism.

The delusions of Alchemy were exposed by Guibert, Gassendi, and Kepler. Libavius answered Guibert in a tone which demonstrated the weakness of his cause. This person, who died in 1616, was the last active experimentalist who believed that transmutation had actually been performed; and in the beginning of the 17th century the processes of rational chemistry were pursued by a number of enlightened persons in different parts of Europe.

A metallurgical school had before this time been founded in Germany. George Agricola published, in 1542, his twelve books, *de Re Metallica*, or, on the methods of extracting and purifying the useful metals; and he was followed by Lazarus Erckern, Assay-Master General of the Empire of Germany, whose works, brought forward in 1574, contain a number of useful practices detailed in a simple and perspicuous manner.

Lord Bacon happily described the Alchemists as similar to those husbandmen who in searching for a treasure supposed to be hidden in their land, by turning up and pulverising the soil, rendered it fertile; in seeking for brilliant impossibilities, they sometimes discovered useful realities; and in speaking of the chemistry of his time, he says, a new philosophy has arisen from the furnaces, which has confounded all the reasonings of the ancients. This illustrious man himself pointed out many important objects of chemical enquiry; but he was a still greater benefactor to the science, by his development of the general system for improving natural knowledge. Till his time there had been no distinct views concerning the art of experiment and observation. Lord Bacon demonstrated how little could be effected by the unassisted human powers, and the weakness of the strongest intellect even without artificial resources. He directed the attention of inquirers to instruments for assisting the senses, and for examining bodies under new relations. He taught that Man was but the servant and interpreter of Nature; capable of discovering truth in no other way but by observing and imitating her operations: that facts were to be collected and not speculations formed: and that the materials for the foundations of true systems of knowledge were to be discovered, not in the books of the ancients, not in metaphysical theories, not in the fancies of men, but in the visible and tangible external world.

Though Van Helmont had formed some just notions respecting the properties of air, yet his views were blended with obscure and vague speculations, and it is to the disciples of Galilæo, that the true knowledge of the mechanical qualities and agencies of elastic fluids is owing. After Torricelli and Pascal had shewn the pressure and weight of the atmosphere, the investigation of its effects in chemical operations became an obvious problem.

John Rey is generally quoted as the first person who shewed by experiments that air is fixed in bodies during calcination: but it appears from the work of this acute and learned man that he reasoned upon the processes of others, rather than upon his own observations.

He quotes Fachsius, Libavius, Cesalpin, and Cardan, as having ascertained the increase of weight of lead during its conversion into a calx, and he mentions an experiment of Hammerus Poppius, who found that antimony calcined by a burning-glass, notwithstanding the loss of vapours, yet was heavier after the process.

Rey ridicules the various notions of the Alchemists on the cause of this phænomenon; and ascribes it to the union of air with the metal; he supposes that air is miscible with other bodies besides metals, and states distinctly that it may be expelled from water.

The observations of John Rey seem to have excited no attention amongst his cotemporaries. The philosophical spirit was only beginning to animate chemistry, and the labourers in this science, occupied by their own peculiar processes, were little disposed to listen to the reasonings of an enquirer in general science; yet, though the most active of the forms of matter were neglected in the processes of the operative chemists of this day, and consequently no just views formed by them, still they discovered a number of important facts respecting the combinations and agencies of solid and fluid bodies. Glauber at Amsterdam, about 1640, made known several neutral salts, and several compounds of metallic and vegetable substances. Kunckel in Saxony and Sweden, pursued technical chemistry with very great success, and was the first person who made any philosophical experiments upon phosphorus, which was accidentally discovered by Brandt in 1669. Barner in Poland, and Glaser in France, published elementary books on the science, and Borichius in Denmark, Bohn at Leipzic, and Hoffman at Halle pursued specific scientific investigations with much zeal and success; and Hoffman was the first person who attempted the philosophical analysis of mineral waters.

About the middle of this century likewise mathematical and physical investigations were pursued in every part of the civilized world with an enthusiasm before unknown. The new mode of improving knowledge by collecting facts, associated together a number of labourers in the same pursuit. It was felt that the whole of nature was yet to be investigated, that there were distinct subjects connected with utility and glory, sufficient to employ all enquirers, yet tending to the common end of promoting the progress of the human mind. Learned bodies were formed in Italy,

England, and France, for the purpose of the interchange of opinions, the combination of labour and division of expense in performing new experiments, and the accumulation and diffusion of knowledge.

The Academy del Cimento was established in 1651 under the patronage of the Duke of Tuscany; the Royal Society of London, in 1660; the Royal Academy of Sciences of Paris, in 1666. And a number of celebrated men, who have been the great luminaries of the different departments of science, were brought together or formed in these noble establishments. The ardour of scientific investigation was excited and kept alive by sympathy: taste was improved by discussion, and by a comparison of opinions. The conviction that useful discoveries would be appreciated and rewarded, was a constant stimulus to industry, and every field of enquiry was open for the free and unbiassed exercise of the powers of genius.

Boyle, Hooke, and Slare, were the principal early chemical investigators attached to the Royal Society of London. Homberg, Geoffroy, and the two Lemerys, a few years later, distinguished themselves in France.

Otto de Guericke of Magdeburgh invented the air-pump; and this instrument, improved by Boyle and Hooke, was made an important apparatus for investigating the properties of air. Boyle[47] and Hooke,[48] from their experiments, concluded that air was absolutely necessary to combustion and respiration, and that one part of it only was employed in these processes. And Hooke formed the sagacious conclusion, that this principle is the same as the substance fixed in nitre, and that combustion is a chemical process, the solution of the burning body in elastic fluid, or its union with this matter.

Mayow of Oxford, in 1674, published his treatises on the nitro-ærial spirit, in which he advanced opinions similar to those of Boyle and Hooke, and supported them by a number of original and curious experiments; but his work, though marked by strong ingenuity, abounds in vague hypotheses. He attempted to apply the imperfect chemistry of his day to physiology; his failure was complete, but it was the failure of a man of genius.

Boyle was one of the most active experimenters, and certainly the greatest chemist of his age. He introduced the use of tests or reagents, active substances for detecting the presence of other bodies: he overturned the ideas which at that time were prevalent, that the results of operations by fire were the real elements of things, and he ascertained a number of important facts respecting inflammable bodies, acids, alkalies, and the phænomena of combination; but neither he nor any of his contemporaries endeavoured to account for the changes of bodies by any fixed principles. The solutions of

---

47. Boyle's Works, Vo. iv. page 90.
48. Hooke's Micrographia, page 45, 104, 105.

the phænomena were attempted either on rude mechanical notions, or by occult qualities, or peculiar subtile spirits or ethers supposed to exist in the different bodies.—And it is to the same great genius who developed the laws that regulate the motions of the heavenly bodies, that chemistry owes the first distinct philosophical elucidations of the powers which produce the changes and apparent transmutations of the substances belonging to the earth.

Sugar dissolves in water, alkalies unite with acids, metals dissolve in acids. Is not this, says Newton, on account of an attraction between their particles? Copper dissolved in aquafortis is thrown down by iron. Is not this because the particles of the iron have a stronger attraction for the particles of the acid, than those of copper: and do not different bodies attract each other with different degrees of force?[49]

A few years after Newton had brought forward these sagacious views, the elder Geoffroy endeavoured to ascertain the relative attractive powers of bodies for each other, and to arrange them in an order in which these forces, which he named, affinities, were expressed.

Chemistry had scarcely begun to assume the form of a science, when the attention of the most powerful minds were directed to other objects of research;—the same great man who bestowed on it its first accurate principles, in some measure impeded its immediate progress, by his more important discoveries in optics, mechanics, and astronomy.

These objects of the Newtonian philosophy were calculated by their grandeur, their simplicity, and their importance, to become the study of the men of most distinguished talents; the effect that they occasioned on the scientific mind may be compared to that which the new sensations of vision produce on the blind receiving sight;—they awakened the highest interest, the most enthusiastic admiration, and for nearly half a century, absorbed the attention of the most eminent philosophers of Britain and France.

Germany still continued the great school of practical chemistry, and at this period it gained an ascendancy of no mean character over the rest of Europe in the philosophy of the science. Beccher, who was born at Spires in 1645, after having studied with minute attention, the operations of metallurgy, and the phænomena of the mineral kingdom, formed the bold idea of explaining the whole system of the earth by the mutual agency and changes of a few elements. And by supposing the existence of a vitrifiable, a metallic, and an inflammable earth, he attempted to account for the various productions of rocks, crystalline bodies, and metallic veins, assuming

---

49. Newton's Works, quarto, Tom. iv. page 242.

a continued interchange of principles between the atmosphere, the ocean, and the solid surface of the globe, and considering the operations of nature as all capable of being imitated by art.

The *Physica subterranea*, and the *Oedipus chemicus* of this author, are very extraordinary productions. They display the efforts of a vigorous mind, the conceptions of a most fertile imagination, but the conclusions are too rapidly formed; there is a want of logical precision in his reasonings; the objects he attempted were grand, but his means of execution comparatively feeble. He endeavoured to raise a perfect and lasting edifice upon foundations too weak, from materials too scanty and not sufficiently solid; and the work, though magnificent in design, was rude[,] unfinished, and feeble, and rapidly fell into decay.

Beccher added very little to the collection of chemical experiments, but he improved the instruments of research, simplified the manipulations, and by the novelty and boldness of his speculations, excited enquiry amongst his disciples.

His most distinguished follower was George Ernest Stahl, born in 1660, who soon attained a reputation superior to that of his master, and developed doctrines which for nearly a century constituted the theory of chemistry of the whole of Europe.

Albertus Magnus had advanced the idea that the metals were earthy substances impregnated with a certain inflammable principle. Beccher supported the idea of this principle, not only as the cause of metallization, but likewise of combustibility: and Stahl endeavoured, by a number of ingenious and elaborate experiments, to prove the existence of phlogiston, as it was called, and to explain its agencies in the phænomena of nature and art.

Glauber, about fifty years before Stahl began his labours, had discovered the combination of fossil alkali and sulphuric acid, which still bears his name. And Stahl, in operating upon this body, thought he had discovered the proof, that the inflammability not only of metals, but likewise of all other substances, was owing to the same principle. Charcoal is entirely dissipated or consumed in combustion, therefore, says this philosopher, it must be phlogiston nearly pure; by heating charcoal with metallic earths, they become metals; therefore they are compounds of metallic earths and phlogiston: by heating Glauber's salt, which consists of sulphuric acid and fossil alkali, with charcoal, a compound of sulphur and alkali is obtained; therefore sulphur is an acid combined with phlogiston. Stahl entirely neglected the chemical influence of air on these phenomena; and though Boyle had proved that phosphorus and sulphur would not burn without air, and had stated that sulphur was contained in sulphuric acid, and not the acid in sulphur, yet the ideas of the Prussian school were received without controversy. Similar opinions were adopted in France by Homberg and Geoffroy, who assumed them without reference to the views of the Prussian philosopher, and opposed them to the more correct and sagacious views of the English school of chemistry.

Though misled in his general notions, few men have done more than Stahl for the progress of chemical science.—His processes were, many of them, of the most beautiful and satisfactory kind: he discovered a number of properties of the caustic alkalies and metallic calces, and the nature of sulphureous acid; he reasoned upon all the operations of chemistry in which gaseous bodies were not concerned, with admirable precision. He gave an axiomatic form to the science, banishing from it vague details, circumlocutions and enigmatic descriptions, in which even Beccher had too much indulged; he laboured in the spirit of the Baconian school, multiplying instances, and cautiously making inductions, and appealing in all cases to experiments which, though not of the most refined kind, were more perfect than any which preceded them.

Dr. Hales, about 1724, resumed the investigations commenced with so much success by Boyle, Hooke, and Mayow; and endeavoured to ascertain the chemical relations of air to other substances, and to ascertain by statical experiments[50] the cases in nature, in which it is absorbed or emitted. He obtained a number of important and curious results; but, misled by the notion of one elementary principle constituting elastic matter, and modified in its properties by the effluvia of solid or fluid bodies, he formed few inferences connected with the refined philosophy of the subject: he disengaged, however, elastic fluids from a number of substances, and drew the conclusion that air was a chemical element in many compound bodies, and that flame resulted from the action and re-action of ærial and sulphurous particles.[51]

In 1756 Dr. Black published his admirable researches on calcareous, magnesian, and alkaline substances, by which he proved the existence of a gaseous body, perfectly distinct from the air of the atmosphere. He shewed that quicklime differed from marble and chalk by containing this substance, and that it was a weak acid, capable of being expelled from alkaline and earthy substances by strong acids.[52]

Ideas so new and important as those of the British philosopher, were not received without opposition; several German enquirers endeavoured to controvert them. Meyer attempted to shew that limestones became caustic, not by the emission of elastic matter, but by combining with a

50. [Experiments relating to weight.]
51. Hales' Statical Essays, 2d ed. 8vo. Vol. i pag. 315.
52. Essays and Observations Physical and Literary, vol. ii. page 159.

peculiar substance in the fire; but the loss of weight was perfectly incon-
sistent with this view: and Bergman at Upsal, Macbride in Ireland, Keir at
Birmingham, and Cavendish in London, demonstrated the correctness of
the opinions of Black; and a few years were sufficient to establish his theory
upon immutable foundations.

The knowledge of one elastic fluid different from air, immediately led to
the enquiry whether there might not be others. The processes of fermenta-
tion which had been observed by the ancient chemists, and those by which
Hales had disengaged and collected elastic substances, were now regarded
under a novel point of view; and the consequence was, that a number of
new bodies, possessed of very extraordinary properties, were discovered.

Mr. Cavendish, about 1765, invented an apparatus for examining elastic
fluids confined by water, which has been since called the hydro-pneumatic
apparatus. He discovered inflammable air, and described its properties;
he ascertained the relative weights of fixed air, inflammable air, and common air, and made a number of beautiful and accurate experiments on the
properties of these elastic substances.

Dr. Priestley, in 1771, entered the same interesting path of enquiry; and
principally by repeating the processes of Hales, added a number of most
important facts to this department of chemical philosophy. He discovered
nitrous air, nitrous oxide, and dephlogisticated air; and by substituting
mercury for water in the pneumatic apparatus, ascertained the existence of
several æriform substances, which are rapidly absorbable by water, muriatic acid air, sulphurous acid air, and ammonia.

Whilst a new branch of the science was making this rapid progress in
Britain, the chemistry of solid and fluid substances was pursued with considerable zeal and success in France and Germany; and Macquer, Rouelle,
Margraff, and Pott, added considerably to the knowledge of fossile[53] bodies, and the properties of the metals. Bergman, in Sweden, developed refined ideas on the powers of chemical attraction, and reasoned in a happy
spirit of generalization on many of the new phænomena of the science;
and in the same country Scheele, independently of Priestley, discovered
several of the same æriform substances: he ascertained the composition
of the atmosphere; he brought to light fluoric acid, prussic acid, and the
substance which has been improperly called oxymuriatic gas.

Black, Cavendish, Priestley, and Scheele, were undoubtedly the greatest
chemical discoverers of the eighteenth century; and their merits are distinct, peculiar, and of the most exalted kind. Black made a smaller number
of original experiments than either of the other philosophers; but being

---

53. [I.e., mineral.]

the first labourer in this new department of the science, he had greater difficulties to overcome. His methods are distinguished for their simplicity; his reasonings are admirable for their precision; and his modest, clear, and unaffected manner, is well calculated to impress upon the mind a conviction of the accuracy of his processes, and the truth and candour of his narrations.

Cavendish was possessed of a minute knowledge of most of the departments of Natural Philosophy: he carried into his chemical researches a delicacy and precision, which have never been exceeded: possessing depth and extent of mathematical knowledge, he reasoned with the caution of a geometer upon the results of his experiments: and it may be said of him, what, perhaps, can scarcely be said of any other person, that whatever he accomplished, was perfect at the moment of its production. His processes were all of a finished nature; executed by the hand of a master, they required no correction; the accuracy and beauty of his earliest labours even, have remained unimpaired amidst the progress of discovery, and their merits have been illustrated by discussion, and exalted by time.

Dr. Priestley began his career of discovery without any general knowledge of chemistry, and with a very imperfect apparatus. His characteristics were ardent zeal and the most unwearied industry. He exposed all the substances he could procure to chemical agencies, and brought forward his results as they occurred, without attempting logical method or scientific arrangement. His hypotheses were usually founded upon a few loose analogies; but he changed them with facility; and being framed without much effort, they were relinquished with little regret. He possessed in the highest degree ingenuousness and the love of truth. His manipulations, though never very refined, were always simple, and often ingenious. Chemistry owes to him some of her most important instruments of research, and many of her most useful combinations; and no single person ever discovered so many new and curious substances.

Scheele possessed in the highest degree the faculty of invention; all his labours were instituted with an object in view, and after happy or bold analogies. He owed little to fortune or accidental circumstances: born in an obscure situation, occupied in the duties of an irksome employment, nothing could damp the ardour of his mind or chill the fire of his genius: with very small means he accomplished very great things. No difficulties deterred him from submitting his ideas to the test of experiment. Occasionally misled in his views, in consequence of the imperfection of his apparatus, or the infant state of the inquiry, he never hesitated to give up his opinions the moment they were contradicted by facts. He was eminently endowed with that candour which is characteristic of great minds, and which induces them to rejoice as well in the detection of their own errors, as in the discovery of truth. His papers are admirable models of the manner in which experimental research ought to be pursued; and they contain details on some of the most important and brilliant phænomena of chemical philosophy.

The discovery of the gasses, of a new class of bodies, more active than any others in most of the phænomena of nature and art, could not fail to modify the whole theory of chemistry. The ancient doctrines were revised; new modifications of them were formed by some philosophers; whilst others discarded entirely all the former hypotheses, and endeavoured to establish new generalizations.

The idea of a peculiar principle of inflammability was so firmly established in the chemical schools, that even the knowledge of the composition of the atmosphere for a long while was not supposed to interfere with it; and the part of the atmosphere which is absorbed by bodies in burning, was conceived to owe its powers to its attraction for phlogiston.

All the modern chemists who made experiments upon combustion, found that bodies increased in weight by burning, and that there was no loss of ponderable matter. It was necessary therefore to suppose, contrary to the ideas of Stahl, that phlogiston was not emitted in combustion, but that it remained in the inflammable body after absorbing gaseous matter from the air. But what is phlogiston? was a question constantly agitated. Inflammable air had been obtained during the dissolution of certain metals, and during the distillation of a number of combustible bodies. This light and subtile matter, therefore, was fixed upon as the principle of inflammability; and Cavendish, Kirwan, Priestley, and Fontana, were the illustrious advocates of this very ingenious hypothesis.

In 1774, Bayen shewed that mercury converted into a calx or earth, by the absorption of air, could be revived without the addition of any inflammable substance; and hence he concluded, that there was no necessity for supposing the existence of any peculiar principle of inflammability, in accounting for the calcination of metals. The subject, nearly about the same time, was taken up by Lavoisier, who had been for some time engaged in repeating the experiments of the British philosophers. Bayen formed no opinion respecting the nature of the air produced from the calx of mercury. Lavoisier, in 1775, shewed that it was an air which supported flame and respiration better than common air, which he afterwards named oxygene; the same substance that Priestley and Scheele had produced from other metallic substances the year before, and had particularly described.[54]

---

54. In the Journal de Physique for 1789, Preliminary Discourse, De la Metherie has given an admirable view of the progress of the investigations concerning the gases. See p.24, &c.

Lavoisier discovered that the same air is produced during the revivification of metallic calces by charcoal, as that which is emitted during the calcination of limestone; hence he concluded, that this elastic fluid is composed of oxygen and charcoal; and from his experiments on nitrous acid and oil of vitriol, he concluded that this gas entered into the composition of these substances.

Dr. Black had demonstrated by a series of beautiful experiments, that when gases are condensed, or when fluids are converted into solids, heat is produced. In combustion gaseous matter usually assumes the solid or the fluid form. Oxygene gas, said Lavoisier, seems to be compound[ed] of the matter of heat, and a basis. In the act of burning, this basis is united to the combustible body, and the heat is evolved. There is no necessity, said this acute philosopher, to suppose any phlogiston, any peculiar principle of inflammability; for all the phænomena may be accounted for without this imaginary existence.

Lavoisier must be regarded as one of the most sagacious of the chemical philosophers of the last century; indeed, except Cavendish, there is no other inquirer who can be compared to him for precision of logic, extent of view, and sagacity of induction. His discoveries were few, but he reasoned with extraordinary correctness upon the labours of others. He introduced weight and measure, and strict accuracy of manipulation into all chemical processes. His mind was unbiassed by prejudice; his combinations were of the most philosophical nature: and in his investigations upon ponderable substances, he has entered the true path of experiment with cautious steps, following just analogies, and measuring hypotheses by their simple relations to facts.

The doctrine of Lavoisier, soon after it was framed, received some important confirmations from the two grand discoveries of Mr. Cavendish, respecting the composition of water, and nitric acid; and the elaborate and beautiful investigations of Berthollet respecting the nature of ammonia; in which phænomena, before anomalous, were shewn to depend upon combinations of æriform matter.

The notion of phlogiston, was however defended for nearly 20 years, by some philosophers in Germany, Sweden, Britain, and Ireland. Mr. Cavendish, in 1784, drew a parallel between the hypothesis, that all inflammable bodies contain inflammable air, and the doctrine in which they are considered as simple substances, in a paper equally remarkable for the precision of the views displayed in it, and for the accuracy and minuteness of the experiments it contains. To this great man, the assumption of M. Lavoisier, of the matter of heat, appeared more hypothetical than that of a principle of inflammability. He states, that the phænomena may be explained on either doctrine; but he prefers the earlier view, as accounting, in a happier manner, for some of the operations of nature.

De Morveau, Berthollet, and Fourcroy, in France, and William Higgins and Dr. Hope, in Britain, were the first advocates for the antiphlogistic chemistry. Sooner or later, that doctrine which is an expression of facts, must prevail over that which is an expression of opinion. The most important part of the theory of Lavoisier was merely an arrangement of the facts relating to the combinations of oxygene: the principle of reasoning which the French school professed to adopt was, that every body which was not yet decompounded, should be considered as simple; and though mistakes were made with respect to the results of experiments on the nature of bodies, yet this logical and truly philosophical principle was not violated; and the systematic manner in which it was enforced, was of the greatest use in promoting the progress of the science.

Till 1786, there had been no attempt to reform the nomenclature of chemistry; the names applied by discoverers to the substances which they made known, were still employed. Some of these names, which originated amongst the alchymists, were of the most barbarous kind; few of them were sufficiently definite or precise, and most of them were founded upon loose analogies, or upon false theoretical views.

It was felt by many philosophers, particularly by the illustrious Bergman, that an improvement in chemical nomenclature was necessary, and in 1787, Messrs. Lavoisier, Morveau, Berthollet, and Fourcroy, presented to the world a plan for an almost entire change in the denomination of chemical substances, founded upon the idea of calling simple bodies by some names characteristic of their most striking qualities, and of naming compound bodies from the elements which composed them.

The new nomenclature was speedily adopted in France; under some modification it was received in Germany; and after much discussion and opposition, it became the language of a new and rising generation of chemists in England. It materially assisted the diffusion of the antiphlogistic doctrine, and even facilitated the general acquisition of the science; and many of its details were contrived with much address, and were worthy of its celebrated authors: but a very slight reference to the philosophical principles of language will evince that its foundations were imperfect, and that the plan adopted was not calculated for a progressive branch of knowledge.

Simplicity and precision ought to be the characteristics of a scientific nomenclature: words should signify things, or the analogies of things, and not opinions. If all the elements were certainly known, the principle adopted by Lavoisier would have possessed an admirable application; but a substance in one age supposed to be simple, in another is proved to be compound; and *vice versa*. A theoretical nomenclature is liable to continued alterations; *oxygenated muriatic acid* is as improper a name as *dephlogisticated marine acid*. Every school believes itself in the right; and if every school assumes to itself the liberty of altering the names of chemical substances, in consequence of new ideas of their composition, or decomposition, there can be no permanency in the language of the science, it must always be confused and uncertain. Bodies which are similar to each other should always be classed together; and there is a presumption that their composition is analogous. Metals, earths, alkalies, are appropriate names for the bodies they represent, and independent of all speculative views; whereas oxides, sulphurets, and muriates, are terms founded upon opinions of the composition of bodies, some of which have been already found erroneous. The least dangerous mode of giving a systematic form to a language, seems to be, to signify the analogies of substances by some common sign affixed to the beginning or the termination of the word. Thus, as the metals have been distinguished by a termination in *um*, as *aurum*, so their calciform or oxidated state, might have been denoted by a termination in *a*, as *aura*; and no progress, however great, in the science, could render it necessary that such a mode of appellation should be changed. Moreover, the principle of a composite nomenclature must always be very limited. It is scarcely possible to represent bodies consisting of five or six elements in this way, and yet it is in such difficult cases that a name implying a chemical truth, would be most useful.

The new doctrines of chemistry, before 1795, were embraced by almost all the active experimental enquirers in Europe; and the adoption of a precise mode of reasoning, and more refined forms of experiment, led not only to the discovery of new substances, but likewise to a more accurate acquaintance with the properties and composition of bodies that had long been known.

New investigations were instituted with respect to all the productions of nature, and the immense variety of substances in the mineral, vegetable, and animal kingdom, submitted to chemical experiments.

The analysis of mineral bodies first attempted by Pott in experiments principally on their igneous fusion, and afterwards refined by the application of acid and alkaline menstrua, by Margraaf, Bergman, Bayen, and Achard, received still greater improvements from the labours of Klaproth, Vauquelin, and Hatchett. Hoffman, in the beginning of the 18th century, pointed out magnesia as a peculiar substance. Margraaf, about fifty years later, distinguished accurately between the silicious, calcareous, and aluminous earths. Scheele, in 1774, discovered barytes. Klaproth, in 1788, made known zircone. Dr. Hope,[55] strontites in 1791. Gadolin, ittria in 1794; and Vauquelin, glucine in 1798.

Seven metals only had been accurately known to the ancients, gold, silver, mercury, copper, [lead,] tin, and iron. Zinc, bismuth, arsenic, and antimony, though mentioned by the Greek and Roman authors, yet were

---

55. Edinburgh Trans. Vol. iv. p. 44.

employed only in certain combinations, and the production of them in the form of reguli or pure metals, was owing to the Alchemists.

Cobalt had been used to tinge glass in Saxony in the sixteenth century; but the metal was unknown till the time of Brandt, and this celebrated Swedish chemist discovered it in 1733. Nickel was procured by Cronstedt in 1751. The properties of manganese, which was announced as a peculiar metal by Kaim in 1770, were minutely investigated by Scheele and Bergman a few years after. Molybdic acid was discovered by Scheele in 1778, and a metal procured from it by Hielm in 1782, the same year that tellurium was made known by Muller. Scheele discovered tungstic acid in 1781; and soon after a metal was extracted from it by Messrs. D'Elhuyars. Klaproth discovered uranium in 1789. The first description of the properties of the oxide of titanium was given by Gregor in 1791. Vauquelin made known chromium in 1797; Hatchett columbium in 1801; and shortly after, the same substance was noticed by Ekeberg, and named by him tantalium. Cerium was discovered in 1804, by Hissinger and Berzelius. Platina had been brought into Europe and examined by Lewis in 1749; and in 1803, Descotils, Fourcroy, and Vauquelin announced a new metallic substance in it; but the complete investigation of the properties of this extraordinary body was reserved for Messrs. Tennant and Wollaston, who in 1803 and 1804 discovered in it no less than four new metallic substances, besides the body which exists in it in the largest proportion, namely, iridium, osmium, palladium, and rhodium.

The attempts made to analyse vegetable substances previous to 1720, merely produced their resolution into the supposed elements of the chemists of those days, namely, salts, earths, phlegm, and sulphur. Boerhaave and Newmann attempted an examination by fluid menstrua, which was pursued with some success by Rouelle, Macquer and Lewis. Scheele, between 1770 and 1780, pointed out several new vegetable acids. Fourcroy, Vauquelin, Deyeux, Seguin, Proust, Jacquin, and Hermbstadt, between 1780 and 1790, in various interesting series of experiments, distinguished between different secondary elements of vegetable matter, particularly extract, tannin, gums, and resinous substances; and investigations of this kind have been pursued with great success by Hatchett, Pearson, Schræder, Chenevix, Gehlen, Thomson, Thenard, Chevreul, Kind, Brande, Bostock, and Duncan. The chemistry of animal substances has received great elucidations from several of the same enquirers; and Berzelius has examined most of their results, and has added several new ones, in a comprehensive work expressly devoted to the subject, published in 1808.

That solid masses fell from above, connected with the appearance of meteors, had been advanced as early as 500 years before the Christian æra, by Anaxagoras; and the same idea had been brought forward in a vague manner by other enquirers amongst the Greeks and Romans, and was revived in modern times; but till 1802 it was regarded by the greater number of philosophers as a mere vulgar error, when Mr. Howard, by an accurate examination of the testimonies connected with events of this kind, and by a minute analysis of the substances said to have fallen in different parts of the globe, proved the authenticity of the circumstance, and shewed that these meteoric productions differed from any substances belonging to our earth; and since that period a number of these phænomena have occurred, and have been minutely recorded.

The philosophy of heat, the foundations of which were laid between 1757 and 1785, by Black, Wilcke, Crawford, Irvine, and Lavoisier, since that period has received some new and very important additions, from the inquiries of Pictet, Rumford, Herschel, Leslie, Dalton, and Gay Lussac. The circumstances under which bodies absorb and communicate heat, have been minutely investigated; and the important discoveries of the different physical and chemical powers of the different solar rays, and of a property analogous to polarity in light, bear immediate relation to the most refined doctrines of corpuscular science, and promise to connect, by close analogies, the chemical and mechanical laws of matter.

A general view of the philosophy of chemistry was published under the name of Chemical Statics, in 1803, by the celebrated Berthollet. It is a work remarkable for the new views that it contains on the doctrines of attraction; views which are still objects of discussion, and which bear an immediate relation to some of the conclusions depending upon very recent discoveries.

At the time when the antiphlogistic theory was established, electricity had little or no relation to chemistry. The grand results of Franklin, respecting the cause of lightning, had led many philosophers to conjecture, that certain chemical changes in the atmosphere might be connected with electrical phænomena;—and electrical discharges had been employed by Cavendish, Priestley, and Vanmarum, for decomposing and igniting bodies; but it was not till the era of the wonderful discovery of Volta, in 1800, of a new electrical apparatus, that any great progress was made in chemical investigations by means of electrical combinations.

Nothing tends so much to the advancement of knowledge as the application of a new instrument. The native intellectual powers of men in different times, are not so much the causes of the different success of their labours, as the peculiar nature of the means and artificial resources in their possession. Independent of vessels of glass, there could have been no accurate manipulations in common chemistry; the air pump, was necessary for the investigation of the properties of gaseous matter; and without the Voltaic apparatus, there was no possibility of examining the relations of electrical polarities to chemical attractions.

By researches, the commencement of which is owing to Messrs. Nicholson and Carlisle, in 1800, which were continued by Cruickshank, Henry,

Wollaston, Children, Pepys, Pfaff, Desormes, Biot, Thenard, Hissinger, and Berzelius, it appeared that various compound bodies were capable of decomposition by electricity; and experiments, which it was my good fortune to institute, proved that several substances which had never been separated into any other forms of matter in the common processes of experiment, were susceptible of analysis by electrical powers: in consequence of these circumstances, the fixed alkalies and several of the earths have been shewn to be metals combined with oxygene; various new agents have been furnished to chemistry, and many novel results obtained by their application, which at the same time that they have strengthened some of the doctrines of the school of Lavoisier, have overturned others, and have proved that the generalizations of the Antiphlogistic philosophers were far from having anticipated the whole progress of discovery.

Certain bodies which attract each other chemically, and combine when their particles have freedom of motion, when brought into contact, still preserving their aggregation, exhibit what may be called electrical polarities; and by certain combinations these polarities may be highly exalted; and in this case they become subservient decompositions; and by means of electrical arrangements the constituent parts of bodies are separated in an uniform order, and in define proportions.

Bodies combine with a force, which in many cases is correspondent to their power of exhibiting electrical polarity by contact; and heat, or heat and light, are produced in proportion to the energy of their combination. Vivid inflammation occurs in a number of cases in which gaseous matter is not fixed; and this phænomenon happens in various instances without the interference of free or combined oxygene.

Experiments made by Richter and Morveau had shewn that, when there is an interchange of elements between two neutral salts, there is never an excess of acid or basis; and the same law seems to apply generally to double decompositions. When one body combines with another in more than one proportion, the second proportion appears to be some multiple or divisor of the first; and this circumstance, observed and ingeniously illustrated by Mr. Dalton, led him to adopt the atomic hypothesis of chemical changes, which had been ably defended by Mr. Higgins in 1789, namely, that the chemical elements consist of certain indestructible particles which unite one and one, or one and two, or in some definite numbers.

Whether matter consists of indivisible corpuscles, or physical points endowed with attraction and repulsion, still the same conclusions may be formed concerning the powers by which they act, and the quantities in which they combine; and the powers seem capable of being measured by their electrical relations, and the quantities on which they act of being expressed by numbers.

In combination certain bodies form regular solids; and all the varieties of crystalline aggregates have been resolved by the genius of Haüy into a few primary forms. The laws of crystallization, of definite proportions, and of the electrical polarities of bodies, seem to be intimately related; and the complete illustration of their connection, probably will constitute the mature age of chemistry.

To dwell more minutely upon the particular merits of the chemical philosophers of the present age, will be a grateful labour for some future historian of chemistry; but for a contemporary writer, it would be indelicate to assume the right of arbitrator, even where praise only can be bestowed. The just fame of those who have enlightened the science by new and accurate experiments, cannot fail to be universally acknowledged; and concerning the publication of novel facts there can be but one judgment; for facts are independent of fashion, taste, and caprice, and are subject to no code of criticism; they are more useful perhaps even when they contradict, than when they support received doctrines, for our theories are only imperfect approximations to the real knowledge of things; and in physical research, doubt is usually of excellent effect, for it is a principal motive for new labours, and tends continually to the developement of truth.

The slight sketch that has been given of the progress of chemistry, has necessarily been limited to the philosophical details of discovery. To point out in historical order the manner in which the truths of the science have been applied to the arts of life, or the benefits derived by society from them, would occupy many volumes. From the first discovery of the production of metals from rude ores, to the knowledge of the bleaching liquor, chemistry has been continually subservient to cultivation and improvement. In the manufacture of porcelain and glass, in the arts of dyeing and tanning, it has added to the elegancies, refinement, and comforts of life; in its application to medicine it has removed the most formidable of diseases; and in leading to the discovery of gunpowder, it has changed the institutions of society, and rendered war more independent of brutal strength, less personal, and less barbarous.

It is indeed a double source of interest in this science, that whilst it is connected with the grand operations of nature, it is likewise subservient to the common processes as well as the most refined arts of life. New laws cannot be discovered in it, without increasing our admiration of the beauty and order of the system of the universe; and no new substances can be made known which are not sooner or later subservient to some purpose of utility.

When the great progress made in chemistry within the last few years is considered, and the number of able labourers who are at present actively employed in cultivating the science, it is impossible not to augur well concerning its rapid advancement and future applications. The most important truths belonging to it are capable of extremely simple numerical expressions, which may be acquired with facility by students; and the apparatus for pursuing original researches is daily improved, the use of it rendered more easy, and the acquisition less expensive.

Complexity almost always belongs to the early epochs of every science; and the grandest results are usually obtained by the most simple means. A great part of the phænomena of chemistry may be already submitted to calculation; and there is great reason to believe, that at no very distant period the whole science will be capable of elucidation by mathematical principles. The relations of the common metals to the bases of the alkalies and earths, and the gradations of resemblance between the bases of the earths and acids, point out as probable a similarity in the constitution of all inflammable bodies; and there are not wanting experiments, which render their possible decomposition far from a chimerical idea. It is contrary to the usual order of things, that events so harmonious as those of the system of the earth, should depend on such diversified agents, as are supposed to exist in our artificial arrangements; and there is reason to anticipate a great reduction in the number of the undecompounded bodies, and to expect that the analogies of nature will be found conformable to the refined operations of art. The more the phænomena of the universe are studied, the more distinct their connection appears, the more simple their causes, the more magnificent their design, and the more wonderful the wisdom and power of their Author.

6. From Erasmus Darwin, *The Temple of Nature* (1803)

[Erasmus Darwin (1731–1802) was an early theorist of evolution. The Temple of Nature was published posthumously. It is a long poem accompanied by extensive explanatory notes: I reprint here a note to a reference in the poem to "spontaneous birth." According to Mary Shelley a passage in this note was discussed in her presence by Percy Shelley and Byron, and influenced her in the invention of her novel; it must be this text that Percy Shelley had in mind when he claimed that the story of the novel was "not of impossible occurrence."]

SPONTANEOUS VITALITY OF MICROSCOPIC ANIMALS.

Hence without parent by spontaneous birth

Rise the first specks of animated earth.   Canto I. l. 227.

Prejudices against this doctrine.

I. From the misconception of the ignorant or superstitious, it has been thought somewhat profane to speak in favour of spontaneous vital production, as if it contradicted holy writ; which says, that God created animals and vegetables. They do not recollect that God created all things which exist, and that these have been from the beginning in a perpetual state of improvement; which appears from the globe itself, as well as from the animals and vegetables, which possess it. And lastly, that there is more dignity in our idea of the supreme author of all things, when we conceive him to be the cause of causes, than the cause simply of the events, which we see; if there can be any difference in infinity of power!

Another prejudice which has prevailed against the spontaneous production of vitality, seems to have arisen from the misrepresentation of this doctrine, as if the larger animals had been thus produced; as Ovid supposes after the deluge of Deucalion, that lions were seen rising out of the mud of the Nile, and struggling to disentangle their hinder parts. It was not considered, that animals and vegetables have been perpetually improving by reproduction; and that spontaneous vitality was only to be looked for in the simplest organic beings, as in the smallest microscopic animalcules; which perpetually, perhaps hourly, enlarge themselves by reproduction, like the roots of tulips from seed, or the buds of seedling trees, which die annually, leaving others by solitary reproduction rather more perfect than themselves for many successive years, till at length they acquire sexual organs or flowers.

A third prejudice against the existence of spontaneous vital productions has been the supposed want of analogy; this has also arisen from the expectation, that the larger or more complicated animals should be thus produced; which have acquired their present perfection by successive generations during an uncounted series of ages. Add to this, that the want of analogy opposes the credibility of all new discoveries, as of the magnetic needle, and coated electric jar, and Galvanic pile; which should therefore certainly be well weighed and nicely investigated before distinct credence is given them; but then the want of analogy must at length yield to repeated ocular demonstration.

Preliminary observations.

II. Concerning the spontaneous production of the smallest microscopic animals it should be first observed, that the power of reproduction distinguishes organic being, whether vegetable or animal, from inanimate nature. The circulation of fluids in vessels may exist in hydraulic machines, but the power of reproduction belongs alone to life. This reproduction of plants and of animals is of two kinds, which may be termed solitary and sexual. The former of these, as in the reproduction of the buds of trees, and of the bulbs of tulips, and of the polypus, and aphis, appears to be the first or most simple mode of generation, as many of these organic beings afterwards acquire sexual organs, as the flowers of seedling trees, and of seeding tulips, and the autumnal progeny of the aphis. See Phytologia.

Secondly, it should be observed, that by reproduction organic beings are gradually enlarged and improved; which may perhaps more rapidly and uniformly occur in the simplest modes of animated being; but occasionally also in the more complicated and perfect kinds. Thus the buds of a seedling tree, or the bulbs of seedling tulips, become larger and stronger in the second year than the first, and thus improve till they acquire flowers or sexes; and the aphis, I believe, increases in bulk to the eighth or ninth generation, and then produces a sexual progeny. Hence the existence of spontaneous vitality is only to be expected to be found in the simplest modes of animation, as the complex ones have been formed by many successive reproductions.

Experimental facts.

III. By the experiments of Buffon, Reaumur, Ellis, Ingenhouz, and others, microscopic animals are produced in three or four days, according to the warmth of the season, in the infusions of all vegetable or animal matter. One or more of these gentlemen put some boiling veal broth into a phial previously heated in the fire, and sealing it up hermetically or with melted wax, observed it to be replete with animalcules in three or four days.

These microscopic animals are believed to possess a power of generating others like themselves by solitary reproduction without sex; and these gradually enlarging and improving for innumerable successive generations. Mr. Ellis in Phil. Transact. V. LIX. gives drawings of six kinds of animalcula infusoria, which increase by dividing across the middle into two distinct animals. Thus in paste composed of flour and water, which has been suffered to become acescent, the animalcules called eels, vibrio anguillula, are seen in great abundance; their motions are rapid and strong; they are viviparous, and produce at intervals a numerous progeny: animals similar to these are also found in vinegar; Naturalist's Miscellany by Shaw and Nodder, Vol. II. These eels were probably at first as minute as other microscopic animalcules; but by frequent, perhaps hourly reproduction, have gradually become the large animals above described, possessing wonderful strength and activity.

To suppose the eggs of the former microscopic animals to float in the atmosphere, and pass through the sealed glass phial, is so contrary to apparent nature, as to be totally incredible! and as the latter are viviparous, it is equally absurd to suppose, that their parents float universally in the atmosphere to lay their young in paste or vinegar!

Not only microscopic animals appear to be produced by a spontaneous vital process, and then quickly improve by solitary generation like the buds of trees, or like the polypus and aphis, but there is one vegetable body, which appears to be produced by a spontaneous vital process, and is believed to be propagated and enlarged in so short a time by solitary generation as to become visible to the naked eye; I mean the green matter first attended to by Dr. Priestley, and called by him conferva fontinalis. The proofs, that this material is a vegetable, are from its giving up so much oxygen, when exposed to the sunshine, as it grows in water, and from its green colour.

Dr. Ingenhouz asserts, that by filling a bottle with well-water, and inverting it immediately into a basin of well-water, this green vegetable is formed in great quantity; and he believes, that the water itself, or some substance contained in the water, is converted into this kind of vegetation, which then quickly propagates itself.

Mr. Girtanner asserts, that this green vegetable matter is not produced by water and heat alone, but requires the sun's light for this purpose, as he observed by many experiments, and thinks it arises from decomposing water deprived of a part of its oxygen, and laughs at Dr. Priestley for believing that the seeds of this conferva, and the parents of microscopic animals, exist universally in the atmosphere, and penetrate the sides of glass jars; Philos. Magazine for May 1800.

Besides this green vegetable matter of Dr. Priestley, there is another vegetable, the minute beginnings of the growth of which Mr. Ellis observed by his microscope near the surface of all putrefying vegetable or animal matter, which is the mucor or mouldiness; the vegetation of which was amazingly quick so as to be almost seen, and soon became so large as to be visible to the naked eye. It is difficult to conceive how the seeds of this mucor can float so universally in the atmosphere as to fix itself on all putrid matter in all places.

Theory of Spontaneous Vitality.

IV. In animal nutrition the organic matter of the bodies of dead animals, or vegetables, is taken into the stomach, and there suffers decompositions and new combinations by a chemical process. Some parts of it are however absorbed by the lacteals as fast as they are produced by this process of digestion; in which circumstance this process differs from common chemical operations.

In vegetable nutrition the organic matter of dead animals, or vegetables, undergoes chemical decompositions and new combinations on or beneath the surface of the earth; and parts of it, as they are produced, are perpetually absorbed by the roots of the plants in contact with it; in which this also differs from common chemical processes.

Hence the particles which are produced from dead organic matter by chemical decompositions or new consequent combinations, are found proper for the purposes of the nutrition of living vegetable and animal bodies, whether these decompositions and new combinations are performed in the stomach or beneath the soil.

For the purposes of nutrition these digested or decomposed recrements of dead animal or vegetable matter are absorbed by the lacteals of the stomachs of animals or of the roots of vegetables, and carried into the circulation of their blood, and these compose new organic parts to replace others which are destroyed, or to increase the growth of the plant or animal.

It is probable, that as in inanimate or chemical combinations, one of the composing materials must possess a power of attraction, and the other an aptitude to be attracted; so in organic or animated compositions there must be particles with appetencies to unite, and other particles with propensities to be united with them.

Thus in the generation of the buds of trees, it is probable that two kinds of vegetable matter, as they are separated from the solid system, and float in the circulation, become arrested by two kinds of vegetable glands, and are then deposed beneath the cuticle of the tree, and there join together, forming a new vegetable, the caudex of which extends from the plumula at the summit to the radicles beneath the soil, and constitutes a single fibre of the bark.

These particles appear to be of two kinds; one of them possessing an appetency to unite with the other, and the latter a propensity to be united with the former; and they are probably separated from the vegetable blood by two kinds of glands, one representing those of the anthers, and the others those of the stigmas, in the sexual organs of vegetables; which is spoken of at large in Phytologia, Sect. VII. and in Zoonomia, Vol. I. Sect. XXXIX. 8. of the third edition, in octavo; where it is likewise shown, that none of these parts which are deposited beneath the cuticle of the tree, is in itself a complete vegetable embryon, but that they form one by their reciprocal conjunction.

So in the sexual reproduction of animals, certain parts separated from the living organs, and floating in the blood, are arrested by the sexual glands of the female, and others by those of the male. Of these none are complete embryon animals, but form an embryon by their reciprocal conjunction.

There hence appears to be an analogy between generation and nutrition, as one is the production of new organization, and the other the restoration of that which previously existed; and which may therefore be supposed to require materials somewhat similar. Now the food taken up by animal lacteals is previously prepared by the chemical process of digestion in the stomach; but that which is taken up by vegetable lacteals, is prepared by chemical dissolution of organic matter beneath the surface of the earth. Thus the particles, which form generated animal embryons, are prepared from dead organic matter by the chemico-animal processes of sanguification and of secretion; while those which form spontaneous microscopic animals or microscopic vegetables are prepared by chemical dissolutions and new combinations of organic matter in watery fluids with sufficient warmth.

It may be here added, that the production and properties of some kinds of inanimate matter, are almost as difficult to comprehend as those of the simplest degrees of animation. Thus the elastic gum, or caoutchouc, and some fossile bitumens, when drawn out to a great length, contract themselves by their elasticity, like an animal fibre by stimulus. The laws of action of these, and all other elastic bodies, are not yet understood; as the laws of the attraction of cohesion, to produce these effects, must be very different from those of general attraction, since the farther the particles of elastic bodies are drawn from each other till they separate, the stronger they seem to attract; and the nearer they are pressed together, the more they seem to repel; as in bending a spring, or in extending a piece of elastic gum; which is the reverse to what occurs in the attractions of disunited bodies; and much wants further investigation. So the spontaneous production of alcohol or of vinegar, by the vinous and acetous fermentations, as well as the production of a mucus by putrefaction which will contract when extended, seems almost as difficult to understand as the spontaneous production of a fibre from decomposing animal or vegetable substances, which will contract when stimulated, and thus constitutes the primordium of life.

Some of the microscopic animals are said to remain dead for many days or weeks, when the fluid in which they existed is dried up, and quickly to recover life and motion by the fresh addition of water and warmth. Thus the chaos redivivum of Linnæus dwells in vinegar and in bookbinders paste: it revives by water after having been dried for years, and is both oviparous and viviparous; Syst. Nat. Thus the vorticella or wheel animal, which is found in rain water that has stood some days in leaden gutters, or in hollows of lead on the tops of houses, or in the slime or sediment left by such water, though it discovers no sign of life except when in the water, yet it is capable of continuing alive for many months though kept in a dry state. In this state it is of a globulous shape, exceeds not the bigness of a grain of sand, and no signs of life appear; but being put into water, in the space of half an hour a languid motion begins, the globule turns itself about, lengthens itself by slow degrees, assumes the form of a lively maggot, and most commonly in a few minutes afterwards puts out its wheels, swimming vigorously through the water as if in search of food; or else, fixing itself by the tail, works the wheels in such a manner as to bring its food to its mouth; English Encyclopedia, Art. Animalcule.

Thus some shell-snails in the cabinets of the curious have been kept in a dry state for ten years or longer, and have revived on being moistened with warmish water; Philos. Transact. So eggs and seeds after many months torpor, are revived by warmth and moisture; hence it may be concluded, that even the organic particles of dead animals may, when exposed to a due degree of warmth and moisture, retain some degree of vitality, since this is done by more complicate animal organs in the instances above mentioned.

The hydra of Linnæus, which dwells in the rivers of Europe under aquatic plants, has been observed by the curious of the present time, to revive after it has been dried, to be restored after being mutilated, to multiply by being divided, to be propagated from small portions, to live after being inverted; all which would be best explained by the doctrine of spontaneous reproduction from organic particles not yet completely decomposed.

To this should be added, that these microscopic animals are found in all solutions of vegetable or animal matter in water; as black pepper steeped in water, hay suffered to become putrid in water, and the water of dunghills, afford animalcules in astonishing numbers. See Mr. Ellis's curious account of Animalcules produced from an infusion of Potatoes and Hempseed, Philos. Transact. Vol. LIX. from all which it would appear, that organic particles of dead vegetables and animals during their usual chemical changes into putridity or acidity, do not lose all their organization or vitality, but retain so much of it as to unite with the parts of living animals in the process of nutrition, or unite and produce new complicate animals by secretion as in generation, or produce very simple microscopic animals or microscopic vegetables, by their new combinations in warmth and moisture.

And finally, that these microscopic organic bodies are multiplied and enlarged by solitary reproduction without sexual intercourse till they acquire greater perfection or new properties. Lewenhoek observed in rainwater which had stood a few days, the smallest scarcely visible microscopic animalcules, and in a few more days he observed others eight times as large; English Encyclop. Art. Animalcule.

Conclusion.

There is therefore no absurdity in believing that the most simple animals and vegetables may be produced by the congress of the parts of decomposing organic matter, without what can properly be termed generation, as the genus did not previously exist; which accounts for the endless varieties, as well as for the immense numbers of microscopic animals.

The green vegetable matter of Dr. Priestley, which is universally produced in stagnant water, and the mucor, or mouldiness, which is seen on the surface of all putrid vegetable and animal matter, have probably no parents, but a spontaneous origin from the congress of the decomposing organic particles, and afterwards propagate themselves. Some other fungi, as those growing in close wine-vaults, or others which arise from decaying trees, or rotten timber, may perhaps be owing to a similar spontaneous production, and not previously exist as perfect organic beings in the juices of the wood, as some have supposed. In the same manner it would seem, that the common esculent mushroom is produced from horse dung at any time and in any place, as is the common practice of many gardiners; Kennedy on Gardening.

7. From Giovanni Aldini, *An Account of the Late Improvements in Galvanism* (1803)

[Giovanni Aldini, 1762–1834, was the nephew of Luigi Galvani (1737–1798) and succeeded his uncle as professor of physics at Bologna. He was in London in 1803 and applied electric shocks to the body of a recently executed criminal. This text records these experiments, and also discusses "reanimation."]

PART III, SECTION III.

Application of Galvanism[56] in cases of asphyxia and drowning.

I mentioned in the second part of this work the great influence which Galvanism has in cases of asphyxia, and the preference which ought to be

---

56. [I.e., an electric shock.]

given to it in comparison of other stimulants. Though the observations offered in that part are sufficient to prove my proposition, I shall add to them the following experiments:

EXPERIMENT I.

Some dogs and cats were immersed in a large pond till they gave no external signs of respiration, or of muscular motion; and Galvanism being immediately administered to them, according to the methods already described, they were sometimes restored to life. I make use of the term 'sometimes,' because, if animals are immersed in water for a longer period than their organization can bear, and if the vital powers are really destroyed, it is evident that it will be impossible to restore them to life by any physical process whatever. I obtained the same results from to [sic] animals thrown into a state of asphyxia in different ways.

EXPERIMENT II.

Having applied Galvanism to the trunk of a dog, in the *Hôpital de la Charité* at Paris, air seemed to escape from the tracheal artery on every application of the arc. Being requested to repeat and confirm this interesting experiment, I found myself under the necessity of sacrificing a new victim to my Galvanic researches. As it was necessary to examine the phænomenon while the body was in that state of vitality most proper for the observation, I exposed the trunk of another dog recently killed to the Galvanic action; and having placed a taper near to the tracheal artery, it was extinguished twice in succession by two applications of Galvanism. By repeating this experiment, in Mr. Wilson's anatomical theatre, Great Windmill-street, and in the theatres of Guy's and St. Thomas's Hospital, London, I found that the taper could be extinguished a greater number of times.

These experiments give me sufficient reason to hope that Galvanism may be administered with some advantage in cases of drowning. But as I never had an opportunity of trying the effects of this stimulant in such cases, I have requested several medical practitioners to pay attention to this application of Galvanism, which may be of the utmost importance to the cause of humanity. I have already mentioned that the method which I propose is exceedingly simple; that no anatomical operation whatever is required; that it is attended with no danger; and that the possibility of saving the life is in every case respected. Nothing is necessary but to immerse in salt water one of the hands of the person subjected to the operation, and then to apply the Galvanic current to one of the ears and to the surface of the salt water.

Dr. Lettsom, a very zealous member of the Humane Society, having been present at some of my experiments, I requested that he would recommend the application of Galvanism in cases of drowning. He assured me that he would use his endeavours to cause my method to be tried, and I had several conferences with him on the subject, that I might communicate to him such information as might tend to facilitate the application of it. As the Galvanism in such cases ought to be administered with great promptitude, we agreed that the apparatus of the trough is preferable to that of the pile; and we contrived the plan of a portable box to contain a trough, two arcs, and a solution of common salt. Such an apparatus will be exceedingly convenient, and may easily be employed in all cases of drowning and of asphyxia.

[. . .]

APPENDIX. No. I.

An Account of the Experiments performed by J. Aldini on the Body of a Malefactor executed at Newgate Jan. 17th 1803.

INTRODUCTION.

THE unenlightened part of mankind are apt to entertain a prejudice against those, however laudable their motives, who attempt to perform experiments on dead subjects; and the vulgar in general even attach a sort of odium to the common practice of anatomical dissection. It is, however, an incontrovertible fact, that such researches in modern times have proved a source of the most valuable information, in regard to points highly interesting to the knowledge of the human frame, and have contributed in an eminent degree to the improvement of physiology and anatomy. Enlightened legislators have been sensible of this truth; and therefore it has been wisely ordained by the British laws, which are founded on the basis of humanity and public benefit, that the bodies of those who during life violated one of the most sacred rights of mankind, should after execution be devoted to a purpose which might make some atonement for their crime, by rendering their remains beneficial to that society which they offended.

In consequence of this regulation, I lately had an opportunity of performing some new experiments, the principal object of which was to ascertain what opinion ought to be formed of Galvanism as a mean of excitement in cases of asphyxia and suspended animation. The power which exists in the muscular fibre of animal bodies some time after all other signs of vitality have disappeared, had before been examined according to the illustrious Haller's doctrine of irritability; but it appeared to me that muscular action might be excited in a much more efficacious manner by the power of the Galvanic apparatus.

In performing these experiments, I had another object in view. Being favoured with the assistance and support of gentlemen eminently well skilled in the art of dissection, I proposed, when the body should be opened, to perform some new experiments which I never before attempted, and to confirm others which I had made above a year ago on the bodies of two robbers decapitated at Bologna.

To enlarge on the utility of such researches, or to point out the advantages which may result from them, is not my object at present. I shall here only observe, that as the bodies of valuable members of society are often found under similar circumstances, and with the same symptoms as those observed on executed criminals; by subjecting the latter to proper experiments, some speedier and more efficacious means than any hitherto known, of giving relief in such cases, may, perhaps, be discovered. In a commercial and maritime country like Britain, where so many persons, in consequence of their occupations at sea, on canals, rivers, and in mines, are exposed to drowning, suffocation, and other accidents, this object is of the utmost importance in a public view, and is entitled to every encouragement.

Forster, on whose body these experiments were performed, was twenty-six years of age, seemed to have been of a strong, vigorous constitution, and was executed at Newgate on the 17th of January 1803. The body was exposed for a whole hour in a temperature two degrees below the freezing point of Fahrenheit's thermometer; at the end of which long interval it was conveyed to a house not far distant, and, in pursuance of the sentence, was delivered to the College of Surgeons. Mr. Keate, master of that respectable society, having been so kind as to place it under my direction, I readily embraced that opportunity of subjecting it to the Galvanic stimulus, which had never before been tried on persons put to death in a similar manner: and the result of my experiments I now take the liberty of submitting to the public.

Before I conclude this short introduction, I consider it as my duty to acknowledge my obligations to Mr. CARPUE, lecturer on anatomy, and Mr. HUTCHINS, a medical pupil, for the assistance they afforded me in the dissection. I was also much indebted to Mr. CUTHBERTSON, an eminent mathematical instrument maker, who directed and arranged the Galvanic apparatus. Encouraged by the aid of these gentlemen, and the polite attention of Mr. KEATE, I attempted a series of experiments, of which the following is a brief account.

EXPERIMENT I.

ONE arc being applied to the mouth, and another to the ear, wetted with a solution of muriate of soda (common salt), Galvanism was communicated by means of three troughs combined together, each of which contained forty plates of zinc, and as many of copper. On the first application of the arcs the jaw began to quiver, the adjoining muscles were horribly contorted, and the left eye actually opened.

EXPERIMENT II.

On applying the arc to both ears, a motion of the head was manifested, and a convulsive action of all the muscles of the face: the lips and eyelids were also evidently affected; but the action seemed much increased by making one extremity of the arc to communicate with the nostrils, the other continuing in one ear.

EXPERIMENT III.

The conductors being applied to the ear, and to the rectum, excited in the muscles contractions much stronger than in the preceding experiments. The action even of those muscles furthest distant from the points of contact with the arc was so much increased as almost to give an appearance of re-animation.

EXPERIMENT IV.

In this state, wishing to try the power of ordinary stimulants, I applied volatile alkali to the nostrils and to the mouth, but without the least sensible action: on applying Galvanism great action was constantly produced. I then administered the Galvanic stimulus and volatile alkali together; the convulsions appeared to be much increased by this combination, and extended from the muscles of the head, face, and neck, as far as the deltoid. The effect in this case surpassed our most sanguine expectations, and vitality might, perhaps, have been restored, if many circumstances had not rendered it impossible.

EXPERIMENT V.

I next extended the arc from one ear to the biceps flexor cubiti, the fibres of which had been laid bare by dissection. This produced violent convulsions in all the muscles of the arm, and especially in the biceps and the coraco brachialis even without the intervention of salt water.

EXPERIMENT VI.

An incision having been made in the wrist, among the small filaments of the nerves and cellular membrane, on bringing the arc into contact with this part, a very strong action of the muscles of the fore-arm and hand was immediately perceived. In this, as in the last experiment, the animal moisture was sufficient to conduct the Galvanic stimulus without the intervention of salt water.

EXPERIMENT VII.

The short muscles of the thumb were dissected, and submitted to the action of the Galvanic apparatus, which induced a forcible effort to clench the hand.

EXPERIMENT VIII.

The effects of Galvanism in this experiment were compared with those of other stimulants. For this purpose, the point of the scalpel was applied to the fibres, and even introduced into the substance of the biceps flexor cubiti without producing the slightest motion. The same result was obtained from the use of caustic volatile alkali and concentrated sulphuric acid. The latter even corroded the muscle, without bringing it into action.

EXPERIMENT IX.

Having opened the thorax and the pericardium, exposing the heart *in situ,* I endeavoured to excite action in the ventricles, but without success. The arc was first applied upon the surface, then in the substance of the fibres, to the carneæ columnae, to the septum ventriculorum, and lastly, in the course of the nerves by the coronary arteries, even with salt water interposed, but without the slightest visible action being induced.

EXPERIMENT X.

In this experiment the arc was conveyed to the right auricle, and produced a considerable contraction, without the intervention of salt water, but especially in that part called the appendix auricularis: in the left auricle scarcely any action was exhibited.

EXPERIMENT XI.

Conductors being applied from the spinal marrow to the fibres of the biceps flexor cubiti, the gluteus maximus, and the gastrocnemius, separately, no considerable action in the muscles of the arm and leg was produced.

EXPERIMENT XII.

The sciatic nerve being exposed between the great trochanter of the femur and the tuberosity of the ischium, and the arc being established from the spinal marrow to the nerve divested of its theca, we observed, to our astonishment, that no contraction whatever ensued in the muscles, although salt water was used at both extremities of the arc. But the conductor being made to communicate with the fibres of the muscles and the cellular membrane, as strong an action as before was manifested.

EXPERIMENT XIII.

By making the arc to communicate with the sciatic nerve and the gastrocnemius muscle, a very feeble action was produced in the latter.

EXPERIMENT XIV.

Conductors being applied from the sciatic to the peronæal nerve, scarcely any motion was excited in the muscles.

EXPERIMENT XV.

The sciatic nerve being divided about the middle of the thigh, on applying the conductors from the biceps flexor cruris to the gastrocnemius, there ensued a powerful contraction of both. I must here observe that the muscles continued excitable for seven hours and a half after the execution. The troughs were frequently renewed, yet towards the close they were very much exhausted. No doubt, with a stronger apparatus we might have observed muscular action much longer; for, after the experiments had been continued for three or four hours, the power of a single trough was not sufficient to excite the action of the muscles: the assistance of a more powerful apparatus was required. This shows that such a long series of experiments could not have been performed by the simple application of metallic coatings. I am of opinion that, in general, these coatings, invented in the first instance by Galvani, are passive. They serve merely to conduct the fluid pre-existent in the animal system; whereas, with the Galvanic batteries of Volta, the muscles are excited to action by the influence of the apparatus itself.

FROM the above experiments there is reason to conclude:

I.

That Galvanism exerts a considerable power over the nervous and muscular systems, and operates universally on the whole of the animal œconomy.

II.

That the power of Galvanism, as a stimulant, is stronger than any mechanical action whatever.

III.

That the effects of Galvanism on the human frame differ from those produced by electricity communicated with common electrical machines.

IV.

That Galvanism, whether administered by means of troughs, or piles, differs in its effects from those produced by the simple metallic coatings employed by Galvani.

V.

That when the surfaces of the nerves and muscles are armed with metallic coatings, the influence of the Galvanic batteries is conveyed to a greater number of points, and acts with considerably more force in producing contractions of the muscular fibre.

VI.

That the action of Galvanism on the heart is different from that on other muscles. For, when the heart is no longer susceptible of Galvanic influence, the other muscles remain still excitable for a certain time. It is also remarkable that the action produced by Galvanism on the auricles is different from that produced on the ventricles of the heart, as is demonstrated in Experiment the tenth.

VII.

That Galvanism affords very powerful means of resuscitation in cases of suspended animation under common circumstances. The remedies already adopted in asphyxia, drowning, &c. when combined with the influence of Galvanism, will produce much greater effect than either of them separately.

TO conclude this subject, it may be acceptable to the reader to have a short but accurate account of the appearances exhibited on the dissection of the body, which was performed with the greatest care and precision by Mr. Carpue. "The blood in the head was not extravasated, but several vessels were prodigiously swelled, and the lungs entirely deprived of air; there was a great inflammation in the intestines, and the bladder was fully distended with urine. In general, upon viewing the body, it appeared that death had been immediately produced by a real suffocation."

It may be observed, if credit can be given to some loose reports, which hitherto it has not been in our power to substantiate, that after this man had been for some time suspended, means were employed with a view to put an end to his sufferings.

From the preceding narrative it will be easily perceived, that our object in applying the treatment here described was not to produce re-animation, but merely to obtain a practical knowledge how far Galvanism might be employed as an auxiliary to other means in attempts to revive persons under similar circumstances.

In cases when suspended animation has been produced by natural causes, it is found that the pulsations of the heart and arteries become totally imperceptible; therefore, when it is to be restored, it is necessary to re-establish the circulation throughout the whole system. But this cannot be done without re-establishing also the muscular powers which have been suspended, and to these the application of Galvanism gives new energy.

I am far from wishing to raise any objections against the administration of the other remedies which are already known, and which have long been used. I would only recommend Galvanism as the most powerful mean hitherto discovered of *assisting* and increasing the efficacy of every other stimulant.

Volatile alkali, as already observed, produced no effect whatever on the body when applied alone; but, being used conjointly with Galvanism, the power of the latter over the nervous and muscular system was greatly increased: nay, it is possible that volatile alkali, owing to its active powers alone, might convey the Galvanic fluid to the brain with greater facility, by which means its action would become much more powerful in cases of suspended animation. The well known method of injecting atmospheric air ought not to be neglected; but here, likewise, in order that the lungs may be prepared for its reception, it would be proper previously to use Galvanism, to excite the muscular action, and to assist the whole animal system to resume its vital functions. Under this view, the experiments of which I have just given an account, may be of great public utility.

It is with heartfelt gratitude that I recall to mind the politeness and lively interest shown by the members of the College of Surgeons in the prosecution of these experiments. Mr. Keate, the master, in particular proposed to make comparative experiments on animals, in order to give support to the deductions resulting from those on the human body.

Mr. Blicke observed that on similar occasions it would be proper to immerse the body in a warm salt bath, in order to ascertain how far it might promote the action of Galvanism on the whole surface of the body. Dr. Pearson recommended oxygen gas to be substituted instead of the atmospheric air blown into the lungs. It gives me great pleasure to have an opportunity of communicating these observations to the public, in justice to the eminent characters who suggested them, and as an inducement to physiologists not to overlook the minutest circumstance which may tend to improve experiments that promise so greatly to relieve the sufferings of mankind.

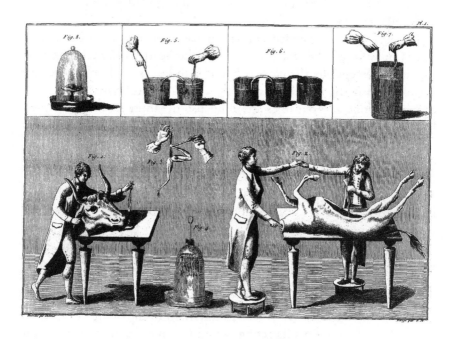

8. From John Abernethy, *An Enquiry into the Probability and Rationality of Mr. Hunter's Theory of Life* (1814)

[Abernethy (1764–1831) was appointed lecturer in anatomy to the Royal College of Surgeons in 1814 and these were his first lectures. His Enquiry *modestly claimed simply to expound the views of the great anatomist John Hunter (1728–1793): but it went far beyond anything in Hunter. Hunter had held*

that "the living principle is inherent in the blood" and that this principle "preserves the body from dissolution . . . and is the cause of all its actions."[57] Abernethy's theory of life was soon attacked by William Lawrence, and defended, as being compatible with Christianity, by opponents of materialism and atheism.]

LECTURE 1.

. . .

Muscles have the power of contracting with surprizing celerity and force. It seems indeed wonderful that the biceps muscle of the arm, which in the dead state would be torn by the weight of a few ounces appended to it, shall in the living state be capable of lifting and sustaining more than 100 lbs. The matter in the muscle seems neither to be increased nor diminished during its contraction, what is lost in length being gained in bulk. The voluntary contraction of muscles cannot be long continued; they become weary and painful, the contraction remits and recurs, causing a tremulous motion. Yet this phænomenon does not seem to be the effect of absolute inability, in the irritable property, to continue in action, for some muscles continue to act without experiencing fatigue. For instance, those of the jaws and back; for whenever they relax, the jaw drops, and the head and body fall forwards, as we see in persons who are going to sleep in a sitting posture. Certain sphincter muscles likewise remain in action without experiencing fatigue. Some sphincters also, I may add, are disposed to yield considerably without impatience; so that their irritability resembles that of those muscles which Bichât has considered as a distinct class, and subservient alone to what he calls the organic life. The contractile power of muscles is also capable of remaining in vehement action for a great length of time, as we see in some cases of cramps, and still more in some cases of tonic tetanus, [*sic*]

Yet though the irritable power is not incapable of continued exertion, it seems evidently to be in general susceptible of fatigue, and inclines to be at rest. If we stimulate the muscles of a limb of a frog severed from the body, by voltaic electricity, the muscular actions are at first vivid and forcible, but they grow fainter and feebler on repeated excitement. Yet if we wait a little till they seem to regain their power, they become vivid and forcible as at first from the same degree of excitement. Such actions may be excited at intervals for twenty-four hours, though with a gradual diminution in their power, after which, in general, they can be no longer excited, and then the

---

57. [John Hunter, *Observations on Certain Parts of the Animal Oeconomy* (London: Sold at no. 13, Castle-Street, 1786), 116.]

muscles become permanently and rigidly contracted. The foregoing facts appear to me to shew the impropriety of the phrase, exhausted irritability, which is in common use to express our inability by the effort of our will to continue the actions of our voluntary muscles: it seems manifest that the irritability is not exhausted but fatigued.

The rigid contraction of the muscles after death, is the effect of irritability: it is its last act. A considerable force is required to overcome this contraction, or to bend the rigid limbs of the dead body, when it has recently taken place. The force required to effect this, gradually diminishes till the muscles become quite pliant; and then, and not till then, does putrefaction ensue.

Mr. Hunter has known this last vital contraction to occur in parts severed from the body sixty hours after their separation, upon the removal of causes which had impeded the contraction before that period; a proof that life in a certain degree was still resident in the part. He observed that death produced by lightning, or large charges of electricity, or by certain kinds of injuries and diseases, prevented this contraction, and even the coagulation of the blood; and that putrefaction would in such cases very rapidly take place. From facts of this kind, as well as from many others, he drew an inference, which has not I believe been disputed, and therefore I need not enter into the discussion of it at length, that the principle of life may in some instances be suddenly removed, or have its power abolished, whilst in general it is lost by degrees.

The contraction of irritability takes place in some animals in a very slow and gradual manner, and their muscles in general are incapable of sudden contraction. Yet though the action of their muscles is very slow, it is very powerful and very permanent. The American sloth, supports its weight for a very long time in one attitude by fixing its claws into the branches of trees; an act which would speedily weary muscles of an ordinary character. The muscles of the legs of birds that roost, seem to have a similar power of permanent contraction.

Mr. Carlisle has lately demonstrated a peculiar distribution of the arteries in the limbs of these tardigrade animals, as they are called, and Doctor Macartney has shewn that a similar arrangement of vessels exists in the legs of fowls. Such a distribution of the arteries may be subservient without being essential to these modes of action.

In the human body we see instances of irritability exerting itself after the manner it does in general in tardigrade animals. If the iris had possessed the ordinary powers of muscles, and none else, it could not have remained, as it is known to do, permanently contracted in a strong light, and permanently dilated in a weak one. Indeed, an anatomist who is fond of tracing structure as connected with function, might readily persuade himself, that there is in the iris a distribution of arteries, similar to that which Mr. Carlisle has demonstrated in the limbs of sloths. We find, however, that sphincter muscles in general have the power of continuing their contraction, though no peculiar distribution of vessels is discoverable in them. In the gall bladder, the function of which requires this slow but permanently acting irritability, in order to express its contents in small and equal quantities into the bowels, as the digested aliment passes into them, we discover no peculiar arrangement of arteries. Though we cannot excite any sudden contraction of that bag, yet we know that it can gradually reduce itself into a very small compass. The skin has every where this slow but permanently acting, and gradually relaxing irritability, the effects of which are most evident in lax and pendulous portions of it. Accordingly we sometimes observe the scrotum and prepuce condensed into a surprizingly small and very compact mass.

Thus have we even in the human body evidences of irritability acting in various modes, whilst we can equally perceive that in tardigrade animals some of their muscles act with celerity. In the Lori, of whose habits Vosmaer has given so interesting an account, and which manifested no signs of alacrity, save in eating the food that it liked, no stimulation nor injury could induce it to mend its pace, but it shewed its resentment of the attempt to make it perform impossibilities, by suddenly snapping at the stick or instrument with which it was goaded; and thus again demonstrated that the muscles of its jaw were endowed with an irritability of the more common character.

Having thus briefly described the principal phænomena of muscular action, for I forbear to notice others of less importance, I proceed to review the conjectures that have been formed as to the cause of these curious, sudden, and powerful contractions. Not to speak of exploded hypotheses, I trouble you only with those which are modern.

First, then, the contraction has been supposed to be the effect of some chemical change occurring in the part. This opinion is I think invalidated by the reiterated contractions which may be produced in the limbs of some animals when removed from the body, even during twenty-four hours, if excited by voltaic electricity, and consequently when no supply of materials can be supposed to exist within the limb, to produce such reiterated chemical changes. The opinion is still further refuted by observing, that these vivacious contractions will equally take place, upon the same excitement, in the exhausted receiver of an air pump and in the open air. They may also be excited under water, under oil, in a great variety of gases; in short, under circumstances which exclude the presence of any chemical agent from without, to which such changes could reasonably be imputed.

Secondly. The contraction of irritability has been supposed to be a property of the muscular fibres. Properties are generally considered as permanent qualities. Thus, the property of gravitation is continually operating, equally when bodies remain at rest and when it produces motion in them, equally whilst I support this book in my hand, and when I suffer it to fall on the table. If, however, so curious an occasional property could belong to matter, we should naturally expect that it would belong to some peculiar quality, or arrangement of matter. But irritability is connected with matter of different qualities and arrangements. The flesh of animals and that of fish are different in quality; the mucilaginous bladders which float in the sea differ from vegetables; yet all are irritable, or possess this power of occasional contraction. Though in general we find irritability connected with a fibrous structure, yet, if we may trust our senses, it is not so in every instance. In the hydatid, where no such structure is apparent even with the aid of lenses, we still have evidence of the irritability of life. If also, as I strongly suspect, the muscular fibres be not continued from one end of the muscle to the other, irritability could not in that case be considered as a property belonging to them, since any breach of continuity would completely frustrate the contraction of the whole muscle.

Thirdly, I proceed to enquire into Mr. Hunter's opinion, that irritability is the effect of some subtile, mobile, invisible substance, superadded to the evident structure of muscles, or other forms of vegetable and animal matter, as magnetism is to iron, and as electricity is to various substances with which it may be connected. Mr. Hunter doubtless thought, and I believe most persons do think, that in magnetic and electric motions, a subtile invisible substance, of a very quickly and powerfully mobile nature, puts in motion other bodies which are evident to the senses, and are of a nature more gross and inert. To be as convinced as I am of the probability of Mr. Hunter's Theory as a cause of irritability, it is, I am aware, necessary to be as convinced as I am that electricity is what I have now supposed it to be, and that it pervades all nature. To obtain this conviction it is necessary that the facts connected with this subject should be attentively considered; but for such an examination I have no time; neither would it be considered as suitable to the general design of these lectures.

Whatever notions philosophers may be pleased to form respecting matter in general, it does not appear to me that our physiological opinions can be affected by their decisions. Of the matter which for the most part presents itself to our notice, and is cognizable by the eye and touch, we know that it has a property called by Sir Isaac Newton *vis inertiæ*, an indisposition to move unless impelled to motion, and a disposition to continue in motion unless retarded.

There are some philosophers who think, that properties similar to those which in the aggregate mass become an object of our senses, likewise belong to every atom of which it is composed; whilst others, on the contrary, think, that the atoms have very different qualities, and that the vis inertiæ is the property only of the aggregate mass. The matter of animals and vegetables is, however, an aggregate mass; it is as we express it, common matter, it is inert; so that the necessity of supposing the superaddition of some subtile and mobile substance is apparent.

Taking it for granted that the opinions generally entertained concerning the cause of electrical motions are true, analogy would induce us to suppose, that similar motions might be produced, by similar causes, in matter organized as it is found to be in the vegetable and animal systems.

The phænomena of electricity and of life correspond. Electricity may be attached to, or inhere, in a wire; it may be suddenly dissipated, or have its powers annulled, or it may be removed by degrees or in portions, and the wire may remain less and less strongly electrified, in proportion as it is abstracted. So life inheres in vegetables and animals; it may sometimes be suddenly dissipated, or have its powers abolished, though in general it is lost by degrees, without any apparent change taking place in the structure; and in either case putrefaction begins when life terminates.

The motions of electricity are characterized by their celerity and force; so are the motions of irritability. The motions of electricity are vibratory; so likewise are those of irritability. When by long continued exertion the power of muscles is fatigued, or when it is feeble, their vibratory or tremulous motions are manifest to common observation, but the same kind of motion may be perceived at all times by attention, as has been shewn by Doctor Woolaston in the Croonian Lecture for the year 1810. It is then I think manifest, that Mr. Hunter's conjectures are the most probable of any that have been offered as to the cause of irritability.

My allotted time does not permit me at present to consider the other vital functions; yet I relinquish the subject with reluctance, because I have been speaking only on that point in which it seems most difficult to persuade the incredulous, of the probability and rationality of Mr. Hunter's Theory.

When hereafter I shall have to speak of the other vital functions, I think it will appear that it is impossible to account for the phænomena in any other manner than that which Mr. Hunter has suggested.

In ascending the difficult and lofty ladder of knowledge, men of great talent and industry seem to have affixed to it certain resting places, on which, reposing for a time from their labours, they could tranquilly assemble their followers, and contemplate more extensive views of nature, and of nature's laws, than had before been taken. If after having stood by the side of the great teacher Newton, and learned from him the properties of common and inanimate matter, we afterwards attend to Mr. Hunter, our great instructor in the functions of living beings, he points out to us how matter, starting from the general mass, springs up into life in vegetation. We see vegetables as it were self formed and producing their own species. We observe them also exerting most of the powers which animals possess. That they have irritability is evident from the current of their sap and their secretions; nay, in some we observe those vivacious motions which seem chiefly to belong to animal life, as is evident in the Mimosæ, the Dionæa Muscipula, and Heydysarum gyrans. We see them like animals having alternate seasons of action and repose; and though in general vegetables like animals are in action during the day and rest in the night, yet also some vegetables like some animals rest in the day and are in action during the common season of repose.

We see animals scarcely differing from vegetables in their functions, like them doomed to a stationary existence, with even less appearance of organization than we usually discover in vegetables, and of a structure so simple as to admit of propagation like vegetables by cuttings. Yet in all the diversity of living beings we recognize certain processes peculiar and essential to life; as the power of converting other kinds of matter into that appropriate to the individual it is to form and support; the power of distributing the nutriment, thus converted, to every part for its formation and supply; the ventilation, as I may call it, of the nutritive fluids; the power of preparing various dissimilar substances from the nutritive fluids; and the propagation of the species. As what is deemed the complexity of animal life increases, we find distinct organs allotted for each of these functions; thus we have organs of digestion, circulation, respiration, secretion, and generation, which are various in their structure in the different tribes of animals.

In vegetables, and in some moluscæ, no traces of nerves are discoverable. The nervous system begins in a simple form, and seems to increase in complexity up to man. But this will make the subject of the next lecture. Mr. Hunter also shews us that there are animals, as for instance the torpedo and gymnotus, which have organs liberally supplied with nerves, forming an electric battery which they can charge at will. Such facts shew to what a degree electricity exists in these animals, and how greatly it is under the influence or control of the nervous system; and they could not fail to make a strong impression on the contemplative and deeply meditating mind of Mr. Hunter.

What then, may I ask, is the natural inference to be drawn from the examination of this great chain of being, which seems to connect even man with the common matter of the universe? What but that which Mr. Hunter drew, that life must be something independent of organization, since it is able to execute the same functions with such diversified structure, and even in some instances with scarcely any appearance of organization at all.

The experiments of Sir Humphrey Davy seem to me to form an important link in the connexion of our knowledge of dead and living matter. He has solved the great and long hidden mystery of chemical attraction, by shewing that it depends upon the electric properties which the atoms of different species of matter possess. Nay, by giving to an alkali electric properties which did not originally belong to it, he has been able to control the ordinary operations of nature, and to make potash pass through a strong acid, without any combination taking place. That electricity is something, I could never doubt, and therefore it follows as a consequence in my opinion, that it must be every where connected with those atoms of matter, which form the masses that are cognizable to our senses; and that it enters into the composition of every thing, inanimate or animate. If then it be electricity that produces all the chemical changes, we so constantly observe, in surrounding inanimate objects, analogy induces us to believe that it is electricity which also performs all the chemical operations in living bodies; that the universal chemist resides in them, and exercises in some degree peculiar powers because it possesses a peculiar apparatus.

Sir Humphrey Davy's experiments also lead us to believe, that it is electricity, extricated and accumulated in ways not clearly understood, which causes those sudden and powerful motions in masses of inert matter, which we occasionally witness with wonder and dismay; that it is electricity which causes the whirl-wind, and the water spout, and which "with its sharp and sulphurous bolt splits the unwedgeable and gnarled oak,"[58] and destroys our most stabile edifices; that it is electricity which by its consequences makes the firm earth tremble, and throws up subterraneous matter from volcanos.

When therefore we perceive in the universe at large, a cause of rapid and powerful motions of masses of inert matter, may we not naturally conclude that the inert molecules of vegetable and animal matter, may be made to move in a similar manner, by a similar cause?

It is not meant to be affirmed that electricity is life. There are strong analogies between electricity and magnetism, and yet I do not know that any one has been hardy enough to assert their absolute identity. I only mean to prove, that Mr. Hunter's Theory is verifiable, by shewing that a subtile substance of a quickly and powerfully mobile nature, seems to pervade every thing, and appears to be the life of the world; and therefore it is probable that a similar substance pervades organized bodies, and produces similar effects in them.

The experiments of Sir H. Davy seem to realize the speculations of philosophers, and to verify the deductions of reason, by demonstrating the existence of a subtile, active, vital principle, pervading all nature as has heretofore been surmized, and denominated the Anima Mundi. The opinions which in former times were a justifiable hypothesis, seem to me now to be converted into a rational theory.

It is then, I think, manifest, that Mr. Hunter's Theory of Life, presents us with the most probable solution of the phænomena of irritability, of any that has hitherto been proposed.

---

58. [A quotation from Shakespeare's *Measure for Measure*.]

The human mind has been the same at all periods of the world; in all ages there have been men of a sceptical disposition, disinclined to believe any thing that was not directly an object of their senses. At all periods there have been other men of a contemplative, and perhaps more credulous character, who have been disposed to believe that there were invisible causes, operating to produce the alterations which are visible, and who from much less numerous facts have drawn the same inferences that I have done. And many of these, from Pythagoras downwards, have expressed their sentiments, though with some variety, yet pretty much to the same effect. The Greek philosophers recognized in man, the Σῶμα, Ψυχή, and Νοῦς, the body, vital principle, and mind, whilst some used words significant of intellect, to express the energizing principle in nature, without apparently having any clear ideas of intelligence.

What was called the Anima Mundi, was, however, by many considered as a distinct and active principle, and was not confounded with intelligence of any kind. I know not how I can better exhibit to my audience the subject I am alluding to, or better acquaint them with the general tenour and tendencies of these opinions, than by quoting that portion of these philosophical notions, which Virgil is said to have put into the mouth of Anchises,

> Spiritus intus alit, totamque infusa per artus
> Mens agitat molem, & magno se corpore miscet.

> [A spirit within sustains; in all the limbs mind moves the mass and mingles with the mighty frame.—Virgil, *Aeneid, bk.* 4, lines 726–27 in *Eclogues. Georgics. Aeneid: Books 1–6*, trans. H. Rushton Fairclough, rev. G. P. Goold, Loeb Classical Library 63 (Cambridge, MA: Harvard University Press, 1999), 582–83.]

And please to observe, gentlemen, it is Virgil says, it is Anchises speaks, that which I also this day have been saying;—

> Inde hominum pecudumque genus, vitæque volantum
> Et quæ marmoreo fert monstra sub æquore pontus.

> [Thence spring the races of man and beast, the life of winged creatures, and the monsters that ocean bears beneath his marble surface.— Virgil, *Aeneid*, bk. 4, lines 728–29 in *Eclogues*, trans. Fairclough, rev. Goold (1999), 582–83.]

LECTURE II.

I proceed to speak of the structure and functions of the nervous fibres.

The nerves which we observe pervading the body, appear to be packets of very minute threads, seemingly distinct from each other. The nerves divide and subdivide, and in so doing a certain number of threads separate from the original packet, and appear as a distinct nerve. It is, therefore, possible to trace a minute nerve, up to its origin, from the toe or finger, by splitting it off from the various packets with which it has been conjoined. So far does anatomical fact concur with the physiological opinion, that every nervous filament communicates distinctly with the brain or some process of that organ.

This apparent continuity is, however, lost, whenever we find those intumescences on nerves which are called ganglia, for in these there seems to be a mixture or consolidation of the nervous matter. It is also lost wherever various nerves unite together, and form a plexus; in which case the nervous fibrils either coalesce, or become inextricably interwoven with one another.

The nerve from which the thoracic and abdominal viscera are chiefly supplied, is beset with numerous ganglia and plexuses; and as we cannot by our will influence the actions of those viscera, and as the iris, the motions of which are also involuntary, is supplied with nerves from a ganglion, it has been thought that ganglia, by intercepting the direct communications between the brain and the extreme branches of nerves, might render parts thus supplied less amenable to the will, and less under the influence of the general affections of the nervous system. It is also thought that ganglia might serve the office of subsidiary brains, each affording a separate source of nervous energy.

On the one hand, it ought to lie observed, that all the vertebral nerves, supplying parts over which the will exerts the most perfect control, have ganglia at their commencement; and that the nerves of the leg and arm form a plexus near their origin. The actions of the cremaster muscle are involuntary; yet I believe it is supplied by the same nerves, which supply muscles that are subject to voluntary actions; therefore this opinion does not appear to me to be such as we should receive with entire confidence. Again, it it[*sic*] is further apparent, that the functions of the abdominal and other viscera are greatly affected by disorders of the brain, and that the brain is greatly affected by disorders of these viscera.

The ingenious and industrious French anatomist, Bichât, has classed the living functions into the organic and animal: the distinction seems a natural and useful one, and throws light on the physiology of the visceral nerve. In vegetables, and in some moluscæ, no traces of a nervous system are discoverable. In some of the lower order of animals, that have organs for the preparation and distribution of nutriment, they are supplied by a visceral nerve, which it is probable maintains amongst those organs a concurrence of impressions and actions. In some of these animals no traces of nerves subservient to the voluntary regulation of their motions can be found. In the ascending complexity of the nervous system, we find a nervous chord more or less beset with ganglia, which supplies other parts of the body besides the viscera, and which probably serves to maintain amongst them likewise a concurrence of impressions and actions. We next find at one end of this chord a kind of ganglion, or brain, which gradually becomes larger and more complex as we trace the series of links upwards to man, in whom it bears a much larger proportion to the nervous system in general than in any other animal. The visceral nerve, in the ascending series of animals, appears connected with the animal nerves; and so numerous are these connections that this nerve has in the human subject obtained the title of the great sympathetic nerve.

The vital organs are required to carry on their functions with a degree of regularity and order, under the varying circumstances of life; and the possession of a distinct nerve may enable them to continue their functions without so materially participating in the disturbances of the animal system, as they must otherwise have done: yet the numerous connections of the visceral with the animal nerves must render both participators in each other's disorders.

The nerves, then, may be said to proceed from the brain, medulla spinalis, and visceral nerve, to all parts of the body for their supply. In thus expressing a fact, however, we should guard against an idea which the analogous distribution of arteries is apt to engender. Arteries become minute in proportion as they send off branches, whilst on the contrary, the branches of nerves are often larger than the trunk from which they proceeded. It is no unfrequent occurrence for malformed children to be born without a brain, yet with a perfect nervous system. The most rational idea, therefore, we can entertain on the present subject, is, that the nerves are formed in the parts where we find them, and that they are connected to those parts of the organs from which we are accustomed to say they proceed. Nerves are vascular, and we can inject them with subtile injections.

The nerves, then, proceeding from, or being connected with the brain, medulla spinalis, and visceral nerve, may be traced, ramifying throughout the body in the manner already mentioned, till they arrive at the part for the supply of which they are designed. They then split into numerous branches which communicate with each other and again subdivide and rejoin, their communications appearing to multiply as they become more minute; so that every part of the body has a kind of net work of nerves, which is minute in proportion to the susceptibility and sensibility it possesses.

This general and imperfect sketch of the anatomy of the nervous system, relates only to what may be discovered by our unassisted sight. If by means of the microscope we endeavour to observe the ultimate nervous fibres, persons in general are as much at a loss as when by the same means they attempt to trace the ultimate muscular fibres.

Those fibres which we can split off from a nervous packet, in the manner before mentioned, though too minute to admit of further subdivision, appear by the microscope to be themselves packets of smaller threads. It is generally asserted by microscopical observers, that the nerves and medullary matter of the brain and spinal marrow are the same, and are composed of very minute fibres. Fontana speaks confidently on this point; and he further says, that he has seen these nervous fibres regenerated in the medium which has been formed to unite a divided nerve. He describes the nervous fibres in every part of the nervous system as cylindrical, pursuing a slightly undulating course, and being in a considerable degree transparent. He states also that they are larger than the ultimate fibres of muscles.

Microscopical observers also tell us, that though the nervous fibrils in each packet appear distinct, and may be separated from each other in the manner already described, yet they have nevertheless transverse communications with each other. Each nervous fibre has been supposed to be covered by investing membranes similar to those of the brain; but this opinion is founded on an analogy with what is observed in the optic nerve, rather than on actual observation with respect to others. That they have investing membranes is clear, and we are told that we may dissolve the medullary or nervous matter by an alkali, and leave these investing membranes; or on the other hand, that we may dissolve the investing membranes by nitric acid, and leave the medullary fibres.

Having thus spoken of the chief circumstances relating to the anatomy of the nervous system, I shall not dwell on this part of the subject, but hasten to the principal object of the lecture, to consider its Physiology, in order to examine how far Mr. Hunter's Theory of Life, seems adequate to explain the phænomena of the nervous functions.

First then, it is generally believed that all sensation is in the brain, and that all volition proceeds from that organ. This proposition requiring to be impressed so as to produce conviction, for it is the foundation on which all our future reasoning is founded, I shall state the principal causes of this opinion. First, If the continuity of a nerve be intercepted at any point between that extremity which receives impressions from the objects of sense, and which therefore may be called the impressible or tangible extremity, and that which communicates with the brain, and is usually called its sensorial extremity, both feeling and volition by means of that nerve are suspended.

2dly. If a certain degree of pressure be made upon the brain, both feeling and voluntary motion cease whilst it continues and return when it is removed.

3dly. As we have evidence that the perceptions and intellect of animals increase in proportion as the brain becomes larger and more complex, so we have reason to conclude that these faculties are connected with that part of the nervous system.

4thly. The conviction which we generally though not constantly experience, that feeling exists in the part which receives impressions, is shewn to be deceptive by the following facts. If a nerve be irritated midway between the brain and its extremities, severe pain is supposed to be felt in those extremities; and if it supplies muscles, those muscles become convulsed. Thus when a disease forms about the hip joint, or in the loins, many persons have applied poultices to their knees, from a conviction that as the pain was felt in the knee, it was the seat of the disorder. In like manner, persons who have had their limbs amputated, can scarcely believe that they are removed, because of the pain and other sensations they still seem to feel in them. In either of these cases, motions being excited in the middle of nerves, and transmitted to the brain, are attributed to a disordered state of those parts from which such motions have heretofore originated.

If then it be admitted that sensation exists in the brain, and that volition proceeds from that organ, it necessarily follows that motions must be transmitted to and fro along the nervous chords, whenever they take place. It was formerly supposed that these chords were passive, and might be made mechanically to vibrate, but their want of elasticity and tension, and their pulpy origins and terminations, are circumstances which render such a supposition inadmissible. Physiologists were therefore led to conjecture that the nervous fibrils were tubular, and that they contained a subtile fluid, by means of which such motions were transmitted.

Of the extensive knowledge and high intellectual powers of Baron Haller no one can entertain a doubt; and yet, he could devise no other theory to account for the phænomena of the nervous functions. His opinions have always appeared to me very sensible, and they were accordant to the philosophy of his own times. He says, Si vero, cogitata nostra de ipsa natura spirituum proferre juberemur, activum ad motum, a voluntate & a sensu concipiendum, aptissimum, celerrimum, omne sensuum acie subtilius, tamen hactenus igne & aethere, & electro, & magnetica materie crassius facere elementum, ut et contineri vasis, & a vinculis coerceri aptum sit: & denique manifestum ex cibis nasci & reparare queat.[59]

Mr. Hunter's opinion of a subtile and mobile substance, inhering in the nervous chords, is not essentially different from that of Haller. He does

---

59. ["If I were obliged to give my opinion, however, concerning the nature of this spirit, I should conceive it to be an active element, most apt for sense and voluntary motion; flowing with the greatest rapidity; so subtile as to escape the most accurate observation of our senses, yet so far more substantial than the matter of heat, æther, electricity, or magnetism, as to be capable of being contained and confined in vessels, or by other mechanical means; and, finally, it must manifestly be of such a nature as to be regenerated and repaired by our food." Translation from John Cooke, *A Treatise of Nervous Diseases*, 2 vols. (London: Longman, 1820), 1:23.]

not indeed suppose it to be confined in tubes, neither does the philosophy of the present time require such a supposition, for no one at present will doubt that a subtile substance may be attached to or inhere in a chord without mechanical confinement. Will not a wire when electrified continue to be so, if surrounded by non-conductors? Experiments made on the limbs of animals with electricity, produced in the manner first explained by Volta, shew that different parts of the body have different conducting powers. Skin and membrane being very bad conductors, and brain, muscle, and blood being remarkably good ones.

The celerity with which motions are transmitted from the tangible extremities of nerves most distant from the brain, and the celerity with which volition is transmitted to the muscles, in consequence of sensations thus induced, are sufficient to convince us that such effects must be produced by the motions of a very mobile substance. It is not necessary to suppose that when such motions are transmitted along the nervous chords, an evident motion of the visible matter of those chords should be induced. Electrical motions take place along a wire without occasioning any visible motion of the metal itself.

Formerly, it was thought that the motions of the nerves that cause sensation, were the effect of an impulse made on their tangible extremities, which was propagated along the chord to the brain. It seems to be an improvement in modem physiology, to attribute sensation to an action begun in the nervous fibrils, in consequence of the stimulation which they suffer from such impulses. This opinion is contended for by Doctor Darwin, in his paper on Ocular Spectra, published in the Philosophical Transactions; and Sir Everard Home has further shewn, that the living principle of nerves has an irritability belonging to it, resembling that of muscles, and capable of causing a contraction in them when they are divided.[60]

The opinion that sensation is the consequence of an action begun in and transmitted through the nervous fibrils, assists us in understanding how our sensations may be very vivid from the slightest impulses; such, for instance, as take place in the application of odour to the olfactory nerves, for it is not the impulse, but the consequent action, that is transmitted to the sensorium: and why we may have no sensation from the most violent impulses; for such we cannot but suppose to occur, when a man is shot through the body, or has a limb removed by a cannon ball; occurrences which have however happened without any distinct feeling intimating the event.

In supposing a principle of life in nerves, similar to what is conceived to exist in muscles, we might naturally expect to find certain analogies of functions in those organs. The facility, celerity, and accuracy of the nervous

---

60. Croonian lecture.

actions, seem like those of the muscles to be improved by use; as is exemplified in the quick and correct perceptions of those who are accustomed to exercise their auditory nerves in attending to musical sounds. A train of nervous actions having often taken place they, like similar actions in muscles, become concatenated, and are liable to occur in succession, when one of them is accidentally induced. Both nerves and muscles require temporary respites from action, and are refreshed by sleep.

The supposition of actions occurring in the nerves, explains many circumstances connected with diseases. Vehement actions may occur in the tangible extremities of nerves, independent of impulses, and occasion severe pain. This seems to happen in the disease called tic douloureux. Ordinarily, actions beginning in the tangible extremities of nerves, are regularly transmitted to the brain; but in cases of nervous pains, actions sometimes seem to begin in the middle of nerves; and it is probable, that actions beginning in the sensorial extremities of nerves may be productive of illusory sensations, and excite fallacious ideas.

If this theory of nervous actions could be proved, the extent of our knowledge would only lead to this conclusion, that motions of a subtile substance, propagated to and fro in the nervous fibrils, took place in consequence of excitement by impulses and volition; but from such motions it seems impossible to account for sensation or volition. We can conceive no variety in these motions, but what relates to degree, duration, and succession, and it seems impossible to believe that sensation can be the result of such motions, or that ideas can arise from any succession or train of them. Certain persons will therefore I doubt not continue to think that sensation, remembrance, comparison, judgment, and volition, are properties of some distinct substance.

The essences or primitive parts of what we call matter, are too subtile to be perceived by our senses, and seem even to elude our conceptions. Is it not then most philosophical to acknowledge our ignorance on these points, and to speak of what we do know, the properties of the different species of substances in nature. Thus we seem to be acquainted with the properties of the aggregate forms of that substance which is cognizable to the eye and touch, and which we then call matter; we seem to be assured of the existence, and to know something of the properties, of a subtile substance which pervades all nature; and if we are allowed to know any thing, we surely may be admitted to know the properties of our own minds.

How diversified are our perceptions, how admirably are they adapted to our wants and gratifications! for all beauty of prospect, all melody of sound, all variety of odour, must by the eye of reason be perceived to result from the masses or molecules of surrounding matter, being in various states of motion or of rest; of which circumstances we have notice by the actions they induce in our nervous fibrils. Such variety of perception I can only consider as the effect of the peculiar properties of that which feels, remembers, reasons, and wills, and which seems connected with the brain alone.

The conclusion to be drawn from this examination of the functions of the nervous system is curious and interesting. We perceive an exact correspondence between those opinions which result from physiological researches, and those which so naturally arise from the suggestions of reason that some have considered them as intuitive. For most reflecting persons in all ages have believed, and indeed it seems natural to believe, what modern physiology also appears to teach, that in the human body there exists an assemblage of organs, formed of common inert matter, such as we see after death, a principle of life and action, and a sentient and rational faculty, all intimately connected, yet each apparently distinct from the other.

So intimate, indeed, is the connection as to impose on us the opinion of their identity. The body springs and bounds as though its inert fabric were alive; yet have we good reasons for believing that life is distinct from organization. The mind and the actions of life affect each other. Failure or disturbance of the actions of life prevent or disturb our feelings, and enfeeble, perplex, or distract our intellectual operations. The mind equally affects the actions of life, and thus influences the whole body. Terror seems to palsy all its parts, whilst contrary emotions cause the limbs to struggle, and become contracted from energy. Now though these facts may countenance the idea of the identity of mind and life, yet have we good reasons for believing that they are perfectly distinct. Whilst, therefore, on the one hand, I feel interested in oppugning those physiological opinions which tend to confound life with organization; I would, on the other, equally oppose those which confound perception and intelligence with mere vitality.

In the first lecture I endeavoured to shew that Mr. Hunter's Theory of Life was verifiable, and that it afforded the most rational solution of the cause of irritability, which had hitherto been offered to the public. It now appears that it does not essentially differ from that of the best physiologists, with regard to the explanation it affords of the nervous functions. As it is impossible to review all the phænomena of these functions in a lecture, I shall on the present occasion merely direct your attention to the consideration of one other subject, which is, the opinions we may be warranted in forming, respecting the connection of irritability and sensibility.

This subject has been the cause of much controversy. Haller maintained that irritability was a distinct property inherent in muscles; to use his own words, that they had a vis insita, independent of the vis nervea; which opinion has of late received additional corroboration from some experiments of Mr. Brodie. Those who object to this opinion, can, I think, only oppose it on the following grounds. They must contend either that the muscles have a kind of perception of injury which causes them to contract, even though they are unconnected with the brain; or that the nerves are the organs which prepare and supply the muscles with something which is the cause of irritability.

Concerning the first of these suppositions, that muscles may have a perceptibility of injury, distinct from that which we understand to be feeling, I have to observe, that we can have no idea of sensation but what results from our own experience, which may be defined to be perception attended with consciousness; which kind of sensation is confined to the brain alone. Of any other kind of perception, it is evident we can never form any idea.

If a man's leg be amputated, and by voltaic electricity I excite contraction in its muscles for some hours, how can I know whether they feel or not? We naturally judge of other subjects from ourselves, and knowing that we shrink from whatever pains us, some persons seem to conclude that the muscles contract because they have been hurt. To the patient who has suffered amputation, such a supposition would seem absurd. He may feel pain when no stimulus is applied to the limb, or he may feel ease when it is. Nay, he continues to feel pain, or sensations, in the limb when it is rotten, or no longer in existence; which seems to shew the integrity of the sentient principle remaining in the brain.

In vegetables, and in some moluscæ, no traces of a nervous system are discoverable, yet the irritability of life is manifest in all. In the ascending series of animals, in proportion as the brain becomes large and complex, we have evidence of the perceptions and intelligence increasing; a circumstance which would lead us to believe that these faculties were connected with that part of the nervous system. We have also equal reason to believe, that neither such perception nor intelligence is requisite for the mere functions of life, for these appear to be carried on as effectually in animals that have no brains, nay, in those which seem destitute of any nervous system, as in those which possess such organs. Indeed, many of the most vivacious and irritable animals have the least nervous system. The nerves in the lower order of animals, that have no common sensorium, may contribute to produce effects, which, in tracing the ascending series, I have endeavoured to express by the words concurrence of impressions and actions; because intimations of impressions and actions occurring in one part may be communicated to others by these inter-nunciate chords, as Mr. Hunter called them, in cases where we are not warranted in supposing there is any sensation such as I have defined.

Assuredly, motion does not necessarily imply sensation; it takes place where no one ever yet imagined there could be sensation. If I put on the table a bason containing a saturated solution of salt, and threw into it a single crystal; the act of crystallization would begin from the point touched, and rapidly and regularly pervade the liquor till it assumed a solid form. Yet I know I should incur your ridicule, if I suggested the idea that the stimulus of the salt had primarily excited the action, or that its extension was the effect of continuous sympathy. If also I threw a spark amongst gun-powder, what would you think were I to represent the explosion as a struggle resentful of injury, or the noise as the clamorous expression of pain?

Now though chemists may solve the cause of these phænomena, physiologists have yet to learn, and probably they never may learn, why certain actions succeed to certain causes in living bodies. Causes which induce muscular or nervous actions in one part do not induce similar actions in another. Both muscles and nerves have peculiar habitudes and modes of action, and require the application of various peculiar excitements. Causes which produce no bad effect upon one person, will have a detrimental influence upon another, and this we say is the result of idiosyncrasy. Thus the odour of a cat, or the effluvia of mutton, the one imperceptible, the other grateful to the generality of persons, has caused individuals to fall on the ground as though bereaved of life, or to have their whole frame agitated by convulsions. Substances which induce disease in one person or animal, do not induce disease in others. That pain is not the cause of action, is I think evident. Nervous motions, induced by the will, cause our muscles to act, but such motions occasion no sensation in the obedient muscles. When, therefore, we employ the terms in common use of a stimulus being applied, and an action or disease excited, we should remember that neither the infliction of pain, nor absolute injury, is essential to the production of such consequences.

With respect to the second proposition, into which I have resolved the objections that may be made to Haller's opinion of irritability being independent on sensibility, I have only to remark, that the effects of pressure made on nerves, as well as other observations, have induced the general belief that some fluid or energy pervades the nerves for the supply of the body. Pressure on a nerve benumbs and paralyzes the parts which it supplies, which regain sensation and motion on the removal of the pressure; yet if irritability exist in vegetables and some animals that have no nervous system, it shews the possibility of irritability being produced without the intervention of nerves.

It has been my object to shew that Mr. Hunter's Theory of Life is a verifiable Theory, and that it affords the most rational explanation of the phænomena of irritability, and of those nervous functions that have been considered. It is, however, impossible in the compass of a lecture, as I have before observed, to review all the phænomena of the nervous functions, which it is necessary to do in order to establish it as a rational Theory. The contemplation of this subject at large, is fitter for meditation in the closet than for discussion in the lecture-room. I shall, therefore, merely mention by way of exciting attention to some of the phænomena alluded to, that it seems impossible to account for those which Mr. Hunter considered as the effect of sympathies between remote organs, or for those consequences of idiosyncrasy which have been mentioned, upon any other supposition than that of a subtile substance, prone to act, or liable to fail in action, pervading the body, the affections of which can with electrical celerity be propagated throughout the system.

I have further to shew that Mr. Hunter's Theory of Life is adequate to explain the cause of the prevention of putrefaction, and the regulation of temperature. If the vital principle of Mr. Hunter be not electricity, at least we have reason to believe it is of a similar nature, and has the power of regulating electrical operations. That electricity is the great chemist both in organized and unorganized bodies, will be generally credited; and that the power which combines may also prevent decomposition is too obvious to need discussion. That electricity is capable of augmenting and diminishing the temperature of unorganized matter is well known. Does not Platina wire drop like wax in fusion when it intervenes between the different ends of the voltaic battery? and do not the spherules of rain fall to the ground at midsummer as firmly frozen as in the depth of winter, when they pass through a stratum of air refrigerated by electrical operations? I believe I need say no more on these subjects.

The varying and the strong retention of life by seeds, and some kinds of vegetables and animals, are facts which seem more satisfactorily solved by Mr. Hunter's Theory of Life than by any other.

Impressed with the difficulties of the task I have undertaken, of giving lectures in the presence of men of superior knowledge and talents, respecting subjects on which every one has formed his own opinions, which of course he thinks correct; though desirous of fulfilling the design of these lectures to the extent of my ability, I feel unable to display the subjects of them in any other way than that to which I have been accustomed. Thinking as Mr. Hunter taught, with regard to life and its functions, in health and disorder, I must use his language as expressive of the phænomena we observe. That an attention to the sympathies of parts and organs is necessary to our understanding disorder and disease, I shall hereafter endeavour to shew. That Mr. Hunter did observe these sympathies in a manner and to an extent that surprized most professional men, is well known to all those who were present at his lectures on this subject. Their surprize was indeed natural, because they were not then fully acquainted with his views and motives.

I mention these things, because I am aware that there are some who say sympathy is a term without any direct meaning, and that all which Mr. Hunter said on the subject of life, explains nothing. What Mr. Hunter meant, I believe I understand; what persons of different sentiments, whom I acknowledge possess great information and ability, mean, when they talk in this manner, I am not so well able to discover. They seem to deny that life can be any thing which may not be seen or felt. They seem to wish us to believe that they have that philosophical turn of mind which exempts them from vulgar prejudices, and that no Theory appears to them satisfactory, neither do they propose any for our adoption.

Thinking being inevitable, we ought . . . to be solicitous to think correctly. Opinions are equally the natural result of thought, and the cause of conduct. If errors of thought terminated in opinions, they would be of less consequence; but a slight deviation from the line of rectitude in thought, may lead to a most distant and disastrous aberration from that line in action. I own I cannot readily believe any one who tells me, he has formed no opinion on subjects which must have engaged and interested his attention. Persons both of sceptical and credulous characters form opinions, and we have in general some principal opinion, to which we connect the rest, and to which we make them I subservient; and this has a great influence on all our conduct. Doubt and uncertainty are so fatiguing to the human mind, by keeping it in continual action, that it will and must rest somewhere; and if so, our enquiry ought to be where it may rest most securely and comfortably to itself, and with most advantage to others? In the uncertainty of opinions, wisdom would counsel us to adopt those which have a tendency to produce beneficial actions.

If I may be permitted to express myself allegorically, with regard to our intellectual operations, I would say, that the mind chooses for itself some little spot or district where it erects a dwelling, which it furnishes and decorates with the various materials it collects. Of many apartments contained in it, there is one to which it is most partial, where it chiefly reposes, and where it sometimes indulges its visionary fancies. At the same time it employs itself in cultivating the surrounding grounds, raising little articles for intellectual traffic with its neighbours, or perhaps some produce worthy to be deposited amongst the general stores of human knowledge.

Thus my mind rests at peace in thinking on the subject of life, as it has been taught by Mr. Hunter; and I am visionary enough to imagine, that if these opinions should become so established as to be generally admitted by philosophers, that if they once saw reason to believe that life was something of an invisible and active nature superadded to organization; they would then see equal reason to believe that mind might be superadded to life, as life is to structure. They would then indeed still farther perceive how mind and matter might reciprocally operate on each other by means of an intervening substance. Thus even would physiological researches enforce the belief which I may say is natural to man; that in addition to his bodily frame, he possesses a sensitive, intelligent, and independent mind: an opinion which tends in an eminent degree to produce virtuous, honorable, and useful actions.

THE END.

9. William Lawrence, "On Life," from *An Introduction to Comparative Anatomy and Physiology* (1816)

[William Lawrence, 1783–1867, was a protégé of Abernethy's, but in his lectures to the Royal College of Surgeons, of which this is one, he set out to attack the views which Abernethy had propounded to the same audience (though without mentioning Abernethy by name). The result was a long and bitter controversy; Lawrence had to recant his views in order to save his career, which went on to be extraordinarily successful.]

THE structure and functions of animals—their organization and life—are the subjects of two sciences; *anatomy* and *physiology*. Although the functions are the offspring of the structure—or the life is the result of the organization—and the two are consequently connected, as cause and effect, they might undoubtedly be treated distinctly. It would be quite possible to describe an animal body, to enumerate all its organs, to detail the size, figure, connexions, and various sensible properties of each, without saying one word of the living powers with which they are endowed, the uses to which they are subservient, or the sympathies and mutual influences by which they are bound together for the great purposes of their creation. We might certainly describe the heart, measure the size of its cavities, and detail their various openings and communications, without once speaking of the blood, or its course,—without mentioning the contracting power of the organ, or the order and succession of its movements. But who would undertake the wearisome task of such a dry and uninteresting detail? or what patience could sustain the attention of the hearer? What would you think of the person who should describe to you a watch or a steam engine in this way? who should exhibit to you all the parts, and shew their position, without any explanation of their uses, without any reference to that nice adjustment, and mutual action, which render the one subservient to the important purpose of marking the division of time, and enable us, by the other, to execute the most stupendous monuments of human labour, or to produce the most striking results of human ingenuity? As I cannot for my own part discern what purpose of utility, much less what end of interest or amusement, could be answered by such a merely anatomical detail, and as the separation of the science of organization from that of life seems to me most violent and unnatural, I shall not disjoin anatomy and physiology.

Our object being to take a survey of structure, and of the functions which it executes, through the whole animal kingdom, I shall inquire first, what we are to understand by an animal, and what idea we are to attach to life.

On this and all other occasions I shall endeavour to convey to you clear notions of the subjects which I propose for your attention; I will therefore carefully explain to you the sense of the terms employed, and avoid all those which have an equivocal meaning.

I exhort you to be particularly on your guard against loose and indefinite expressions: they are the bane of all science; and have been remarkably injurious in the different departments of our own.

Equal caution is necessary in verifying facts; the authenticity of which should always undergo a close examination. They are the foundation of our physiological reasonings; if they are insecure, the whole structure erected on them is at every moment liable to fall. So long as we attend to these two points, the scrutiny of facts and the definition of terms, our progress, though slow, will be sure. On subjects not sufficiently examined, it is better to confess our ignorance, than to attempt to hide it by arbitrary assumption and vague language. We thus mark out objects for further investigation. Most of the physical sciences afford us excellent models for the method of proceeding. Unfortunately the various branches of medical science abound with examples of all abuses; of facts loosely admitted, of words vaguely employed, of reasonings most incorrect and inconclusive.

I shall not be anxious to attract your attention by novelty, nor by multitude of details; but shall rather attempt to exhibit the various parts of the subject in their natural connexion and order; to lead you to a correct mode of reasoning; and to the best method of investigating and cultivating the science.

Organization means the peculiar composition, which distinguishes living bodies; in this point of view they are contrasted with inorganic, inert, or dead bodies. Vital properties, such as sensibility and irritability, are the means, by which organization is capable of executing its purposes; the vital properties of living bodies correspond to the physical properties of inorganic bodies; such as cohesion, elasticity, &c. Functions are the purposes, which any organ or system of organs executes in the animal frame; there is of course nothing corresponding to them in inorganic matter. Life is the assemblage of all the functions, and the general result of their exercise. Thus organization, vital properties, functions, and life are expressions related to each other; in which organization is the instrument, vital properties the acting power, function the mode of action, and life the result.

The matter that surrounds us is divided into two great classes, living and dead; the latter is governed by physical laws, such as attraction, gravitation, chemical affinity; and it exhibits physical properties, such as cohesion, elasticity, divisibility, &c. Living matter also exhibits these properties, and is subject in great measure to physical laws. But living bodies are endowed moreover with a set of properties altogether different from these, and contrasting with them very remarkably. These are the vital properties or forces, which animate living matter, so long as it continues alive, are the source of the various phenomena, which constitute the functions of the living animal body, and distinguish its history from that of dead matter.

It is justly observed by Cuvier that the idea of life is one of those general and obscure notions produced in us by observing a certain series of phenomena, possessing mutual relations, and succeeding each other in a constant order. We know not the nature of the link, that unites these phenomena, though we are sensible that a connexion must exist; and this conviction is sufficient to induce us to give it a name, which the vulgar regard as the sign of a particular principle, though in fact that name can only indicate the assemblage of the phenomena, which have occasioned its formation. Thus, as the bodies of animals appear to resist, during a certain time, the laws which govern inanimate bodies, and even to act on all around them in a manner entirely contrary to those laws, we employ the term life to designate what is at least an apparent exception to general laws. It is by determining exactly, in what the exceptions consist, that we shall fix the meaning of the term. For this purpose it is necessary to consider living bodies in their various relations with the rest of nature; and to contrast them carefully with inert substances; as it is only from the result of such a comparison that we can expect to derive a clear notion of life.

In reviewing the characters of organized bodies, this very name will lead us to consider, in the first place, the nature of their composition, and the points in which it differs from that of inorganic substances. Organization then, by the meaning of the term, denotes the possession of organs, or instruments for accomplishing certain purposes. The character of an inorganic substance is to be found in the properties of its integral particles; the mass, which they may compose, whether solid, fluid, or gaseous, is unlimited; but its extent, whether great or small, neither adds nor takes away any thing that can change the nature of the body; that nature residing completely in each of the particles of which the whole is an aggregate. Thus a single grain of marble has the same characters as an entire mountain. A living body, on the contrary, derives its character from the whole mass, from the assemblage of all the parts. This character, which is more simple or complicated according to the place which the body occupies in the scale of being, is altogether different from that of its component particles. Even in so simple a creature as the polype, the individuality of the whole animal is quite different from that of its component atoms; but this difference is much more striking when we ascend in the scale, as for instance in a quadruped.

Inorganic bodies are for the most part homogeneous in their composition; but they may be heterogeneous. This depends on the accidental circumstances, under which the aggregation has taken place. All living bodies, however simple in their organization, are necessarily heterogeneous, or composed of dissimilar particles.

An inert substance may present a perfectly solid, fluid, or gaseous mass; but all bodies possessing life exhibit in their structure both solid and fluid parts. We find in no inert body that fibrous and cellular texture, nor that multiplicity of volatile elements which form the characters of organized bodies, whether in those that are alive, or in those that have lived.

The masses of dead matter have no form peculiar to the species; even where they are crystallized, the form of the mass is not constantly the same. Living bodies however have always a form characterizing the species to which they belong, and not capable of change without producing a new race.

The component atoms of an inert body are all independent of each other: whether the mass they form be a solid, liquid or gas, each particle exists by itself, and derives its character from the number, properties, and state of combination of its principles, borrowing or deriving nothing from the similar or dissimilar atoms which are near it. On the contrary, the particles which make up a living body are dependent on each other; they are all subject to the influence of a cause which animates them. This cause makes them all concur in the production of a common purpose, either in each organ, or in the individual: and its variations produce corresponding changes in the state of the particles or organs.

Hitherto I have considered organized bodies in respect to their composition, to what we may call their passive condition, or state of rest. But it is from a different order of phenomena that the most impressive notions of life will be derived. We must view them in activity; we must observe them, surrounded by chemical agents, yet preserved from chemical action; maintaining a composition apparently constant and identical, yet keeping up an incessant motion and change of their particles, in which the old materials are discharged and new ones converted into their own substance; producing new bodies, the seat of similar active powers with themselves, yet terminating their own existence by the very action of the principle that has so long preserved them.

You well know what happens to the body after death: its heat is lost, and it soon reaches the temperature of the surrounding medium: the eyes become dim, the lips and cheeks livid; the hue of the skin is altered: the fluids contained in the vessels, or cavities, and the substances lodged in the viscera of the body, penetrate their receptacles, and tinge all the surrounding parts. The flesh soon turns green or livid, diffuses ammoniacal effluvia or noxious exhalations in the atmosphere, or melts away into an offensive ichor. Such are the effects produced by the chemical action of the solids and fluids of the body on each other, and by the affinities of the surrounding agents air, moisture and heat to both. Yet the animal solids and fluids, and the visceral contents were in mutual contact during life; and the body was surrounded by the same external agents. But the vital forces were superior to these chemical affinities, and superseded their action: the destructive power of these agents was suspended by the preservative power of life. So striking an operation could not fail to attract observation; and life has been even defined by Stahl and his followers, from this exemplification of its effects, that which prevents decomposition, *putredini contrarium*; now, although this is too limited a view of the subject, inasmuch as the phenomenon in question is only one out of several included under our notion of vitality, yet it belongs to the very essence of it, as we could not conceive life to last a moment if this power were withdrawn.

The regulation of animal temperature is a remarkable illustration of the operation of vital powers: it attracted the notice of Mr. Hunter, and was made by him the subject of numerous and highly interesting experiments[61]. You know how soon heat becomes equally diffused through all surrounding inert bodies, the temperature of any one, that is either higher or lower than those around it, being speedily reduced or exalted to a level with them. Animals however maintain a certain standard temperature under all circumstances. The human body has one and the same heat in the intense colds[62] of Siberia, Spitzbergen, and Greenland, where mercury freezes in the open air; and in the parched atmosphere of equinoctial Africa or America, where the thermometer has exceeded 120°[63]; in the heated rooms of experimenters, where it has stood at 260°; and in the stoves used for drying grain, where it has been as high as 290°, and where a heat of 270° was borne for a quarter of an hour[64].

In continuing our investigation we soon find that the force, which binds together the particles of a living body, does not confine its operation to this passive result. We see at least that living bodies can act on other matter; that they can convert it into their own substance, and thus augment the number of their component particles. We find this operation as constant as the exertion of that force, by which they resist decomposition. For the absorption of alimentary matter, its conversion into nutritive fluid, and the subsequent transmission of that fluid to all parts of the body,

---

61. Observations on the Animal Economy.
62. [Here there is a long note on the degrees of cold measured at various locations.]
63. [And here, a long note on the extreme heat that can be survived by the human body.]
64. [And here, a long note on this case.]

experience no interruption: and, in plants at least, there seems to be a constant absorption from the external surface.

Since however living bodies cannot increase indefinitely, but are confined in each case within certain limits, they must lose on one side what they gain on the other. Accordingly we find, besides the immense loss by transpiration, that there are constant movements of the internal parts, changes in their condition, and losses of substance connected with these alterations; thus we arrive at a very different view from that which we took at first; instead of a constant union among the component particles, we see a continued change, so that the body cannot be called the same in any two successive instants. We see a kind of circulation established, in which the old and useless elements are thrown out, and their place is supplied by new materials. The latter are deposited in the interstices of the particles already existing; or, technically speaking, they grow by introsusception.

In all these points there is a strong contrast in inorganic bodies; they are exposed to the action of all surrounding media: instead of exhibiting a constant motion, they can only remain unchanged in a state of rest; for, when any motion of the particles is excited, the body loses its form and consistence, if the agent be mechanical, its very nature, if it be chemical: their increase in volume is unlimited, and dependent on accidental circumstances; it is effected by juxtaposition, that is, by the addition of new particles on the outside of the old ones.

Having thus proceeded, as far as we can, in ascertaining the nature of life by the observation of its effects, we are naturally anxious to investigate its origin, to see how it is produced, and to inquire how it is communicated to the beings in which we find it. We endeavour therefore to observe living bodies in the moment of their formation, to watch the time, when matter may be supposed to receive the stamp of life, and the inert mass to be quickened. Hitherto, however, physiologists have not been able to catch nature in the fact. Living bodies have never been observed otherwise than completely formed, enjoying already that vital force and producing those internal movements, the first cause of which we are desirous of knowing. However minute and feeble the parts of an embryo may be, when we are first capable of perceiving them, they then enjoy a real life, and possess the germ of all the phenomena, which that life may afterwards develop. These observations, extended to all the classes of living creatures, lead to this general fact, that there are none, which have not heretofore formed part of others similar to themselves, from which they have been detached. All have participated in the existence of other living beings, before they exercised the functions of life themselves. Thus we find that the motion proper to living bodies, or in one word, Life, has its origin in that of their parents. From these parents they have received the vital impulse; and hence it is evident, that in the present state of things, life proceeds only from life; and there exists no other but that, which has been transmitted from one living body to another, by an uninterrupted succession.

Inorganic bodies and their masses grow up from the accidental union of particles, or combination of elements; that is, they are formed in obedience to chemical and physical laws, of which we do not notice the action.

Foiled in our attempts to ascend to the origin of organized beings, we seek to inform ourselves concerning the real nature of the powers, which animate them, by examining their composition, by investigating their texture, and the union of their elements. In them only can the vital impulse have its source and foundation. In this branch of the inquiry nothing has been neglected; all the animal organs have been most closely scrutinized, examined in their mass and in detail, and analized into their constituent textures; each of which has been exposed to every variety of anatomical, chemical, and microscopic research. The animal fluids have been subjected, in like manner, to all the inquiries that the advanced state of modern chemical science could suggest, or its zealous cultivators execute. The result of all these inquiries, I have no hesitation in affirming, to be, that no connexion has been established, in any one case, between the organic texture and its vital power; that there is nothing, either in the nature of the tissue, or in the combination of the elements, of any animal structure, that could enable us to determine beforehand what kind of living phenomena it will exhibit: and consequently that this, like all other branches of human knowledge, consists simply in an observation of the succession of events. Would the mere examination of muscular fibres, without any observation of their living action, have ever enabled you to determine that they possess the power of contraction? Would a comparison of the fibres of the deltoid, the heart and the diaphragm have shewn you that the former will contract in obedience to the will: that the second are uninfluenced by the will, and that the third act both spontaneously and voluntarily? Would any length of contemplation have led you to discover, that medullary substance is capable of sensation and of thought? Could you have known from the structure of the stomach that it digests, or from that of the liver that it secretes?

These, and all the other particulars we know about the nature of living properties and functions, are simply the result of observation: consequently our labours on the organic economy must be confined to its history.

Lastly, the destruction of living beings is effected in a peculiar and characteristic manner. The very nature of life is to produce, after a time, which varies in the different species, a state of the organs incompatible with the continuance of their functions; this mode of termination, by death, is therefore one of the laws, to which organized beings are subject.

To these considerations I might add others, tending to establish still further the difference between physical and vital laws, and consequently between physical and vital phenomena: but it is sufficient to have proved, as I shall now recapitulate, that inert solids are composed only of similar particles, which attract each other, and never move except to separate: that they are resolvable into a very small number of elementary substances: that they are formed by chance, as we term it, or by the combination of those substances, and the juxta-position of new particles: that they grow only by the juxta-position of new particles, the strata of which envelope the preceding mass: and that they are destroyed, only by some mechanical agent separating their particles, or some chemical agent, altering their combinations. While, on the contrary, organized bodies, made up of fibres and laminæ, having their interstices filled with fluids, and resolvable almost entirely into volatile products, are produced by a determinate function, that of generation; growing on bodies similar to themselves, from which they do not separate, until they are sufficiently developed to act by their own powers: that they exhibit a constant internal movement of composition and decomposition, assimilating to their own substance foreign matters, which they deposit between their own particles: that they grow by an internal power, and finally perish by that internal principle, or by the effect of life itself, exhibiting, in their natural destruction or death, a phenomenon as constant, as that of their first production.

We may establish then, as the general and common characteristics of all organized bodies, that they are produced by GENERATION, that they grow by NUTRITION, and that they end by DEATH. Such are the particular notions included under the term LIFE, when we employ that word in its widest acceptation. This description applies to vegetables, as well as animals. But if there are many living beings that exhibit only the degree of life just described, there are many others, in whom the process is much more complicated; in whom there are numerous organs, executing appropriate functions. Our idea of life must therefore be modified according to what we have learned by observation in each instance. Thus the life of a quadruped will be very different from that of an insect or worm.

In the study of the physical sciences, we observe the succession of events, ascertain their series and order, and refer the phenomena ultimately to those general properties or principles, of which the name does not indicate any independent existence, but is to be regarded merely as the generalized expression of the facts. Thus the chemist traces all the mutual actions between the component particles of bodies to their elective attractions or chemical affinities; the natural philosopher sees every where the exertion of gravity, elasticity, &c. These words denote what we call the properties of matter, and what are said to be the causes of the phenomena in question.

Experience does not shew us in what the essential action of any of these causes whatever consists, nor *how* any of the effects are produced: for example (to take a most common occurrence) we know not how motion is produced in a body by impulse. Experience can only exhibit the order and rule of succession of the phenomena, which indicate the action of the cause. When one event is observed constantly to precede another, the first of these is called cause, and the latter effect; and we believe that the preceding event has a power of producing that which succeeds; although, in reality, we know only the fact of succession. Hence, in natural philosophy, we only know the general causes by those laws which experience has established in the succession of the phenomena. These general causes, which have been called experimental, inasmuch as they are only known through the medium of experience, have been termed indifferently principles, powers, forces, faculties.

In our examination of the phenomena exhibited by living beings, we follow a method analogous to that pursued in the physical sciences. We trace the succession of events as far as observation and experiment will enable us to pursue them, and we refer them ultimately to a peculiar order of properties or forces, called vital, as their causes. These vital properties are the causes of vital functions in the same way as chemical affinity is the cause of the combinations and decompositions exercised among the component particles of bodies, or as attraction is the cause of the motions that occur among the great masses of matter.

Whatever we see in astronomy, hydraulics, mechanics, &c. must be ultimately referred, through the concatenation of causes, to gravity, elasticity, &c. In the same way the vital properties are the main spring at which we arrive, whatever phenomena we may be contemplating in respiration, digestion, secretion, and inflammation.

Among the most remarkable of these vital properties are sensibility and irritability—the power of perceiving or feeling, and that of contracting. To such properties we refer, in our ultimate analysis of the functions, as the mechanician does to elasticity, when he is explaining the motions of a watch, or the astronomer to gravitation, in accounting for the course of the heavenly bodies.

But are these the only vital properties? will they account for all the phenomena exhibited by organized beings? Probably not, probably the analysis is not yet complete, or at least the powers, which observation has led us to discover, are not yet sufficiently distinguished. Sensibility implies consciousness; it is equivalent to the power of feeling; there is not only the capability of receiving an impression, but the additional power of referring that impression to a common centre; and this sense of the word is so strongly fixed by universal consent and long use, that its application to the vital acts, which are not attended with consciousness, strikes us at once not only as improper, but as contradictory. We cannot however avoid recognising that an impression is made, in various cases, on the animal organs, when no perception takes places. The blood excites the heart to contract—it excites the capillaries of the glands to those motions, which produce secretion, and the capillaries of the various organs to those operations, which constitute nutrition, yet we have no word in physiology to denote the impressions made in these cases, unless we employ, with a late acute and most promising physiologist, whose premature death I cannot but regard as a very great loss to our science, sensibility; to which I have already stated my objections. Irritability again, more particularly as it has been consecrated by long custom to that species of motion, which is exhibited by the muscular fibres, is not well calculated to denote the invisible operations of capillary circulation, secretion, &c. which are known only by their effects.

If we cast a comparative glance along the series of living beings, we shall observe the vital properties, either the fewest, or the least active at the lower end of the scale, and gradually increasing in energy to the upper. Vegetables are traversed by fluids, which circulate in innumerable capillary tubes, which ascend and descend, and afford the materials of growth and of various secretions. All parts of the vegetable must be acted on by these fluids, and the vessels must react on them to produce the various effects, of vegetable circulation, of secretion, absorption and exhalation. Their vitality resembles that of the bones and some other parts in animals. In the commencement of the animal kingdom, as in the zoophytes, there is a digestive cavity, alternately distended and emptied; here then the vital processes are attended with obvious motion. Hitherto organized bodies are fitted for supporting a mere existence: but, as we ascend, they begin to exhibit relations to surrounding objects; the senses and voluntary motion gradually make their appearance in worms, insects, and mollusca; the vital properties necessary to the exercise of these functions being added to what they possessed before. As we ascend through reptiles, fishes, birds, and quadrupeds, the powers of sensation and motion become much more energetic, much more active, and the internal life is at the same time more and more developed. Finally, the cerebral functions, which are much more numerous and diversified in the higher orders of the mammalia, than in any of the preceding divisions of the animal kingdom, receive their last development in man; where they produce all the phenomena of intellect, all those wonderful processes of thought, known under the names of memory, reflexion, association, judgment, reasoning, imagination, which so far transcend any analogous appearance in animals, that we almost feel a repugnance to refer them to the same principle.

If therefore we were to follow strictly the great series of living bodies through its whole extent, we should see the vital properties gradually increased in number and energy from the last of plants—the mosses or the algae—to the first of animals—Man.

I have pointed out to you the numerous and obvious differences between organized and inert bodies in their composition, and in the history of the phenomena which they exhibit. The vital properties of the former present an equally strong contrast to the physical powers of the latter.

The vital properties, constantly variable in their intensity, often pass with the greatest rapidity from the lowest to the highest degree of energy, are successively exalted and weakened in the different organs, and assume, under the influence of the slightest causes, a thousand different modifications. Compare the muscular energy of the same individual, when fainting, with that which he can display in a fit of rage, or in a paroxysm of mania. The physical powers, on the contrary, constantly the same at all times, give rise to a series of phenomena always uniform. Contrast sensibility and attraction; the latter is always in proportion to the mass of the body, in which it is observed, while the former is constantly changing in the same organ, in the same mass of matter.

The invariable nature of the laws, which preside over physical phenomena, enables us to submit to calculation all the facts in those sciences; but the application of the mathematics to vital action can only lead to very general formulæ, both because the different data are uncertain quantities, and because we cannot be sure that we have taken them all into consideration. The resistance experienced by a fluid in passing through a dead tube, the velocity of a projectile, the rate at which a body falls through the air, may be easily reduced to a fixed law; but to calculate the power of a muscle, the velocity of the blood, or the action of the stomach, is, to use the comparison of Bichat, like building on a moving sand an edifice, which is solid in itself, but which quickly falls from the insecurity of its foundation.

From the circumstances just explained, the vital and physical phenomena derive, respectively, the characters of irregularity and uniformity. Inert fluids are known, when they have once been accurately analyzed; but one or even many examinations do not inform us of the nature of the living fluids. Chemical analysis gives us a kind of anatomy of them; but their physiology consists in a knowledge of the innumerable varieties they exhibit according to the condition of their respective organs, or of the system in general; and to the mutual influences, which connecting the organs to each other, produce most important modifications of their functions. The urine differs as it is voided after a meal or after sleep; that is, according to the state of the digestive organs, and of the blood: in winter and in summer, or in proportion to the greater or less activity of the cutaneous capillaries, the mere passage from a warm to a cold temperature alters its composition. It is not the same in the child, the adult, and the old man; in the male and in the female; in a quiet state of the mind, and in the agitation of the passions. Add to these differences the innumerable alterations produced by disease, and you will be immediately sensible that the mere analysis of common urine constitutes a very inconsiderable share of the physiological history of that fluid.

The science of organized bodies should therefore be treated in a manner entirely different from those, which have inorganic matter for their object. We should employ a different language, since words transposed from the physical sciences to the animal and vegetable economy, constantly recal to us ideas of an order altogether different from those which are suggested by the phenomena last mentioned. Although organized bodies are subjected in many respects to physical laws, their own peculiar phenomena present no analogy to those which are treated in chemistry, mechanics, and other physical sciences: the reference therefore to gravity, to attraction, to chemical affinity, to electricity or galvanism, can only serve to perpetuate false notions in physiology, and to draw us away from the proper point of view, in which the nature of living phenomena and the properties of living beings ought to be contemplated. We might just as rationally introduce the language of physiology into physical science; explain the facts of chemistry by irritability, or employ sensibility and sympathy to account for the phenomena of electricity and magnetism, or for the motions of the planetary system.

The application of physical science to physiology was begun when the latter was in its infancy; when organization had been little studied, and its phenomena still less observed. The successful employment of the just method of philosophizing, exhibited in the stupendous discoveries of Newton, did not advance the science of life. On the contrary, dazzled by the brilliancy of his progress, physiologists were even led by it into the error of seeking every where in the animal economy for attraction and impulse, and of subjecting all the functions to mathematical calculations. To Haller principally we must ascribe the merit of placing physiology on its proper basis, as a peculiar and independent science, by his unwearied industry in dissection, and more particularly by his numerous researches, in living animals, on all the parts of their vital economy.

The same means were pursued by Mr. Hunter to a much greater extent, and with superior success. He did not attempt to explain life by barren a priori speculations, or by the illusory analogies of other sciences; but he sought to discover its nature in the only way, which can possibly lead to any useful and satisfactory result; that is, by a patient examination of the fabric, and a close observation of the actions of living creatures. He surveyed the whole system of organized beings, from plants to man; he developed their structure by numberless dissections, of which the evidences are contained in the adjoining collection; and he discovered their functions by patient observation and well contrived experiments, of which you have the results recorded in his works. He thus not only strengthened and secured the foundations laid by Haller, but supplied many deficiencies, rectified several inconsistencies, and gave to the whole structure an unity of character and solidity, that will ensure its duration.

Such is the path, difficult and tedious, but the only one, by which we can arrive at a knowledge of vitality: to frame an hypothesis, or even many, is a much shorter and easier business. To represent that Mr. Hunter is the first or the only inquirer, who saw the subject in a right point of view, and prosecuted it on the right principles, who contemplated physiology as a distinct science, that must be cultivated by itself, embracing a peculiar order of phenomena, not to be elucidated by electricity, attraction, or what not, would be an act of injustice to many enlightened inquirers. But his labours, more than those of any one man, embraced so wide a field of inquiry into the composition and vital phenomena of animals, that we might deduce from them a rational explanation of many of the actions of living beings, and thus lay the foundation for a general theory of life, that would not disgrace the name of Hunter.

In the science of physiology we proceed on the observation of facts, of their order and connexion; we notice the analogies between them; and deduce the general laws, to which they are subject. We are thus led to admit the vital properties, already spoken of, as causes of the various phenomena; in the same way as attraction is recognised for the cause of various physical events. We do not profess to explain *how* the living forces in one case, or attraction in the other, exert their agency. But some are not content to stop at this point; they wish to draw aside the veil from nature, to display the very essence of the vital properties, and penetrate to their first causes; to shew, independently of the phenomena, what is life, and how irritability and sensibility execute those purposes, which so justly excite our admiration. They endeavour to give a physical explanation of the contraction of a muscle, and to teach us how a nerve feels. They suppose the structure of the body to contain an invisible matter or principle, by which it is put in motion. Such is the ενορμουν or impetum faciens of Hippocrates, the Archeus of Van Helmont, the Anima of Stahl, Materia Vitæ of Hunter, the calidum innatum, the vital principle, the subtle and mobile matter of others;—there are many names for it, as each successive speculator seems to have fancied that he should establish his own claim to the offspring by baptizing it anew. Either of the names, and either of the explanations may be taken as a sample: they are all equally valuable, and equally illustrative.

Most of them indeed have long lain in cold obstruction amongst the rubbish of past ages; and the more modern ones are hastening after their predecessors to the vault of all the Capulets.

The object of explanation is to make a thing more intelligible. Explaining a phenomenon consists in shewing that the facts, which it presents, follow each other in an order analogous to that which is observed in the succession of other more familiar facts. In shewing that the motions of the heavenly bodies follow the same law as the descent of a heavy substance to the earth does, Newton explained the fact. The opinion under our review is not an explanation of that kind; unless indeed you find, what I am not sensible of, that you understand muscular contraction better by being told that an Archeus, or a subtle and mobile matter sets the fibres at work.

This pretended explanation, in short, is a reference, not to any thing that we understand better, than the object to be explained; but to something, that we do not understand at all—to something which cannot be received as a deduction of science, but must be accepted as an object of faith.

If animals want such an aid for executing their functions, how is it that vegetables proceed without the same assistance? They perform vital motions, and exhibit some of the most important functions: do they accomplish them without an Archeus or a vital principle? have they no subtle fluid of life?

If the properties of living matter are to be explained in this way, why should not we adopt the same plan with physical properties, and account for gravitation or chemical affinity by the supposition of appropriate subtle fluids? Why does the irritability of a muscle need such an explanation, if explanation it can be called, more than the elective attraction of a salt?

To make the matter more intelligible, this vital principle is compared to magnetism, to electricity, and to galvanism; or it is roundly stated to be oxygen. 'Tis like a camel, or like a whale, or like what you please. You have only to grant that the phenomena of the sciences just alluded to depend on extremely fine and invisible fluids, superadded to the matters in which they are exhibited; and to allow further that life and magnetic, galvanic and electric phenomena, correspond perfectly: the existence of a subtle matter of life will then be a very probable inference. On this illustration you will naturally remark, that the existence of the magnetic, electric, and galvanic fluids, which is offered as a proof of the existence of a vital fluid, is as much a matter of doubt, as that of the vital fluid itself. It is singular also that the vital principle should be like both magnetism and electricity, when these two are not like each other.

It would have been interesting to have had this illustration prosecuted a little further. We should have been pleased to learn whether the human body is more like a loadstone, a voltaic pile, or an electrical machine: whether the organs are to be regarded as Leyden jars, magnetic needles, or batteries.

The truth is, there is no resemblance, no analogy between electricity and life: the two orders of phenomena are completely distinct; they are incommensurable. Electricity illustrates life no more than life illustrates electricity. We might just as well say that an electrical machine operates by means of a vital fluid, as that the nerves and muscles of an animal perform sensation and contraction by virtue of an electric fluid. By selecting one or two minor points, to the neglect of all the important features, a distant similarity may be made out; and this is only in appearance. In the same way life might be shewn to be like any thing else whatever, or any thing else to be like life.

Identity or similarity of cause can only be inferred from identity or resemblance of effect. Which electric operation is like sensation, digestion, absorption, nutrition, generation? which vital phenomenon resembles the attraction of bodies dissimilarly electrified, or the repulsion of those in similar states of electricity? what function resembles the ignition of metals, and the firing of gases; the decomposition of water, and the subversion of the strongest chemical affinities?

Another assertion, which has been employed to prove the existence of an independent living principle, superadded to the structure of animal bodies, is, that the various beings composing the animal kingdom, and differing from each other so remarkably as they do, nevertheless exhibit the same functions. This argument, which has been adduced on other occasions, and for other purposes, is completely ungrounded. The fact is just the reverse. Comparative anatomy affords the strongest and most numerous proofs of the dependance of function on structure. Every variation in the construction of an organ is accompanied with a corresponding modification of function; and whenever an organ ceases to exist altogether, its office also ceases. The stomach indeed is very different in a man, a cow, a fish, a worm, and each of these different stomachs digests—but it digests after its own manner. If any organ can execute any function, why may not the urinary bladder digest, or the lungs form urine; why should not one organ execute all purposes. Were it indeed otherwise, all the interest and all the utility of the science would be at an end. All our praises of the wise adaptation of structure to situation and habits, of the modification of organs according to their uses, presuppose the truth I have just asserted. If this were not so, what end would it answer to classify animals according to their structure? How would this lead us to a natural arrangement, in which the place occupied by the animal indicates its construction, economy, and way of life? However, to cut the matter short by an example or two, is the vital economy of an insect the same as that of a fish? or does that of either resemble the physiology of a quadruped? Do the very different teeth, jaws, muscles, stomach, and intestines of a cow and a lion perform the same offices? The visible fabric of the brain differs most widely in quadrupeds, birds, fishes, insects: is there not an equal difference in their intellectual phenomena, appetites, and instincts?

It seems to me that this hypothesis or fiction of a subtle invisible matter, animating the visible textures of animal bodies, and directing their motions, is only an example of that propensity in the human mind, which has led men at all times to account for those phenomena, of which the causes are not obvious, by the mysterious aid of higher and imaginary beings. Thus in the earlier ages of the world, and in less advanced states of civilization, all the appearances of nature, which the progress of science enables us to explain by means of natural causes, have been referred to the immediate operation of the divinity[.]

The storm was the work of Jupiter, who is sculptured with the thunderbolt in one hand, and grasping the lightning with the other: Eolus produced the winds; Neptune agitated the ocean; Vulcan and Pluto shook the globe with volcanos and earthquakes. So far was this belief in invisible agencies carried, that each grove and each tree, each fountain and each river, was regarded as the abode of its peculiar deity;—the fawns, the dryads, the nymphs of the elegant Grecian mythology; the sprites, the elves, the fairies of more modern credulity. Poetry, which speaks the language of the people, and appeals to their common feelings, is full of illustrations of this observation. Personification is its most common figure; and, so strong is our disposition to clothe all surrounding objects with our own sentiments and passions, to animate the dead matter around us with human intellect and expression, that the boldest examples of this figure do not shock us. In his sublime description of a tempest, Virgil not only makes the monarch of Olympus "ride in the whirlwind and direct the storm," but brings him before our eyes in the very act of hurling the lightning, and casting down mountains with the bolt.

Ipse pater, media nimborum in nocte, corusca
Fulmina molitur dextra: quo maxuma motu
Terra tremit; fugere feræ, et mortalia corda
Per gentes humilis stravit pavor: ille flagranti
Aut Atho, aut Rhodopen, aut alta Cerania telo
Dejicit.

[The Father himself, in the midnight of storm clouds, wields his bolts with flashing hand. At that shock the mighty earth shivers; far flee the beasts and all over the world prostrating terror lays low men's hearts: he with blazing bolt dashes down Athos or Rhodope or the Ceraunian peaks.— Virgil, *Georgics*, bk. 1, lines 329–33 in *Eclogues*, trans. Fairclough, rev. Goold (1999), 120–23.]

Thus we find at last that the philosopher with his archeus, his anima, or his subtle and mobile vital fluid, is about on a level, in respect to the mental process, by which he has arrived at it, with the

"Poor Indian, whose untutor'd mind,
Sees God in clouds, and hears him in the wind."[65]

It may appear unnecessary to disturb those, who are inclined to indulge themselves in these harmless reveries. The belief in them, as in sorcery and witchcraft, is not grounded in reasoning, and therefore has nothing to fear from argument. I only oppose such hypotheses, when they are adduced with the array of philosophical deduction, because they involve suppositions without any ground in observation or experience, the only sources of our information on these subjects. I repeat to you that the science of physiology, in its proper acceptation, is made up of the facts, which we learn by observation and experiment on living beings, or on those which have lived; of the comparison of these with each other; of the analogies which such comparison may discover, and the general laws to which it may lead. So long as we proceed in this path, every step is secure; when we endeavour to advance beyond its termination, we wander without any guide or direction, and are liable to be bewildered at every moment. To say, that we can never arrive at the first cause of the vital phenomena, would be presumptuous; but it is most true, that all the efforts to penetrate its nature have been equally unsuccessful, from the commencement of the world to the present time. Their complete failure in every instance has now led almost universally to their abandonment, and may induce us to acquiesce on this point in the observations of Lucretius on a parallel subject;

Ignoratur enim quæ sit natura animai;
Nata sit, an contra, nascentibus insinuetur,
Et simul intereat nobiscum morte dirempta,
An tenebras orci visat, vastasque lacunas.

[For there is ignorance what is the nature of the soul, whether it be born or on the contrary find its way into men at birth, and whether it perish together with us when broken up by death, or whether it visit the gloom of Orcus and his vasty chasms. . . .—Lucretius, *De rerum natura*, bk. 1, lines 112–15 in *On the Nature of Things*, trans. W. H. D. Rouse, rev. Martin F. Smith, Loeb Classical Library 181 (Cambridge, MA: Harvard University Press, 2014), 12–13.]

---

65. [A quotation from Alexander Pope's "Essay on Man."]

10. From John Barrow, "Lord Selkirk and the North-west Company," in the *Quarterly Review,* Volume 16, Number 31 (nominally October 1816, but actually February 11, 1817), pp. 129–72

[Sir John Barrow (1764–1848) was second secretary to the Admiralty. This left him enough free time to be a regular reviewer for the Quarterly Review. *This was the first of a series of essays he wrote advocating a new program of arctic exploration; these led to a series of failed expeditions in search of the Northwest Passage. He was the author of* Mutiny on the Bounty *(1831). Barrow's essay includes (pp. 153–65) an extended account of the search for a Northwest Passage from 1500 to the present day. He writes: "We firmly believe . . . that a navigable passage from the Atlantic to the Pacific round the northern coast of America does exist, and may be of no difficult execution. . . ." The following excerpt begins on p. 166.]*

Never was man more sanguine of success in any undertaking than Mr. Duncan. In 1790 he went out in the Company's ship Sea-horse, to take the command of a sloop in Hudson's Bay, called the Churchill. He found, on his arrival, a crew who affected to be terrified at the idea of going on discovery; the [Hudson's Bay] Company's servants told him the vessel was totally unfit for such a purpose, and that she could not be made sea-worthy in that country; though Mr. Duncan says he has since learned that she had been constantly employed for *twenty years* afterwards. Seeing nothing to be done there he immediately returned to England, resolving to have no further concern with the Hudson's Bay Company—but the governors expressed so much regret and disappointment, and Mr. Dalrymple was so urgent for following up the discovery, that he consented to take the command of a strong well-built ship of eighty-four tons, called the Beaver, fitted to his mind, and stored for eighteen months. He left the Thames on the 2d May, 1791, but did not reach the height of Charles's Island in 63° lat. till the 2d August, nor Churchill River till the 5th September, when all hope of accomplishing any thing that year was at an end. It is remarkable that our early adventurers, at a time when the art of navigation was in its infancy, the science but little understood, the instruments few and imperfect, in barks of twenty-five or thirty tons burthen, ill-constructed, ill-found and apparently ill-suited to brave the mountains of ice through which they had to force their way, and the dark and dismal storms which beset them—that these men should have succeeded in running through the straits to high latitudes and home again in less time than Mr. Duncan required to reach one of the Hudson's Bay Company's establishments, the route to which was then as well known as that to the Shetland islands.

Mr. Duncan remained in Churchill River till the 15th July in the following year, got into Chesterfield Inlet and returned to Churchill about the end of August; his crew having mutinied, encouraged, as he states, by his first officer, who was a servant of the Company.—Here grief and vexation so preyed on his mind as to render a voyage which promised every thing, completely abortive:—thus terminated the last and the least efficient of the expeditions (excepting that of Gibbons) for the discovery of the North-west Passage!

All these failures, however, are by no means conclusive against its existence. We must bear in mind that not one of the adventurers proceeded, on the eastern side of America, beyond the Arctic circle; and that on the western side, or Strait of Behring, three points of land only to the northward of Cape Prince of Wales have been seen at a distance, the northernmost (Icy Cape) in lat. 70° 29′; the next, (Cape Lisburne,) in 69° 5′, and the third (Cape Mulgrave) in 67° 45′. Could we only be certain then that Hearne and Mackenzie actually arrived at the shore of the northern ocean,[66] as the title of their books and all the charts assert, the existence of a passage would amount nearly to a certainty. The distance between Baffin's Sea and Behring's Strait is not more than 1,200 miles, of which that between the mouths of the Mackenzie and Copper-mine rivers is about 400. On the charts the mouths of these rivers are nearly on the same parallel of latitude, i.e. about 69½°. Now there can be but little doubt that the two continents of America and Asia have once been united, the trending of the coast of the latter continuing on the opposite side of Behring's Strait for more than 1000 miles nearly in the same line. On the American side, no land has been seen to the northward of the Icy Cape, and none between it and Cape Lisburne; Icy Cape is very low land, the Russians, whose regular establishments on the American continent extend as far north as 67° north lat. say that it is an island; and so strong is the impression at Petersburgh of a practicable passage from the Pacific to the Atlantic, round the northern coast of America, that Count Romanzoff, at his own expense, has fitted out a stout vessel called the Rurick, commanded by Lieut. Kotzebue, son of the celebrated writer of that name, to make the attempt. She passed Plymouth last summer, where she was supplied with a life-boat, and during the

---

66. [I omit here a lengthy note in which Barrow discusses whether Hearne and Mackenzie had in fact reached the ocean.]

summer of the present year, she is to endeavour to penetrate into the northern sea between Icy Cape and Cape Lisburne, or, on meeting with any impediment, to proceed round the former: it will be a singular event if the last, and we may almost say least of the maritime powers of Europe, should be the first to make this important discovery—so often attempted before she had a single ship on the ocean.

Thus then the coast of America may be presumed to preserve a line from Behring's Strait to Mackenzie's River, and from thence to Copper-mine River, a distance of 800 miles, fluctuating between the parallels of 69° and 70°, and we see not the slightest reason to question its continuance, in or near that line, for the remaining 400 miles to Baffin's Sea, or to the strait which connects it with Hudson's Sea: this is the only point to be discovered.—No human being has yet approached the coast of America, on the eastern side, from 66½° to 72°. Davies, Baffin, and Foxe came nearest to it; but the attempts of the rest were chiefly confined to the southward. Middleton was in the way of making discoveries, if, instead of losing his time in Wager River, he had continued to coast to the northward.

The solution of this important problem is the business of *three months* out and home. The space to be examined, at the very utmost, is from the 67th to the 71st parallels, or four degrees of latitude.

Two small schooners of 80 or 100 tons, under the command of a skilful Naval Officer, with a couple of Greenland fishermen to act as pilots through the ice, would be sufficient for the purpose. They should proceed at once up the very middle of Davis's Strait, keeping to the westward so as not to raise their latitude higher than 72°, and having cleared Cumberland Island, edge away to the southward. Hitherto most of our adventurers have worked their way through Hudson's Strait, which is generally choked up with ice; then standing to the northward they have had to contend with ice drifting to the southward, with contrary winds and currents; these inconveniences would be obviated by standing first to the latitudes of 71° or 72° and from thence southerly and westerly till they either reached Hudson's Bay, which would decide the question in the negative, or till they saw the north coast of America, which would go far to complete the discovery.

Disappointment is generally fertile in apologies for failures; we need not therefore be surprized if we find some assert that no such passage exists, and others pronounce its inutility if it should be discovered, from the uncertainty of its being free from ice any one year, and perhaps practicable only once in three or four years. Such an apology for our present ignorance of every thing that regards the geography, the hydrography, and meteorology of the north-eastern shores of America, might be pleaded by mercantile speculators, but can have little weight with those who have the interests of science at heart, or the national honour and fame, which

are intimately connected with those interests. When the government offered a reward of £20,000 for the discovery of the North-west Passage,
and £5000 to him who should approach within one degree of the North
Pole, it was not with a view to any immediate commercial advantages that
this liberal encouragement was held out, but with the same expanded object that sent Cook in search of a 'Southern Continent.' If, however, the
continent of America shall be found to terminate, as is most likely, about
the 70th degree of latitude, or even below it, we have little doubt of a free
and practicable passage round it for seven or eight months in every year;
and we are much mistaken if the North-west Company would not derive
immediate and incalculable advantages from a passage of three months to
their establishment in Columbia River, instead of the circuitous voyage
of six or seven months round Cape Horn; to say nothing of the benefit
which might be derived from taking in their cargoes of furs and peltry
for the China market at the mouths of Mackenzie and Copper-mine rivers, to which the northern Indians would be too happy to bring them, if
protected by European establishments, at these or other places, from their
enemies the Esquimaux.

The polar reaches of the globe within the arctic circle offer a wide field
for the researches of a philosophic mind; yet, in point of science, very little
is known beyond what is contained in the account of Captain Phipps's
voyage to the neighbourhood of Spitzbergen. The natural history, though
the best, is still but imperfectly known; the sea and land swarm with animals in these abodes of ice and snow, and multitudes of both yet remain
to be discovered and described. It is an important object to obtain more
accurate observations on those huge mountains of ice which float on the
sea; it is no longer a question that the *field* or *flaked* ice is frozen sea-water,
though itself perfectly fresh; and it is almost as certain, though doubted
by some, that the huge masses which the Dutch call *icebergs*, are formed
on the steep and precipitous shores, from whence those 'thunderbolts of
snow' are occasionally hurled into the deep, bearing with them fragments
of earth and stones. 'I came,' says Foxe, 'by one piece of ice higher than
the rest, whereupon a stone was of the contents of five or six tonne weight,
with divers other smaller stones and mud thereon.'

It is a common but we believe an erroneous opinion, that the temperature of our climate has regularly been diminishing, and that it is owing to
the ice having permanently fixed itself to the shores of Greenland, which,
in consequence, from being once a flourishing colony of Denmark, is now
become uninhabitable and unapproachable. We doubt both the fact and
the inference. It is not the climate that has altered, but we who feel it
more severe as we advance in years; the registers of the absolute degree of
temperature, as measured by the thermometer, do not warrant any such

conclusion; and more attempts than one to land on the coast of Greenland must be made, before we can give credit to its being bound up in eternal ice—which is known to shift about with every gale of wind—to be drifted by currents—and to crumble and consume below the surface of the water. We suspect indeed, that the summer heat, which in the latitude of 80½° Phipps found to be on the average of the month of July at 42° of Fahrenheit, during the whole twenty-four hours, and once, when exposed to the sun, as high as 86½°, dissolves fully as much of the ice and snow on the surface of the sea as the preceding winter may have formed.[67] It appears too, that there are times in the depth of winter when the temperature is exceedingly mild; and the intense frosts are undoubtedly moderated by the caloric given out from the Aurora borealis, which in these regions affords not only an admirable compensation for the short absence of the moon[68], but imparts a considerable degree of warmth to the lower regions of the atmosphere, filling the whole circle of the horizon, and approaching so near the surface of the globe as to be distinctly *heard* in varying their colours and positions. 'I have frequently,' says Hearne, 'heard them making a rustling and crackling noise, like the waving of a large flag in a fresh gale of wind.' The electric *aura*, it is well known, will raise the mercury in the tube of the thermometer, but no experiments have been made to ascertain the degree of heat given out by these *henbanes* or *petty dancers*, as Foxe calls them, which must be very considerable; as Button says, 'the stream in the element is like the flame that cometh forth from the mouth of a hot oven.' Almost every voyager into Hudson's and Baffin's seas complains of the occasional hot weather, and the great annoyance of mosquitoes on the shores. Duncan, when surrounded with ice, had the thermometer in August at 56° in the shade, and 82° in the sun. Yet the cold in winter is more intense than they have yet been able to measure either by a mercurial or spirit thermometer. It is a well established fact, that on the eastern sides of great continents, the temperature is greatly below that in the same degree of latitude on the western sides: thus, while the whole of Hudson's Bay, the coast of Labrador and Newfoundland, down to 46° may be said to be, in winter, one mass of ice, not a particle of ice was ever seen in the sea on the western side of America, to the southward of 64° or 65°. The delicate humming-bird is not uncommon at Nootka, and was seen by Mackenzie at Peace River, in latitude 54° 24′. The cold of Halifax, in latitude 44° 40′, is much more intense than that of London in 51½°. Pekin, in less than latitude 40°, has generally a constant frost for three months every year; and

---

67. [Again, I omit a footnote discussion.]
68. [Barrow takes it for granted that the sun never rises in winter; the moon does often, but not always.]

ice, the thickness of a dollar, is not uncommon at Canton, under the tropics. On the coast of Jesso, in latitude 45° 24', Captain Krusenstern found the ground covered with snow in the middle of May, and vegetation more backward than at Archangel, in latitude 64½°, in the middle of April.

Some of our old navigators ascribed the great variation and irregularity of the magnetic needle in Hudson and Baffin's Seas, to the effects of cold;[69] and others to the attraction of particular islands. In the northern regions, near Spitzbergen, Phipps observed nothing remarkable in the variation of the needle, but Baffin found it at 5 points, or 56°, 'a thing almost incredible, and almost matchless in all the world besides.' Duncan supposed the needle to be attracted by Charles's Island, as the variation amounted to 63° 51', nearly 6 points; and on the same parallel, when the island was out of sight, only 45° 22'; and he states, that when near Merry and Jones's Islands, in a violent storm of thunder, lightning and heavy rain, the night being very dark and dismal, all the compasses in the ship were running round, and so unsteady, that they could not trust one moment to the course they were steering.

Many other meteorological phenomena peculiar to these regions afford curious matter for investigation; but our geographical knowledge of every part of Hudson's and Baffin's seas is most defective. We need only cast an eye over the different charts made by Arrowsmith, from 1793 to 1811, no two of which are alike—large islands being inserted in some and omitted in others—the north-eastern side of the continent is, in one, cut into islands—in another, islands are joined to the continent—here a strait is filled up—there another opened—in short—

'Vidi ego quod fuerat quondam solidissima tellus
Esse fretum. Vidi factas ex æquore terras'—
[I have seen what was once most solid earth
Become ocean. I have seen dry land made out of the sea.
Ovid, *Metamorphoses*, xv.262.]

These flourishes *ad libitum* (for not one iota of additional information of the northern parts has been received for the last sixty years) are not very commendable, in a geographical point of view; and in the absence of all knowledge, we should deem it preferable to leave *blank* (as Purdey has left Baffin's Sea in his General Chart) those coasts and islands which fancy only has created.

---

69. Foxe observed that the needle near Nottingham Island had lost its powers, which, among other things, he ascribed to the cold air interposed between the needle and the point of its attraction. Ellis conceived the cold to be the cause of the irregular action of the needle, and he says, that the compasses on being brought into a warm place recovered their action and proper direction.

11. The Reviews

a. *La Belle Assemblée, or Bell's Court and Fashionable Magazine*, 2d Series, 17 (March 1818): 139–42.
b. *The Edinburgh Magazine and Literary Miscellany; A New Series of "The Scots Magazine"* 2 (March 1818): 249–53.
c. *Blackwood's Edinburgh Magazine* 2 (March 1818): 613–20—by Walter Scott.
d. *The British Critic*, N.S., 9 (April 1818): 432–38; also rpt. in *The Port Folio* [Philadelphia] 6 (September 1818): 200–207.
e. *The Literary Panorama, and National Register*, N.S., 8 (1 June 1818): 411–14.
f. *Quarterly Review* 18 (January [delayed until 12 June] 1818): 379–85—by John Wilson Croker.
g. *The Athenæum*, 10 November 1832, p. 730 [review of 1818 edition, written in either 1817 or 1818]—by Percy Bysshe Shelley.

a. *La Belle Assemblée, or Bell's Court and Fashionable Magazine*, 2d Series, 17 (March 1818): 139–42.

This is a very *bold* fiction; and, did not the author, in a short Preface, make a kind of apology, we should almost pronounce it to be *impious*. We hope, however, the writer had the moral in view which we are desirous of drawing from it, that the *presumptive* works of man must be frightful, vile, and horrible; ending only in discomfort and misery to himself.

But will all our readers understand this? Should not an author, who has a moral end in view, point out rather that application which may be more generally understood? We recommend, however, to our fair readers, who may peruse a work which, from its originality, excellence of language, and peculiar interest, is likely to be very popular, to draw from it that meaning which we have cited above.

The story of *Frankenstein* is told in a letter from a Captain Walton to his sister, Mrs. Saville, residing in England. Walton is almost as much of an enthusiast as the wretched Frankenstein, whom, as the Captain is in search of finding the north west passage, and penetrating as far as possible to the extremities of the pole, he meets, engaged in the pursuit of the demon-being of his own creation: Walton rescues Frankenstein from the imminent danger of losing his life in this pursuit, amongst the floating flakes of ice; and after this Prometheus recovers, in part, his bodily strength, and relates his history to Walton.

Frankenstein is a Genevese; (these people are not naturally romantic) but Frankenstein's mind has been early warped by a perusal of those authors who deal in the marvellous. His father is a respectable Syndic, and has taken under his protection a niece, born in Italy. In due time, Frankenstein and his fair cousin become lovers, and their union is sanctioned by his father. He has also the blessings of a sincere friend, Henry Clerval, of a stronger mind than the Prometheus, who is absorbed in the study of natural philosophy, which he declares as "the genius that regulated his fate."—When he becomes a student at the University of Ingoldstadt, he bewails, as his first misfortune, the death of his mother; and when his grief has begun to subside, he devotes himself entirely to chemistry and his favourite science: the structure of the human frame particularly excites his attention, and, indeed, every animal endowed with life: he then proceeds to examine *the cause of life and death*—(how vain)—and finds himself capable (we use the writer's own words) "of bestowing animation on lifeless matter!!!"

This reminds us of the famous philosopher who declared, that, give him but matter enough, and he could create a world! Why, then, could he not form one in miniature, about the size of an egg or a walnut?

To return to Frankenstein; he had no longer any doubt but what he could create a perfect man! But his workshop, and the process he was compelled to observe, disgusted him; for he tells Walton, that "the dissecting-room, and the slaughter-house, furnished him with materials." On a dark night of November he completes his work, and the eye of the creature opens; whom, in order to make superior to his species, he has formed eight feet high! He is soon after surprised by a visit from his friend Clerval; and trembles at the idea of his seeing the monster he has created: he steals up softly to his apartment, and finds that the demon has fled.

After a fit of illness, which causes a cessation of his studies, he is afflicted, on his return to them, by a letter from his father, acquainting him that his little brother William is murdered; the picture he wore round his neck being found in the pocket of an interesting young girl, the attendant on Elizabeth, Frankenstein's cousin, she is accused, and suffers innocently. After visiting the parental roof, as the unfortunate Prometheus is wandering among the Alps, he beholds the frightful being he has formed, and he feels convinced in his own mind that he is the murderer of his brother.—This being seems, indeed, to have a supernatural power of following his maker wherever he goes, and he soon after meets with him near Mont Blanc. He here relates to Frankenstein how he has supported his miserable existence; but he feels the charm, and the imperious want of society, by having beheld, in a cottage, an old peasant and his daughter, with a young man; they are indigent, but, in comparison with his forlorn state, most happy. Delighted with the picture of social life and its affections, he seeks to contribute to their wants; piles wood before their cottage, when they want fuel, and other offices unperceived: by listening, he gains speech, and understands the meaning of different words. The arrival of an Arabian lady serves to complete the savage's education: he hears the young man read to her, and obtains a slight knowledge of history. This part of the work is rather prolix and unnatural; the monster learns to read, and is delighted with *Paradise Lost, Plutarch's Lives,* and *The Sorrows of Werter*!

The demon then confesses himself the murderer of Frankenstein's brother; and, moreover, declares his intention of immolating the rest of his family, if he does not create a female like himself, with whom he may retire to undiscovered wilds, and molest mankind no more. Frankenstein, at first, positively refuses, but at length consents.

After pausing some time in travelling, Frankenstein and Clerval visit Scotland; and the former retires from the society of his friend, to undertake, in the solitude of the Orkney Islands, the dreadful task assigned him. When he has half finished the wretched work, he reflects that, perhaps, he is bringing a curse on future generations, and he tears the thing to pieces on which he is engaged. The monster presents himself, and after some severe upbraidings, he tells him he will be with him on his wedding night.

The fragments of a human being lying before him, urge Frankenstein to seek his safety by flight; he packs them in a basket, sails from the Orkneys, and sinks them when he has attained the midst of the sea: he next arrives at a good harbour, where he is taken up for murder; and for the murder, too, of Clerval, his friend, whose mangled body is presented before him: this deprives him of reason; and in a gaol, loaded with irons, like a malefactor, he suffers all the agonies of the mind, accompanied with frenzied fever. He is, however, at length, honourably acquitted, and accompanies his father, who comes for him, back to Geneva, where preparations take place for his wedding; for which, when the day is arrived, Elizabeth is found dead, after coming from the sacred ceremony, and lying across her bridal bed. He now makes a solemn vow to find out the fiend of his creation, and to destroy him, though the work of his own hands. He traverses wild and barbarous countries; where, in some places, he beholds inscriptions on the rocks and trees, as, "My reign is not yet over"—"You live, and my power is complete," &c. &c. By perseverance, Frankenstein, at length, meets with him, where Captain Walton first discovers him; and whom Frankenstein, after bringing his narrative to a close, intreats to avenge his cause by killing the monster, should he die. He expires soon after; and this *wonderful* work of *man* comes in at the cabin-window of Captain Walton's ship, breathes a soliloquy over the coffin of his creator, and then plunges into the icy waves, the same way as he entered.

This work, which we repeat, has, as well as originality, extreme interest to recommend it, and an easy, yet energetic style, is inscribed to Mr. Godwin; who, however he once embraced novel systems, is, we are credibly informed, happily converted to what he once styled *ancient prejudices*.

We are sorry our limits will not allow us a more copious review of *Frankenstein*. The few following extracts will serve to shew the excellence of its style and language:—

ENTHUSIASM OF FRANKENSTEIN IN
HIS WORK OF FORMING MAN.

"Life and death appeared to me ideal bounds, which I should first break through, and pour a torrent of light into our dark world. A new species would bless me as its creator and source; many happy and excellent natures would owe their being to me. No father could claim the gratitude of his child so completely as I should deserve theirs. Pursuing these reflections, I thought, that if I could bestow animation upon lifeless matter, I might in process of time (although I now found it impossible) renew life where death had apparently devoted the body to corruption."

DESCRIPTION OF FRANKENSTEIN'S MAN
WHEN FIRST ENDOWED WITH LIFE.

"It was on a dreary night of November, that I beheld the accomplishment of my toils. With an anxiety almost amounting to agony, I collected the instruments of life around me, that I might infuse a spark of being into the lifeless thing that lay at my feet. It was already one in the morning; the rain pattered dismally against the panes, and my candle was nearly burnt out, when, by the glimmer of the half-extinguished light, I saw the dull yellow eye of the creature open; it breathed hard, and a convulsive motion agitated its limbs.

["]How can I describe my emotions at this catastrophe, or how delineate the wretch whom with such infinite pains and care I had endeavoured to form? His limbs were in proportion, and I had selected his features as beautiful. Beautiful!—Great God! His yellow skin scarcely covered the work of muscles and arteries beneath; his hair was of a lustrous black, and flowing; his teeth of a pearly whiteness; but these luxuriances only formed a more horrid contrast with his watery eyes, that seemed almost of the same colour as the dun white sockets in which they were set, his shrivelled complexion, and straight black lips."

HIS REPENTANCE AT HAVING FORMED HIM.

"I considered the being whom I had cast among mankind, and endowed with the will and power to effect purposes of horror, such as the deed which he had now done, nearly in the light of my own vampire, my own spirit let loose from the grave, and forced to destroy all that was dear to me."

ARGUMENTS HELD OUT BY THE MONSTER.

"All men hate the wretched; how, then, must I be hated, who am miserable beyond all living things! Yet you, my creator, detest and spurn me, thy creature, to whom thou art bound by ties only dissoluble by the annihilation of one of us. You purpose to kill me. How dare you sport thus with life? Do your duty towards me, and I will do mine towards you and the rest of mankind. If you will comply with my conditions, I will leave them and you at peace; but if you refuse, I will glut the maw of death, until it be satiated with the blood of your remaining friends.

"God, in pity, made man beautiful and alluring, after his own image; but my form is a filthy type of yours, more horrid from its very resemblance. Satan had his companions, fellow-devils, to admire and encourage him; but I am solitary and detested."

FRANKENSTEIN'S AGONY ON THE DEATH OF ELIZABETH.

"Great God! why did I not then expire!—Why am I here to relate the destruction of the best hope, and the purest creature of earth. She was there, lifeless and inanimate, thrown across the bed, her head hanging down, and her pale and distorted features half covered by her hair. Every where I turn I see the same figure—her bloodless arms and relaxed form flung by the murderer on its bridal bier. Could I behold this, and live? Alas! life is obstinate, and clings closest where it is most hated. For a moment only did I lose recollection; I fainted."

THE MONSTER'S REFLECTIONS OVER THE DEAD BODY OF FRANKENSTEIN.

"'That is also my victim!' he exclaimed; 'in his murder my crimes are consummated; the miserable series of my being is wound to its close! Oh, Frankenstein! generous and self-devoted being! what does it avail that I now ask thee to pardon me? I, who irretrievably destroyed thee by destroying all thou lovedst.—Alas! he is cold; he may not answer me.'"

b. *The Edinburgh Magazine and Literary Miscellany; A New Series of "The Scots Magazine"* 2 (March 1818): 249–53.

Here is one of the productions of the modern school in its highest style of caricature and exaggeration. It is formed on the Godwinian manner, and has all the faults, but many likewise of the beauties of that model. In dark and gloomy views of nature and of man, bordering too closely on impiety,—in the most outrageous improbability,—in sacrificing every thing to effect,—it even goes beyond its great prototype; but in return, it possesses a similar power of fascination, something of the same mastery in harsh and savage delineations of passion, relieved in like manner by the gentler features of domestic and simple feelings. There never was a wilder story imagined, yet, like most of the fictions of this age, it has an air of reality attached to it, by being connected with the favourite projects and passions of the times. The real events of the world have, in our day, too, been of so wondrous and gigantic a kind,—the shiftings of the scenes in our stupendous drama been so rapid and various, that Shakespeare himself, in his wildest flights, has been completely distanced by the eccentricities of actual existence. Even he would scarcely have dared to have raised, in one act, a private adventurer to the greatest of European thrones,—to have conducted him, in the next, victorious over the necks of emperors and kings, and then, in a third, to have shewn him an exile, in a remote speck of an island, some thousands of miles from the scene of his triumphs; and the chariot which bore him along covered with glory, quietly exhibited to a gaping mechanical rabble under the roof of one of the beautiful buildings on the North Bridge of Edinburgh,—(which buildings we heartily pray may be brought as low as the mighty potentate whose Eagles are now to be seen looking out of their windows, like the fox from the ruins of Balclutha.) Our appetite, we say, for every sort of wonder and vehement interest, has in this way become so desperately inflamed, that especially as the world around us has again settled into its old dull state of happiness and legitimacy, we can be satisfied with nothing in fiction that is not highly coloured and exaggerated; we even like a story the better that it is disjointed and irregular, and our greatest inventors, accordingly, have been obliged to accommodate themselves to the taste of the age, more, we believe, than their own judgment can, at all times, have approved of. The very extravagance of the present production will now, therefore, be, perhaps, in its favour, since the events which have actually passed before our eyes have made the atmosphere of miracles that in which we most readily breathe.

The story opens with a voyage of discovery to the North Pole. A young Englishman, whose mind has long been inflamed with this project, sets sail from Archangel, soon gets inclosed, as usual, among ice mountains, and is beginning to despair of success, when all his interest and thoughts are diverted suddenly into another channel, in consequence of a very singular adventure. One day a gigantic figure was seen moving northwards on a sledge, drawn by dogs, and a short time afterwards a poor emaciated wretch was picked up from a sledge that drifted close to the vessel. The Englishman soon formed a violent friendship for this stranger, and discovers him to be a person of the greatest virtues, talents, and acquirements, which are only rendered the more admirable and interesting, from the deep cloud of melancholy which frequently overshadowed them. After a time, he gets so far into his confidence, as to obtain from him the story of his life and misfortunes. His name was Frankenstein, son of a Syndic of Geneva, and of an amiable mother, who very properly dies at the beginning of the book, to leave her son and a young female cousin, who resided in the family, so disconsolate, that they could find no comfort except by falling in love. Frankenstein had been left much to his own disposal in the conduct of his studies, and, at a very early period, he had become quite *entêté* with some of the writings of the alchemists, on which he accidentally lighted; and we were at first in expectation that, like St Leon, he was to become possessed of the philosopher's stone, or of the *elixir vitae*. He is destined, however, to obtain a still more extraordinary power, but not from the alchemists, of the futility of whose speculations he soon became convinced, but whose wild conceptions continued to give to his mind a strong and peculiar bias.

At the university, stimulated by the encouragement of some distinguished philosophers, he applied himself, with the utmost perseverance and ability, to every department of natural science, and soon became the general object of envy and admiration. His researches led him to investigate the principle of life, which he did in the old and approved manner by dissecting living animals, groping into all the repositories of the dead, and making himself acquainted with life and death in all their forms. The result was a most wonderful discovery,—quite simple, he says, when it was made, but yet one which he very wisely does not communicate to his English acquaintance, and which, of course, must remain a secret to world,—no less than the discovery of the means of communicating life to an organized form. With this our young philosopher sets himself to make a man, and that he might make no blunder from taking too small a scale, unfortunately, as it turns out, his man is a giant. In a garret of his apartments, to which none but himself was ever admitted, he employs four months on this wonderful production. Many of the ingredients seem to have been of a very disgusting description, since he passed whole nights in sepulchres raking them out; he thought, however, that he had succeeded in making a giant, as gainly in appearance as least as O'Brien, or the Yorkshire Boy, and every thing was now ready for the last touch of the master, the infusion of life into the inanimate mass. In breathless expectation, in the dead of night, he performed this last momentous act of creation; and the creature opened upon him two immense ghastly yellow eyes, which struck him with instant horror. He immediately hated himself and his work, and flew, in a state of feverish agony, to his room below; but, finding himself followed thither by the monster, he rushed out into the streets, where he walked about in fearful agitation, till the morning dawned, and they began to be frequented by their inhabitants. Passing along, he saw step from a coach an intimate friend of his from Geneva. For the moment he forgot every thing that had happened, was delighted to find that his friend had come to pursue his studies along with him, and was conducting him to his apartments, when on a sudden he recollected the dreadful inmate who would probably be found in them. He ran up and examined them, and, on finding that the monster had disappeared, his joy became quite foolish and outrageous; he danced about like a madman, and his friend was not surprised when immediately after he was seized by a delirious fever, which confined him for some weeks, alleviated, however, by all the attentions which friendship could bestow.

Scarcely had he recovered, when a sad piece of intelligence arrives from home. His father writes him that his little brother had strayed from them in an evening walk, and was at last found dead, and apparently strangled. He flies home to comfort his family, but it is night ere he reaches Geneva, and the gates being shut, he remains in the neighbourhood, and walks out in the dark towards the hills. The monster on a sudden stalks past him, and moving with inconceivable rapidity, is seen by him perched on one of the highest cliffs. The thought instantly strikes him, that this fiend, the creation of his own hand, must have been the murderer of his brother, and he feels all the bitterness of despair. Very ill able to comfort others, he next morning went to his father's house, and learns, as an additional misery, that a young servant girl, who had been beloved as a friend in the family, was taken up on suspicion of the murder, and was to be tried for her life. A picture, which the child had worn on the fateful night, was found in her pocket. Though, in his own mind, he could not doubt of the real author of the murder, and his beloved Elizabeth was equally convinced that it could not be her favourite Justine, still circumstances were so strong against her, that the poor girl was condemned and executed. No wonder that Frankenstein now fell into a deep melancholy; to relieve him from which, his father took him and Elizabeth on a tour to the valley of Chamounix. This part of the book is very beautifully written; the description of the mountain scenery, and of its effect on Frankenstein's mind, is finely given. One rainy day they did not proceed on their journey, but Frankenstein, in a state of more than common depression, left them early in the inn, for the purpose of scaling the summit of Montarvet.

"It was nearly noon (he says) when I arrived at the top of the ascent. For some time I sat upon the rock that overlooks the sea of ice. A mist covered both that and the surrounding mountains. Presently a breeze dissipated the cloud, and I descended upon the glacier. The surface is very uneven, rising like the waves of a troubled sea, descending low, and interspersed by rifts that sink deep. The field of ice is about a league in width, but I spent nearly two hours in crossing it. The opposite mountain is a bare perpendicular rock. From the side where I now stood Montarvet was exactly opposite, at the distance of a league; and above it rose Mont Blanc, in awful majesty. I remained in a recess of the rock, gazing on this wonderful and stupendous scene. The sea, or rather the vast river of ice, wound among its dependent mountains, whose aërial summits hung over its recesses. Their icy and glittering peaks shone in the sunlight over the clouds. My heart, which was before sorrowful, was swelled with something like joy; I exclaimed, 'Wandering spirits, if indeed ye wander, and do not rest in your narrow beds, allow me this faint happiness, or take me, as your companion, away from the joys of life.' As I said this, I suddenly beheld the figure of a man, at some distance, advancing towards me with superhuman speed. He bounded over the crevices in the ice, among which I had walked with caution; his stature also, as he approached, seemed to exceed that of man. I was troubled: a mist came over my eyes, and I felt a faintness seize me, but I was quickly restored by the cold gale of the mountains. I perceived, as the shape came nearer, (sight tremendous and abhorred,) that it was the wretch whom I had created. I trembled with rage and horror, resolving to wait his approach, and then close with him in mortal combat. He approached; his countenance bespoke bitter anguish, combined with disdain and malignity, while its unearthly ugliness rendered it almost too horrible for human eyes."

Frankenstein at first addresses him in words of violent rage,—the monster, however, endeavours to soften him.

"Will no entreaties cause thee to turn a favourable eye upon thy creature who implores thy goodness and compassion? Believe me, Frankenstein, I was benevolent, my soul glowed with love and humanity, but am I not alone, miserably alone? You, my creator, abhor me; what hope can I gather from your fellow-creatures who owe me nothing? They spurn and hate me. The desart mountains and dreary glaciers are my refuge. I have wandered here many days; the caves of ice, which I only do not fear, are a dwelling to me, and the only one which man does not grudge. These black skies I hail, for they are kinder to me than your fellow beings. If the multitude of mankind knew of my existence, they would do as you do, and arm themselves for my destruction. Shall I not then hate them who abhor me?—Hear my tale; it is long and strange, and the temperature of this place is not fitting to your fine sensations; come to the hut upon the mountain. The sun is yet high in the heavens; before it descends to hide itself behind yon snowy precipices, and illuminate another world, you will have heard my story and can decide. On you it rests whether I quit for ever the neighbourhood of man, and lead a harmless life, or become the scourge of your fellow creatures, and the author of your own speedy ruin."

The monster now begins his story, and a very amiable personage he makes himself to be. The story is well fancied and told. Immediately on his creation he wandered out into the forest of Ingoldstadt, where he remained for some days, till his different senses learnt to perform their appropriate functions, and he discovered the use of fire and various other rudiments of knowledge; and thus accomplished, he ventured forth into the great world. But in the first village that he reached he was hooted and stoned, and was obliged to take shelter in a hovel at the back of a cottage. Through a crevice in the wall, he soon became intimate with all the operations in the cottage, the inhabitants of which were an old blind man, his son and daughter. After the reception he had met with in the village, he kept himself very snug in his hole through the day, but being really a good-natured monster, and finding the young man was much overwrought in cutting fuel for the family, what does he, but betake him to the wood in the night time, and collect quantities of fuel, which he piles up beside the door? The good people think themselves the favourites of some kind spirit or *brownie*. In the mean time, he learns how to apply their language, which he found he could imitate tolerably well. He gradually, too, becomes acquainted with more of their circumstances and feelings; and there was so much affection between the venerable blind man (who moreover played beautifully on a musical instrument) and his children, and they were so loving to each other,—and they were so interesting withal from their poverty, that the worthy monster took a vehement passion for them, and had the greatest inclination to make himself agreeable to them. By close study, and the occurrence of favourable opportunities, he also acquires a knowledge of written language; and one day on his rambles, lighting on a portmanteau, which contained the Sorrows of Werter, a volume of Plutarch, and Milton's Paradise Lost,—he becomes quite an adept in German sentiment, ancient heroism, and Satanic sturdiness. He now thought himself qualified to make himself acquainted with the family,—though aware of his hideous appearance, he very wisely began with the blind gentleman, on whom he ventured to make a call when the rest of the family were out of doors. He had just begun to interest the old man in his favour, when their *tête-a-tête* is unluckily interrupted, and the poor monster is abused and maltreated as heretofore by the villagers. He flies to the woods, furious with rage, and disappointed affection; and, finding on his return that the cottagers had forsaken the place, scared by his portentous visit, he amuses himself in his rage with setting it on fire, and then sets out in search of his creator. Other circumstances occur in his journey to give him a greater antipathy to the human race. He confesses the murder of the boy, whom, lighting upon, he wished to carry off, in the hope that he might find in him an object to attach himself to;—the murder was partly accidental,—but the slipping the picture into Justine's pocket was a piece of devilish malice. He concludes with denouncing vengeance against Frankenstein and all his race, if he does not agree to one request, to create a female companion for him like himself, with whom he proposes to retire to the wilds of North America, and never again to come into contact with man.

It is needless to go minutely through the remainder of this wild fiction. After some demurring, Frankenstein at last accedes to the demand, and, begins a second time the abhorred creation of a human being,—but again repents, and defies the demon; who thenceforth recommences his diabolical warfare against the unhappy philosopher,—destroys his friends and relations one by one, and finally murders his beloved Elizabeth, on the very evening of their marriage. Frankenstein, alive only to vengeance, now pursues the fiend over the world,—and it was in this chace that he had got into the neighbourhood of the North Pole, where he was but a little way behind him, but had quite spent himself in the pursuit. So ends the narrative of Frankenstein, and worn out nature soon after yields to the bitterness of his thoughts and his exhausted frame. He dies, and, to the astonishment of our Englishman and the crew, the monster makes his appearance,—laments the fate of his creator,—says that his feelings of vengeance are for ever at an end,—departs, and is heard of no more.

Such is a sketch of this singular performance, in which there is much power and beauty, both of thought and expression, though, in many parts, the execution is imperfect, and bearing the marks of an unpractised hand. It is one of those works, however, which, when we have read, we do not well see why it should have been written;—for a *jeu d'esprit* it is somewhat too long, grave, and laborious,—and some of our highest and most reverential feelings receive a shock from the conception on which it turns, so as to produce a painful and bewildered state of mind while we peruse it. We are accustomed, happily, to look upon the creation of a living and intelligent being as a work that is fitted only to inspire a religious emotion, and there is an impropriety, to say no worse, in placing it in any other light. It might, indeed, be the author's view to shew that the powers of man have been wisely limited, and that misery would follow their extension,—but still the expression "Creator," applied to a mere human being, gives us the same sort of shock with the phrase, "the Man Almighty," and others of the same kind, in Mr Southey's "Curse of Kehama." All these monstrous conceptions are the consequences of the wild and irregular theories of the age; though we do not at all mean to infer that the authors who give into such freedoms have done so with any bad intentions. This incongruity, however, with our established and most sacred notions, is the chief fault in such fictions, regarding them merely in a critical point of view. Shakespeare's Caliban (though his simplicity and suitableness to the place where he is found are very delightful) is, perhaps, a more *hateful* being than our good friend in this book. But Caliban comes into existence in the received way which common superstition had pointed out; we should not have endured him if Prospero had created him. Getting over this original absurdity, the character of our monster is in good keeping;—there is a grandeur, too, in the scenery in which he makes his appearances,—the ice-mountains of the Pole, or the glaciers of the Alps;—his natural tendency to kind feelings, and the manner in which they were blighted,—and all the domestic picture of the cottage, are very interesting and beautiful. We hope yet to have more productions, both from this author and his great model, Mr Godwin; but they would make a great improvement in their writings, if they would rather study the established order of nature as it appears, both in the world of matter and of mind, than continue to revolt our feelings by hazardous innovations in either of these departments.

c. *Blackwood's Edinburgh Magazine* 2 (March 1818): 613–20—by Walter Scott.

[Sir Walter Scott (1771–1832) published his first novel, Waverley, *which immediately became a publishing sensation, in 1814. He had long been a well-known poet, and had been and continued to be an influential reviewer. Praise from Scott was thus important. At the time he wrote the review he believed the novel had been written by Percy Shelley; Mary later wrote to him from Italy to set him straight: "I am anxious to prevent your continuing in the mistake of supposing Mr. Shelley guilty of a juvenile attempt of mine; to which—from its being written at an early age, I abstained from putting my name—and from respect to those persons from whom I bear it.[70] I have therefore kept it concealed except from a few friends" (Shelley,* Letters, *ed. Bennett [1980–1988], 1:71).]*

> Did I request thee, Maker, from my clay
> To mould me man? Did I solicit thee
> From darkness to promote me?—
>
> > *Paradise Lost.*

---

70. [She signs herself Mary Wollst^ft Shelley, but she presumably means to include Godwin among those from whom she bears her name.]

This is a novel, or more properly a romantic fiction, of a nature so peculiar, that we ought to describe the species before attempting any account of the individual production.

The first general division of works of fiction, into such as bound the events they narrate by the actual laws of nature, and such as, passing these limits, are managed by marvellous and supernatural machinery, is sufficiently obvious and decided. But the class of marvellous romances admits of several subdivisions. In the earlier productions of imagination, the poet, or tale-teller does not, in his own opinion, transgress the laws of credibility, when he introduces into his narration the witches, goblins, and magicians, in the existence of which he himself, as well as his hearers, is a firm believer. This good faith, however, passes away, and works turning upon the marvellous are written and read merely on account of the exercise which they afford to the imagination of those who, like the poet Collins, love to riot in the luxuriance of oriental fiction, to rove through the meanders of enchantment, to gaze on the magnificence of golden palaces, and to repose by the water-falls of Elysian gardens. In this species of composition, the marvellous is itself the principal and most important object both to the author and reader. To describe its effect upon the mind of the human personages engaged in its wonders, and dragged along by its machinery, is comparatively an inferior object. The hero and heroine, partakers of the supernatural character which belongs to their adventures, walk the maze of enchantment with a firm and undaunted step, and appear as much at their ease, amid the wonders around them, as the young fellow described by the Spectator, who was discovered taking a snuff with great composure in the midst of a stormy ocean, represented on the stage of the Opera.

A more philosophical and refined use of the supernatural in works of fiction, is proper to that class in which the laws of nature are represented as altered, not for the purpose of pampering the imagination with wonders, but in order to shew the probable effect which the supposed miracles would produce on those who witnessed them. In this case, the pleasure ordinarily derived from the marvellous incidents is secondary to that which we extract from observing how mortals like ourselves would be affected,

> By scenes like these which, daring to depart
> From sober truth, are still to nature true.

Even in the description of his marvels, however, the author who manages this stile of composition with address, gives them an indirect importance with the reader, when he is able to describe with nature, and with truth, the effects which they are calculated to produce upon his dramatis personæ. It will be remembered, that the sapient Partridge was too wise to be terrified at the mere appearance of the ghost of Hamlet, whom he knew to be a man dressed up in pasteboard armour for the nonce—it was when he saw the "little man," as he called Garrick, so frightened, that a sympathetic horror took hold of him. Of this we shall presently produce some examples from the narrative before us. But success in this point is still subordinate to the author's principal object, which is less to produce an effect by means of the marvels of the narrations, than to open new trains and channels of thought, by placing men in supposed situations of an extraordinary and preternatural character, and then describing the mode of feeling and conduct which they are most likely to adopt.

To make more clear the distinction we have endeavoured to draw between the marvellous and the effects of the marvellous, considered as separate objects, we may briefly invite our readers to compare the common tale of Tom Thumb with Gulliver's Voyage to Brobdingnag; one of the most childish fictions, with one which is pregnant with wit and satire, yet both turning upon the same assumed possibility of the existence of a pigmy among a race of giants. In the former case, when the imagination of the story-teller has exhausted itself in every species of hyperbole, in order to describe the diminutive size of his hero, the interest of the tale is at an end; but in the romance of the Dean of St Patrick's, the exquisite humour with which the natural consequences of so strange and unusual a situation is detailed, has a canvass on which to expand itself, as broad as the luxuriance even of the author's talents could desire. Gulliver stuck into a marrow bone, and Master Thomas Thumb's disastrous fall into the bowl of hasty-pudding, are, in the general outline, kindred incidents; but the jest is exhausted in the latter case, when the accident is told; whereas in the former, it lies not so much in the comparatively pigmy size which subjected Gulliver to such a ludicrous misfortune, as in the tone of grave and dignified feeling with which he resents the disgrace of the incident.

In the class of fictitious narrations to which we allude, the author opens a sort of account-current with the reader; drawing upon him, in the first place, for credit to that degree of the marvellous which he proposes to employ; and becoming virtually bound, in consequence of this indulgence, that his personages shall conduct themselves, in the extraordinary circumstances in which they are placed, according to the rules of probability, and the nature of the human heart. In this view, the *probable* is far from being laid out of sight even amid the wildest freaks of imagination; on the contrary, we grant the extraordinary postulates which the author demands as the foundation of his narrative, only on condition of his deducing the consequences with logical precision.

We have only to add, that this class of fiction has been sometimes applied to the purposes of political satire, and sometimes to the general illustration of the powers and workings of the human mind. Swift, Bergerac, and others, have employed it for the former purpose, and a good illustration of the latter is the well known Saint Leon of William Godwin. In this latter work, assuming the possibility of the transmutation of metals, and of the *elixir vitæ,* the author has deduced, in the course of his narrative, the probable consequences of the possession of such secrets upon the fortunes and mind of him who might enjoy them. Frankenstein is a novel upon the same plan with Saint Leon; it is said to be written by Mr Percy Bysshe Shelley, who, if we are rightly informed, is son-in-law to Mr Godwin; and it is inscribed to that ingenious author.

In the preface, the author lays claim to rank his work among the class which we have endeavoured to describe.

"The event on which this fiction is founded has been supposed by Dr. Darwin, and some of the physiological writers of Germany, as not of impossible occurrence. I shall not be supposed as according the remotest degree of serious faith to such an imagination; yet, in assuming it as the basis of a work of fancy, I have not considered myself as merely weaving a series of supernatural terrors. The event on which the interest of the story depends is exempt from the disadvantages of a mere tale of spectres or enchantment. It was recommended by the novelty of the situations which it developes; and, however impossible as a physical fact, affords a point of view to the imagination for the delineating of human passions more comprehensive and commanding than any which the ordinary relations of existing events can yield.

"I have thus endeavoured to preserve the truth of the elementary principles of human nature, while I have not scrupled to innovate upon their combinations. The *Iliad,* the tragic poetry of Greece,— Shakespeare, in the *Tempest* and *Midsummer Night's Dream,*—and most especially Milton, in *Paradise Lost,* conform to this rule; and the most humble novellist, who seeks to confer or receive amusement from his labours, may, without presumption, apply to prose fiction a license, or rather a rule, from the adoption of which so many exquisite combinations of human feeling have resulted in the highest specimens of poetry."

We shall, without farther preface, detail the particulars of the singular story, which is thus introduced.

A vessel, engaged in a voyage of discovery to the North Pole, having become embayed among the ice at a very high latitude, the crew, and particularly the captain or owner of the ship, are surprised at perceiving a gigantic form pass at some distance from them, on a car drawn by dogs, in a place where they conceived no mortal could exist. While they are speculating on this singular apparition, a thaw commences, and disengages them from their precarious situation. On the next morning they pick up, upon a floating fragment of the broken ice, a sledge like that they had before seen, with a human being in the act of perishing. He is with difficulty recalled to life, and proves to be a young man of the most amiable manners and extended acquirements, but, extenuated by fatigue, wrapped in dejection and gloom of the darkest kind. The captain of the ship, a gentleman whose ardent love of science had engaged him on an expedition so dangerous, becomes attached to the stranger, and at length extorts from him the wonderful tale of his misery, which he thus attains the means of preserving from oblivion.

Frankenstein describes himself as a native of Geneva, born and bred up in the bosom of domestic love and affection. His father—his friend Henry Clerval—Elizabeth, an orphan of extreme beauty and talent, bred up in the same house with him, are possessed of all the qualifications which could render him happy as a son, a friend, and a lover. In the course of his studies he becomes acquainted with the works of Cornelius Agrippa, and other authors treating of occult philosophy, on whose venerable tomes modern neglect has scattered no slight portion of dust. Frankenstein remains ignorant of the contempt in which his favourites are held, until he is separated from his family to pursue his studies at the university of Ingolstadt. Here he is introduced to the wonders of modern chemistry, as well as of natural philosophy in all its branches. Prosecuting these sciences into their innermost and most abstruse recesses, with unusual talent and unexampled success, he at length makes that discovery on which the marvellous part of the work is grounded. His attention had been especially bound to the structure of the human frame and of the principle of life. He engaged in physiological researches of the most recondite and abstruse nature, searching among charnel vaults and in dissection rooms, and the objects most insupportable to the delicacy of human feelings, in order to trace the minute chain of causation which takes place in the change from life to death, and from death to life. In the midst of this darkness a light broke in upon him.

"Remember," says his narrative, "I am not recording the vision of a madman. The sun does not more certainly shine in the heavens than that which I now affirm is true. Some miracle might have produced it, yet the stages of the discovery were distinct and probable. After days and nights of incredible labour and fatigue, I succeeded in discovering the cause of generation and life; nay, more, I became myself capable of bestowing animation upon lifeless matter."

This wonderful discovery impelled Frankenstein to avail himself of his art, by the creation (if we dare to call it so) or formation of a living and sentient being. As the minuteness of the parts formed a great difficulty, he constructed the figure which he proposed to animate of a gigantic size, that is, about eight feet high, and strong and large in proportion. The feverish anxiety with which the young philosopher toils through the horrors of his secret task, now dabbling among the unhallowed reliques of the grave, and now torturing the living animal to animate the lifeless clay, are described generally, but with great vigour of language. Although supported by the hope of producing a new species that should bless him as his creator and source, he nearly sinks under the protracted labour, and loathsome details, of the work he had undertaken, and scarcely is his fatal enthusiasm sufficient to support his nerves, or animate his resolution. The result of this extraordinary discovery it would be unjust to give in any words save those of the author. We shall give it at length, as an excellent specimen of the style and manner of the work.

"It was on a dreary night of November that I beheld the accomplishment of my toils. With an anxiety that almost amounted to agony, I collected the instruments of life around me, that I might infuse a spark of being into the lifeless thing that lay at my feet. It was already one in the morning; the rain pattered dismally against the panes, and my candle was nearly burnt out, when, by the glimmer of the half-extinguished light, I saw the dull yellow eye of the creature open; it breathed hard, and a convulsive motion agitated its limbs.

"How can I describe my emotions at this catastrophe, or how delineate the wretch whom with such infinite pains and care I had endeavoured to form? His limbs were in proportion, and I had selected his features as beautiful. Beautiful!—Great God! His yellow skin scarcely covered the work of muscles and arteries beneath; his hair was of a lustrous black, and flowing; his teeth of a pearly whiteness; but these luxuriances only formed a more horrid contrast with his watery eyes, that seemed almost of the same colour as the dun white sockets in which they were set—his shrivelled complexion, and straight black lips.

"The different accidents of life are not so changeable as the feelings of human nature. I had worked hard for nearly two years, for the sole purpose of infusing life into an inanimate body. For this I had deprived myself of rest and health. I had desired it with an ardour that far exceeded moderation; but now that I had finished, the beauty of the dream vanished, and breathless horror and disgust filled my heart. Unable to endure the aspect of the being I had created, I rushed out of the room, and continued a long time traversing my bedchamber, unable to compose my mind to sleep. At length lassitude succeeded to the tumult I had before endured; and I threw myself on the bed in my clothes, endeavouring to seek a few moments of forgetfulness. But it was in vain: I slept indeed, but I was disturbed by the wildest dreams. I thought I saw Elizabeth, in the bloom of health, walking in the streets of Ingolstadt. Delighted and surprised, I embraced her; but as I imprinted the first kiss on her lips, they became livid with the hue of death; her features appeared to change, and I thought that I held the corpse of my dead mother in my arms; a shroud enveloped her form, and I saw the grave-worms crawling in the folds of the flannel. I started from my sleep with horror; a cold dew covered my forehead, my teeth chattered, and every limb became convulsed; when, by the dim and yellow light of the moon, as it forced its way through the window shutters, I beheld the wretch—the miserable monster whom I had created. He held up the curtain of the bed; and his eyes, if eyes they may be called, were fixed on me. His jaws opened, and he muttered some inarticulate sounds, while a grin wrinkled his cheeks. He might have spoken, but I did not hear; one hand was stretched out, seemingly to detain me, but I escaped, and rushed down stairs. I took refuge in the court-yard belonging to the house which I inhabited; where I remained during the rest of the night, walking up and down in the greatest agitation, listening attentively, catching and fearing each sound as if it were to announce the approach of the demoniacal corpse to which I had so miserably given life.

"Oh! no mortal could support the horror of that countenance. A mummy again endued with animation could not be so hideous as that wretch. I had gazed on him while unfinished; he was ugly then; but when those muscles and joints were rendered capable of motion, it became a thing such as even Dante could not have conceived.

"I passed the night wretchedly. Sometimes my pulse beat so quickly and hardly, that I felt the palpitation of every artery; at others, I nearly sank to the ground through languor and extreme weakness. Mingled with this horror, I felt the bitterness of disappointment: dreams, that had been my food and pleasant rest for so long a space, were now become a hell to me; and the change was so rapid, the overthrow so complete!

"Morning, dismal and wet, at length dawned, and discovered to my sleepless and aching eyes, the church of Ingolstadt, its white steeple and clock, which indicated the sixth hour. The porter opened the gates of the court, which had that night been my asylum, and I issued into the streets, pacing them with quick steps, as if I sought to avoid the wretch whom I feared every turning of the street would present to my view. I did not dare return to the apartment which I inhabited, but felt impelled to hurry on, although wetted by the rain which poured from a black and comfortless sky.

"I continued walking in this manner for some time, endeavouring, by bodily exercise, to ease the load that weighed upon my mind. I traversed the streets without any clear conception of where I was or what I was doing. My heart palpitated in the sickness of fear; and I hurried on with irregular steps, not daring to look about me:

'Like one who, on a lonely road,
Doth walk in fear and dread,
And, having once turn'd round, walks on,
And turns no more his head;
Because he knows a frightful fiend
Doth close behind him tread.'"[71]

He is relieved by the arrival of the diligence from Geneva, out of which jumps his friend Henry Clerval, who had come to spend a season at the college. Compelled to carry Clerval to his lodgings, which, he supposed, must still contain the prodigious and hideous specimen of his Promethean art, his feelings are again admirably described, allowing always for the extraordinary cause supposed to give them birth.

"I trembled excessively; I could not endure to think of, and far less to allude to, the occurrences of the preceding night. I walked with a quick pace, and we soon arrived at my college. I then reflected, and the thought made me shiver, that the creature whom I had left in my apartment might still be there, alive, and walking about. I dreaded to behold this monster; but I feared still more that Henry should see him. Entreating him therefore to remain a few minutes at the bottom of the stairs, I darted up towards my own room. My hand was already on the lock of the door before I recollected myself. I then paused; and a cold shivering came over me. I threw the door forcibly open, as children are accustomed to do when they expect a spectre to stand in waiting for them on the other side; but nothing appeared. I stepped fearfully in: the apartment was empty; and my bed-room was also freed from its hideous guest. I could hardly believe that so great a good fortune could have befallen me; but when I became assured that my enemy had indeed fled, I clapped my hands for joy, and ran down to Clerval."

The animated monster is heard of no more for a season. Frankenstein pays the penalty of his rash researches into the *arcana* of human nature, in a long illness, after which the two friends prosecute their studies for two years in uninterrupted quiet. Frankenstein, as may be supposed, abstaining, with a sort of abhorrence, from those in which he had once so greatly delighted. At the lapse of this period, he is made acquainted with

---

71. Coleridge's "Ancient Mariner."

a dreadful misfortune which has befallen his family, by the violent death of his youngest brother, an interesting child, who, while straying from his keeper, had been murdered by some villain in the walks of Plainpalais. The marks of strangling were distinct on the neck of the unfortunate infant, and a gold ornament which it wore, and which was amissing, was supposed to have been the murderer's motive for perpetrating the crime.

At this dismal intelligence Frankenstein flies to Geneva, and impelled by fraternal affection, visits the spot where this horrid accident had happened. In the midst of a thunder-storm, with which the evening had closed, and just as he had attained the fatal spot on which Victor[*sic*] had been murdered, a flash of lightning displays to him the hideous demon to which he had given life, gliding towards a neighbouring precipice. Another flash shews him hanging among the cliffs, up which he scrambles with far more than mortal agility, and is seen no more. The inference, that this being was the murderer of his brother, flashed on Frankenstein's mind as irresistibly as the lightning itself, and he was tempted to consider the creature whom he had cast among mankind to work, it would seem, acts of horror and depravity, nearly in the light of his own vampire let loose from the grave, and destined to destroy all that was dear to him.

Frankenstein was right in his apprehensions. Justine, the maid to whom the youthful Victor had been intrusted, is found to be in possession of the golden trinket which had been taken from the child's person; and, by a variety of combining circumstances of combined evidence, she is concluded to be the murtheress, and, as such, condemned to death and executed. It does not appear that Frankenstein attempted to avert her fate, by communicating his horrible secret; but, indeed, who would have given him credit, or in what manner could he have supported his tale?

In a solitary expedition to the top of Mount Aveyron, undertaken to dispel the melancholy which clouded his mind, Frankenstein unexpectedly meets with the monster he had animated, who compels him to a conference and a parley. The material demon gives an account, at great length, of his history since his animation, of the mode in which he acquired various points of knowledge, and of the disasters which befell him, when, full of benevolence and philanthropy, he endeavoured to introduce himself into human society. The most material part of his education was acquired in a ruinous pig-stye—a Lyceum which this strange student occupied, he assures us, for a good many months undiscovered, and in constant observance of the motions of an amiable family, from imitating whom he learns the use of language, and other accomplishments, much more successfully than Caliban, though the latter had a conjuror to his tutor. This detail is not only highly improbable, but it is injudicious, as its unnecessary minuteness tends rather too much to familiarize us with the being whom it regards, and who loses, by this *lengthy* oration, some part of the mysterious sublimity annexed to his first appearance. The result is, this monster, who was at first, according to his own account, but a harmless monster, becomes ferocious and malignant, in consequence of finding all his approaches to human society repelled with injurious violence and offensive marks of disgust. Some papers concealed in his dress acquainted him with the circumstances and person to whom he owed his origin; and the hate which he felt towards the whole human race was now concentrated in resentment against Frankenstein. In this humour he murdered the child, and disposed the picture so as to induce a belief of Justine's guilt. The last is an inartificial circumstance: this indirect mode of mischief was not likely to occur to the being the narrative presents to us. The conclusion of this strange narrative is a peremptory demand on the part of the demon, as he is usually termed, that Frankenstein should renew his fearful experiment, and create for him an helpmate hideous as himself, who should have no pretense for shunning his society. On this condition he promises to withdraw to some distant desert, and shun the human race for ever. If his creator shall refuse him this consolation, he vows the prosecution of the most frightful vengeance. Frankenstein, after a long pause of reflection, imagines he sees that the justice due to the miserable being, as well as to mankind, who might be exposed to so much misery, from the power and evil dispositions of a creature who could climb perpendicular cliffs and exist among glaciers, demanded that he should comply with the request; and granted his promise accordingly.

Frankenstein retreats to one of the distant islands of the Orcades, that in secrecy and solitude he might resume his detestable and ill-omened labours, which now were doubly hideous, since he was deprived of the enthusiasm with which he formerly prosecuted them. As he is sitting one night in his laboratory, and recollecting the consequences of his first essay in the Promethean art, he beings to hesitate concerning the right he had to form another being as malignant and bloodthirsty as that he had unfortunately already animated. It is evident that he would thereby give the demon the means of propagating a hideous race, superior to mankind in strength and hardihood, who might render the very existence of the present human race a condition precarious and full of terror. Just as these reflections lead him to the conclusion that his promise was criminal, and ought not to be kept, he looks up, and sees, by the light of the moon, the demon at the casement.

> "A ghastly grin wrinkled his lips as he gazed on me, where I sat fulfilling the task which he had allotted to me. Yes, he had followed me in my travels; he had loitered in forests, hid himself in caves, or

taken refuge in wide and desert heaths; and he now came to mark my progress, and claim the fulfilment of my promise.

"As I looked on him, his countenance expressed the utmost extent of malice and treachery. I thought with a sensation of madness on my promise of creating another like to him, and, trembling with passion, tore to pieces the thing on which I was engaged. The wretch saw me destroy the creature on whose future existence he depended for happiness, and, with a howl of devilish despair and revenge, withdrew."

At a subsequent interview, described with the same wild energy, all treaty is broken off betwixt Frankenstein and the work of his hands, and they part on terms of open and declared hatred and defiance. Our limits do not allow us to trace in detail the progress of the demon's vengeance. Clerval falls its first victim, and under circumstances which had very nearly conducted the new Prometheus to the gallows as his supposed murderer. Elizabeth, his bride, is next strangled on her wedding-night; his father dies of grief; and at length Frankenstein, driven to despair and distraction, sees nothing left for him in life but vengeance on the singular cause of his misery. With this purpose he pursues the monster from clime to clime, receiving only such intimations of his being on the right scent, as served to shew that the demon delighted in thus protracting his fury and his sufferings. At length, after the flight and pursuit had terminated among the frost-fogs, and icy islands of the northern ocean and just when he had a glimpse of his adversary, the ground sea was heard, the ice gave way, and Frankenstein was placed in the perilous situation in which he is first introduced to the reader.

Exhausted by his sufferings, but still breathing vengeance against the being which was at once his creature and his persecutor, this unhappy victim to physiological discovery expires just as the clearing away of the ice permits Captain Walton's vessel to hoist sail for their return to Britain. At midnight, the dæmon, who had been his destroyer, is discovered in the cabin, lamenting over the corpse of the person who gave him being. To Walton he attempts to justify his resentment towards the human race, while, at the same time, he acknowledges himself a wretch who had murdered the lovely and the helpless, and pursued to irremediable ruin his creator, the select specimen of all that was worthy of love and admiration.

"Fear not," he continues, addressing the astonished Walton, "that I shall be the instrument of future mischief. My work is nearly complete. Neither yours nor any man's death is needed to consummate the series of my being, and accomplish that which must be done; but it requires my own. Do not think that I shall be slow to perform this sacrifice. I shall quit your vessel on the ice-raft which brought me hither, and shall seek the most northern extremity of the globe; I shall collect my funeral pile and consume to ashes this miserable frame, that its remains may afford no light to any curious and un-hallowed wretch, who would create such another as I have been.—"

"He sprung from the cabin-window, as he said this, upon the ice-raft which lay close to the vessel. He was soon borne away by the waves, and lost in darkness and distance."

Whether this singular being executed his purpose or no must necessarily remain an uncertainty, unless the voyage of discovery to the north pole should throw any light on the subject.

So concludes this extraordinary tale, in which the author seems to us to disclose uncommon powers of poetic imagination. The feeling with which we perused the unexpected and fearful, yet, allowing the possibility of the event, very natural conclusion of Frankenstein's experiment, shook a little even our firm nerves; although such and so numerous have been the expedients for exciting terror employed by the romantic writers of the age, that the reader may adopt Macbeth's words with a slight alteration:

"We have supp'd full with horrors:
Direness, familiar to our "callous" thoughts,
Cannot once startle us."

It is no slight merit in our eyes, that the tale, though wild in incident, is written in plain and forcible English, without exhibiting that mixture of hyperbolical Germanisms with which tales of wonder are usually told, as if it were necessary that the language should be as extravagant as the fiction. The ideas of the author are always clearly as well as forcibly expressed; and his descriptions of landscape have in them the choice requisites of truth, freshness, precision, and beauty. The self-education of the monster, considering the slender opportunities of acquiring knowledge that he possessed, we have already noticed as improbable and overstrained. That he should have not only learned to speak, but to read, and, for aught we know, to write—that he should have become acquainted with Werter, with Plutarch's Lives, and with Paradise Lost, by listening through a hole in a wall, seems as unlikely as that he should have acquired, in the same way, the problems of Euclid, or the art of book-keeping by single and double entry. The author has however two apologies—the first, the necessity that his monster should acquire those endowments, and the other, that his neighbours were engaged in teaching the language of the country to a young foreigner. His progress in self-knowledge, and the acquisition of information, is, after all, more wonderful than that of Hai Eben Yokhdan, or Automathes, or the hero of the little romance called The Child of Nature, one of which works might perhaps suggest the train of ideas followed by the author of Frankenstein.

We should also be disposed, in support of the principles with which we set out, to question whether the monster, how tall, agile, and strong however, could have perpetrated so much mischief undiscovered, or passed through so many countries without being secured, either on account of his crimes, or for the benefit of some such speculator as Mr Polito, who would have been happy to have added to his museum so curious a specimen of natural history. But as we have consented to admit the leading incident of the work, perhaps some of our readers may be of opinion, that to stickle upon lesser improbabilities, is to incur the censure bestowed by the Scottish proverb on those who start at straws after swallowing *windlings*.

The following lines, which occur in the second volume, mark, we think, that the author possesses the same facility in expressing himself in verse as in prose.

> We rest; a dream has power to poison sleep.
> We rise; one wand'ring thought pollutes the day.
> We feel, conceive, or reason; laugh, or weep,
> Embrace fond woe, or cast our cares away;
> It is the same: for, be it joy or sorrow,
> The path of its departure still is free.
> Man's yesterday may ne'er be like his morrow;
> Nought may endure but mutability!

Upon the whole, the work impresses us with a high idea of the author's original genius and happy power of expression. We shall be delighted to hear that he has aspired to the *paullo majora*;[72] and, in the meantime, congratulate our readers upon a novel which excites new reflections and untried sources of emotion. If Gray's definition of Paradise, to lie on a couch, namely, and read new novels, come any thing near truth, no small praise is due to him, who, like the author of Frankenstein, has enlarged the sphere of that fascinating enjoyment.

d. *The British Critic*, N.S., 9 (April 1818): 432–38; also rpt. in *The Port Folio* [Philadelphia] 6 (September 1818): 200–207.

This is another anomalous story of the same race and family as Mandeville; and, if we are not misinformed, it is intimately connected with that strange performance, by more ties than one. In the present instance, it is true,

---

72. [From Virgil's *Eclogues*: *paulo maiora canamus*: let us sing about a rather more elevated subject.]

we are presented with the mysteries of equivocal generation, instead of the metaphysics of a bedlamite; but he who runs as he reads, might pronounce both novels to be *similis farinæ*. We are in doubt to what class we shall refer writings of this extravagant character; that they bear marks of considerable power, it is impossible to deny; but this power is so abused and perverted, that we should almost prefer imbecility; however much, of late years, we have been wearied and ennuied by the languid whispers of gentle sentimentality, they at least had the comfortable property of provoking no uneasy slumber; but we must protest against the waking dreams of horror excited by the unnatural stimulants of this later school; and we feel ourselves as much harassed, after rising from the perusal of these three spirit-wearing volumes, as if we had been over-dosed with laudanum, or hag-ridden by the night-mare.

No one can love a real good ghost story more heartily than we do; and we will toil through many a tedious duodecimo to get half a dozen pages of rational terror, provided always, that we keep company with spectres and skeletons, no longer than they maintain the just dignity of their spiritual character. Now and then too, we can tolerate a goule, so it be not at his dinner-time; and altogether, we profess to entertain a very due respect for the whole anierarchy[73] of the dæmoniacal establishment. Our prejudices in favour of legitimacy, of course, are proportionably shocked by the pretensions of any pseudo-diabolism; and all our best feelings of ghostly loyalty are excited by the usurpation of an unauthorized hobgoblin, or a non-descript fee-fa-fum.

It will be better, however, to say what little we mean to add on this point, by and by, when our readers are fairly put in possession of the subject, and enabled to form their own estimate of our opinions. In a sort of introduction, which precedes the main story of this novel, and has nothing else to do with it, we are introduced to a Mr. Walton, the Christopher Sly of the piece, with whose credulity the hero of the tale is afterwards to amuse himself. This gentleman, it seems, has had his imagination fired by an anticipation of the last number of the Quarterly Review, and is gone out to the North Pole, in quest of lost Greenland, magnetism, and the parliamentary reward. In justice to our author, we must admit that this part is well done, and we doubt whether Mr. Barrow, in plain prose, or Miss Porden herself, in more ambitious rhyme, can exceed our novelist in the description of frozen desarts and colliding ice-bergs. While employed in this pursuit, and advancing into a very high latitude, one day,

---

73. [A made-up word meaning "not-hierarchy," or, presumably, "upside-down hierarchy."]

"About two o'clock the mist cleared away, and we beheld, stretched out in every direction, vast and irregular plains of ice, which seemed to have no end. Some of my comrades groaned, and my own mind began to grow watchful with anxious thoughts, when a strange sight suddenly attracted our attention, and diverted our solicitude from our own situation. We perceived a low carriage, fixed on a sledge and drawn by dogs, pass on towards the north, at the distance of half a mile: a being which had the shape of a man, but apparently of gigantic stature, sat in the sledge, and guided the dogs. We watched the rapid progress of the traveller with our telescopes, until he was lost among the distant inequalities of the ice.

"This appearance excited our unqualified wonder. We were, as we believed, many hundred miles from any land; but this apparition seemed to denote that it was not, in reality, so distant as we had supposed. Shut in, however, by ice, it was impossible to follow his track, which we had observed with the greatest attention.

"About two hours after this occurrence, we heard the ground sea; and before night the ice broke and freed our ship. We, however, lay to until the morning, fearing to encounter in the dark those large loose masses which float about after the breaking up of the ice. I profited of this time to rest for a few hours.

"In the morning, however, as soon as it was light, I went upon deck, and found all the sailors busy on one side of the vessel, apparently talking to someone in the sea. It was, in fact, a sledge, like that we had seen before, which had drifted towards us in the night on a large fragment of ice. Only one dog remained alive; but there was a human being within it, whom the sailors were persuading to enter the vessel. He was not, as the other traveller seemed to be, a savage inhabitant of some undiscovered island, but an European. When I appeared on deck the master said, 'Here is our captain, and he will not allow you to perish on the open sea.'

"On perceiving me, the stranger addressed me in English, although with a foreign accent. 'Before I come on board your vessel,' said he, 'will you have the kindness to inform me whither you are bound?'

"You may conceive my astonishment on hearing such a question addressed to me from a man on the brink of destruction and to whom I should have supposed that my vessel would have been a resource which he would not have exchanged for the most precious wealth the earth can afford. I replied, however, that we were on a voyage of discovery towards the northern pole.

"Upon hearing this he appeared satisfied and consented to come on board." Vol. I. p. 22.

After proper applications, the stranger is recovered, and of course a strong attachment, takes place between him and his preserver; and, in due season, after much struggling with melancholy and sullenness, he prevails upon himself to tell his own story.

Frankenstein was a Genevese by birth, of honorable parentage, and betrothed, from his earliest years, to an orphan cousin, with whom he had been brought up, Elizabeth Lavenza. In his youth, he manifested a strong bent for natural philosophy, at first, indeed, a little perverted by an accidental acquaintance with the early masters of this science, and an initiation into the mystical fancies of Cornelius Agrippa, Albertus Magnus, and Paracelsus; a short residence at the University of Ingolstadt, however corrected this bias, and he soon distinguished himself among the students, by his extraordinary proficiency in the various branches of chemical knowledge. One of the phænomena which particularly engrossed his attention, was no less than "the principle of life;" to examine this, he had recourse to death, he studied anatomy, and watched the progress of decay and corruption in the human body, in dissecting rooms and charnel-houses; at length, "after days and nights of incredible labour and fatigue, I succeeded in discovering the cause of generation or life: nay, more, I became myself capable of bestowing animation upon lifeless matter."

When once in possession of this power, it is not to be supposed that he could long leave it unemployed; and, as the minuteness of parts formed a great hindrance to the speedy execution of his design, he determined to make the being which he was to endow with life, of a gigantic stature, "that is to say, about eight feet in height, and proportionably large." We pass over the months which he employed in this horrible process, and hasten to the grand period of consummation.

"It was on a dreary night of November that I beheld the accomplishment of my toils. With an anxiety that almost amounted to agony, I collected the instruments of life around me, that I might infuse a spark of being into the lifeless thing that lay at my feet. It was already one in the morning; the rain pattered dismally against the panes, and my candle was nearly burnt out, when, by the glimmer of the half-extinguished light, I saw the dull yellow eye of the creature open; it breathed hard, and a convulsive motion agitated its limbs.

"How can I describe my emotions at this catastrophe, or how delineate the wretch whom with such infinite pains and care I had endeavoured to form? His limbs were in proportion, and I had selected his features as beautiful. Beautiful!—Great God! His yellow skin scarcely covered the work of muscles and arteries beneath; his hair was of a lustrous black, and flowing; his teeth of a pearly whiteness; but these luxuriances only formed a more horrid contrast with his watery eyes, that seemed almost of the same colour as the dun white sockets in which they were set, his shrivelled complexion and straight black lips.

"The different accidents of life are not so changeable as the feelings of human nature. I had worked hard for nearly two years, for the sole purpose of infusing life into an inanimate body. For this I had deprived myself of rest and health. I had desired it with an ardour that far exceeded moderation; but now that I had finished, the beauty of the dream vanished, and breathless horror and disgust filled my heart. Unable to endure the aspect of the being I had created, I rushed out of the room, and continued a long time traversing my bed-chamber, unable to compose my mind to sleep. At length lassitude succeeded to the tumult I had before endured; and I threw myself on the bed in my clothes, endeavouring to seek a few moments of forgetfulness. But it was in vain: I slept, indeed, but I was disturbed by the wildest dreams. I thought I saw Elizabeth, in the bloom of health, walking in the streets of Ingolstadt. Delighted and surprised, I embraced her; but as I imprinted the first kiss on her lips, they became livid with the hue of death; her features appeared to change, and I thought that I held the corpse of my dead mother in my arms; a shroud enveloped her form, and I saw the grave-worms crawling in the folds of the flannel. I started from my sleep with horror; a cold dew covered my forehead, my teeth chattered, and every limb became convulsed; when, by the dim and yellow light of the moon, as it forced its way through the window-shutters, I beheld the wretch—the miserable monster whom I had created. He held up the curtain of the bed; and his eyes, if eyes they may be called, were fixed on me. His jaws opened, and he muttered some inarticulate sounds, while a grin wrinkled his cheeks. He might have spoken, but I did not hear; one hand was stretched out, seemingly to detain me, but I escaped, and rushed down stairs. I took refuge in the court-yard belonging to the house which I inhabited; where I remained during the rest of the night, walking up and down in the greatest agitation, listening attentively, catching and fearing each sound as if it were to announce the approach of the demoniacal corpse to which I had so miserably given life." Vol. I. P. 97.

While in this state of horror, he is agreeably surprized by the arrival of the friend of his youth, Henry Clerval, who had been dispatched by his family, under some alarm at the long silence which his genethliacal[74] studies had occasioned. We shall not pretend to trace this story through the remainder of its

---

74. [*Genethliacal* normally means "astrological," but here it means "to do with giving birth."]

course, suffice it to say, that the being whom he has created, pursues his steps, and operates, like his evil genius, upon every subsequent event of his life. His infant brother is murdered by the hands of this anonymous androdæmon;[75] the servant girl, who attended the child, is executed upon circumstantial evidence; and Frankenstein himself, suspecting the real author of this foul deed, and stung with remorse, that he should have been its primary cause, commences a life of wandering, to throw off, if possible, the agony which haunts him. In the glacier of Montauvert, he has an interview with his persecutor, who succeeds, by threats, promises, and intreaties, in obtaining a hearing. The narrative which he relates, has some ingenuity in it; it is the account of a being springing at one bound into the full maturity of physical power, but whose understanding is yet to be awakened by degrees; this manhood of body, and infancy of mind, is occasionally well contrasted. Some of the steps in his intellectual progress, we confess, made us smile. He learns to read by accidentally finding *Paradise Lost*, a volume of *Plutarch's Lives, the Sorrows of Werter*, and *Volney's Ruins*; and his code of ethics is formed on this extraordinary stock of poetical theology, pagan biography, adulterous sentimentality, and atheistical jacobinism: yet, in spite of all his enormities, we think the monster, a very pitiable and ill-used monster, and are much inclined to join in his request, and ask Frankenstein to make him a wife; it is on the promise of this alone, that he consents to quit Europe for ever, and relieve his undutiful father from the horrors of an interminable pursuit.

In order to perform this promise, our hero is under the necessity of making a journey to England, for he "has heard of some discoveries made by an English philosopher," (and we wish he had revealed his name,) "the knowledge of which was material;" accordingly, in company with Harry Clerval, he sets off for London. By the way, they ["]saw Tilbury Fort, and remembered the Spanish Armada," (how came they to forget Whiskerandos?) "Gravesend, Woolwich, and Greenwich, places which they had heard of, even in their own country." After collecting such information as could be obtained at Surgeon's Hall, the Royal Institution, and the new drop,[76] on the subject of his enquiry, he determines to fix his workshop of vivification in the Orkneys, picking up all the medical skill that was to be learnt at Edinburgh, *en passant*. Here he labours many months, not very agreeably it seems, on what he tells us is but, at best, a "filthy work;" the woman is almost completed, and wants only the last Promethean spark to enliven her, when, one evening, as he is moulding the body to its final shape, he is suddenly struck by the thought, that he may be assisting in the propagation of a race of dæmons; and, shuddering at his own fiendish work, he

---

75. [I.e., man-dæmon.]
76. [I.e., the new gallows.]

destroys the creature upon which he is employed. The monster is at hand, and, fired by this unexpected breach of promise of marriage, "wrinkles his lip with a ghastly grin," and "howls devilish despair and revenge," bidding him remember that he will be with him on his wedding-night.

Henry Clerval is found dead on the coast of Ireland, to which we are next conveyed, with marks of violence. Frankenstein is thrown into prison on suspicion of the murder, and his knowledge of the perpetrator, joined to the inability of clearing himself, produces a paroxysm of lunacy. His father succeeds in proving his innocence; and they return in peace to Geneva, with no farther mishap by the way, than a fit of the night-mare at Holyhead. He is married to Elizabeth Lavenza; the monster is true to his promise, and murders her on their wedding-night; in his despair, Frankenstein devotes himself to revenge, and resolves to track the steps of the destroyer of his peace, for the remainder of his days; he pursues him successively though Germany, the Mediterranean, the Black Sea, Tartary, and Russia, and appears to have been gaining upon his flight, at the time the ground sea split the island of ice upon which both were travelling, and separated them for ever.

In a few days after he has finished his tale, Frankenstein dies, and Mr. Walton is surprized by a visit from the monster, who most unceremoniously climbs in at his cabin window. We fear it is too late to give our arctic explorers the benefit of his description; *mais le voila.*

> "I entered the cabin where lay the remains of my ill-fated and admirable friend. Over him hung a form which I cannot find words to describe; gigantic in stature, yet uncouth and distorted in its proportions. As he hung over the coffin his face was concealed by long locks of ragged hair; but one vast hand was extended, in colour and apparent texture like that of a mummy. When he heard the sound of my approach, he ceased to utter exclamations of grief and horror, and sprung towards the window. Never did I behold a vision so horrible as his face, of such loathsome, yet appalling hideousness. I shut my eyes involuntarily, and endeavoured to recollect what were my duties with regard to this destroyer. I called on him to stay." P. 179

After a short conversation, which Mr. Walton was not very anxious to protract, he takes his leave, with the very laudable resolution of seeking the northern extremity of the globe, where he means to collect his funeral pile, and consume his frame to ashes, that its remains may afford no light to any curious and unhallowed wretch who would create such another. We cannot help wishing, that our ships of discovery had carried out the whole impression of his history, for a similar purpose.

We need scarcely say, that these volumes have neither principle, object, nor moral; the horror which abounds in them is too grotesque and *bizarre* ever to approach near the sublime, and when we did not hurry over the pages in disgust, we sometimes paused to laugh outright; and yet we suspect, that the diseased and wandering imagination, which has stepped out of all legitimate bounds, to frame these disjointed combinations and unnatural adventures, might be disciplined into something better. We heartily wish it were so, for there are occasional symptoms of no common powers of mind, struggling through a mass of absurdity, which well nigh overwhelms them; but it is a sort of absurdity that approaches so often the confines of what is wicked and immoral, that we dare hardly trust ourselves to bestow even this qualified praise. The writer of it is, we understand, a female; this is an aggravation of that which is the prevailing fault of the novel; but if our authoress can forget the gentleness of her sex, it is no reason why we should; and we shall therefore dismiss the novel without further comment.

e. *The Literary Panorama, and National Register,* N.S., 8 (1 June 1818): 411–14.

This novel is a feeble imitation of one that was very popular in its day,— the St. Leon of Mr. Godwin. It exhibits many characteristics of the school whence it proceeds; and occasionally puts forth indications of talent; but we have been very much disappointed in the perusal of it, from our expectations having been raised too high beforehand by injudicious praises; and it exhibits a strong tendency towards *materialism.*

The main idea on which the story of Frankenstein rests, undoubtedly affords scope for the display of imagination and fancy, as well as knowledge of the human heart; and the anonymous author has not wholly neglected the opportunities which it presented to him: but the work seems to have been written in great haste, and on a very crude and ill-digested plan; and the detail is, in consequence, frequently filled with the most gross and obvious inconsistencies. We shall hereafter point out a few of those to which we allude.

The story begins at the end. Walton, an enthusiastic traveller, bound on a voyage of discovery in the north seas, after having been for some time surrounded with ice, is astonished by the appearance of a human being of apparently savage character who passes the vessel at a distance, in a sledge drawn by dogs. The day after this extraordinary adventure the ice breaks up; but previously to the vessel sailing away from it, they encounter another human being, nearly exhausted with fatigue and privation. This last, who is taken into the vessel, proves to be Frankenstein, the hero of the tale; who at the time he had been nearly destroyed by the breaking up of

the ice, was in pursuit of the being that had passed the vessel on the preceding day. After a time Frankenstein contracts a friendship with Walton,
the Captain of the vessel, and relates to him his supernatural story.—In
his youth he had been led by accident to study chemistry; and becoming
deeply interested by the results of his experiments, he at length conceived
the idea of its being possible to discover the principle of vital existence.
Taking this possibility as the leading point of his studies, he pursues them
with such effect as at last actually to gain the power of endowing inanimate
matter with life!!! He instantly determines to put his newly acquired power
into practice; and for this purpose collects the materials with which to
form a living human being. From the difficulty of arranging some of the
parts, arising from their minuteness, he determines to chuse them of more
than ordinary size. In short, after incredible pains and perseverance, he at
length succeeded in producing a living human being, eight feet high, and
of proportionate powers. From this moment Frankenstein commences a
life of unmixed and unceasing misery. The being which he has formed becomes his torment, and that of every one connected with him. He causes
one by one the death of all Frankenstein's dearest connections; his brother,
his friend, and lastly his wife—whom he murders on their wedding night.
The fiend then quits the country where he has committed these horrors;
and Frankenstein, in dispair, determines to pursue him until he shall either
destroy him, or die by his hand. The story ends shortly after what we have
related in the beginning. Frankenstein dies on board the vessel of Walton;
and the fiend may, for any thing we know to be the contrary, be wandering
about upon the ice in the neighbourhood of the North Pole to this day;
and may, in that case, be among the wonderful discoveries to be made by
the expedition which is destined there.

We have mentioned that there are gross inconsistencies in the minor details of the story. They are such, for example, as the following: the moment
Frankenstein has endowed with life the previously inanimate form of the
being which he has made, he is so horror-struck with the hideousness of
the form and features, when they are put in motion, that he remains fixed
to the spot, while the gigantic monster runs from the horizontal posture in
which he lay, and *walks away*; and Frankenstein never hears any more of
him for nearly two years. The author supposes that his hero has the power
of communicating *life* to dead matter: but what has the vital principle
to do with *habits*, and actions which are dependent on the moral will? If
Frankenstein could have endowed his creature with the vital principle of
a hundred or a thousand human beings, it would no more have been able
to walk without having previously acquired *the habit* of doing so, than it
would be to talk, or to reason, or to judge. He does not pretend that he
could endow it with *faculties* as well as life: and yet when it is about *a year*

old we find it reading *Werter*, and *Plutarch* and *Volney*! The whole detail of the development of the creature's mind and faculties is full of these monstrous inconsistencies. After the creature leaves Frankenstein, on the night of *its birth*, it wanders for sometime in the woods, and then takes up its residence in a kind of shed adjoining to a cottage, where it remains for many months without the knowledge of the inhabitants; and learns to talk and read thro' a chink in the wall! "*Quod mihi ostendit*," &c

We have heard that this work is written by Mr. Shelley; but should be disposed to attribute it to even a less experienced writer than he is. In fact we have some idea that it is the production of a daughter of a celebrated living novelist.

f. *Quarterly Review* 18 (January [delayed until 12 June] 1818): 379–85—by John Wilson Croker.

[John Wilson Croker (1780–1857) was a politician, civil servant, and historian who reviewed frequently for the Quarterly Review, *a journal opposed to the radicalism of the Godwins and the Shelleys.]*

Frankenstein, a Swiss student at the university of Ingolstadt, is led by a peculiar enthusiasm to study the structure of the human frame, and to attempt to follow to its recondite sources 'the stream of animal being.' In examining the causes of *life*, he informs us, antithetically, that he had first recourse to *death*.—He became acquainted with anatomy; but that was not all; he traced through vaults and charnel houses the decay and corruption of the human body, and whilst engaged in this agreeable pursuit, examining and analyzing the minutiae of mortality, and the phenomena of the change from life to death and from death to life, a sudden light broke in upon him—

> 'A light so brilliant and wondrous, yet so simple, that while I became dizzy with the immensity of the prospect which it illustrated, I was surprized that among so many men of genius, who had directed their inquiries towards the same science, I alone should be reserved to discover so astonishing a secret.
>
> 'Remember, I am NOT recording the vision of a madman. The sun does not more certainly shine in the heavens, than that which I now affirm is true. Some miracle might have produced it, yet the stages of the discovery were distinct and probable. After days and

nights of incredible labour and fatigue, I succeeded in discovering the cause of generation and life; nay, more, I became myself capable of bestowing animation upon lifeless matter.'—p. 84–85.

Having made this wonderful discovery, he hastened to put it in practice; by plundering graves and stealing, not bodies, but parts of bodies, from the church-yard: by dabbling (as he delicately expresses it) with the unhallowed damps of the grave, and torturing the living animal to animate lifeless clay, our modern Prometheus formed a filthy image to which the last step of his art was to communicate being:—for the convenience of the process of his animal manufacture, he had chosen to form his figure about eight feet high, and he endeavoured to make it as handsome as he could—he succeeded in the first object and failed in the second; he made and animated his giant; but by some little mistake in the artist's calculation, the intended beauty turned out the ugliest monster that ever deformed the day. The creator, terrified at his own work, flies into one wood, and the work, terrified at itself, flies into another. Here the monster, by the easy process of listening at the window of a cottage, acquires a complete education: he learns to think, to talk, to read prose and verse; he becomes acquainted with geography, history, and natural philosophy, in short, 'a most delicate monster.' This credible course of study, and its very natural success, and brought about by a combination of circumstances almost as natural. In the aforesaid cottage, a young *Frenchman* employed his time in teaching an *Arabian* girl all these fine things, utterly unconscious that while he was

'whispering soft lessons in his fair one's ear,'

he was also tutoring Frankenstein's hopeful son. The monster, however, by due diligence, becomes highly accomplished: he reads Plutarch's Lives, Paradise Lost, Volney's Ruin of Empires, and the Sorrows of Werter. Such were the works which constituted the Greco-Anglico-Germanico-Gallico-Arabic library of a Swabian hut, which, if not numerous, was at least miscellaneous, and reminds us, in this particular, of Lingo's famous combination of historic characters—'Mahomet, Heliogabalus, Wat Tyler, and Jack the Painter.' He learns also to decypher some writings which he carried off from the laboratory in which he was manufactured; by these papers he becomes acquainted with the name and residence of Frankenstein and his family, and as his education has given him so good a taste as to detest himself, he has also the good sense to detest his creator for imposing upon him such a horrible burden as conscious existence, and he therefore commences a series of bloody persecutions against the unhappy Frankenstein—he murders his infant brother, his young bride, his bosom friend; even the very nursery maids of the family are not safe from his vengeance, for he contrives that they shall be hanged for robbery and murder which he himself commits.

The monster, however, has some method in his madness: he meets his Prometheus in the valley of Chamouny, and, in a long conversation, tells him the whole story of his adventures and his crimes, and declares that he will 'spill much more blood and become worse,' unless Frankenstein will *make* (we should perhaps say *build*) a wife for him: the Sorrows of Werter had, it seems, given him a strange longing to find a Charlotte, of a suitable size, and it is plain that none of Eve's daughters, not even the enormous Charlotte[77] of the Variétés herself, would have suited this stupendous fantoccino. A compliance with this natural desire his kind-hearted parent most resonably promises; but, on further consideration, he becomes alarmed at the thought of reviving the race of Anak, and he therefore resolves to break his engagement, and to defeat the procreative propensities of his ungracious child—hence great wrath and new horrors—parental unkindness and filial ingratitude. The monster hastens to execute his promised course of atrocity, and the monster-maker hurries after to stab or shoot him, and so put an end to his proceedings. This chase leads Frankenstein through Germany and France, to England, Scotland, and Ireland, in which latter country, he is taken up by a constable called Daniel Nugent, and carried before Squire Kirwan a magistrate, and very nearly hanged for a murder committed by the monster. We were greatly edified with the laudable minuteness which induces the author to give us the names of these officers of justice; it would, however, have been but fair to have given us also those of the impartial judge and enlightened jury who acquitted him, for acquitted, as our readers will be glad to hear, honourably, acquitted, he was at the assizes of Donegal.—Escaped from this peril, he renews the chase, and the monster, finding himself hard pressed, resolves to fly to the most inaccessible point of the earth; and, as our Review had not yet enlightened mankind upon the real state of the North Pole, he directs his course thither as a sure place of solitude and security; but Frankenstein, who probably had read Mr. Daines Barrington and Colonel Beaufoy on the subject, was not discouraged, and follows him with redoubled vigour, the monster flying on a sledge drawn by dogs, according to the Colonel's proposition, and Prometheus following in another—the former, however, had either more skill or better luck than the latter, whose dogs died, and who must have been drowned on the breaking up of the ice, had he not been fortunately picked up in the nick of time by Mr. Walton, the master of an English whaler, employed on a voyage of discovery towards the North Pole. On board this ship poor Frankenstein, after telling his story to Mr. Walton, who has been so kind as to write it down for our use, dies of cold, fatigue, and horror; and soon after, the monster, who had borrowed (we presume from the flourishing colony of East Greenland) a kind of raft, comes alongside the ship, and notwithstanding his huge bulk, jumps in at Mr. Walton's cabin window, and is surprised by that gentleman pronouncing a funeral oration over the departed Frankenstein; after which, declaring that he will go back to the Pole, and there burn himself on a

---

77. In the parody of Werter, at the Variétés in Paris, the Charlotte is ludicrously corpulent.

funeral pyre (of ice, we conjecture) of his own collecting, he jumps again out the window into his raft, and is out of sight in a moment.

Our readers will guess from this summary, what a tissue of horrible and disgusting absurdity this work presents.—It is piously dedicated to Mr. Godwin, and is written in the spirit of his school. The dreams of insanity are embodied in the strong and striking language of the insane, and the author, notwithstanding the rationality of his preface, often leaves us in doubt whether he is not as mad as his hero. Mr. Godwin is the patriarch of a literary family, whose chief skill is in delineating the wanderings of the intellect, and which strangely delights in the most afflicting and humiliating of human miseries. His disciples are a kind of *out-pensioners of Bedlam*, and like 'Mad Bess' or 'Mad Tom,' are occasionally visited with paroxysms of genius and fits of expression, which makes sober-minded people wonder and shudder.

We shall give our readers a very favourable specimen of the vigour of fancy and language with which this work is written, by extracting from it the three passages which struck us the most on our perusal of it. The first is the account of the animation of the image.

'It was on a dreary night of November, that I beheld the accomplishment of my toils. With an anxiety that almost amounted to agony, I collected the instruments of life around me, that I might infuse a spark of being into the lifeless thing that lay at my feet. It was already one in the morning; the rain pattered dismally against the panes, and my candle was nearly burnt out, when, by the glimmer of the half-extinguished light, I saw the dull yellow eye of the creature open; it breathed hard, and a convulsive motion agitated its limbs.

'How can I describe my emotions at this catastrophe, or how delineate the wretch whom with such infinite pains and care I had endeavoured to form? His limbs were in proportion, and I had selected his features as beautiful. Beautiful!—Great G—! His yellow skin scarcely covered the work of muscles and arteries beneath; his hair was of a lustrous black, and flowing; his teeth of a pearly whiteness; but these luxuriances only formed a more horrid contrast with his watery eyes, that seemed almost of the same colour as the dun white sockets in which they were set, his shrivelled complexion, and straight black lips.

'The different accidents of life are not so changeable as the feelings of human nature. I had worked hard for nearly two years, for the sole purpose of infusing life into an inanimate body. For this I had deprived myself of rest and health. I had desired it with an ardour that far exceeded moderation; but now that I had finished, the beauty of the dream vanished, and breathless horror and disgust filled my heart. Unable to endure the aspect of the being I had created, I rushed out of the room, and continued a long time traversing my bed-chamber, unable to compose my mind to sleep. At length lassitude succeeded to the tumult I had before endured; and I threw myself on the bed in my clothes, endeavouring to seek a few moments of forgetfulness. But it was in vain: I slept indeed, but I was disturbed by the wildest dreams. I thought I saw Elizabeth, in the bloom of health, walking in the streets of Ingolstadt. Delighted and surprized, I embraced her; but as I imprinted the first kiss on her lips, they became livid with the hue of death; her features appeared to change, and I thought that I held the corpse of my dead mother in my arms; a shrowd enveloped her form, and I saw the grave-worms crawling in the folds of the flannel. I started from my sleep with horror; a cold dew covered my forehead, my teeth chattered, and every limb became convulsed; when, by the dim and yellow light of the moon, as it forced its way through the window-shutters, I beheld the wretch—the miserable monster whom I had created. He held up the curtain of the bed; and his eyes, if eyes they may be called, were fixed on me. His jaws opened, and he muttered some inarticulate sounds, while a grin wrinkled his cheeks. He might have spoken, but I did not hear; one hand was stretched out, seemingly to detain me, but I escaped, and rushed down stairs. I took refuge in the court-yard belonging to the house which I inhabited; where I remained during the rest of the night, walking up and down in the greatest agitation, listening attentively, catching and fearing each sound as if it were to announce the approach of the demoniacal corpse to which I had so miserably given life.'—vol. i. pp. 97–101.

The next is a description of the meeting in the valley of Chamouny.

'It was nearly noon when I arrived at the top of the ascent. For some time I sat upon the rock that overlooks the sea of ice. A mist covered both that and the surrounding mountains. Presently a breeze dissipated the cloud, and I descended upon the glacier. The surface is very uneven, rising like the waves of a troubled sea, descending low, and interspersed by rifts that sink deep. The field of ice is almost a league in width, but I spent nearly two hours in crossing it. The opposite mountain is a bare perpendicular rock. From the side where I now stood Montanvert was exactly opposite, at the distance of a league; and above it rose Mont Blanc, in awful majesty. I remained in a recess of the rock, gazing on this wonderful and stupendous scene. The sea, or rather the vast river of ice, wound among its dependent mountains, whose aërial summits hung over its recesses. Their icy and glittering peaks shone in the sunlight over the clouds. My heart, which was before sorrowful, now swelled with something like joy; I exclaimed—"Wandering spirits, if indeed ye wander, and do not rest in your narrow beds, allow me this faint happiness, or take me, as your companion, away from the joys of life."

'As I said this, I suddenly beheld the figure of a man, at some distance, advancing towards me with superhuman speed. He bounded over the crevices in the ice, among which I had walked with caution; his stature also, as he approached, seemed to exceed that of man. I was troubled: a mist came over my eyes, and I felt a faintness seize me; but I was quickly restored by the cold gale of the mountains. I perceived, as the shape came nearer, (sight tremendous and abhorred!) that it was the wretch whom I had created. I trembled with rage and horror, resolving to wait his approach, and then close with him in mortal combat. He approached; his countenance bespoke bitter anguish, combined with disdain and malignity, while its unearthly ugliness rendered it almost too horrible for human eyes. But I scarcely observed this; anger and hatred had at first deprived me of utterance, and I recovered only to overwhelm him with words expressive of furious detestation and contempt.'–vol. ii. pp. 21–23.

The last with which we shall agitate the nerves of our readers is Captain Walton's description of the monster he found in his cabin.

'O! what a scene has just taken place! I am yet dizzy with the remembrance of it. I hardly know whether I shall have the power to detail it; yet the tale which I have recorded would be incomplete without this final and wonderful catastrophe.

'I entered the cabin, where lay the remains of my ill-fated and admirable friend. Over him hung a form which I cannot find words to describe; gigantic in stature, yet uncouth and distorted in its proportions. As he hung over the coffin, his face was concealed by long locks of ragged hair; but one vast hand was extended, in colour and apparent texture like that of a mummy. When he heard the sound of my approach, he ceased to utter exclamations of grief and horror, and sprung towards the window. Never did I behold a vision so horrible as his face, of such loathsome, yet appalling hideousness. I shut my eyes involuntarily, and endeavoured to recollect what were my duties with regard to this destroyer. I called on him to stay.

'He paused, looking on me with wonder; and, again turning towards the lifeless form of his creator, he seemed to forget my presence, and every feature and gesture seemed instigated by the wildest rage of some uncontrollable passion.

'"That is also my victim!" he exclaimed; "in his murder my crimes are consummated; the miserable series of my being is wound to its close! Oh, Frankenstein! generous and self-devoted being! what does it avail that I now ask thee to pardon me? I, who irretrievably destroyed thee by destroying all thou lovedst. Alas! he is cold; he may not answer me."

'His voice seemed suffocated; and my first impulses, which had suggested to me the duty of obeying the dying request of my friend, in destroying his enemy, were now suspended by a mixture of curiosity and compassion. I approached this tremendous being; I dared not again raise my looks upon his face, there was something so scaring and unearthly in its ugliness. I attempted to speak, but the words died away on my lips. The monster continued to utter wild and incoherent self-reproaches.'—vol. iii. pp. 178–181.

It cannot be denied that this is nonsense—but it is nonsense decked out with circumstances and clothed in language highly terrific: it is, indeed,
——————————————————'a tale
Told by an ideot, full of sound and fury,
Signifying nothing—'
but still there is something tremendous in the unmeaning hollowness of its sound, and the vague obscurity of its images.

But when we have thus admitted that Frankenstein has passages which appal the mind and make the flesh creep, we have given it all the praise (if praise it can be called) which we dare to bestow. Our taste and our judgment alike revolt at this kind of writing, and the greater the ability with which it may be executed the worse it is—it inculcates no lesson of conduct, manners, or morality; it cannot mend, and will not even amuse its readers, unless their taste have been deplorably vitiated—it fatigues the feelings without interesting the understanding; it gratuitously harasses the heart, and wantonly adds to the store, already too great, of painful sensations. The author has powers, both of conception and language, which employed in a happier direction might, perhaps, (we speak dubiously,) give him a name among those whose writings amuse or amend their fellow-creatures; but we take the liberty of assuring him, and hope that he may be in a temper to listen to us, that the style which he has adopted in the present publication merely tends to defeat his own purpose, if he really had any other object in view than that of leaving the wearied reader, after a struggle between laughter and loathing, in doubt whether the head or the heart of the author be the most diseased.

g. *The Athenæum,* 10 November 1832, p. 730 [review of 1818 edition, written in either 1817 or 1818]—by Percy Bysshe Shelley.

The novel of 'Frankenstein; or, the Modern Prometheus,' is undoubtedly, as a mere story, one of the most original and complete productions of the day. We debate with ourselves in wonder, as we read it, what could have been the series of thoughts—what could have been the peculiar experiences that awakened them—which conduced, in the author's mind, to the astonishing combinations of motives and incidents, and the startling catastrophe, which compose this tale. There are, perhaps, some points of subordinate importance, which prove that it is the author's first attempt. But in this judgment, which requires a very nice discrimination, we may be mistaken; for it is conducted throughout with a firm and steady hand. The interest gradually accumulates and advances towards the conclusion with the accelerated rapidity of a rock rolled down a mountain. We are led breathless with suspense and sympathy, and the heaping up of incident on incident, and the working of passion out of passion. We cry "hold, hold! enough!"—but there is yet something to come; and, like the victim whose history it relates, we think we can bear no more, and yet more is to be borne. Pelion is heaped on Ossa, and Ossa on Olympus. We climb Alp after Alp, until the horizon is seen blank, vacant, and limitless; and the head turns giddy, and the ground seems to fail under our feet.

This novel rests its claim on being a source of powerful and profound emotion. The elementary feelings of the human mind are exposed to view; and those who are accustomed to reason deeply on their origin and tendency will, perhaps, be the only persons who can sympathize, to the full extent, in the interest of the actions which are their result. But, founded on nature as they are, there is perhaps no reader, who can endure anything beside a new love story, who will not feel a responsive string touched in his inmost soul. The sentiments are so affectionate and so innocent—the characters of the subordinate agents in this strange drama are clothed in the light of such a mild and gentle mind—the pictures of domestic manners are of the most simple and attaching character: the father's is irresistible and deep. Nor are the crimes and malevolence of the single Being, though indeed withering and tremendous, the offspring of any unaccountable propensity to evil, but flow irresistibly from certain causes fully adequate to their production. They are the children, as it were, of Necessity and Human Nature. In this the direct moral of the book consists; and it is perhaps the most important, and of the most universal application, of any moral that can be enforced by example. Treat a person ill, and he will become wicked. Requite affection with scorn;—let one being be selected, for whatever cause, as the refuse of his kind—divide him, a social being, from society, and you impose upon him the irresistible obligations—malevolence and selfishness. It is thus that, too often in society, those who are best qualified to be its benefactors and its ornaments, are branded by some accident with scorn, and changed, by neglect and solitude of heart, into a scourge and a curse.

The Being in 'Frankenstein' is, no doubt, a tremendous creature. It was impossible that he should not have received among men that treatment which led to the consequences of his being a social nature. He was an abortion and an anomaly; and though his mind was such as its first impressions framed it, affectionate and full of moral sensibility, yet the circumstances of his existence are so monstrous and uncommon, that, when the consequences of them became developed in action, his original goodness was gradually turned into inextinguishable misanthropy and revenge. The scene between the Being and the blind De Lacey in the cottage, is one of the most profound and extraordinary instances of pathos that we ever recollect. It is impossible to read this dialogue,—and indeed many others of a somewhat similar character,—without feeling the heart suspend its pulsations with wonder, and the "tears stream down the cheeks." The encounter and argument between Frankenstein and the Being on the sea of ice, almost approaches, in effect, to the expostulations of Caleb Williams with Falkland. It reminds us, indeed, somewhat of the style and character of that admirable writer, to whom the author has dedicated his work, and whose productions he seems to have studied.

There is only one instance, however, in which we detect the least approach to imitation; and that is the conduct of the incident of Frankenstein's landing in Ireland. The general character of the tale, indeed, resembles nothing that ever preceded it. After the death of Elizabeth, the story, like a stream which grows at once more rapid and profound as it proceeds, assumes an irresistible solemnity, and the magnificent energy and swiftness of a tempest.

The churchyard scene, in which Frankenstein visits the tombs of his family, his quitting Geneva, and his journey through Tartary to the shores of the Frozen Ocean, resemble at once the terrible reanimation of a corpse and the supernatural career of a spirit. The scene in the cabin of Walton's ship—the more than mortal enthusiasm and grandeur of the Being's speech over the dead body of his victim—is an exhibition of intellectual and imaginative power, which we think the reader will acknowledge has seldom been surpassed.